Prais … ell

'As good as it gets.' Lee Child

'A great book written by a great girl.' Martina Cole

'Zippy, twisty plot…and a bevy of memorable supporting goodies and baddies.' The Sunday Times

'Thrilling.' Sunday Express Books of the Year

'Awesome tale from a talented writer.' Sun

'Fast paced and full of twists and turns.' Crime Scene Magazine

'Mitchell outguns Martina Cole for pure, shocking East End gangster grit.' Mirror

BLOOD SECRETS

Flesh and Blood Series: Book 4

Dreda Say Mitchell

This is a work of fiction.
Names, characters, places and incidents are the product of the author's imagination or are used fictitiously. Any resemblance to actual events, locales, or persons, living or dead, is purely coincidental.

Cover design © Stuart Bache
https://www.bookscovered.co.uk

Formatting by Polgarus Studio
https://www.polgarusstudio.com

Published by Emma Joseph and Anthony Mason
London, UK.
ISBN: 978-1-9164202-0-5
ISBN: 978-1-9164202-1-2

For Kat, Anne, Rob, Ellen,
Casey and Adam
Thank you awesome people for
your time, advice and for being there xx

Prologue

Babs and Pearl faced off like a pair of alley cats ready to do some serious damage.

Babs got straight down to it. 'Did you have a word with you know who?'

Pearl snapped back, 'He can't help. I told you that was a long shot.' Her eyes narrowed, her mouth turned ugly. 'Although he did have one helpful suggestion that I couldn't really face up to at the time. Perhaps I'll have to now though - I'm not sure I've got any other choice.'

Babs' face burned red at the threat in the smaller woman's tone. 'If you've got something to say gob it out.'

Pearl waved her small hand in the air. 'It's not just him saying it, but also the spirits are telling me—'

Babs butted in with a nasty scoffing sound. 'Spirits my East End arse. The only spirits you commune with are the ones drifting drunkenly out of a bottle of rum.'

Pearl moved closer. So did Babs. They stood nose-to-nose. Toe-to-toe. Their hot, angry breaths bounced off each other's face.

'Listen Pearl, I don't know exactly what's gone on here,' Babs snarled behind gritted teeth. 'Maybe you got caught up in the moment. Or maybe someone's leaned on ya, I dunno. I don't care.' She wriggled her head provocatively. 'Let's just say if you put things right, I'll say no more about it. Let bygones be bygones, know what I mean?' That was supposed to be the end of it but her temper got the better of her. 'Which I think is pretty generous of me in the circumstances.'

Pearl lost it big time, her head rearing back in outrage. 'Me? 'You're saying it was me? You've got the nerve of the Devil and all the evil spirits in hell—'

'Oh, pack it in with your spirits malarkey, I'm not a mug down the fairground.'

Pearl folded her arms, tilted her chin back and looked down her nose. 'I should have guessed you were behind it all along. What an idiot I've been.' She slapped her forehead, her bangles jangling. 'Trusting you of all people! Are the rest of the Millers in on the deal as well? I bet they are – a right little coven of teefs, the lot of ya.'

Her Jamaican accent was righteous with molten rage as she pronounced 'thief' as 'teefs'.

Pearl's mouth wouldn't stop. 'No wonder your gangster boyfriend couldn't help, he's already helped you out with this, hasn't he? You get me? What kind of fool do you take me for? And you know what really hurts? You and the rest of the gang having a laugh at my expense – that's what really stings. You bitch! You utter, fucking bitch.'

Babs' jaw dropped south. She'd never heard Pearl turn the air blue before. Then she reminded herself that this woman hadn't been banged up with her, less than a year ago, in the prison cell next door for being an angel.

Babs got right into her face. 'Now you listen to me. I've

tried being being upfront but you ain't having it. You're gonna put things right, whatever it takes. And if you don't you'll be bloody sorry. I'll chase you down to the gates of hell if I have to…'

Crack!

Babs' head rocked back with the force of Pearl's considerable slap to her face. She could've dealt with the blow – it wasn't the first and no doubt wouldn't be the last time someone took a swing at her – what tipped her over the edge was the smug, self-satisfied expression of glee on her former mate's face.

'Right, you've gone and done it now!'

Babs flew at Pearl, grabbing her headscarf and dragging her to the floor, arms flailing as if they were two girls hating on each other in the playground. Babs went down with her. Pearl might be in her sixties but she gave as good as she got. The pair of them wrestled on the floor, grappling and spitting venom instead of landing blows.

'You piece of crap!'

'You two-faced slag!'

'Fuck you!'

'No, fuck you!'

A roaring fizz and whistle sound shuddered with an almighty thud against the outside of the closed door, followed by an explosion that sounded like a hand grenade going off.

The two women froze in shock staring straight into each other's eyes, more like lovers than enemies. Babs hurriedly shook herself free from Pearl, rushed over to the door and threw it open. People were screaming and shouting. Hooded figures attacked anyone that didn't scarper quickly enough.

Complete, fucking bedlam.

Part One: 2007

A week ago

'She'd come to think the yellow stuff might actually be cursed.'

One

A stone came whizzing over one of the balconies, missing Babs and Natty by inches as she pushed him around the estate. Babs went bananas, frothing at the mouth, murder in her heart, as she looked up at the block. No sod in sight. Typical! At the first sign of trouble, no one on the Essex Lane Estate, aka The Devil's Estate, stuck around long enough to put their hands up to a little stone throwing. Babs narrowed her eyes. They were there alright. She could sense their sniggers and Jack the lad high-fiving behind whichever balcony they hid behind.

So she wagged her finger heavenwards and gave it to them with both barrels.

'Oi! I know you're up there you bunch of toe rags. I'm telling ya now, if you'd hurt my grandbaby I'd fecking hunt your arses down, day and bloody night…'

Abruptly, Babs snapped her gob shut. After doing a three-year stretch for the manslaughter of her former husband, gangster Stanley Miller, she'd made a silent vow to keep a low profile. She had more than enough drama to give the writers of 'Eastenders' a run for their money. Peace and quiet, that's all she wanted. Was that too much to ask for, eh? To let her hair down with her family, especially her grandkids. Running her mouth from one end of The Devil to the next wasn't going to help. Of course, she still had that one ticklish little problem outstanding...but she wasn't going to pay that any mind at present. There was a time and place for everything. Now was a time to spend with her naughty but nice grandkid.

Babs' face lit up as bright as a neon light up the Dilly.

'Aww, there he is,' Babs said with a grandmother's pride and delight, cooing and tickling his tum-tum.

Tucked up, as cosy as a kitten he was, inside a multi-coloured crocheted blanket she'd picked up for a song down The Roman. The pram was a bit of a let down. If it was a car, it would be up for the scrap yard. Its large wheels wobbled and shook and the holes in the black hood were covered with plasters. She didn't give a toss. Her kids, Jen and Tiff, had been pushed around in that pram when they were nippers. If it was good enough for them it was good enough for the next generation of Millers. Anyways, it beat all those boy racer type prams kids were wheeled around in nowadays.

Some of the good cheer drained out of her. The one baby who hadn't graced the inside of her pram was Natty's mum, Dee. She'd given birth to Dee back in '72. It hadn't been easy for a white woman to have a brown baby back in those days but Babs had cherished her. That was until Dee had been taken away from her...Babs shook her head against the heart-wrenching memories. She would've given anything – anything! - to have paraded her eldest daughter around the estate.

Tears burned the back of Babs' eyes. She'd been so young

then, so trusting. Full of dreams and reaching for the moon. And what had she got? Two bastard blokes who had done her over, good and proper. That wasn't going to happen again. No fucking way! No geezer was ever going to be wiping the soles of his doozy doos on her front doormat ever again. They were trouble, the lot of 'em.

'Except my darlin' Natty, o' course.'

He squealed with glee, kicking his chubby baby legs in the air. Babs' proud smile slipped slightly. There was a lot of Dee in him - that was plain to see - with his light-brown skin and loose curly hair. Funny thing though was she couldn't see a single lick of his dad, John, in him. Babs felt wicked even thinking it. John was laid to rest almost a year now. Another naughty but nice character. One minute he was there, the next gone. Her fingers tightened and trembled around the metal handle of the pram.

Thinking about John made her instantly think of the stolen gold.

Sensing the mood shift in his Nanna Babs, Natty's face crumbled and scrunched up. He wailed piercing and loud.

Babs clucked him gently under the chin, soothing him. ''Ere, we'll have none of that my lad. Don't want to muck up that beautiful boat of yours.' Her voice became distant. 'Ain't your fault your Nanna Babs is neck deep in this crap...'

'What a gorgeous baby,' a woman's voice burst over her troubled thoughts.

Startled, Babs twisted round. Fuck me! It was Angelina Jolie with bouncing platinum hair. That wasn't the only thing that bounced, Babs decided, copping an eyeful of her jugs. And legs...blimey, they were so long they went up to the fourth floor. The clobber was top drawer and the slap wasn't cheap neither.

The woman wasn't threatening, but Babs instantly moved to an attack dog position in front of the pram. No matter how she'd tried she'd never gotten over that time, years back, when having a dark skinned baby was asking for trouble.

The woman hesitantly stepped back. 'Oh, I'm sorry, didn't mean anything by it. Just…' she waved at the pram as she smiled with a sweet shyness, 'everyone loves a baby, you know…' She hitched her Chanel bag more securely to her shoulder. 'Gotta dash —'

'No. You're alright.' Babs felt like a proper prat. What person in their right mind wouldn't want to have a gander at her handsome grandson?

'It ain't you babe. It's just around these parts we get all sorts out an' about. Even a baby ain't safe these days and I don't want my Natty copping any of that. You hear all sorts of stories.' She eyed the woman as another thought came to her. 'And I ain't seen your face round here before.'

'Natty? Is that his name?'

Babs nodded. 'Short for Nathan.'

Babs stepped aside giving the woman silent permission to come closer. And when she did she let out a long coo as she gazed down at Natty who gave her one of his killer smiles. Her boy knew how to put on a show for a pretty face.

"What a cutie.'

Her finger instinctively reached out towards him. Babs growled low in the back of her throat in warning. She didn't have a problem with folk getting soppy over Natty, but no one touched him without her say-so. First off, she didn't have a clue who this woman was and you didn't know where her hands might have been. He was as innocent as driven snow and that's the way it was going to stay.

Babs' warning didn't put the woman off her stride as she gushed, 'It's just me and my fella are trying for our first. We're planning to tie the knot first o' course.'

A slow, dreamy sigh escaped her lips, her brown eyes gleaming with joy. Babs knew that look. Same one she'd worn in those first years of her marriage to that chancer Stan. She only hoped this stunner of a lady had more luck than she'd had.

Rihanna's 'Umbrella' ring tone peeled from Babs' mobile. Natty went wild in his pram, thrusting his arms and legs. The old wheels on the pram juddered and shook. He loved this song, which was why Babs had changed her ringtone to it.

As she fished out her phone the woman smiled gratefully at her. 'Thanks for letting me have a little peek at your grandson. Let's hope I get a little man just like him. Be seeing ya.'

'Stay lucky.'

Babs clocked the name on the mobile's screen and connected the call.

'Alright Babsie, it's me, Pearl.'

'I know who it is,' Babs replied in a rush to the older woman.

Pearl's light Jamaican accent dipped low. 'Thing is, we need to talk about...the oranges.'

Babs' eyebrows shot up. 'Oranges? What are you on about?'

'You know, the fruit I've been looking after. The oranges,

the apples, the pears that I've been looking after for us, in my settee.'

Comprehension flashed across Babs' face. 'Ahhh! *Those* oranges.'

'Thing is, we need to sort something out here a bit lively. Or they might go off - '

'Yeah, we don't want them going off,' Babs cut in, feeling the weight of the world on her shoulders.

Pearl was right on the money, of course. That gold was hot property which they needed to get rid of, as soon as. Oh, how she wished she'd never got mixed up in the whole business in the first place. Truth be told, she wanted to do a Dorothy - click her heels three times - and have done with the whole palaver. That gold had caused nothing but trouble and nearly torn her family apart.

Babs' mind cast back to how all this mess had started. Dee's old man John had done a major league blag with her foster son Kieran Scott that netted them a wagonload of bullion. John, the silly sod, had only gone and double-crossed Kieran and hidden the gold. Then John had cocked up his toes, leaving an almighty shit storm on Dee's doorstep when the owner of the gold, a craft old codger called the Commander, had sent along a well-known heavy of the old school to get his property back. Turned out the Commander was the grandfather of Florence, her bastard ex-hubbie's wrong side of the blanket daughter with some posh tart from North London. Chuck in her daughters squabbling and scrapping and ultimately falling out about the newly discovered houses she owned in Mile End, World War Three had broken out. She'd felt helpless as she languished behind bars watching her family fall apart.

That was until Pearl discovered, by chance, the gold hidden in a settee in one of Babs' houses. On Babs' say-so Pearl had spirited the gold away with no one any the wiser. Pearl had risked life and limb to get it away from Babs' family. Sure she wanted her cut but that was only to be expected. As Babs saw it she owed Pearl, big time.

Babs had wanted to tell her girls what she'd done, but couldn't bring herself to because she couldn't take the chance it might send her family into meltdown again. But what was she going to do with the gold? Pearl had literarily been sitting on it for the last three months and Babs couldn't blame her for getting shirty.

'I'll pop around today–'

'Not today,' Pearl shoved in quickly, 'it's the fourth of the month.'

'And what's that got to do with the price of fish?'

'It's the number four Babsie,' the other woman answered as if instructing a child. 'It's unlucky. In China the number four is a bit too close to the word for death—'

'Well, the fruit isn't in China, is it?' Babs rolled her eyes. Give me strength. Pearl and her fairground magic act. Mind you, it was that very same act which had got Pearl to sniff out the gold in the first place when she was cleansing Babs' houses of Stan's evil spirit.

'Anyway, I'm off on a little outing today,' Pearl added. Whatever her day trip out was she didn't sound very happy about it.

'Alright. I'll come over tomorrow…that's unless there's something dodgy about the number five as well.'

Pearl didn't like the joke. 'Even if there is, we have to get this sorted out. Be seeing you tomorrow my girl.'

After she cut the call Babs held her mobile to her chest her brain ticking furiously away. What the heck were they going to do about *that* gold?

Two

Mizz Long Legs gave the man in the driver's seat the tonguing of a lifetime. When she left Babs and Natty she'd made her way to the white van parked up near the old cemetery round the back of The Devil's Estate.

Kieran Scott wasn't in the mood but got into the kiss anyway. Then he gently pushed his girlfriend of a couple of months away. She could be a right octopus. Clinging and winding herself round him way too much for his liking. Kieran was a geezer who needed space to breath.

'How was Babs?'

Lisa Connor flicked her lush, long hair off her shoulder as she answered, 'The old bird was playing the doting granny to the hilt.'

Kieran almost reached across and wrapped his hand round her beautiful, slim neck. 'Don't. Call. Her. That.'

'Ouch!' Lisa sulkily pursed those luscious lips. That mouth could suck the life from a fella and not just on the mouth. 'No need to get techy treacle. I'm just reporting back.' She crossed those unforgettable legs and shifted closer to him. 'Who is this Babs to you anyways?'

Kieran didn't answer. He pulled out a pack of ciggies and

lit up as he considered the question. Truth was he didn't know who Babs was to him anymore. Last year she'd told him she never wanted to see his mug again and slammed the door in his face. He still couldn't get his head around it. Babs was his second mum. No, she was the only mum he'd ever known. His blood mother didn't deserve the title and God help anyone who tried to tell him otherwise. He still had the scars and nightmares from her knocking him about as a boy, leaving him to roam all hours around The Devil's Estate. He'd been neglected and unloved until Babs had taken him in hand. She'd taken a smelly, neglected, troubled boy with a plaster covering his lazy eye into her heart and loved him unconditionally.

It hurt worse than his old mum whacking him one that Babs didn't want to know him anymore. And the real thump in the guts was her telling him that he reminded her of her evil, ex-husband, Stan Miller. That had hurt. Really hurt. Still hurt. Kieran conceded he'd gone too far using her girls to help to try to find the gold, but, for fucks sake, that gold was his. He'd been the one to blag and bag it and he didn't give a toss what Babs or her girls claimed; he knew that John Black had been trying to rip him off. But all his lines weren't going to talk her round. Trouble was he couldn't stay away either.

'And the lad?' He sounded so casual. Inside he was wound up tighter than a finger on a trigger.

Lisa's palm clasped his knee as she leaned into him, her face spreading into a huge grin. 'Aww, what a lovely little man. Natty's gonna grow up to be a total heartbreaker.'

Kieran couldn't keep down the emotion that grew in his chest. He didn't want to feel it, but that was his boy for

God's sake. Not only had he lost Babs, he'd lost all rights to his son. *His* son. Not that two-faced, rip-off merchant John Black's lad. Kieran had had a one-nighter with Dee, John's wife, and Natty had been the result. John had once been his guiding hand in the underworld, but bad blood had torn them apart.

Kieran had agreed with Dee to back off. To keep the lie going that John was the real father. Yeah, but what if Dee turned out to be a carbon copy of his real mum? What if she gave his boy the back of her hand and told him he was a loser? It would cripple Kieran if that happened to a kid of his.

'What does he look like?' Seeing the confusion on her face he roughly added, 'you know, his features. What colour eyes? Hair? That kinda stuff.'

Lisa lightly laughed. 'The interest you're showing that kid anyone would think he was your son.'

'My boy? Don't talk bollocks,' he sputtered.

The laughter died on Lisa's lips when she saw the blush on his face. 'Bloody hell Kieran, that lad's your son, ain't he?'

'Nah, you're on the wrong track there doll.'

She rubbed her palm soothingly down his thigh. 'So what if you've had a kid with another bird. These things happen, don't they?'

He said nothing, so she inched ever so closer to him. 'You should've seen him Kieran. All that lovely, glossy hair and gorgeous skin.' Now she delivered her ace. 'He's got a couple of teeth as well.'

Those milk teeth represented all the time he was missing out watching his son grow up. All parents said it - they grow up so fast. And Kieran wasn't there to witness any of it.

'He's mine alright,' Kieran finally admitted with pride puffing out his chest. 'I agreed with his mum to stay out of the picture. In fact, everyone thinks the kid's her dead husband's.'

Lisa leaned closer to him so that he could feel her breath brush against his cheek. 'I know that you're a man of his word, but really Kieran — that's your son. *Your flesh and blood.* He's got the right to see his dad.'

He blasted back, 'Yeah, I know, I don't need telling!'

She ran her palm down his arm. 'Don't get me wrong, I'm not saying Natty's mum is a wrong un, but what if she hooks up with another fella, eh? And he turns out to be a not right, know what I mean?'

His face grew red with rage. 'If anyone lays a finger on my kid, they're dead. I don't care who they are—'

She cut him off. 'Don't get the hump babe. I don't like to see you all twisted outta shape.'

Kieran shook his head. Hot pain filled his gaze. 'But I gave my promise and a man's not a man if he breaks his word.'

'I know, I know,' she soothed. 'But then again, is a man a man if he doesn't look out for his own kid?'

Three

'Get me security and do it fast!' Adam, the receptionist on the ground floor, was in a right ol' panic as he spoke urgently into the phone keeping an eagle eye glued on the barney taking place on the street outside.

He'd been working on the reception at this fuck-off plate glass tower near Liverpool Street for six months and not once had there been a bit of bother. His job involved dishing out ID badges to the booted and suited brigade and directing them to the right company on the right floor. Truthfully though, he spent most of his time surfing the net. Some of the staff knowingly whistled the Baywatch tune as they walked by. Cheeky piss-takers.

'Yeah – what's up?' The guy from the security team sounded like he couldn't be arsed. They weren't used to having to shift themselves.

Properly worried now, Adam shot to his feet scarcely able to believe what he was witnessing outside.

'Get down here, pronto. A van's mounted the pavement and about ten, angry wrinklies have got out and they look like they're here for a ruck. They're carrying hockey sticks and cricket bats. Now they're gawping through the windows and banging on the door.'

Adam looked more closely. 'The ringleaders look like a bowed-legged old bloke in the leeriest blue suit I've ever seen and a mad, old, black woman wrapped in a gay rainbow flag…no, it's a kaftan. She's got bangles on and a green and black headscarf.'

The security man stifled a yawn. 'What do they want?'

Was this chump having a laugh? Adam spat, 'How the fuck would I know? But I tell you this – I don't think they're here to close a deal.'

'We're on our way down.'

Adam quickly put down the phone and hesitantly resumed his seat waiting for the back up to arrive. The man in the suit and the old girl in the kaftan seemed to be having words, which she put a stop to by jabbing a finger in his face. The others jostled around her as she took charge and pressed the intercom.

This was trouble, no doubt about it, but the first rule Adam had learned about the job was be polite to visitors. *All* visitors.

'Good morning. How may I help you?'

'Good morning.' She answered in a voice that was a dead ringer for his girlfriend's Caribbean mum putting him on the spot for not putting a ring on her finger. 'We're residents of Happy Hill Care Home and we want to speak to Mister Jerome Saint-Aubin about a serious matter please.'

Before Adam could even open his mouth the geezer in the suit elbowed the woman out of the way. 'I told you to let me handle this Pearl. I know how to deal with these people.' He gave the intercom his full attention. 'Oi! You still there mate?'

'Yes, I'm still here.'

The old boy shouted the odds. 'We wanna have it out with that crook Saint-Aubin and we ain't budging an inch until we see that ponce face-to-face. Now get these doors moving sonny.'

Adam's lips tightened into a grim line. He should've guessed this was about Jerome Saint-Aubin. He was the financier that had gone from Romford dustman's son to city slicker with the Midas touch. That was until he'd been declared bankrupt last month and scarpered into thin air. There'd been a steady stream of people since then who 'wanted a word' with him but nothing like this. Adam thought the guy was the scum of the earth personally and bang out of order, but he still had his job to do.

'May I ask your name sir?'

'Frederick Marshall. Fred the Red to me mates.' The next words came behind gritted, NHS false teeth. 'Now open the door or we'll kick it in.'

Adam desperately checked for any sign of security. What was taking those lazy twats so long? 'Unfortunately, Mr Saint-Aubin isn't on the premises today.'

Rumour was he'd done a bunk to Spain with a wheelbarrow load of tenners he'd made out of timeshares, pensions and investment schemes.

'Would you like to leave a message?'

'Yeah, we'll leave him a message alright.' Fred the Red snarled as he turned to the tallest person in the group, a bald-headed man with an eye patch and a triple chin that hung the same way as his belly. 'Alright Gazza, let's have this door down.'

Gazza disappeared from view and then, to Adam's shock, leaving him slack-jawed, came back with a chair and hurled it full force at the glass.

Crash! A large crack appeared in the glass. Passers-by watched in horror. Gazza picked up the chair again and smashed it into the glass like it was an Olympic sport, leaving another crack as it buckled. The army of angry greys stormed forward like an avenging army battering the door with sticks and bats. Adam leapt for the blower and dialled the cops as shattered glass scattered and spun across the reception floor tiles.

The operator came on. 'What service do you require sir? Police, fire or ambulance?'

'All three of them by the looks of it.'

Adam's call was cut short as the old folks filled the reception and Fred the Red snatched the phone out of his hand and slammed it down.

Up close Adam saw that Fred had a gold side tooth as he menacingly growled, 'Where is the little Herbert? Quit stalling, we know he's in here.'

'I told you, Mr Saint Aubin's not in today.'

Fred bristled, leaned over the desk and, with surprisingly strong hands, took Adam by the lapels and dragged him close. 'Are you deaf, my friend? I said where is he?'

Adam was scared out of his trousers. He breathed a sigh of utter relief when security finally put in an appearance… What the effing heck? His jaw dropped when they turned tail as soon as they clocked the seething mass of OAPs who looked well up for venting their fury on human punch bags.

Instead it was Pearl who bailed him out of trouble. Adam could now see that the scarf on her head was the design of the Jamaican flag.

'Leave off Fred, let him go. ' Fred grizzled at her command, refusing to do as told, so she warned him, 'When they fling your skin in Pentonville I won't be coming to get you, I'll leave you there to rot.'

Thoroughly fed up with him she kissed her teeth and prised his fingers from Adam's clothing and pushed him backwards. Then she astonished one and all by climbing on the desk. For an older lady Adam had to admit she knew how to move.

'Right. Will everyone calm down please.' Her chunky silver bangles jingled to the beat of her voice. 'We're not taking anything out on this unfortunate young boy. It's not his fault. We want justice not vengeance.'

Fred the Red heckled, 'He'll get justice up his Khyber if he don't find Saint Aubin.'

He was shut up by Pearl's forceful glare.

Adam was transfixed by what she did next. She closed her index fingers onto her thumbs and raised them. 'Peace. We want peace.' She turned in a full circle. 'There can be no justice without peace and harmony.'

Everyone heard Fred scoff, 'Oh blimey, she's off again,' but it didn't put her off her stride. In fact the crowd fell into a calm sea of silence.

Satisfied that her appeal to the spirit of harmony had done the trick, Pearl climbed down and turned to the trembling receptionist. 'What's your name darlin'?'

'Adam.'

'OK Adam, we all live in a care home in Stratford. Your Mr Saint Aubin was kind enough to visit the residents and arrange for a number of us to invest in a high earning investment scheme. We know he works here coz it's on his business card.' Pearl's voice cracked with emotion. 'All of us, including me, sank much of our life savings into it. Now we're having difficulties tracing the money and we're very upset. All we want is to have a word with him so we can find out what's happened.'

Now that they were quiet and no longer waving weapons, Adam saw the fear and desperation etched in their faces along with the lines that showed their ages. His Nan and Granddad were about the age of these people. How would he feel if some tealeaf in a suit, clutching a briefcase and a gold-plated smile had screwed them over? Fucking knock his block into next year if he got his hands on him.

He leaned over the desk with open sympathy. 'Look Pearl, I'll be honest with you, your guy's done a runner. The bird has flown, to Spain apparently. If you want proof, go up to the fifth floor. He was working as a freelancer with a company run by Mister Olson. When the shit hit the fan, Olson wiped his hands of him but gave him a desk and chair to work from, hoping he might be able to set things right. Obviously that isn't what happened.' He pointed. 'The stairs are over there. But be quick, the law will be here shortly.'

Adam couldn't get the image of this happening to his own grandparents out of his head so he decided, 'Actually, tell you what, to make it simple, I'll take you.'

Pearl turned to the forlorn group. 'Me and Fred will go up. Go back to the van, especially you Vi, your hips must be murder.'

On the fifth floor Adam introduced them to this Olson character. He didn't seem the least surprised or alarmed to see them. Not a good sign. Even Fred's bluster seemed to vanish.

'Saint Aubin?' Olson protested, his body stiffening. 'He's nothing to do with us.'

'I'll bet,' Fred seethed bitterly, 'but I'm sure he was when he was making you a few bob.'

Olson carried on unruffled; didn't even have the cheek to look embarrassed. 'He did have a desk for a while but he left sometime ago. You don't believe me? See for yourself.'

He took them over to an empty desk in the corner of the office. A few cables where a computer had once been and a silent phone with no line attached were the only evidence that someone had once worked there. Fred pulled open some of the drawers. Nothing inside except a few cards and some takeaway menus.

Fred slowly closed the drawer and whispered, 'Fuck him'.

In the streets below, police sirens could be heard.

When Pearl looked upset at the sound, Adam reassured, 'don't worry about it. The owners won't press charges. They won't want their connection with Saint Aubin becoming public.'

A dejected Fred forlornly said to Pearl, 'what are we going to tell our people? They've been skinned alive.'

Pearl seemed uncertain. 'We'll tell them we'll get their money back.'

Fred laughed, not a lick of humour in it but plenty of anguish. 'How? Take the van to Spain to track the bellend down?'

A glimmer of hope suddenly shone in Pearl's sharp eyes.

'Didn't Vi say she knew someone who might be able to help us?'

Four

The sound of a major league row going on in the squat made Tiffany half open one sleepy eye. By rights she should've jumped out of bed scared out of her wits. But Tiff - being Tiff - was still feeling the affects of a booze and ecstasy bender from a night on the razz and so she couldn't be arsed. She'd only dossed down on the mattress on the floor a couple of hours back and the only thing that was going to shift her any time soon was someone chucking money in the air.

'Keep the bloody racket down will ya,' she yelled, properly miffed.

Was it too much to ask for a girl to get some beauty sleep around here? Tiff checked the time on her Nokia: eleven in the morning for Pete's sake. What was the world coming to when a girl couldn't get some shut-eye?

She yanked the sleeping bag over her head and tried to forget about the banging and shouting. Sounded like it was coming from the hallway. Why, oh why, was there always some bat-shit drama going in this squat? Tiff didn't mind the bare floorboards, the peeling wallpaper and the damp. She could put up with there being no gas or lecky too. It was the petty slanging matches that went on for what felt like 24/7 that did her head in. It was always the same. Someone had pinched someone else's drugs, milk, pillow or girlfriend. A right royal den of shysters. But then again there was no rent or rates to worry about.

That was certainly a big factor in Tiff taking up residence here. After she'd made a dog's dinner at her first shot of independence, she'd had no alternative but to slink back to her mum's on The Devil's Estate, tail firmly between her legs,. Tiff had hated that. Though, truth be told, as much as she'd despised being back on The Devil at least it had been a safe place to put her head down. Unlike her life in that flash duplex on the Island where the good times had been derailed by her borrowing blunt like it was going out of fashion. Her mum had put a spanner in the works of her coming back home of course. Told her in no uncertain terms she had a week to find her own gaff. If it hadn't been for the girl she was snogging at the time giving her a steer on this squat, she'd have been well on her uppers, just another homeless with a can of lager and a dog on a string.

Tiff put her past troubles aside and got on with the business of sleeping. She'd nearly nodded off again when the door was flung open and crashed against the wall. Some maniac rushed across the creaking boards to the window and flung open the curtains. Or, more like, lifted the towel that was nailed there.

Tiff squeezed her eyes tight. If someone thought she was budging from her snug bug nest they had another thing coming. 'Will you sod off whoever you are?'

'They're here. And they've come mob-handed.'

It was the voice of one of the girls who bedded down in the

living room. Tiff couldn't recall her name but she'd obviously ignored the government's warning to, 'Just say no'.

Tiff snuggled deeper. 'Who's here?'

'The bailiffs. And the filth are sitting in their motors as back up.'

The Bill didn't scare Tiff, nor did the bailiffs. She'd been dragged up on The Devil; take more than that lot to put the frighteners on her. 'What do they want?'

'Well, they're not here to service the boiler, are they?' came the sarky reply. 'We're being slung out, you dopey cow. Some of the boys are barricading the front door with the furniture.'

Tiff sniggered as she finally popped her head out of the sleeping bag. Her hair was shaved around the sides with a dyed-silver Mohican in the middle and she wore a nose ring. 'That'll be a good trick; we ain't got no furniture. It all went on the fire along with half the floorboards.'

The girl was in a right two and eight, moving in an agitated state from one foot to the other as she kept a nervous watch at the window.

She let the towel fall back and tried to pep Tiff up. 'Come on, move yourself, we're making a fight of it. We might get another couple of days outta it.'

'Can't see the point.' Tiff threw her head back in a large yawn.

No-name-junkie fisted her hands on her hips like an angry mother. 'You really are crap, aren't you Tiff? There's no zip in you at all.'

'Got that right in one. I've been evicted before and I expect I'll be evicted again before I finally get my rose covered cottage out in the sticks.'

The other woman scratched the needle tracks on her arm as she made her way to the door. 'Suit yourself. If you've got any gear, best flush it down the John before they kick their way in.'

Did she have any stuff? It had been one hell of a rave the night before so she thought not. There was a lull for about ten minutes and it was nearly long enough for Tiffany to drift back to snoozeville. In a half dream, she saw her mum standing over her, stabbing a finger at her going into her usual Judge Judy routine:

'What's the matter with ya girl? When you gonna grow up and do something with your life? How much longer are you gonna ponce, skive and thieve? Eh? And don't give me any lip or think you're too old to feel the back of my hand across your bonce.'

Tiff woke with a start. There was a crash but it wasn't Babs' hand across her head. It was the front door being booted in.

'Nazis! Sieg heil!' one of the guy's mocked from the hallway.

Another voice yelled, 'You feel no shame chucking homeless people on the street?'

The druggie, who'd been in her room, joined the chorus, her tone beyond hysterical. 'How would you like it if someone did this to your old gran?' To which a stern male voice replied, 'my old gran would have more self-respect than to squat on someone else's property.'

The sound of a brief, half-hearted struggle took place before the voices moved onto the street. Smash, crash, wallop! Tiff didn't need to see to know what that was; the sound of the squatters' belongings being unceremoniously dumped in the gutter.

Tiff pulled a face in the sleeping bag. So much for the fight they were going to put up.

Her room door was flung open again.

'There's another one in here.'

To Tiff's surprise it was a woman's voice. She didn't know girls did this kind of work. Whatever! Tiff wasn't moving.

'Oi! Sleepyhead! Rise and shine. Get your shit together, time to go.'

Tiff toughed it out inside the sleeping bag. 'Gimme a break luv - I'm knackered. Why don't you board up the doors and windows and I'll let myself out across the lean-to later?'

Tiff howled in pain as a hard kick sunk into her belly. She didn't even have enough time to get her breath back before a second blow knocked her, along with her sleeping bag, clean off the mattress, sending her rolling, like Cleopatra, across the dodgy floorboards. Tiff had been around long enough to figure out that the blows were professionally placed to cause maximum pain. This woman obviously knew how to dish it out and had learnt her trade somewhere nasty.

Gasping, chest rising high, Tiff shoved back her sleeping bag and begged, 'Alright, alright, steady on, there's no need for that, I'm going, I'm going.'

The woman was smirking at her. She was a proper bruiser. Thick set with cropped hair, tats popping out like greeting cards and a dead ringer for a tough off 'Bad Girls'. More importantly she was wielding a wicked looking baseball bat.

Suddenly Cell Block H's finest peered at her more closely. 'Hold up a minute! I know you!'

She proceeded to stroll over to Tiff, who was in no mood for another kicking so she did her best to manoeuvre, quick as a flash, out of reach, but the sleeping bag hampered her progress. The woman caught up and lorded it over her.

Holding her aching belly with both hands, Tiff babbled, 'No, you don't.'

'Yeah I do – you're Babs Miller's girl. Jen, ain't it?'

One of the basic rules Tiff had learned in life was never to admit to anything. 'No, it ain't.'

The woman rocked back on her heels. 'Yeah, it is, but I think you're the lippy one, Tiffany. I did bird with your ol' girl. I remember you and your sisters coming up on visiting days. Jen was the looker, Dee the gorgeous black daughter and you're the one with the gob.' She grinned but that only upped her menace quota. 'The name's Knox. I expect your mum told you all about me. Sorry about the rough stuff babe but everyone's gotta earn a living, haven't they?'

Tiff was in no mood to swap prison tales with this hatchet-faced horror story.

Knox got back on with her job, slapping her baseball bat menacingly in the palm of her hand. 'Give Babs my love. Now fuck off.'

Tiff didn't need telling twice. She pulled on her trackie bottoms and a torn T-shirt, rolled up her sleeping bag and threw her shit into twin, blue plastic bags. It didn't take long; there wasn't much. While she did so, Knox wrote something in a notebook and then ripped it out.

'Ere – this is my number. Give it to your mum. I'd like to catch up with her and yarn about our days on the block. I lost touch with her when I got my jam roll. She's a good ol' sort is Babs.'

Tiff snatched the note and stuffed it in her pocket. Without a word, she made for the door, headed down the stairs and out through the broken front door where chippies were already measuring up. The other squatters were long gone. Down the road a carload of coppers was sitting patiently although with Knox on the case Tiffany wasn't sure they were really needed. That bird was a one-woman heavy mob.

Tiff's pace slowed to a crawl as she turned a corner with her bags already weighing her down. She was out of other places to go. Jen and Dee had long since stopped putting her up. Her other mates were fed up with her and squats were hard to come by.

It was going to have to be her mum's again. Inwardly she groaned. She couldn't face it. As soon as she crossed the threshold of her mum's, Babs started up with her earache routine. Finger wagging, lectures on earning a living, warnings about drugs and bad company; it was like being a long-suffering teen all over again. Even being kicked around by mad girl Knox was better than that. Plus, who in their right mind wanted to live on The Devil's Estate? Been there, done that, never going back. Except it was looking like she had no alternative. Why was life such a B.I.T.C.H?

Tiff's mobile pinged in her pocket. A text from big sis Dee.

'You'd better be on your way or else.'

Bollocks! She was meant to be meeting her sisters at Dee's new club in Stratford, which was opening its doors for the first time on Saturday. There'd been talk of Tiff running the bar but that had tailed off lately and she knew why. Probably Jen bitching and moaning for all she was worth:

'Give Tiff a job? Are you off your rocker? She'll help herself to your first night's takings along with a selection of the optics and then be away on her toes.'

Tiff had a think as she pulled out a fag and lit up. She didn't really want to go to Dee's new club, no doubt to be bossed only the way older sisters knew how. But then she had nowhere else to go. And there was always the possibility that she might be able to find a room there where she could crash for a while. Her mood brightened. It was worth a punt before she ended up back on The Devil with her mum.

Five

'Ruddy Nora, they're here already,' Fred the Red warned tightly as the van full of deflated OAPs moved into the care home driveway.

Fred, a bloke who usually had way too much to say for himself, hadn't exercised his gob much since they'd left Liverpool Street. Neither had Pearl, who sat next to him. There was a hopeless, defeated atmosphere. The old folks in the back looked like they'd aged ten years. Much of their hard earned savings were gone and they knew it. If Pearl ever got her hands on that scheming, scamming, cheating Saint Aubin she'd choke him slowly until his lying eyes popped clean out of his deceitful head. But what ate her up the most was it was all her fault.

Feeling wretched she didn't look up. 'Who's here?'

She didn't give a monkey's who'd put in an appearance. No doubt another so-called entertainment outfit the care home's top brass insisted on putting on for them, like they were brainless, dribbling ninnies. If she had to sit through another long-haired Hippy-Mary and guitar strumming sidekick singing Kum-friggin'-baya she'd be doing some serious damage with the same said guitar.

Mind you she loved this care home. The one she'd previously lived in in Ilford had been a right morgue.

'Old Bill,' Fred answered briskly.

Pearl's head shot up in an instant. A cop car sat on the grass near her room. Her heart accelerated as one thing swerved into her mind – the gold. What if the cops had found out? But how could they have? Only she and Babs knew where it was. Fred's next words calmed her down.

'That kid up Liverpool Street must've changed his mind and given the plod the full SP and told them where to find us.'

Vi, seated next to her identical twin, Di, cried out in horror, 'we're not going to end up in the slammer are we Fred?'

The sisters shared a room and were devoted to each other. Where you saw one you usually saw the other. They might be knocking on but they never left their room without rose-red lippy, bold-blue eye shadow and retro, silver screen Diana Dors hair.

Fred puffed out his chest in a manly fashion as he caught Vi's alarmed expression in the rear-view mirror. 'Not on my watch. I'll protect you with my life luv.'

Everyone, except Vi it appeared, knew he was sweet on her. He became cocky as he added, 'Leave it to me. I'll talk to 'em. I know how to get round the law. Cross their palms with a pony and they'll soon decide it's not in the public interest to press charges.'

Pearl slapped him, with feeling, on the thigh and scoffed, 'I don't think so; you'll just kick off as usual. You could start a fight on a desert island. Leave the chat to me. I'll go on the attack and demand to know why they aren't chasing that crook Saint Aubin.'

Fred parked the van round the back. He got out to open the back doors and, wearing a huge grin, gallantly offered his hand to Vi to help her down.

'Thanks Fred.' She patted his hand gently.

Fred leaned in, his face going slightly red. 'Anytime Vi, anytime.'

If he got any closer to his secret crush he'd be slobbering all over her, Pearl observed, resisting the urge to roll her eyes.

'Fred, find your feet and step to it,' she ordered.

As they drew closer, Pearl saw two uniformed cops and some of the Home's staff peering through an open window and inspecting the walls. When she drew closer still, she almost keeled right over.

Merciful God in heaven! They were looking in *her* room. Her hand instinctively clamped over her mouth in shock. The iron bars on her windows were hanging off. There were black marks around the frame and up the exposed brickwork where the paint had been burned off.

Fred seemed even more shocked than she was. 'What the fuck?'

One of the two officers turned towards them. 'Good afternoon sir – madam. Is this your room?'

A cloud of doom descended over Pearl. She felt sick to her very soul. Almost turned tail and ran. Instead she went into her feeble, old lady routine, shifting slowly, shoulders hunched, muttering mumbo jumbo as she headed towards the blown out window. She peered inside.

No! No! No! Her settee had been slashed to ribbons. Not the gold! Please not the gold! Her troubles with Jerome Saint Aubin and a savings scam were child's play compared to this. In a daze she saw the tyre marks on the grass and flower beds.

They were deep and wide and obviously made by a van or truck. Her sharp gaze zeroed in on an object lying a few yards away that no one else seemed to have clocked. And that's the way she wanted to keep it.

When she didn't speak, one of the cops said, very slowly and loudly, as if talking to a three-year-old, 'Is. This. Your. Room. Madam? Only there seems to have been some kind of incident here. An explosion it looks like. Have you got any information that could help?'

Pearl drew a deep breath but no words came out when she tried to speak.

She knew she was in shock so she tried again. 'Yes… No…' her voice squeaked. 'No, I've been out all day.' Then she remembered she was meant to be a doddering old dear. 'Well, I think it was today. Might've been yesterday or last week.' Her eyes darted around as she played the confused old bat to the hilt.

The cop pursed his lips. 'It was today. We've heard all about that. A posse of you old dears went down to Liverpool Street to sort out that scam merchant Jerome Saint Aubin?' He sighed. 'I hope you had better luck catching him than we did.'

Distract him. Steer him away from the subject of your room, Pearl mentally chanted anxiously to herself.

'Are we in trouble officer over the business at Liverpool Street?'

'Nah, they don't want any grief over that. Having a crook who'd operated out of their premises is a bit of a red face for them.' His gaze narrowed. 'Now then, why would anyone want to blow the window off your room? Did you keep any valuables in there? Only your room seems to be the only one with bars on.'

Both cops stared hard at her now, putting her on the spot. Pearl had lived much of her adult life wheedling her way out of trouble. She knew every trick in the book, but at that precise moment all she could think about was some light-fingered prick had nicked hers and Babs' gold. But who? Who? Who, when only Babs and her knew about it or where it was hidden?

It was Fred who came to her rescue when he blurted out, 'Gas.'

'Gas?' The cop frowned down his nose at him.

'Yeah, that's right.' Fred's voice gathered confidence. He levelled his knowing gaze at Pearl. 'You cook on the ol' gas heater in your room, don't ya Pearl?' He gave the cops a sidelong, 'she ain't all there, know what I mean?' look.

'You was probably brewing up a cup of char and was so wound up about scumbag Saint Aubin, you forgot to turn it off afore we went out and then – boom! Up it goes while we're out.'

'Oh yes,' Pearl admitted weakly, for once in her life grateful for that motor mouth of Fred's. 'Gas. Boom! Up it goes!'

The officers escorted Pearl inside to see if any of her belongings had disappeared in the gas explosion. Instead of doing a proper check, she stood in front of the sofa, waving her kaftan like a pair of gigantic, multi-coloured bird wings in an attempt to hide the damage from the two cops.

'Are you feeling OK madam?' one of the officers asked as he stared at her pityingly.

'What?' Pearl flapped her arms some more looking startled. 'Where am I? Is this my room?' Her gaze skidded towards Fred. 'Is it dinner time yet?'

Fred sidled up to the cops and whispered, 'Let me take care of this.' Then he turned to Pearl and bellowed, 'has anything been taken from your room Pearl my dear?'

'Taken?' She slapped on a terrified expression. 'Is someone trying to take me? Who?'

Both cops appeared thoroughly fed up now. 'Valuables,' one said. 'Have any valuables been taken?'

'Oh no,' She smiled softly. 'I don't keep any valuables in my room and I haven't got any valuables to steal anyway.'

The boys in blue were staring suspiciously at the iron bars, so Pearl added, 'I'm worried about men breaking in.' Her voice lowered as she dramatically placed her palm at her throat. 'You know, an old lady's not safe anywhere these days.' She shook her head. 'What a bad, bad world we live in gentlemen, a very bad world.'

'Very wise madam. Well, if nothing's gone and you're sure the damage is a can of cooking gas blowing its top and there's no crime here, there's nothing more we can do.'

Pearl needed to find out if there was a witness. But she couldn't simply blurt it out because that would put her squarely in the spotlight again. How to get around this...She straightened slightly as a light bulb flashed on in her mind.

She was all innocence as she remarked wildly, 'Thanks heaven no one was here!'

'It seems everyone was up Liverpool Street so no harm done. There was one person around though.'

Bingo!

She let him continue. 'The woman who lives three rooms down. Lin? Said she heard a bit of a muffled bang but didn't think anything of it so she didn't investigate.'

The cops looked at each other, gently warned her about

the pitfalls of having gas in her room and left when they were radioed about a nasty mugging on the High Street.

But Fred the Red didn't leave.

When they were alone, he got to work trying to find out what had really gone on. 'You're not in any kind of trouble, are you Pearl? Coz your barmy ol' dear act ain't fooling me. You're sharper than a butcher's cleaver.' His voice lowered. 'Maybe I can help?'

She waved him away as she unfurled her backbone fully. 'Of course not. You said it yourself. It was a gas explosion.'

Fred burst out laughing, his gold tooth twinkling. 'Oh, do me a favour! The lock on the window was blown off. That's professionals, that is. An opportunist skaghead don't use plastic explosives to break into rooms. Nah, this is a proper job by proper people.'

His bowlegs took him to her settee. 'Look at the state of it. Like Freddie Kruger's been at it.' He stared at her shrewdly. 'What was you hiding in there? Eh? They must've known what they was looking for, they ain't touched nowt else. I mean, I don't want to poke my snout in but if you've got a problem, I might be able to give you a steer. Used to be in the business myself, know what I mean?' He tapped his nose.

It was a popular boast of Fred's that he'd been 'in the know' and had gone drinking with all the top East End villains. A likely tale. If he'd been in the biz, how come he was living out his days in Happy Hill Home in Stratford instead of on the Costa Del Crime? Fairy stories, every last word of them.

Her voice was leaden. 'I thank you for the gas story, but turns out this really was a gas explosion. Now if you wouldn't mind, I need to start clearing up.'

He shrugged, but those eyes of his still drilled into her. 'Suit yourself. But if you change your mind, you know where I am. I could put some feelers out, get a tickle.'

In way of an answer she clicked her fingers and went, 'Boom!'

When he was gone Pearl pulled up her kaftan and took out the only spirits she could really commune with - a quart bottle of Wrey and Nephew Overproof rum. She kept it tucked between her racy, lilac garter and thigh. Funny what a body could keep hidden under loose clothing and a scarf. Pearl downed a good slug and shuddered. Man, the stuff could make your eyes roll and nose twitch at the same time. But it couldn't bring back the gold.

Pearl tucked her secret stash of booze back in its hiding place, gave it thirty minutes until she was sure the coast was clear and then went outside to recover the object that she'd seen lying on the grass earlier. Then she went to Lin Chen's room three doors down while clutching it and knocked.

Pearl's ears pricked up. That was shuffling inside alright, but no one answered. She knocked again, more loudly. Still no answer. Finally, she hammered on the door and shouted, 'Open up Lin, I know you're in there.'

The door opened a fraction and a bird-like woman with a pale face appeared.

Before Pearl could say a word, Lin barked, 'I didn't see anything and I didn't hear anything, OK? Don't ask me about it again.'

The door started to shut. Oh no, you don't! Pearl got her foot in there.

'I've got something for you. You must've dropped it earlier.'

She showed Lin the walking stick she'd recovered from the lawn. 'I know it's yours because it's got your name etched on it. Your daughter got it laser engraved for you a few months back, remember?'

As soon as Lin saw the walking stick her frail hand flew to her throat and she started rubbing it. Pearl held back a gasp. One of the many tricks up her sleeve was reading people. She'd honed the skill as part of her essential routine as a bogus fortune-teller. Whoever had nicked the gold had pressed Lin's walking stick against her throat to scare the bejabbers out of her. The old girl was lucky to still be standing because she had a very delicate heart condition.

The other woman's hand dropped as she peered out through the narrow gap and opened the door wider. She hesitantly took her stick. 'Thanks. I dropped it earlier while I was out for a walk.'

Pearl seized her chance. 'What happened? Who was it? I just need to know. I won't get you involved.'

The fierce little woman in front of her clutched her stick as if to strike someone and whispered behind her teeth, 'this is the last time I'm going to say this to you. I didn't see anything and I didn't hear anything.'

Lin's breathing was coming short and frantic. Pearl was terrified that her old ticker was going to give out, so she eased off on the pressure.

'If that's how you want to play it.' She reluctantly turned to go.

But the other woman called out, voice trembling, 'But I will say this. I don't know what you're up to in that room of yours but you're mixing it with some very dangerous people. If I were you, I'd change my name and move. A very long way away.'

Six

'Right people, prick up your ears and listen up.'

Dee Black's commanding voice boomed from the steel balcony of the VIP lounge in her club as she gazed down at her staff gathered below. Her legs were braced apart, hands gripping the steel railing so they got it, loud and clear, she meant business with a capital B.

Gone were her usual go-to figure-hugging clothes, replaced by a Marc Jacob's midnight-black pants suit with belted waist and plain white blouse. She might be projecting the ultimate image of a successful businesswoman, but the shoes and hair of the old Dee she couldn't let go. Five inch heels, which were bright green, including the soles and Queen Latifah look-a-like weave, short on one side, longer on the other with an electric blue fringe that flopped over her right eye.

'Every last one of you knows that we'll be launching on Saturday night.'

Her alert eyes did a sweep. They'd better be opening their ears to every last word coming out of her mouth.

Satisfied she continued, 'I'll give you this, you've worked your nuts and clits off to get this place right. Don't get me wrong, there's still shit to do before the doors open.' She smiled, but anyone who knew Dee Black would sus it didn't reach her eyes. 'We get this right on the night, there's gonna be a hundred nicker top up in your take home.'

A ripple of excitement spread through the group as Dee clicked-clacked her way down the steel staircase with hip swaying style. She positioned herself in front of them on the main dance floor.

'You're good to me I'm good to you. See, I'm different from the other club owners round these parts who will pay you bottom dollar for a hard day's graft. I take care of my people and reward your loyalty in all kinds of ways, including hard cash.' Dee fixed a deadly expression on her face. 'If anyone of you feel you can't be loyal to me you need to hit the door now.'

No one moved. An ominous silence filled the air as Dee resumed. 'So, I take it that means I've got everyone on my side?' The silence deepened. Dee bit out, 'I can't hear ya.'

'Yes Mizz Dee,' they chorused smartly, but there was confusion in some of the replies. Something was obviously up.

'Here's the thing, can someone explain to me what's happening here?'

She pulled out the remote for the enormous video-music screen on the wall and hit play.

The screen was grainy for a few seconds and then it filled with footage from one of the security cams. It proceeded to show the back view of one of the female staff, quickly and furtively, loading up a good-sized sports bag with bottles of fizz. Once the deed was done she bolted for the door finally revealing her five-finger discount mug.

The staff gasped as Dee turned her fierce gaze onto the culprit, one of the waitresses. She was a girl more than a woman really but clearly already sliding down the greasy pole.

Bug-eyed, the tealeaf started backing away trying to wriggle her way out of trouble. 'Mizz Dee, it ain't what it looks like—'

Dee stabbed a dangerous finger her way. 'You're fucking lucky I'm rigged out in one of my best suits and don't care to get it dry cleaned or else I'd personally slice off your thieving fingers - real slow - one at a time.'

Lips rippling in disgust, Dee nodded curtly at the head of her security team, who swiftly frogmarched the blubbing waitress out of Dee's new empire. She was fizzing now and wanted all her people to fully understand what would go down if they tried to mug her off.

'Anyone else wanna take the rise, you'd best remember that I'm the baddest bitch you will ever – you hear me – *ever* meet.' She levelled her accusing finger at the lot of them. 'The next wanker to try it on…' Dee dropped her hand, straightened her shoulders and in a tight, soft voice finished, 'Let me put it this way. It will take your dear mum a whole bloody year before she recognises you again.'

Her chest rose and fell heavily with her warning. 'Right people, what you standing round looking like a bunch of gorms for?' She clapped her hands. 'Chop! Chop! We've got work to do.'

They scattered. Dee didn't move an inch, still fuming. She was trying to restrain herself, holding back an almighty urge to bolt after that sticky-fingered slag and give her what for, right there in the street. But she wouldn't; that was the old Dee. The new model Dee didn't get her hands dirty. She had people to do that for her now.

'You look like you're ready to batter someone just for smiling.'

The sound of her sister, Jen's voice, pulled her out of her murderous ravings.

The sisters embraced and kissed on the cheek. Dee still found it hard to get accustomed to this new look Jen with her bottle red, brutal short cut and caked on slap. Not that Jen was looking slutty or anything, but the trademark softness that had been pure Jennifer Miller was long gone and, truth be told, Dee missed it. But then again, Jen needed all the toughness she could muster in her new role as manager of the club.

'Had to get the staff in line.' Dee added pointedly, 'which, last time I looked, was part of your job description as is being on time.'

'Yeah, sorry bout that,' Jen answered as they made their way to the bar. 'Courtney's class assembly took a lot longer than I thought and the trains were murder on the way back.'

Dee ordered a couple of Tia Maria cocktails as they settled down on the leather kettle stools.

'My little princess getting on alright in her new school?' Dee asked.

Dee loved Jen's girls, Courtney and Little Bea, as if she'd given birth to them. At one time she'd thought they'd be the only kids in her life, along with her Nicky. Now she had her very own slice of royalty, her little prince, Natty.

Her heart squeezed tight with grief. Dee still found it hard to come to terms with her John never being there for their boy. And he was *their* boy, nobody else's, no matter what that handy prat Kieran Scott had to say on the matter. Not that he'd blabbed about their secret to give him his due. She stayed clear of him and he stayed clear of her and that's the way she wanted to keep it. It weren't right, just not right. That John would never get to be there at Natty's first birthday, teach him how to play footie, hold him in his big, strong, safe arms. Life could be such a cruel bitch, a fact Dee had learned early in life.

The gentle touch of Jen's palm covering her own brought her back to the present. Jen smiled sadly, as if reading her thoughts. 'John would be tickled pink and so proud of you starting up your own place.'

Tears blurred Dee's vision. She could barely look at Jen with the heartache churning inside her. 'I wake up in the nights sometimes and reach for him and when my arms come up all empty I can't believe that my big man has gone.'

'I know, I know,' Jen comforted with the tenderness of a mother. 'But you know what? John was a top geezer who loved life to the max and that's what he'd want you to be doing. Getting out there and putting your stamp on the world.' She swivelled on her stool and waved her arms in wonder. 'Look around you Dee; this club is proper, it could be in Vegas.'

Dee's dried her eyes. Jen was right. No expense had been spared to bring Dee's club to life. The building had been a mashed down, neglected joint in Stratford when Dee had managed to nab it for a song; John had taught her well about the ins and outs of haggling. And then Dee had lucked out again - Stratford was picked as the spot for the 2012 London Olympics in five years time. Over night the club's real estate value rocketed and it become part of what those in the know were saying would be the trendiest part of East London. You couldn't make that shit up! Yeah, John would be done up for her.

When they were both facing the bar again Jen took a sip of her drink and then smacked her wet lips sourly together. 'I see that Tiff ain't put in an appearance.'

Dee arched her brow. 'I've text a reminder.'

Jen slammed her glass down irritated to the core. 'If you ask me, you're making a top mistake asking her to look after the bar staff. I love my sis, even though she can be as painful as a splinter in your jacksie when she wants to be, but let's face it, she can barely look after herself much less an important part of your club. Plus, how can you trust her after that stunt she pulled last year…you know, with the gold.'

Dee's razor-sharp expression cut Jen to the bone. It reminded her younger sister clearer than an exploding bomb that they never talked about the gold. It had nearly destroyed their family. Sister fighting sister, John dead, Jen and Tiff's half-sister Flo sticking her oar in before the Miller family was nigh on wrecked by the fall out. Dee shuddered. She didn't know what had happened to the gold. No one did or at least no one was saying. And Dee liked it that way. She'd come to think the yellow stuff might actually be cursed. She was glad it was gone.

'Hope I ain't too late for the proceedings.'

Dee and Jen gave each other the eye before turning to greet their very late baby sister. Dee gave her an all-over up and down. She didn't know where Tiff had rolled in from, but she was a mess. Looked like she was fleeing some war torn country. Dee took pointed note of her bulging plastic bags. She knew what that meant. Their kid sister was on her travels again.

Dee and Jen looked meaningfully at each again and announced, in unison, their gazes targeted on Tiff's manky luggage, 'You ain't stopping at mine.'

Tiff tutted as if she couldn't believe the nerve of them. 'Ain't been here two seconds and you're already on my case. And, I might add, with no offer of something to wet my beak.'

Dee wasn't in the mood for an all out barney but she had to draw a line. 'If you're gonna work here you need to get it through that bonce of yours that we don't work on Tiff time but Dee time, got it?'

'Whatever,' came the glib response as Tiff moved towards them with her customary cocksure swagger. Instead of joining them she made her way round the bar zeroing in on a bottle of super expensive voddy.

Dee was on her feet in a flash. 'What the fuck are you doing?'

'You said I was in charge of the bar, innit.' She tilted the bottle to her lips and swallowed away.

As Jen wore a 'I told you so' expression, Dee blew her stack. 'If you don't put that slosh down I'll use the bottle to bang the house rules into your homeless nut.'

Tiff smirked, but she got the message and did as big sis asked. She wiped her mouth cheekily with the back of her hand as she joined them on a stool. 'Just need to check the goods before we start selling.'

Dee resumed her seat, barely able to keep her backside still as she continued to fume. 'I think you mean *I'm* selling. I've just had to let someone go for taking the piss. Don't think coz we share half of the same gene pool you won't be going the same way if you try any of your sly shit moves here.'

That knocked the stuffing out of Tiff. 'Don't be like that Dee, only having a wind up.'

Before Dee could put her further in her place the head of her security appeared. 'Mizz Dee, some guy wants a word.'

'About…?' Her security team were under strict orders not to admit anyone who didn't have an appointment. Time wasters she could do without.

'I told him you wouldn't see him, but he won't take no for answer. He's suited and booted and looks official like.'

Dee had a think. It might be a suit from up the council. She needed to keep them sweet because just as they'd had the power to give her a license they could as easily take it away.

It was Jen who made the decision for her by announcing, 'I'll take Tiff for a tour of the wine cellar…without the taste test this time.'

When her sisters were gone Dee gave the nod for her unexpected guest to present himself. Her head of security was spot on; the fella looked the part, clobbered out in a well-made, dark grey suit and briefcase in hand.

'Mrs Black?'

Dee hitched her head back and flicked her blue fringe out of her eye. 'Who wants to know?'

He smiled with professional politeness. 'My name is Jacob Smith. I wonder if I might have a word?'

It dawned on Dee that he wasn't from the Council. Her mouth turned down at the corners. 'You flogging something?'

He burst out laughing, flashing a well-kept set of teeth. 'Yes, I'm afraid I am, in a manner of speaking.'

By rights she should tell him to sling his hook, but curiosity got the better of her. 'OK – let's hear it.'

Smith took out a business card and passed it to her.

'I represent a consortium of local firms who've clubbed together to offer each other support in the face of the rising tide of criminality in the area. As I'm sure you're aware, this is a subject close to the heart of anyone trying to run a successful business in these difficult times.'

He rubbed his palms together. 'And, as I'm sure you're also aware, the local police are hopeless. They can't and won't help. We, on the other hand, can provide effective assistance in the event of you being targeted by criminals. By paying a small joining fee and making a regular contribution to our mutual defence fund, we ensure you can conduct your trade in peace.'

He even sounded like a proper salesman but Dee was an old hand and realised straight away what he was up to.

She slid his card back without looking at it. 'No thanks, ta, Mister Smith. I'm quite capable of ensuring my own security thank you very much.'

He persisted, his smile dimming ever so slightly. 'I'm sure you are. But I'm afraid many local businesses have made the mistake of assuming they could cope with these kinds of problems without support only to find themselves sunk by trouble later. And you never know what direction crime might come from - theft, criminal damage, arson and assaults. Many an honest trader has been put out of business by this kind of delinquent activity.'

He leaned in and whispered, 'You may not be aware of this Mrs Black, but I'm afraid there are a number of protection rackets active in the area. Going up against these evil people on your own would be very unwise. Dangerous in fact.'

This was rich. Dee nearly hooted with laughter. A bloke from a protection racket offering her protection against protection rackets? He must think she'd fallen off last year's Christmas tree.

'Like I said, no thanks Smithy. You see, I'm the widow of John Black. I expect you're familiar with the name in your line of work? I know how to look after myself – you may want to pass that information on to your *consortium.*'

Smith was still smiling but she could see from his eyes that he knew he'd drawn a blank.

'Of course.' He looked around the club. 'Very nice place you have here. I wish you every success with it.'

As he left, Dee eyeballed him all the way. She knew already that either Mister Smith or his 'consortium' would come a-calling again.

Ten minutes later Dee forgot all about protection rackets as she and her sisters waited outside on the pavement with bated breath as the lights of the club's name lit up for the very first time. They linked arms as they stared with excitement at the neon blue sign.

Three Sisters.

Seven

Jacob Smith – not his real name - aka The Salesman was shitting himself as he sat in his motor outside the boxing gym. His bosses were liable to rip him a new one when he passed on the bad news that Dee Black wasn't playing ball. He hated being called the Salesman. He wanted a moniker that was either cool or menacing. But he kept that to himself because it was the two brothers, his bosses, who'd given him his nick. Once they made up their minds about something they rarely changed it. But Jacob had to admit that The Salesman tag pretty much summed up the work he did for them.

The two brothers drove around their patch in their big Caddy SUV, Tony Soprano style, and when they spotted a new business opening its doors it was his job to speak all nicey-nicey to the owners and persuade them to 'insure' against damage to their property. Usually it went down without a hitch. To say the brothers wouldn't be best pleased that he'd left the Three Sisters Club without sealing a deal was the understatement of the year. Especially when they'd figured a load of wonga was being pumped into the club, which meant they could hike up the premium.

£ £ £ was the name of their game.

But the bitch owner had turned nasty. Now the boys were going to turn nasty.

It was a nasty business.

The Salesman pulled as much courage as he could together and exited his wheels. He nodded at the stony-faced huge bastard who was on point by the door and went into the gym. Amy Winehouse's 'Rehab' blasted from speakers mounted on the wall. The place was heaving, smelling of sweat and maleness. Gloved and guarded guys were in the ring swapping punches under the eagle eye of a trainer. Other blokes pulled weights, skipped rope or belted punch bags. The Salesman took no notice of any of that. He focused on the table at the far end of the room where his gaffers kept an eye on proceedings, one in a leather chair, the other sitting on a table.

Their birth names were Lennox and Glenroy, but they were known by one and all as Pinky and Styley. In their early days they'd got into a young designer who used the brand name 'Pink Style' because all her clothing had a dash of pink. To start with she'd peddled her fashion off a stall in Spitalfields Market and the guys were her best customers. Now she had a shop in Hoxton, flogging threads to pop stars and TV people but the brothers remained her number one customers.

Today Pinky was in a pink suit and tie with a black shirt and handmade shoes while his brother was in a leather jacket sporting a pink fur trim, black jeans and a pair of Pink Style brogues. Their gear was a bit out there, but no one dared take the piss. No one took the rise out of these two.

They fixed their cool stares on The Salesman as he

hesitantly approached. They didn't look much like brothers. Styley favoured his father's Irish family, with his white skin and blonde, slightly wavy hair. Pinky, on the other hand, was black like his maternal Jamaican grandparents. And what confused people even more was that Styley had dark eyes and Pinky's were a light, piercing blue.

There was no small talk when The Salesman reached them.

Styley got straight down to business as usual. 'The rich bitch with the club – did you talk to her?'

The Salesman nervously cleared his throat. 'Ummm... Yes.'

'And?' Styley picked up a can of brew and swallowed slowly, his dark eyes never leaving his henchman. He was a good-looking guy with his hair styled out in zigzag cornrows.

The Salesman bit the bullet, finally admitting, 'She won't pay up.'

Pinky eased out of his chair. He was the brains of the outfit, Styley the fists. 'Perhaps you didn't try hard enough. Now you've put us to some trouble. You know we don't like trouble.'

Cold sweat leaked down The Salesman's back. 'I tried boss, but she knows her way round these types of matters. She's John Black's widow.'

Pinky was unimpressed. 'John Black's six feet under, so I don't see what the problem is?'

'Even so, she looks like a bit of handful herself as it happens.'

Pinky rubbed his nose. 'Handful? We'll give her handful.' He turned to his brother. 'Better give our girlfriend down in Bow a bell, get her to pay this clip joint a visit, show the Widow Black what a handful really looks like.'

The Salesman stood to a respectful attention in front of the displeased brothers. It was difficult to tell how this was going to play out. Usually when they ranted and raved it was a good sign; meant you weren't going to get a hiding. When they smiled and fooled around that was when you started worrying; it was often the run-up to one of the brutal beatings they liked to dish out.

Styley took his phone from his jacket and made the call as his brother sat beside him on the table.

'Alright bird? Me and my bruv have got a job for you, so drop by…No, I'm not telling you on the blower – what's the matter with ya? Everyone's phone's bugged these days, you thick twat. Perhaps you'd like me to drop a memo to the Chief Constable while we're at it?'

The Salesman was dismissed by Pinky. 'Jerk off. But do better next time. Practice your hard boy act in the mirror, otherwise people will think you're a pussy ass, which is bad - and we will too, which is worse.' He added with menace, 'You wouldn't want to go a round in the ring with us, now would ya? You might get some fingers broken.'

The Salesman's mouth went bone-dry at that stark final threat. He worked with the brothers on a as-and-when-needed basis, the rest of his time taken up with what he considered to be his real job. A job where the use of his fingers was his very livelihood. The brothers knew full well he couldn't afford for any damage to be done to his hands. Evil bastards!

As he walked with speed he passed a thick-necked trainer heading out to the back of the gym. As the man passed the table, he sent the brothers a cheery grin. 'Here Pinky, what's the deal with that tie then?'

Pinky slowly lifted his head to stare at him. 'Wha'cha mean?'

The trainer nodded at his boss' neckwear. 'Well, it's a bit wide. The cool boys are wearing them a bit narrower…at the moment.'

The Salesman slowed his pace as he closed his eyes in horror. This guy was clearly too new on the premises to know you never dissed the pair's clobber. Now he'd realised his mistake, it was too late. The gym went silent as all the men looked on. Even Amy stopped singing.

Pinky's lips spread in a slow and easy malevolent smile as he got off the table while examining his tie. 'Too wide? Yeah, you think so? I suppose you think my brother's fur trim is a bit girly for this season as well?'

Pasty-skinned, shitting a brick, the trainer sputtered, 'Leave it out Pinky, I was only having a joke wiv ya.'

Pinky put his arm around the trainers shoulder with the strength of barbed wire hooking him close. 'I know you was. Relax matey, we know how to have a hoot in here. I always say the art of good management is knowing when to share a gag with your staff. It keeps morale up, ain't that right Sty?'

Styley chuckled away as he settled back in the comfy padding of the leather chair and he plonked his Pink Style feet on the table. 'That's right bruv. Like one, big happy family here. We'll be holding hands next, singing all the world needs now is love, sweet love.'

Pinky's arm tightened round the trainer's trembling shoulder. 'Just to show you I know how to share a joke, let me take my far too wide tie off and put it in the bin.' Pinky loosened his tie without undoing the knot and pulled it over his head. Then, as easy as you please, he dropped the noose over the trainer's head and pulled it tight before yanking the terror-stricken man backwards like a dog towards a punch bag. He tied the loose end of the tie to the top of the bag and then strung him up. The trainer dangled, choking and kicking for dear life like a man at the gallows.

Pinky declared with the flare of the ringmaster at a boxing bout at Wembley Arena, 'Can I have everyone's attention please? Gather round.' When the crowd had joined Pinky in a semi-circle, he explained, 'the standard of boxing in this place is lower than the odds on me in a fight. You're punching like schoolgirls in the playground. I don't wanna see blows like this…'

He delivered a couple of fierce jabs to the trainer's face, who yelped and howled with pain through his gagging noises.

Pinkie continued his masterclass. 'If you want to box, you need to show some fire in your belly. Really let the other guy know he's in for the battering of a lifetime. More like this.'

He really let rip with his clenched fists. He pummelled his victim, landing blow after blow to his face and body, until the trainer was left slumped, hanging by his neck, face bloodied, black and blue.

Pinky paused for breath and looked ready to go another round when his brother nudged him, indicating they had a visitor.

A Range Rover had pulled up outside and judging by the headlights reflected in the blinds it looked like a big one. Pinky took a blade from his back pocket and cut the noose around the trainer's neck who fell to the floor spluttering and gasping to fill his lungs like a beached whale.

'Lesson over people – get back to it.' When they didn't move quickly enough for his liking Pinky growled, 'come on – knock the living daylights outta something!'

The brothers went back to their table as the door to the gym opened.

A tall, older black guy in a long overcoat wearing a trilby walked in. He paused by the body of the trainer and peered emotionless at him while he peeled off his gloves. Then he went up to the table where Pinky and Styley now anxiously stood to attention like a couple of soldiers.

Pinky spoke first, his Adam's apple bobbing as he swallowed nervously. 'Hello Biggin. This is a nice surprise. We don't usually see you up here. How's things?'

All the men in the gym, except The Salesman, knew the newcomer's real name began with an 'N' but due to his statue in the underworld he had been universally known as Big N. Over time this had morphed into Biggin.

Biggin looked back at Pinky's victim. 'What happened to him?'

Styley wet his lips. 'Oh, you know, the usual locker room banter that ended in a difference of opinion. Can we get you something? A snifter maybe?'

The brothers were falling over themselves to accommodate him.

Biggin's voice was soft. 'Yeah, you can get me something – the rent – I was expecting it yesterday.'

The brothers looked like they were about to be the victims of a fatal car crash.

Pinky turned on his brother in horror. 'You were supposed to do that.'

'No way bruv, that was down to you.'

Biggin swiftly raised his hand to stop the Ping-Pong blame game in its tracks. 'I don't care which of you two lemons it was supposed to be. Go and get it for me now. And put on ten per cent for late payment.'

Styley hurried out back and returned with an envelope, which he handed to Biggin who put it in his coat pocket.

'I won't count it. Even you two aren't stupid enough to try and short me. And I'm very sure indeed you're not stupid enough to make me come up to this flea pit a second time to collect my cash.'

And with that he walked out without another word. His motor's engine burst back into life and glided off the pavement outside.

The two brothers were badly shaken and were whispering frantically to each other. They were so dazed that they barely noticed that The Salesman was still in the background.

He heard Pinky say, 'the curtain's gonna fall if he finds out we messed up the backhander from that club.'

The Salesman had no idea the brothers answered to anyone. They always insisted they were top of the chain. He had no idea who this Biggin character was but he knew one thing - if Biggin could verbally bitch-slap two crazies who'd just choked a man half to death for making a joke about a tie, then he had to be a very big Face indeed.

Eight

Heart beating like the clappers, fourteen-year-old Courtney Miller peeped around the corner of the brick wall near the Ragged School Museum opposite the newly done up Mile End Stadium. All she had to do now was walk through the park, cross over into Bow Common Lane and then be on her merry way to The Devil following the brick wall of the old cemetery. That would sort the fuckers out. No way were they getting her today.

But luck wasn't on her side. Half way through the park her tormentors appeared like birds of prey. One minute they weren't there and the next they were.

As per usual there were three of them, but the one who was yanking the chain was her former best mate, Tasha. What a right jealous bitch Tasha had turned out to be. They'd once been all bestie-bestie, matey-matey but as soon as Courtney had won the scholarship to Egerton Academy, a posh school in the City, Tasha turned all salt and vinegar and didn't want to know her anymore. Courtney could've dealt with that – she'd already felt the hard whack of life in her short time on this earth – but her once time best mate had taken it into her mean loaf to wage all out war on her.

Being a Miller, most figured Courtney knew how to use her fists to look out for herself, but the plain truth was after that horror-filled incident with her granddad Stan she dared not raise her hand to anyone, terrified of what the results might be.

Smirking with evil confidence Tasha sauntered up to her, followed by her two hood monkeys, who snapped and snarled eager to sink their gnashers into something tasty.

Tasha wore her trademark clobber – skimpy skirt and crop top – which put enough flesh on display, as she put it, to get the lads on The Devil sniffing after her. Probably thinks she looks like something off MTV, Courtney thought wickedly; more like Scrubbers TV.

They crowded her and Tasha, the Teenage Bitch, got in her face. 'Oh please Mizz! I've done my Shakespeare homework Mizz! And I sagged my violin lesson to make it extra special for you Mizz! Can I kiss your jacksie Mizz?'

Tasha's she-devils cackled their dumb heads off. Courtney clutched her rucksack, which contained her homework, as her edgy gaze swung between the bullies. She'd tried every trick in the book to avoid their antics. Hanging around the City for a couple of hours in the hope this mob would out be off their heads on the latest high when she got back but that was no use either. Tried blindsiding them by getting off at either Stepney Green or Bow Road tube and then making her way home through the back streets. Nothing seemed to work. Her school had a strict anti-bullying policy but these girls didn't. They had a piss-take and clout very hard policy. Wailing to her mum wasn't an option; in the East End you took care of your own problems.

Tasha growled, the glow in her eyes declaring she was having the time of her pathetic life. 'Think you're better than the rest of us coz you go to that snob joint, don't ya?'

Courtney cut her eyes at the girl she'd once shared all her secrets with and tried to step around her, but the thugs only fenced her tighter in their intimidating snare.

Courtney had had enough. 'Why don't you sod off, you slag.'

Tasha's face turned scarlet as it twisted into an ugly expression. 'Sod off you slag?' Her cruel laughter was even more twisted than her face. ''Ere, I thought posh bitch schools charged top dollar to teach you how to speak proper? Your mum's wasting her dosh.'

'She don't pay actually. I'm on a scholarship.'

Tasha mimicked, 'She *don't pay actually, I'm on a scholarship* - so you're a trampy, snob bitch? Fucking hell Courtney, you can't catch a break can you?'

For the first time one of Tasha's gang chipped in, 'when people cuss at schools like hers, they wash their mouths out with soap and water, don't they?'

Tasha high-fived her goon with glee. 'Good point. Well, I ain't got no soap, but I know where there's plenty of water. Let's take her down the Regent's.'

Courtney's skin turned clammy as she realised these girls were taking their cruel game up a notch. Up until now, Tasha's crew had taken liberties with a load of spiteful verbal. Courtney had bravely shrugged it off with a 'sticks and stones' approach. Now, the way they were closing in, told her, point blank, they were intending to royally sort her out. And, worst of all, The Regent's Canal was only a hop, skip and jump away.

All of a sudden a tidal wave of rage whelmed up inside her. Only one time in her life had she felt this way – watching her granddad trying to throttle the life out of her beloved Nanna Babs.

Courtney twisted her hands into fists at her side, the way Aunty Tiff had taught her, so when she let loose she did maximum damage. Courtney lunged and lashed out, a red mist of manic anger clouding her vision. She'd teach this twat-hag some basic manners she'd never forget. But Tasha dunked neatly out of the way nearly making Courtney loss her balance.

'You're dead,' was all the warning she got.

She tried punching out again but her arms were grabbed and clamped tightly by her side. Courtney was boxed in.

I'm bleedin' done for.

Legging it was no longer an option and screaming would make her look like a proper cry baby. But she wasn't going to blub either, no effing way.

They shoved, jostled and strong-armed her past the curved Mile End Green Bridge to the banks of the canal. She tried one more time to bash her way out, but it was no use. Fuck me! She couldn't go in that water. Just couldn't. There were rats in there. Her cold skin crawled as she imagined them nibbling on her flesh. In her hair. Razor-sharp teeth in her ear. Courtney almost screamed…

But what was the point? Anyone looking out of the flash flats opposite would assume that it was a group of typical teens larking about.

Tasha bent down to grab her legs. 'Time for a dunking.'

Courtney booted her with all the force she could muster. Aunty Tiff had taught her that move too. Roaring in pain

Tasha landed on the grass. Her skirt twisted round her waist displaying a pair of knickers that looked more like your granny's than Victoria's Secret. If the guys on The Devil could see her now they'd be laughing their nuts off. Before Courtney could savour any satisfaction, one of the other girls pinched her hard on her breast making her sag and gasp in pain.

Tasha scrambled to her feet, her body rocking with rage. 'Get her in the water. Now!'

They dragged her towards the water, Courtney kicking and fighting all of the way. They reached the edge. Defiantly she stared down at her reflection in the murky, green water awaiting her watery fate.

'Push the bitch in,' Tasha shouted with relish, clapping along.

'Courtney?' a hesitant, husky voice interrupted.

A youth, with a Pitbull on a lead, advanced on them with a cocksure confidence. Courtney couldn't tell if it was a boy or a girl as the face was hidden by a low slunk hoodie. The newcomer wore grunge-style, three-quarter khaki cargo pants and black Converses.

Tasha crossed her arms with attitude as she insolently slid her withering gaze up the newcomer…and down again.

'Mind your own, unless you fancy some of the same.' Tasha taunted, her head swaying from side to side like she was Queen of the Regent's castle.

The youth flipped their hood back revealing a girl with spiked, jet-black hair and lipstick to match. Courtney's face scrunched up. Don't I know her? She trawled her mind. Where? Where? Nah, she couldn't place her. Whoever she was her steadfast stare announced she wasn't backing down from a rumble. Tasha and her gang must've recognised it too because Courtney's arms were abruptly released.

Hoodie girl tightened her grip on the dog and turned to Tasha. 'What the fuck do you think you're doing?'

Tasha shrugged her shoulders but looked like she was wetting her granny panties. 'Just having a laugh…you know….'

'A laugh?' The words were gobbed Tasha's way. 'Look at my lips. Am I laughing?' The girl looked down at her dog. 'Is my friend here laughing?'

The dog picked up on the threatening tone and strained forward, baring his teeth. Her tormentors backed off a little. But that wasn't enough for the dog owner. 'Do you know who Courtney is covered by?'

The blood drained from Tasha's face as a quivering, 'No,' passed her lips.

'Alright - do you know who I'm covered by?'

'Yeah.' Courtney's tormentor could barely get the word out she was that scared.

The dog was almost on its hind legs jerking furiously against its leash.

'If I ever catch you having a go at Courtney again, I'm gonna send my little bow-wow round your gaff where he'll grab you by your arse and drag you down the river and it won't be for a splash around, you get me?' When there was a shame-faced silence, the girl yelled, 'Are you fucking deaf? I said - do you understand?'

Even Courtney was quaking at this force of nature.

'What are you waiting for?' her saviour bellowed, 'Bug. Right. Off.'

Courtney almost creased up with pure joy as she watched

Tasha and her lapdogs run for their lives. But she didn't dare. This bitch girl assassin might've saved her bacon but she didn't know her from Adam…or more like Eve. Aunty Tiff had warned her never to get chummy before you sussed a body out and this girl was going to take a wagonload of sussing.

Hoodie girl cheered up. 'Hello Courts – you don't remember me, do ya?'

Still not willing to let her guard down she merely shook her head. All she wanted to do was to get herself indoors.

'Yeah, you do! I'm Dodgy! We were in that care home together!'

The penny dropped and Courtney was confronted with memories she'd rather wipe from her mind forever. She'd been placed in a girl's secure care home in Kent while a decision was made about what should be done about her after she'd confessed to delivering the killer blow that had sent her monster granddad to his rightful place in the fires of hell. That had been the lowest point of her life. Locked up and not allowed out had almost killed her. She'd sobbed her heart out most nights missing her family something terrible, especially Nanna Babs. Although she'd only been in the home for a week that had been long enough to get to know all about Dodgy. Her real name was Shannon Fraser, but even the staff called her Dodgy and for a very good reason.

'You can't let other girls treat you like that Courts,' the other girl counselled, dragging Courtney back to the cold present. 'You need to get some back up, especially if you're going to walk the streets dressed like that.' Her face scrunched up with distaste. 'I mean, what the fuck is that you're rigged out in?'

'It's my school uniform.' Mortified, Courtney's cheeks grew hot and bothered. No wonder she'd become a target. The get-up made her stand out like a top hat and tails at a West Ham match, especially the red and black tartan blazer.

It was Foxy, her former therapist, who had helped her mum get her into Egerton Academy. Apparently Foxy was on chummy terms with the headmistress. Mind you, it might have all come to nothing if Courtney hadn't passed the entrance test.

She chewed on her lip as her thoughts became darker. She knew her mum was only trying to do the best for her, make sure she got a flying start in life, but going to a school that wasn't around here meant she'd lost touch with most of her mates. Even Rockers, the boy she'd loved since forever, didn't really hang out with her anymore. Courtney No Mates. She felt like the loneliest soul in the world.

'I go to this private school down by Tower Bridge. And my school don't do back up. They do counselling instead.'

That tickled Dodgy's fancy as she hee-heed. 'Private school? Bad luck babe.' She put her arm around Courtney's shoulder walking down the canal with her. 'So you don't know anyone who can help you out when you're in a bit of bother?'

Rockers had always been her back up, not anymore though. 'Nah.'

Dodgy had a think. 'You don't really need back up anyway, all you need is a bit of a rep and I can help you out there. Hang out with me now and then, word will soon spread that you run with Dodgy and the Dodgy Girls and then you'll be able to wear your poncey uniform where you like. You'll be bomb proof. No problem!'

Dodgy and the Dodgy Girls? Courtney wasn't sure. But then again, she was brassed off with all the ducking and diving, on her jacks, round the streets on her way home trying to avoid the likes of Tasha. Still…

'I dunno Dodgy.'

The other girl encouragingly squeezed her shoulder. 'Come on Courts, do yourself a favour. It's not like I'm in a gang or nuthin. We just muck about, is all.'

She worried her bottom lip again. She wasn't sure…but it hurt being a no mates. 'I suppose we could hang out.' Her words dripped out slowly.

'Good girl.' Dodgy grinned. A bounce entered her step making her dog jump around excitedly. 'My dog's called Mandela.' Seeing the confusion on Courtney's face she explained, 'he's like that Nelson Mandela, ain't he? No matter how much people kick him they won't take him down.'

Courtney remained confused; who the heck was this Nelson Mandela character? Not wanting to appear a total div she nodded.

The other girl's face suddenly contorted with anger. 'I found him roaming the street. He had all bruises up his ribs and a boot mark on his throat. I tell you what Courts, if I ever get my hands…' Her voice shook with emotion.

Dodgy's lips suddenly relaxed as the rage slipped away. 'Come down the Station Car Park in the evenings, we're usually down there sooner or later.'

Then Dodgy remembered something. ''Ere Courts, have you got a blade?' Seeing the wide-eyed alarm on Courtney's face she quickly added, 'Not to stiff anyone or nuthin obviously, I mean just to brandish if trouble comes down the street.'

When she didn't get an answer, Dodgy went on. 'Not to worry babe, you can borrow one of mine.'

Nine

The accusations came thick and fast as soon as Pearl walked into the care home's dayroom the following afternoon.

'This is all your fault Pearl.'

'We would've never met that chancer Saint Aubin if it weren't for you.'

'That money was put aside for my grandkids. What am I going to leave them now – my collection of Spanish pesetas?'

The residents who had been swindled were gathered around a couple of tables with that Daisy Evans lording it over at the head of the table in her wheelchair like she was Queen Bee of the home. Pearl didn't like the woman. That fat body of hers and even bigger gob took up far too much space. And, as if that wasn't bad even, she was always going on and on to anyone with an ear about how well her Darren was doing in the City as some high-flying financial whizz kid. Even had a photo of the chump taped to the arm of her motorised wheelchair. Funny thing though, she obviously thought the world of her boy but he rarely came to visit her.

As much as she hadn't taken to the old windbag she couldn't fault Daisy this time – Pearl had made a right bodge up job of persuading the others to invest their money.

Guilt squeezed in beside her as she took her seat.

For the second time, in two days, Fred rode to her rescue. 'It ain't Pearl's fault, alright? She was only trying to do all of us a kindness by cutting us in on something that would see us through our twilight years.' He sat next to the twins with a protective arm on the back of Vi's chair.

'Bleedin' Twilight Zone more like,' Daisy scoffed, her tight gaze spearing Pearl like a weapon. 'She was the one who bought that rip-off merchant here in the first place.'

Fred was about to come to her defence again, but Pearl could stand on her own two feet and if that Daisy kept giving it some she'd be standing on hers as well.

'You're right, I did bring Saint Aubin in here, but it was only coz I'd been investing with him for some time and making money hand over fist—'

Vi softly cut in, her tiny, soft hands moving in her lap. 'That isn't strictly true. It was me who asked Pearl about where I should put my savings. She didn't come to me, *I* went to *her*.'

She fixed her gaze on Daisy. Vi could've given her a right, royal raking over with her stare, but that wasn't her way.

Her faded, grey eyes were mixed with equal parts gentleness and sadness. 'And my money did good at first,' she turned slowly to Pearl, 'and I will always thank you for that. Seeing as how our investment was increasing Pearl only asked that man to come here because she wanted to help you.'

She cast her gaze across the gathering. 'No one strong-armed any of us to put our money into his scheme. There are people in this world that believe us older folk have lost our marbles. Is that what we're saying here? That Pearl made us do it because our wits have deserted us?'

An uncomfortable silence settled over the group. Vi nodded. 'Yeah, that's what I thought. When my dad came to England as a young lad, after fleeing those Nazis in Germany who butchered his parents in the camps, he always said to me, 'don't blame good people for what bad people do."'

The majority appeared shame-faced at her stirring words.

Fred patted her shoulder proudly as the corners of his eyes crinkled with adoration. 'No truer words have been spoken girl.'

'Hold up Fred.' Daisy wasn't going down without a fight. 'Before you hand Vi there an Oscar for best performance in a movie starring a scam merchant, I say,' she gave it a dramatic pause as she caught each eye in the room, 'maybe that Saint Aubin fella knew he had someone on the inside when he came in here to fleece us.' She slapped her brazen, accusing gaze on Pearl.

Pearl knew where she was going and wasn't having it. 'You saying I was in on his double-dealing act?'

There was a collective indrawn breath. Daisy twisted her substantial lips. 'You know what they say – if it quacks like a duck …'

A few years back she would've been bang to rights. Pearl had, in her day, been one of the most cunning con artists around. She'd used her Madam Pearl fortune-telling routine to reel her gullible punters in and once they were in her web she sucked them dry of every penny she could ponce off them. That was the problem with people, always desperate to know about their future instead of sorting out their shit in the here and now. She'd made a killing. Living it large. A life devoted to spend, spend, spend.

Her biggest shame was instead of using her loot on her kids, she'd skipped out on them for a Flash Bay Rum smothered Harry. He'd known had to use his tally whacker between the sheets alright, but as soon as the money dried up he booted her to the kerb and high-tailed it out of town with a French stripper who really hailed from Halifax. She'd moved heaven and earth to cosy up back to her kids, but they didn't want to know. Pearl didn't blame them really. Still, losing your babies created the type of heartache no quack could cure.

She still touted herself as the woman with the all-seeing eye into the future, without taking anyone's cash these days, because she couldn't let go of it. Almost like it had come out of the womb with her when she was born into this world sixty-three years ago in her mum's corrugated iron-roofed humble home in Jamaica. And look at the great Madam Pearl now, eh? Con artist extraordinaire who'd been almost taken for all she was worth by a con trick she should've seen coming a mile off.

That's why she felt so much guilt. Instead of protecting her friends with her insider knowledge she'd led them to the slaughter.

But still, she wasn't letting an ignorant, too much to say tub of lard, like Daisy Evans blatantly tell porkies about her.

Giving them the best theatre most of them hadn't seen in forever, she spread her arms dramatically wide, silver bangles tinkering in the air, and peered up at the heavens. 'Spirits, I beseech you to forgive Daisy for the evil tongue she has woken up with today. May her heart be filled with peace and love, for all man, and all woman, so she can help use during this terrible—'

'Oh, gimme a break,' Daisy snapped, snorting in disgust. 'Why don't you ask your friends in the spirit world where our money's gone? Where Saint Aubin's holed up? Do something useful for a change.'

Many grumbled agreement, but Pearl levelled her stage act stare shutting them up. She paused for effect. Then quietly uttered, as if they were all linking hands at a séance, 'I don't control the spirits. I am a mere vessel for them. And when Saint Aubin's was amongst us they chose not too appear.' Her voice dipped low, making the few wearing hearing aids lean closer. 'And do you know why that was? They sensed an evil presence in our midst—'

'I say Pearl should be expelled,' Daisy barked completely pissed off with Pearl's claptrap.

'What, from the meeting?' asked a bewildered Fred, scratching his balding head.

Daisy's amble bosoms shook. 'Nah, I mean from the Home. She's put us all in the shit and don't deserve to live among the rest of us. She should find somewhere else to live. And take her bogus spirits with her.'

Pearl snapped out of her act and got to her feet. 'You what?'

With smarmy satisfaction Daisy gave it to her straight. 'You heard. You shouldn't be living with decent people.'

'Decent people?' Pearl gave it back to her in spades. 'I ain't taking that from a dodgy boiler who's only in a wheelchair because her legs can't take the strain.'

Daisy manoeuvred her wheelchair towards Pearl with speed. 'You take that back Pearl Hennessy.'

Pearl slammed her fists on her hips, her bracelets shaking violently, looking down at the other woman who appeared to be on the verge of running her over. 'And if I don't?'

'You'll find out why these,' Daisy shook her fists, 'were nicknamed Mohammed Ali and Joe Frazier back in the day in Poplar.'

'Should I come back later?' a voice interrupted from the doorway.

The room focused its attention on a tall man, with greying, short hair and a smart, black suit. In his fifties, with a handsome face, he had an air about him that captured the eye.

'Patrick,' Vi greeted, clapping her hands in utter pleasure. 'Thanks so much for coming.'

The newcomer returned her smile and kissed her warm cheeks. She held his hand between her palms for a while as if he were a long, lost treasure returned to her. 'Remember I said that there might be someone who can help us – well, this is Patrick.' She beamed at him. 'He's like a son to me. I only wish that you could've met him during happier times.'

As Daisy wheeled herself back to her place she asked, 'So, how can he help?'

The guy stayed on his feet as he addressed the gathering. 'I can't promise that I'll be able to do that, but from what Vi has told me, you've been scammed by a classic pyramid scheme—'

'What's that then?' Fred squinted as his bushy brows drew together.

Vi's friend took his time as he patiently explained. 'A few people are asked to invest and at first their money starts doing well. This builds confidence, so other people then join and that's when things go down hill. This man who conned you made sure he got as much as he could from you all and then disappeared with your money.'

Fred frown deepened, his gold tooth flashing as he snarled, 'Back in my day they had another name for it - daylight robbery.'

'So what can you—?' Before Pearl could finish the receptionist politely tapped on the open door.

'Pearl, you've got a visitor.'

'Me?' Pearl was puzzled. She wasn't expecting anyone. Then her heart lifted with hope. Maybe it was one of her children finally come to forgive her. If it was...Pearl excitedly patted her headscarf like a teenager going on her first date.

When she got to her feet she looked over at Fred. 'If I'm not back fill me in on what's-what later on.'

As Pearl walked away with a spring in her step Daisy jeered, 'Probably getting a visit from those whack-a-do spirits who see fuck all.'

'Will you give it a rest?' This was from Mrs Kowalski who rarely uttered a word.

Pearl didn't hear a word of it, too excited at the prospect at seeing one of her kids. It had been over twenty years. That's a long time to be without the flesh and blood you gave birth to. But when she reached the reception, Pearl was in for a crushing disappointment. It wasn't one of her kids.

'What you doing here?'

'We agreed I'd come over today. I wanna word about the gold,' a grim-faced Babs Miller replied.

Ten

Babs had never seen a black person turn green before. Truth be told, she didn't think it was possible, but that's exactly what happened to Pearl's face. It came all over a green. A very nasty green indeed.

'The...gold?' Pearl stammered, obviously having forgotten about their meeting.

Babs leaned in close, her words only for the other woman's ears. 'Yeah, you know the yellow stuff kipping in your settee.'

Up close Pearl looked like she was about to chunder. There was a line of sweat just under her headscarf and her usually smooth, brown skin looked tired. Blimey, she hoped the old girl wasn't about to collapse on her.

'Pearl, you alright?'

'Alright?...Yeah, yes, of course I am.'

Babs begged to differ. Pearl was blinking like she'd just discovered her eyelashes and her lips were quivering.

Whatever was going on Babs took the matter in hand as she took Pearl gently by the arm. 'Let's get you sat down and a cup of hot Rosie Lee inside ya.'

She gently guided Pearl down the corridor as she

continued, 'Once we're in your room you can tell me what's up. And don't tell me nothing's wrong coz you look like you've just seen the grim reaper.'

'My…room?'

Her former next-door cellie sounded so alarmed Babs increased their pace.

'Yeah, you know the place where you put your head down every night.'

Babs could feel her friend trembling. Poor Pearl! Best get her sat down before her legs gave way. But when they reached her friend's room, to Babs' astonishment, Pearl shifted herself with the speed of lightening and plonked herself squarely in front of the door.

'We can't go in there,' she protested, folding her arms.

'Why not?' Babs didn't get it. One minute Pearl looks like she's ready to take her last breath and now she's coming on like a bouncer.

'Fleas,' Pearl punched out, not budging an inch.

Babs' brows snapped together. 'What are you rabbiting on about?' Then it dawned on her. 'You having a senior moment? Maybe I should go get one of the carers.'

Pearl straightened her back. Babs squinted at her knowingly. While they were doing bird Babs had felt sorry for the old lag next door because she'd been a shuffling, stooped wreck who royally got on the other girls' nerves. Babs hadn't had the heart to turn her away when her little face popped round her cell doorway silently begging for someone to natter with. Babs knew first hand how lonely and scary prison could be. Only on the out did Babs cotton on to the fact that the hunched, poor ol' dear act was exactly that – an act. Pearl had more toughness in her spine than British Steel.

Babs pursed her lips. 'What's going on here Pearl?'

The older woman's eyes danced the same way when she was telling anyone with an ear about her Madam Pearl routine.

'I'm lying in bed last night trying to catch some sleep and all of a sudden I start scratching my arms, then my legs. I tell you Babsie girl before I know it I'm scratching everywhere.' Her little hands fluttered in the air. 'This morning I got the caretaker to come look and he tells me,' she leaned in close but didn't move from the door, 'it's fleas.' Her gaze moved dramatically up and down the corridor. 'Told me to keep it under my headscarf so the others don't find out. He fumigated my room this morning, so I can't go in there until tomorrow.'

Babs' lips tightened. She'd heard all kinds of likely stories in her time and this ranked right up there.

'Fleas? That's a right Jackanory if you ask me. What's going on?'

'Cross my heart, hope to die.' Pearl accompanied her words with the action.

To Babs' surprise she stepped out of the way.

'I ain't stopping you from going in there, but it's *fleas* Babs. Those critters are like spirits, jump on you in the blink of an eye. Then they'll be breeding and hopping with glee in your home. And if your girls come around – which I know they do regular like – they'll be on them too. Next thing you hear your kid's homes have been infested.' She gasped as she covered her mouth in shock. 'What about your grandbaby? They'll have at him too.' Pearl stepped further into the corridor and waved her hand at the door. 'Like I said Babsie girl, I ain't stopping you from going into Flea City.'

Babs reached again for the handle. Hesitated. Fleas in her home. Yuk! Bloody hell she felt like scratching all over. And what if Natty ended up with them? And then flippin' nits? Dee might never let her look after him again…

Suddenly, Babs' expression soured. Stan had taught her all about the 'go ahead and have a look' trick. She'd fly into a rage, challenging him about his story about where he'd been and he'd counter with, all calm and innocent, that she could check his pockets if she didn't believe him. Of course she never did because why would a guilty person put himself on the line if he had anything to hide? Right? Wrong. Now one of her besties thought she could pull the same stunt.

Babs opened the door with determination.

'Babsie…I…I never…' Pearl spluttered behind her.

'What the heck went on here?' Babs' eyes grew round with incredulity as she stared horrified at Pearl's room.

Burn marks on the far wall. The window boarded up. The iron bars, which she'd been pleased that Pearl had installed as a security measure for the gold…

Bloody hell, the gold…

Babs' breath froze as her gaze skidded to the settee. Looked like Edward Scissorhands had done a proper number on it.

An incredible rage swelled inside her. 'Where. Is. The. Gold?'

All Pearl's playacting vanished as she squared her shoulders and confessed, 'It's gone.'

'Wha'cha mean, it's gone? It don't have legs to just up and waltz outta here.'

The older woman's jaw moved, but no words came out. Then she tried again. 'I was out with the others and when I came back the cops were—'

'The Bill?' Could this get any bloody worse? Babs' head started ringing. This was a nightmare, pure and simple.

'Don't worry, I fobbed them off with a story that did the trick,' Pearl tried to reassure her. 'Let's go to the dayroom and I'll tell you how it was.'

In a daze of disbelief Babs followed her to the dayroom. A meeting was going on at one end of the room, with a man, who had his back to her, addressing the audience. Two women were sitting in armchairs, but as soon as they clocked Pearl they stabbed her with nasty looks, got up and stomped off.

When they were sat at a table Babs asked, 'what was all that about? Those two looked at you like you had the plague.'

Pearl let out a weary sigh. 'I tried to do a goodness and it turned bad.' Babs hitched her brow in a question so the other woman carried on. 'I invested much of my savings with this guy I thought was legit and got him to come here to tell the others—'

'Who invested their hard earned cash and then he did a bunk,' Babs finished off for her.

Pearl shook her head sadly. 'You'd think someone like me, who's been around the block a few times, would've known better.' She looked down the room at the meeting. 'Now they all blame me. That's why I never told you about the gold coz I thought you'd blame me for that too.'

Babs let out a lengthy sigh. 'What happened?'

Pearl quickly gave her the low-down and ended on, 'I know what you're going to asked – who knew it was there? Well *I* never told a soul.'

Babs looked affronted as her head snapped back. 'You saying I did?'

Pearl looked incredulous, Babs' words cutting her to the quick. ''Course not. We need to find *our* gold.'

Babs chewed fretfully on her bottom lip and hesitantly offered, 'Now it's gone maybe we let it be gone. It's only bought a storm of trouble to my family. It's like it's cursed.'

'Cursed?' Pearl uttered with derision. 'I don't know about that but It's my gift for a very nice retirement, thank you very much, especially with most of my life savings being robbed.' Her voice turned silky smooth. 'I need the cash it's going to bring me.'

Babs leaned threateningly forward. 'You trying to put the frighteners on me? Coz let me tell you bigger fish than you have tried and have lost.'

Pearl seemed to collapse back in her chair. 'I'd never do that Babsie. I ain't lived an easy life and some would say I've brought that down on my own head. I just wanna be able to put my feet up and not have to worry where my next penny's coming from.'

Babs instantly felt sorry for her outburst. Truth be told, she'd probably think the same thing in Pearl's shoes. Babs was financially sorted having sold her two houses, her girls none the wiser. Those houses had caused enough problems to make the Godfather 4. She'd put most of the money from the sale aside for her grandkids and the rest a nice, little nest egg for her old age. Pearl was low on funds through no fault of her own. Babs didn't have the heart to leave her stranded.

She let her mind tick over before proposing, 'we need to find our gold. And nab the bastard who pinched it. What we need is someone who has their nose to the ground who can put the word out and have a sniff around.' She reluctantly added, 'I know someone who might fit the bill.'

Pearl's brightened up. 'I've got someone too.' Her voice quietened. 'My brother could help. Who's the someone you know?'

Babs was already regretting putting this person in the mix. 'I'd rather keep mum about who that is for now.'

She reached across the table and took her ex-jailbird friend's hand. 'We'll get this sorted out. Never you mind that some here are giving you the bum's rush, I'll always be your friend.'

Pearl placed her hand on top of Babs'. 'Friends forever.'

Eleven

'Oops! Sorry mate.'

Babs apologised after she slammed into a man's chest. A very muscular chest. The gold, understandably, had bent her all out of shape, so much so that as she approached the care home exit she hadn't been looking where she was going.

A strong hand steadied her. 'Babs?'

All thought of the gold fled as her head shot up. Her heart did a double somersault. Then another. Blimey, she could barely catch her breath.

No way…

Can't be…

But it was.

In the flesh.

Tricky Dickie, aka retired cop Patrick Johnson, a former high-ranking guy at the Yard. And God help the dodgy East End girl in her, the love of her life.

They'd met back in the 70s when he'd been hunting a pair of cops who were as bent as Uri Geller's cutlery and who also turned out to be bosom buddies of that prick Stan. She and Tricky Dickie – that's how she'd always think of him – had got into it big time. Sex in his car. Sex in a hotel. Sex that had melted her bones on the inside. For the first time she'd understood what it meant to make love to a *real* man. Even if he was a cop.

Although they hadn't touched each other since then her feelings for him had grown and deepened over the years. Tricky Dickie was her angel in the shadows who'd appeared like magic many-a-time when there was major league bother in her life. But a bird from the East End doing the horizontal Tango with a cop went against the laws of nature. She'd heeded it for nearly thirty years and it had broken her aching, lovesick heart.

'Babs? What are you doing here?'

Patrick's short, cropped grey hair had lost the Poldark look she been so into in the 70s. He still held himself like he had steel instead of a backbone for a spine. And, wow, those gorgeous eyes. Grey and kind with lines that crinkled at the corner. Fancy waking up and gazing into those beauties on the pillow next to you every morning?

Nelly's song, 'Hot In Here', began beating in her head as her cheeks flamed. And man did she feel like ripping her clothes off. But that was never going to happen, was it? She felt bitter to the core. Why was it some people got lucky while others were dumped like rubbish on the 'dreams not meant to be' scrapheap?

Babs forced out a bright and breezy voice, like she'd been having the time of her life without him. 'Been visiting a good mate of mine. Known each other for yonks.'

His thick brows snapped together. 'Oh, who's that then?'

Her eyelashes fluttered as she ignored his question and threw one of her own. 'So, what you doing here? Booking yourself a room?'

He smiled at her cheeky remark making the dimple she'd been head over heels for appear. 'There's been some nasty business going on here – I'm not at liberty to say…'

Nasty business! Bloody hells bells! What if he was here to follow up on the earlier visit by the Bill about what had gone down in Pearl's room? The bloke had the snout of a bloodhound. If there was anyone who could sniff out there was more than meets the eye about Pearl's slashed settee it was Tricky Dickie.

And look at her, chatting for England with him for Pete's sake!

Babs made a big play of coughing and checked her watch. 'Must dash,' she said with enough drama to put Meryl Streep in the shade. 'I'm running late —'

A startled hiccup escaped her when his warm palm settled on her shoulder. He stared intently at her. Cor, those eyes of his were casting a spell over her. Look away! Look away! But Babs couldn't. He was the only fella who'd done right by her. But it couldn't be. Her girls would never accept a former Rozzer in her life. Once a cop always a cop. And, fuck me, if he ever clocked about the gold…

Hot tears gathered in her throat.

Babs half-turned away from him in despair. 'Patrick, look—'

'Say that again,' he said softly with utter wonder.

'What?' She still wouldn't look at him.

He placed his other hand on her shoulder and gently turned her to face him. She had no alternative but to meet his glowing gaze.

'My name. You always call me Tricky Dickie.'

This was killing her. Her heart hurt so much. Babs shook

her head and with whispered anguish implored, 'There's no point to this…Patrick. I know you're gonna ask me out, like you always do, but we're from different worlds.'

His fingers tightened on her shoulders as his features fixed with determination. 'But we're older now Babs. The world has moved on.' He never took his eyes off her. 'I'm not a cop anymore, I'm a middle-aged fella going a bit soft in the tummy.'

'Soft in her head more like,' she muttered. They both smiled at that.

'I want to see you Babs. Hold you close. Never let you go.'

Babs wrenched out of his hold. His words tore up her insides with the power of acid. She wanted to scream that at him and more. But what was the point? Best to cut this off at the legs while she still had strength.

'I'll be seeing you Tricky Dickie.'

Babs held her head up and walked away with leaden steps. Even when he called,

'I'm going to marry you Babs, just you wait and see,' she kept going.

Tie the knot? Was he off his trolley? Babs stepped to it as if a fire had been lit under her bum. Only when she got on the Number 25 bus back home did she let the tears silently fall. Why was life so unfair? Women her age deserved a slice of happiness as well for crying out loud. He was the man of her absolute dreams, but no matter how hard she reached for him the gulf was too wide. Funny how all those years ago Stan, with his silk hankies and slick-backed Brylcreemed hair-do had been the perfect portrait of her soul mate. Her wide-boy knight in shining armour rescuing her from the shame of being up the duff with no man on your arm. Of course, Stanley had turned out to be the devil in disguise, a geezer with badness as his middle name. Throughout almost it all, standing patiently in the shadows, was a man full of goodness. Maybe…? What if…?

Babs shook her head with misery. Who the effing heck was she kidding? Jen might come around eventually, but Tiff and Dee…Nah! That was asking for an out 'n' out war to kick off. Anyways, it was all a non-starter. If Tricky Dickie found out his darling Babs was involved in one of the most infamous blags of recent years he'd have her banged up in a cell In Holloway in a heartbeat.

From her doorway Pearl had zeroed in on Babs marching with purpose away from that Patrick fella who had come to their meeting. From the looks of things Babs knew the geezer very well. Very well indeed. In fact, Pearl would go as far as putting her neck on the chopping block to say her former next door cellie looked like she was on the verge of crying a river. Interesting!

'Pearl ol' girl.' She turned to find Fred standing there. 'Thought I'd give you the full SP on what Vi's friend told us.'

Five minutes later Pearl had the lay of the land – Patrick could do sweet FA. Go to the plods was the advice he gave. Well that wasn't an option as far as Pearl was concerned. The Bill might tumble about the gold. Plus the cops gave her the willies.

'I'm worried about Vi and Di,' Fred interrupted her thoughts. 'I know most times they're in each other's pockets, but they seem to be clinging to each other more than usual.'

Pearl had way too many troubles on her mind to be taking on anyone else's. 'You've been dying to ask Vi out. Go on, take her for a snifter, might take her mind off things.'

'I'm being serious.' Still his face blushed as red as his hair had once been. 'There's something going on…'

He wandered off scratching his nearly baldhead.

Before he got too far Pearl called out, 'What does that Patrick do?'

Fred turned slightly, still distracted. 'He's put up his truncheon for good now, but he was once a high-ranking copper.'

Twelve

Babs wiped the tears from her face. Slapped on some of that Mac powder Dee had got her from Selfridges Up West and got off the bus on Mile End Road.

'You alright me lovely-jubbly Babs?'

The slurred voice of Ryan Mallory greeted her as she entered The Devil's Estate. He sat on his usual spot, the crumbling wall near the offy, nursing his poison of choice, a bottle of cheap brandy. She could smell him from here, his clothes in need of the scrubbing of a lifetime, possibly even fumigation. He was The Devil's resident piss artist. Most took the proper piss out of him, a figure of fun to brighten their miserable lives. Not Babs though. She knew what it felt like to be on your uppers, driven to drink.

Mind you, you had to be careful with Ryan. He'd skin a kitten for a farthing if it meant he could buy more drink if his cash flow had dried up.

Babs reached him, not too close mind; the stench coming off him was eye-watering. 'Thought you'd run off with a supermodel,' she teased, trying her best to wash away the sadness of seeing Tricky Dickie.

His bristled jaw moved as he cackled away. 'Had to give

her up for my real lady love here.' He shook the bottle at her. The laughter left his grizzled face as he touched a dirty fingertip under his eye and then pointed to her block.

Babs drilled a laser stare into him. He might be the neighbourhood drunk, but, from his perch, he was also the all-seeing-eyes of the estate. No one clocked the ins and outs of what was occurring on The Devil's Estate like Ryan Mallory.

'You seen something going on at my place?' Bloody hell, the last thing she needed was more effing trouble. And right on her doorstep this time. 'Come on, spit it out.'

Suddenly his face fell. His bloodshot eyes glazed over.

'Me and my Shirley were going to get a flat in your block, but then, in the end, the council decided to put us somewhere else.' He took a deep, heartfelt breath. 'My Shirley. What a lady.'

He took a deep swig from the hard stuff and then started belting out, all out of key, Simon and Garfunkel's, 'Bridge Over Troubled Waters.'

With a dismissive cluck of her tongue Babs left him. Old fool! Probably pointing at her place wanting to reminisce about old times. Well looking back never got a body anywhere, which she knew all too well after seeing Tricky Dickie.

Babs ran her eye up her block. The four-storey building might not be most people's idea of paradise, but since '72 this had been her castle. She'd been one of the first tenants when the estate had been spanking and sparkling new and full of promise. Babs let out a weary sigh; all good things came to an end.

The lift was out of order – again! – so she trudged up the

stairs. Her dreams of peace vanished as soon as she reached her landing. Now she got it why Ryan had knowingly pointed to her block and then belted out a tune about troubled waters. On her doorstep stood trouble incarnate with two packed bags. She didn't need this.

Babs marched down the landing and tersely asked, 'What the heck are *you* doing here?'

'What do you want Flo?'

Babs wasn't gentle in the asking. After her ding-dong of a day the last thing she needed was Stan's daughter. Born on the wrong side of the blanket daughter. Jeez. What a gut-wrenching business that had been, finding out what filth Stan had been up to behind her back. And what made it worse was Flo and Tiff were only months apart in age. It made her sick to her stomach to think he'd been dipping his wick with her and some Doris at the same time. Fuck me! If Viagra had been around back then Stan's plonker would've seen the inside of half of London.

'My granddad's thrown me out.'

Babs bristled slightly at Flo's lah-di-dah accent. It wasn't the girl's fault Stan had two-timed Babs with some upmarket bint from North London. What added salt to the wounds was Flo's old girl's family were loaded. Brought up in the lap of luxury, no doubt attending the best schools while Babs' girls had gone to the local comp and scarpered as soon as.

The sweater dress she wore, cinched in at the waist with a thick, brown leather belt didn't come cheap. The heels with crystal stone straps must've cost a pretty penny too. Only her Amy Winehouse jet-back, thick eyeliner and almost falling down beehive made her look like she came off the estate. Babs found it hard to look at the girl without seeing that bastard Stan. Flo was the spit of him, right down to those untrustworthy fox-like blue eyes.

And, to top if off, Florence's granddad, The Commander was a sore point in the Miller family. The gold had belonged to him originally – although Babs suspected he'd nicked it off someone else in the first place - and he'd played a very dirty game trying to get it back, including using Flo here as one of his attack dogs.

Flo hunched slightly, pleading, 'I haven't got any other place to go.'

'What about your mum?' Just thinking about the *other* woman brought bile to Babs' throat.

The girl's cold lips tightened. 'Doesn't want me anyway near her.' Her words and accent then became Stan Miller's through and through. 'Thinks I'm a druggie slag, don't she? Told me to do one.'

Babs' heart did break for this girl. That effing Stan had left a trail of wrecked lives in his wake. Babs hardened her heart. She might feel for the girl but, all things being told, she wasn't her problem. Flo wasn't family.

'Maybe you can make it up with your granddad—'

'Nah,' Flo cut in, 'he's had it with me as well. Told me to make myself scarce coz his cat's taken against me.'

Babs was outraged. 'He told you that? His cat? Put some tabby before his own flesh and blood?'

They were strange people, the rich. How they ever built an empire or won wars Babs could never fathom.

Flo nodded vigorously. Her gaze sharpened ever so slightly. 'And Babs, you did say you wanted me to get to know my dad's side of the family.'

That she had. But she'd only meant for the girl to pop around on her invite during special occasions, like birthdays, parties and piss ups. But coming to stop in her gaff? That was crossing a line Babs was adamant would not be crossed.

Babs pushed the key in her door as Flo stepped hopefully and eagerly forward. Babs used her body to bar her entry.

'Go back to your granddad's and make it up with his puss. I'm sorry, I can't have you here.'

Babs quietly closed the door. Fucking Ada! What a bruising day.

As she leaned against the door she heard Stan's daughter's soft sobs as she walked away along the balcony.

Kieran Scott shot his load so hard he thought he'd blown his mind. His sweat soaked body collapsed on top of a breathless Lisa. Her hot breath hit him full in the face making him turn his head in disgust. For once in his life couldn't he find a bird who didn't munch on fags every minute of every day? Baccy breath stank. Put him in mind of his terrible mum and the old days. He was moving up in the world and what he needed was a woman, not a bird, who could comfortably play the part of his other half. Someone who could get through dinner with his business associates without asking a waiter for ketchup.

Despite enjoying Lisa's hot, tasty body she was going to have to go.

Grinning for all she was worth she got out of bed. Taking her sweet time she sashayed slowly across the bedroom of his two mill plus penthouse in Chelsea, no doubt so he got a front row butchers of her lush bot and stunning legs. She hunted in her designer bag and came back to bed with – and he saw it coming – a fag. At least it wasn't ketchup.

Lisa proceeded to curl up next to him and stink the place out. Kieran had had enough.

He got up and put on his boxers and with his back to her announced, 'You know what girl, I think we should cool it for a little while.'

'You what?' She jack-knifed to a sitting position, her perfect boobs bobbing up and down.

He found his black jeans strewn on the floor and shoved them on. 'I got a few important business deals on the go and won't have the time to see ya.'

Her face drained of colour as she mashed the ciggy out against his headboard. He'd had the headboard imported from Thailand for fuck's sake. It hadn't come cheap neither.

Lisa looked like she'd been slapped round the chops. 'But…but I thought we were going to become a family.'

Flippin' heck. That was the other problem with the bird, she'd been dropping hints left, right and sideways about the house they could buy together, the number of kids they were going to have, his and hers matching pillows.

Finally he turned to her and laid it on the line, twisting her words to get her gone and soften the blow. 'See that's the thing babe, I ain't in the market for a family. I'm too busy. Got my life all mapped out for the next five years and not a kid in sight.'

'Except the one you've already got.'

He stared blankly at her. 'What?'

Her face perking up she crawled across the rumpled sheets towards him. 'Natty. You've got a beautiful son.' Her face brimmed with the same energy she put into getting her rocks off. 'You're a father who needs to claim his flesh and blood.'

Kieran flinched as if she'd hammered a stake through his heart. Hot temper poured from his eyes. 'Get your fucking gear and fuck off.'

She looked stumped. 'What's the matter? I'm only speaking the God's honest truth–'

'No, what you're doing is speaking about things that are above your pay grade.'

Lisa had this strange bewildered expression on her face like he'd ripped her guts out. 'But everything to do with you is my business.'

Oh, she was going to be one of those, was she? One of those women who just couldn't take 'no' for an answer. He'd had a few of those in his time. A right, proper nuisance. At least he knew how to deal with one.

He softened his tone as he walked over to her and pulled her naked flesh into his arms. She clung to him, sticky as poison ivy.

He deep-throated her for a time, then softly whispered, 'I've got an important client coming into town, so give me a week, yeah? After that we'll get together, pop some bolly and talk about the future.'

Lisa squealed and hugged him like there was no tomorrow, while all the time he held his breath against the stale smell of ciggies.

He eased her gently away and slapped her bum.

She giggled as he said, 'Get your kit on. I'm already late for a meet coz I've spent way too much time with you.' He ran his gaze slowly down her very fine figure. 'Then you're worth it.'

As far as he was concerned it took her way too long to drag her clothes on. Once he had her at the door he kissed her again. 'Wait by the phone for my call.'

Her eyes shone with hope. 'Me and you together like it's meant to be.'

Kieran leaned heavily against the door once she was gone. She'd soon get the message when he didn't return her calls.

Lisa had been wrong and right.

He didn't want a family.

What he wanted was his son.

Thirteen

'You alright mum?' Jen asked, peering at Babs with concern. 'You're looking a bit peaky. You ain't coming down with that flu doing the rounds?'

'Nah hun.' Babs plastered on her best smile. 'Just glad we're all together. When I was banged up I never thought I'd see a day like this again.'

A sad silence settled over them at Babs' kitchen table, each remembering the horror of her being banged up for Stan's murder. That time away from her treasured family had been the worst years of her life.

Babs' heart swelled with a mother's pride as she looked at each of her daughters in turn. Her eldest Dee was fierce, took no prisoners, but also had a core as soft as pudding once you got to know her. Poor luv had been through the wringer, but her Dee had bounced back, was a proud mum now and on the verge of opening her own club.

Her biggest worry, once upon a time, had been Jennifer. Her middle girl had been too trusting. That old Jen was long gone replaced by one who had teeth that didn't hesitate to snap and bite anyone daring to take the rise, especially when it came to her daughters, Courtney and Little Bea.

And then there was Tiffany. Babs didn't know whether to grind her teeth or smile. She loved her youngest to bits but also itched to wallop her around her loaf because she could be a right sly one on the side. Tiff had shown up today with her belongings like a refugee. All Babs could pray was this new job she'd wangled at Dee's club would finally set her straight.

If her girls twigged the stolen gold was on the loose again...Babs shoved the despairing thought aside but couldn't stop the shivers sliding down her spine.

'This is a cracking dinner mum,' Dee complimented, casting an appreciative eye at the spread Babs had put on.

Steak and Kidney pud, cheesy mash, glazed carrots and string beans from her neighbour Mabel's allotment. They'd already polished off two litre bottles of Lambrusco.

'You found a nanny for Natty yet?' Babs asked as she gazed adoringly down at her cherished grandson dozing in his carrycot.

Dee screwed up her face. 'I'm interviewing tomorrow at the club.'

Her eldest girl wasn't looking forward to handing over her boy to a live-in nanny, but the reality was she couldn't look after the new club and her kid at the same time.

Tiff slouched in her seat, knocked back some fizz and asked Jen, 'How's Courtney doing? Like going to St. Trinian's does she?' She chuckled at her little dig.

Jen pursed her lips, then huffed, 'It's called Egerton Academy, as you well know. It's a proper school.' She cut her eyes at her baby sister. 'Not that you'd know anything about schools since you spent most of your time bunking off.'

Tiff smirked the type that made Babs want to give her a doughboy. 'Weren't my fault that my teachers never understood my peculiar talents. That's why I was bored outta my nut. Blame the school not the child.'

Jen weren't having it, her voice becoming fierce. 'Your only peculiar talent I've seen is rolling spliffs with one hand.'

Dee banged her fork on the table, only stopping when she remembered Natty snoozing by her feet. 'Will you two give it a rest?' She glared at them, pointing her fork in a deadly, stabbing motion at them in turn, her arched eyebrow warning there'd be trouble if they had the brass to interrupt.

'Mum's put on a slap up bit of tuck and all you two wanna do is go at it like two Z Celebs on Big Brother. Have some respect.'

Jen knew better than to respond, but Tiff had never quite mastered the art of not being a mouthy sod. She curled her lip. 'You might be my boss lady down the Three Sisters but not around our mum's, comprende?'

Babs held up her palms before this got out of hand. 'Can we give the verbal a night off, eh? For once in our lives.'

Dee and Tiff still gave each other the eye, but stopped trading verbal blows.

Babs lowered her hands and turned to Jen. 'I'm done up for Courtney that she's liking her new school.'

Jen perked up, face glowing. 'Dead proud of her I am. I will admit I was scared to death of her going across town on her tod and probably being the only girl in her class who weren't from one of them nob families, but my girl has put her head down and done me proud.' She preened, 'Her form mistress says that her grades are one of the best in the class.'

'I'm glad,' Babs replied.

She didn't add anything about the business with Courtney and Stan because it was an unstated rule that they didn't go there. The few times they had it had only brought Jen to tears and how it hurt Babs seeing her girl crippled in pain. Best to let sleeping dogs lie.

The remainder of the meal was spent nattering about this and that 'n' then they settled in the sitting room with a bottle of pink gin, courtesy of Dee's bar at the club, and a large bowl overflowing with sea salt and balsamic vinegar Kettle crisps. Babs popped the latest Bond movie in the DVD, a bootleg copy she'd purchased for a couple of quid on the communal staircase, no questions asked.

'That Daniel Craig's a bit of alright,' Jen uttered breathlessly five minutes into the film. She ran her tongue over her lips watching his high jinx every step of the way.

Then she and Dee, who cradled a sleeping Natty in her arms, started laughing and chanting, 'Go Daniel! Go Daniel!'

Babs shook her head as she munched. 'As if this Danny boy has got a patch on Roger Moore…'

Tiff wasn't joining in. Instead she eyeballed her belongings sitting in the corner of the room. Last night she'd sofa surfed at a mate's in a last ditch attempt not to go to her mum's. The sharp springs had nearly crippled her. No way was there going to be a repeat performance of that tonight.

Her mum pointedly asked, 'Is there something on your mind Tiffany?'

Tiff inwardly groaned. That's what she'd be coming back to if she moved in again. A mum with eyes at the back and side of her head. It would be like being back in school and not Egerton Academy either.

Tiff avoided her mum's suspicious stare to mask the glint in her eye that showed she was up to no good. 'Why? Should there be?'

'You tell me.'

Tiff hesitated for a moment and then made a big show of touching the side of her head as if she'd just remembered something. 'Oh, nearly forgot mum, I need my old room back for a couple of days.'

Jen tutted and Dee muttered with disapproval. Screw 'em, Tiff mentally raged. Since when did they have a say who their mum let stay in her drum? Since for never.

Babs passed the bowl of crisps to Jen and folded her arms. 'I beg your pardon?'

Tiff still avoided her mum's piercing stare and went for the kill with her hard luck story. 'See, thing is, I was renting a room in Bow but the landlord booted me out coz he wants the house back to do it up and sell it on. Got another place sorted out. Can't move in yet though. Being tarted up, ain't it, so I need somewhere to crash for a couple of days…or maybe just a week.'

Babs gave her kid one of her mum looks. 'What did I say to you Tiffany the last time this happened? Told you point blank it was the last time. You're a grown woman now. You can't keep coming back here like the Boomerang Kid every time things go tits up. You should have had your own four walls and a roof sorted out by now.'

'Which she did, let's not forget,' Dee backed up their mum as she passed Natty to Jen.

Jen put in her two pence worth as well. 'But ballsed it up, splashing the cash like a drunk sailor until she had debts coming out of her rear end.'

Tiff turned on her sisters. 'Thanks for your input ladies but I'm not asking you.' She twisted back to Babs and, in a sweet as pie tone, begged, 'ain't got nowhere else to go mum, its here or nowhere.'

'Don't try to guilt trip me, my girl,' Babs threw harshly back. 'I'm sorry, but I'm putting my foot down. Go down the housing and talk to the council; they'll sort you something out. You're not coming back here and that's final.'

Tiff looked like she'd lost her dinner then her hot temper scorched through her rapid-fire words. 'What do you want me to do? Go down a doss house and bunk up with the smack heads? Kip in a shop doorway? Eh? I told ya, it's only for a couple of days.'

'Mum's got a point.' Tiff almost screamed at hearing Dee's interfering gob again. 'It's a bit much you treating her place like a hostel. I mean, how old are you now?'

'Who asked you to stick your beak in?' Tiff scoffed. 'I notice you're not offering me a room at Dee Mansions. Oh no, worried 'bout the neighbours probably.'

Babs was firm. 'Pack it in Tiffany. You're not staying here and that's that. Now then.' She turned back to the telly and squealed, 'look at 007 go! Swinging off that building like Spiderman.'

Tiff rubbed her teeth against each other in a see-saw motion. If mum thought the battle for her old room was lost she had another thing coming.

She got to her feet muttering, 'Fuck James Bond.'

With grim determination she strode across the room and yanked up her plastic bags. When Babs clocked what was happening, she flashed to her feet and grabbed Tiff by the arms to stop her heading across the hallway towards her old room.

'I'm warning you my girl.'

There was a brief struggle as Tiff grappled with her mum before she broke free. Dee and Jen were up and out of their comfy seats as Tiff escaped from the room slamming the door behind her.

Tight-lipped Babs gestured for them to sit down. 'Leave it ladies. Let her go. Your sister will be back very shortly, I can promise you that.'

Babs was right. A few seconds later, an ear-piercing wail filled the hallway followed by shouting. Then the sitting room door banged back open. Tiffany strode in, face white, fists clenched and her body vibrating with rage.

She yelled, 'What the fuck is that fucking dungeon tart, Flo, doing in my fucking room?'

Fourteen

'Ah yeah, I should've told ya, I'm letting Florence stay for a few days.'

The shoe was on the other foot now. It was Babs' turn to pretend to have remembered something.

'Poor kid turned up on my doorstep earlier like a drowned mouse. I will admit I turned her away at first, but then I got to thinking she's my Tiff and Jen's half-sister. Her granddad turned her out with nowhere to go. What a brute, eh? There's something a bit funny about that family if you ask me.'

Tiff had an apoplectic fit. 'Are you off your fucking nut?'

Hyperventilating, she couldn't believe it. She knew it was going to be a struggle getting her old room back. She even admitted to herself that she was taking the Arthur Bliss by asking for it. But never, ever, did she expect to find that high-rent, low budget Paris Hilton wannabe tucked up and cosy in her room. Her fucking room!

Jen and Dee were having trouble coping with their mum's unwelcome news as well. They couldn't have looked more shocked if Babs had informed them that Stanley Miller was popping by for a drink and a yarn later.

Dee's eyes flashed with fury, but kept her tone civil. 'Mum, what's going on?'

'That girl's trouble mum and you know it.' Jen was having trouble keeping her voice hushed, trying not to let her wrath wake the sleeping baby in her arms. 'We've been sat here for a couple of hours and you never said a word. Why didn't you tell us, as soon as, when we got here?'

Babs wrung her hands, but her features remained stubborn. 'Coz I knew there would be ructions and I don't expect to have to answer to my own kids for what happens in *my* own home. To save trouble, I told Flo to stay put in her room.' That explained why Stan's daughter hadn't put in an appearance when the girls arrived.

Babs reached for her drink and knocked the last of it back to give her some much-needed strength. 'There's no point in jumping outta your pram. I've told her she can stay for a couple of days and that's all there is to it. Last time I looked, my name was on the rent book, so it ain't Tiff's room, it's *mine*, which means I can let it to who I like.' She slammed her glass down on the side table and stood. 'Now, who wants a cuppa?'

Tiff dogged her, haranguing her all the way. 'Can you hear that mum?' she blasted as soon as they got inside the kitchen.

'Hear what?'

'The sound of me puking,' Tiff fired back, 'coz how could you let dad's wrong side of the blanket past the doorstep much less park her posh pussy in here? After all she did?' She shook her fists like she wanted to shake her mum. 'All she did to you and all she did to us? How could you?'

Babs knew where her daughter was coming from; she'd

asked herself the same questions before deciding to open her home to Flo. The awful things that Flo had put them through weren't easy to push aside. But after she'd told the girl that kipping at hers was a no-can-do, Babs' heart had almost broken at the wretched sobs coming from Flo as she'd walked away.

The last time Babs had heard such anguished weeping was from a broken teen on her wing in prison who'd howled for forgiveness and her mum every night.

So Babs had called Flo back, sat her down and read her the riot act so she got it through her posh locks that Babs wasn't going to put up with her shenanigans here. Made sure she understood what was in, what was out. None of Flo's old tricks in her drum, thank you very much. And so far, so good.

Babs was tired of having to explain herself inside her own four walls to a daughter who should've sorted her act out yonks ago.

'Now you listen to me.' She turned on Tiff. 'I'm no more a fan of the girl than you are. But at the end of the day she's still your flesh and blood and she's a girl in trouble. Your old man might've been the work of the devil but that's no reason to take it out on the girl. It's ain't her fault.'

Tiff wiggled her head in disbelief. 'I'm your actual flesh and blood and I'm in trouble! And I ain't stabbed you in the back, the front and sides! Now go and tell Lady Muck to piss right off or I'll do it!'

Babs lost her rag and grabbed her daughter's ear, pinching it so tight Tiff yelped. 'Don't you backchat me, little madam. And don't think you're too old to feel the back of my hand across that thick skull of yours. I gave her my word. If you want to sleep on the sofa for a few days, that's alright with me.'

Tiff got her ear back. 'Ta. That's nice. I'll tell you what though,' sarky as thick as butter on bread, 'perhaps I should check with Flo before I lay my hat on the sofa? You know, just to make sure she's alright with it too.'

Suddenly Babs was shagged to the bone, especially after seeing Pearl, the gold doing a Houdini and bumping into Tricky Dickie. And, as if that wasn't enough, she was having a tropical moment. This menopause business was a right headache. She could've lit one of her ciggies easy with the heat coming off her face.

'Let's all just try and get along, eh?'

She jacked open the window. Ah! Heaven. Her face began to cool down.

A seething Tiff sloped off to the sitting room.

But Babs was interrupted from making the tea when she heard Dee shout, 'Oi, what you doing with that?'

More trouble! Babs banged the cup in her hand down and flew into the sitting room to find her youngest marching to the doorway with the ornamental poker. Strangely enough she got out of the way and let Tiff proceed to her old room.

'Mum, bloody well stop her,' Jen barked, the change in her voice making Natty whimper, but mercifully he didn't wake up.

Babs sagged against the wall. 'You know what, those two are both gonna be stopping under this roof, so the sooner they have it out the quicker we can get it outta the way and find some peace.'

Dee shook her head. 'But Tiff will do some serious damage with that bit of iron.'

Babs' face became grim. 'You're both forgetting that Flo's Stan Miller's daughter.'

As soon as Tiff got inside her old room she placed the poker behind her back and used her other hand to close the door quietly. Snob gob Flo was sitting up on the bed, cushioned against a pillow, wearing only a T-shirt and skimpy thongs, her long blonde locks thrown over one shoulder. Her head bopped from side to side in time with the music coming through the earphones stuck in her ears.

Tiff viciously whispered, 'I'll make your head bop, you bitch.'

Her half-sister seemed oblivious of the row she'd engineered or that Tiff stood at the foot of the bed like a doctor with bad news.

When she finally looked up, she pulled off her earphones and shook her head back like a model on a fashion shoot.

'Oh, hello there sis.' Her words were pleasant enough except for the invisible poison dripping from the side of her chops. Well, that's how Tiff saw it anyways.

That lah-di-da-di-da accent of hers grated on Tiff's nerves, big time. 'What are you playing at?'

'It's an old Prince album.'

Oh, it's like that, is it? Think's she's the mutt's nuts, does she? Tiff pulled the poker from behind her back and waved it menacingly. 'Yeah, that's right, you keep running your Notting Hill trap and I'll fill it in for you.'

Flo smirked, not a care in the world. 'I don't think you will. Look at the state of you. You couldn't knock the top off a rice pudding as our old man used to say. You need to pack it in with the poncing about, sofa surfing and squatting sis; such an unhealthy lifestyle.'

Tiff was both needled and slightly alarmed that Flo seemed to know her business. Probably been listening, with her ear pressed to the door at the row going on between her and mum.

'What are you playing at Flo? I mean really playing at?'

The other woman sank back into the pillow. 'Didn't Babs explain? I was staying at my grandfather's – you remember the Commander? Well, he's never really forgiven me for messing up on the gold and when he got the chance, he made me walk the gangplank. I got thrown out. Not that I blame him for having the hump, of course. No one likes to be robbed of gold bullion after all. Anyway, I had nowhere to go, so I thought I'd throw myself on the mercy of the woman who could've been my mum.'

Tiff could feel herself getting riled up again, but reined it back in, playing it cool. 'First off, she could never be your mum. As fucking if! She's *my* mum.'

Flo sighed as if this sit-down wasn't even worth the time o' day or night as it were. 'Alright, step-mum, half-mum, sub-mum - families are all over the place these days, aren't they?'

Tiff ignored her. 'And second, there's a thousand other places you could've found to rest that big head of yours. Dopey boyfriends or dopey wannabe boyfriends, you could even have gone back to your own old lady.'

Flo shivered. Her control was slipping. Her accent became East End girl to the core, no doubt learned at the knee of Stan Miller.

'I ain't going back to that looby-loo, she's one stop on the district line from East Ham, you get me?' Realising what she'd done, she swiftly switched back to her upmarket voice.

'No, I made the right choice coming here. It's not a problem, is it? We can get along, can't we? We share a father's blood after all, you can't deny that.'

Tiff parked herself on the edge of the bed, gaze sharp and knowing. 'You're up to something, I can tell. You're like Stan; he was always up to something. That's why you're here. You've got a plan. What is it? Tell me. I won't grass, especially if there's something in it for me.'

Flo gave her an appraising glance. 'You're right. I am like dad. I've always got a plan just like he did.'

Tiff leaned triumphantly closer. She'd been right; this bint was on the make.

But she was disappointed when Flo continued. 'And my plan was to find somewhere to stay.'

Tiff shot to her feet in disgust.

Flo reached for her earphones and said, 'But then that's the difference between you and me…sister. I've always got a plan and you haven't.'

As soon as the door was shut Flo chucked the earphones and picked up her mobile.

Her thumbs beat away as she texted:

'The daughters know I'm here. Should be no problems now.'

Two minutes later the answering text pinged on her phone.

'Well done. I knew I could rely on you. Now get to work and find your inheritance, the gold.'

Flo sent loads of kisses back to her granddad, The Commander.

Fifteen

'Hang on a moment please,' Dee called out regally as the final candidate for the job of Natty's nanny knocked at the door.

Dee was sitting pretty in her custom-made, red, gold and green executive chair in her office on the top floor of the Three Sisters Club. She leaned back on the headrest, trying to shift some of the anxiety gnawing away at her. You heard all kind of stories about what nannies got up to once the parents were out of sight. Take what happened last year to one of her neighbours. Turns out the nanny had been using the place as a pop up brothel and doing the nasty with all sorts right in their marital bed. Dirty scrubber! And, as if that wasn't enough, she'd had the nipper in the same room. Poor kid! Probably grow up to be a serial killer. No way was that kind of carry-on happening in her beautiful home. Nathan, along with her older son Nicky, were the most precious people in her life and she owed it to John to make sure they grew up right. Ah, John!

'Don't you worry babes,' she whispered with all her heart, 'I'll make sure our Natty turns into a man you would be proud to call your own.'

The knock came again. Dee quickly took out her mint breath freshener and squirted twice in her mouth to get rid of the bolly cocktail she'd downed a while back.

'Enter!'

John had told her once that you got ten seconds to make an impression when you entered a room, including situations where you had to deliver a couple of slaps. Dee's laser eyes burned into the tall woman who came in.

Neat, brown bob – tick.

Black business suit with skirt below the knee – tick.

No strawberry creams on the loose – tick.

No tottering heels, but sensible, black flats – tick.

No slap – tick.

Ten out of ten, so far. The last thing Dee wanted in her house was some floozy swanning around like Her Majesty of bloody Essex on stilettos.

Once the candidate, Miriam Hartley, was sat down Dee deliberately got up and waltzed over to the drinks cabinet and took out a bottle of whisky. 'You must be a bit parched after your journey. Join me in a 'nice to meet ya' drink?'

She waved the bottle invitingly like she was dangling a high-end piece of jewellery.

Miriam Hartley's expression didn't change, she simply, and firmly, responded, 'No, thank you.'

This was one of the tests Dee had lined up to checkout the candidates. Her son wasn't going to be looked after by no alkie, no soddin' way. The third candidate had been shown the door after downing her snifter in one and then asked for another. The nerve of the woman!

As Dee popped the bottle back it occurred to her how cool Miriam had been. Hadn't turned a hair at being offered a drop. Dee liked that; she needed someone with a level head around Natty just in case trouble ever came to her door.

Back at her desk she ran through the usual stock questions – what experience have you had? What would you do if a baby starts choking? How do you put a toddler to sleep? Then proceeded to the next test.

Settling a deceptively sweet smile on her lips, Dee leaned across the desk as if she was about to invite Miriam to become her bestie. 'I've got this massive collection of designer dresses, which I only get to use every now and again. Vera Wang, Versace, Westwood; you name it I've got it. As my kid's nanny I don't mind if you borrow them once in awhile.'

Yeah, as if! Anyone touching her gear would find themselves down to no fingers.

Once again the other woman's face remained neutral. 'That's a very kind offer Mrs Black, but I feel that it's important to maintain professional boundaries at all times. If I started wearing your clothes I would consider that to be a breach of trust.'

Dee leaned back, the smile spreading into one of pleasure. She was liking this Miriam a lot. But it was going to be a hard decision, as she'd also liked the first candidate as well, a jolly granny type whose eyes sparkled when she talked about children.

Dee got ready to deliver the next question when an urgent knock at the door stopped her. The door was thrust back to reveal her head of security.

'Some div has just thrown a brick through the front window.'

Dee was on her feet in double time. 'You catch the bastard?'

First thought that came to her mind was that this must be the local 'consortium' trying to frighten her into paying up. Take more than a broken window for her to join their bullyboy club.

Her head of security shook his head. 'But I clocked him. Should've been in school by the looks of him. I'll know his face if he dares show it again.'

Dee dismissed it having anything to do with the protection racket because anyone worth their salt in that business would know better than to rely on some teen tearaway to tighten the screws.

'Mrs Black.' Dee absently turned having forgotten all about Miriam Hartley. 'I'm happy to wait if you need to sort this out.'

Dee took her up on the offer, but when she came back five minutes later her she was in too foul a mood to continue. After seeing the mess downstairs she was only in the mood to strangle someone…very slowly. The club launch was around the corner so everything had better be Bristol fashion. Stratford might be touting itself as the next London postcode to be, as it got ready to wave the Olympic flag, but underneath it was the East End, dodgy business as usual.

She held the door open so that Miriam got the message that the interview was over. As the other woman picked up her bag and stood, Dee said, 'Thanks for coming in. I'll be in touch within the hour.'

But instead of leaving, the other woman lingered by the door. 'I can see you're a busy person, but there's one question I wanted to ask.'

Dee clenched her jaw. She wasn't in the mood to be questioned. 'If it's about the wages—?'

Miriam shook her head and cut in,' No. It's about your son's father. Will I have the opportunity to meet him as well if I get the job?'

On the word 'father', grief ripped through her. Would she ever get use to her beautiful, mad-bastard of an old man being six feet under?

'Oh, I'm sorry,' the other woman said softly, witnessing Dee's sorrow. 'I didn't mean to upset you.'

Gently she touched Dee's hand. Dee nearly snatched her hand back. The other woman's paw wasn't just cold it was freezing. A shiver ran through her as she quickly took her hand back. She knew she might be over reacting, but she didn't like the icy feeling Miriam left on her skin.

Miriam pulled the strap of her bag tighter against her shoulder. 'Thanks so much for your time and I look forward to hearing from you.'

As soon as the door shut Dee made her decision about who would be Natty's nanny – bubbly granny it was. She poured herself two fingers of whiskey – she wasn't over doing the booze while on the job – and then slung herself into her chair. But when Dee offered her the job she got the shock of her life.

The woman huffed and puffed with outrage on the other end of the phone. 'I should report you to the authorities.'

'You what?' Dee was stunned. What was the old bird going on about?

'I've never heard the like. Sex games and whips.' Sounded like the old girl was about to faint. 'I should report you to Social Services.'

Dee got to her feet snarling, 'You mention my boy's name in the same breath as the SS there's gonna be proper trouble.' She added with menace, 'Don't forget I know where you live.'

The phone connection abruptly clicked off. Dazed, Dee sank slowly back into her chair. What the effing hell was that all about? Sex games? Whips? The woman must be a proper nutter. And to think she'd nearly given her precious boy into her care.

Dee called the other candidate to give her the good news. 'Is that Miriam?'

A hopeful voice answered, 'Yes Mrs Black.'

'I wanna offer you the job as nanny to my Nathan. I'll level with you that you weren't my first choice, but…well, let's just say the other candidate doesn't appear to be the full ticket.'

Dee could picture her grinning like Xmas and her birthday had all come along at the same time. 'Mrs Black I can't thank you enough. I promise that I'll look after your son as if he were my own.'

'You better had. And everyone calls me Mizz Dee.'

'Mizz Dee, thank you from the bottom of my heart.'

Miriam's triumph fell a touch when Mizz Dee went into Sir Alan Sugar Apprentice mode.

'And let me just remind you. I don't like shirkers, moaners, cheats, wasters and nosey parkers. I don't like staff who take a nap when I run up the shops, have a snort from my whiskey bottles and then top it up with tap water. I don't like people who rifle through my mail or borrow things that they think I won't notice are missing. And I definitely don't like employees who bring their man candy round and shag 'em silly in my bed. Got it?'

Miriam stammered, 'Er…Yes, that goes without saying.'

Dee allowed herself a pat on the back smile. 'Welcome to the Black and Miller family.'

It was only after Dee put her mobile down that she noticed the paper with the list of the nanny candidates and their details was on the right hand side of the desk. Dee scowled. She could've sworn she'd left it on the other side.

Sixteen

'Oh, it's you,' Pearl's brother announced – though to Pearl's ear it was a dead ringer for a groan.

He stood in the doorway of his four-storey house in a fuck-off Georgian Square in Camden. He was looking down at her as she stood on the step. It seemed right; he was always looking down on her despite her having eight years on him.

He'd not only done alright for himself, but was also in good nick for a man his age. Tall, muscular and fit, a walking definition of the phrase, 'black don't crack' because there wasn't a line on his good-looking face. He was rigged out in a designer suit with chamois slip-ons. Not a grey strand in sight in his obviously dyed black hair. No change there then: he'd always made a right song and dance about his hair when they were younger.

'Hi bruv, how's tricks?' Pearl cracked a way too sunshine smile on her face.

He folded his arms with a sour twist of his mouth and nodded. 'Good. It's been a long time Pearl.' From the tone of his voice he wished it were longer.

As he kept her on the doorstep like a Jehovah Witness desperate to spread the Good News she had to do the honours. 'Any chance I could have a word?'

With an impatient huff he looked over his shoulder down the hallway and then back at his sister. It seemed like an age before he finally snapped, 'you'll have to make it quick. I'm holding a dinner party and my guests will be here shortly.'

Holding a dinner party? Oooo, get him! Ever since making his first mill in the building trade, he'd put on airs and graces. He'd bought this house as a wreck decades earlier when its foundations were almost giving up the ghost of trying to prop anything up and turned it into a property that rivalled any other in the square. A proper lord of the manor was her baby brother these days it appeared.

Pearl checked the pricey Victorian paintings of foxhunts and shipwrecks on the walls as he led her through the hallway. As she passed the lavish dining room she got an eyeful of expensive china, candles and crystal glasses laid out on a table that would've done Buckingham Palace proud. Probably splashed the cash around to get high-end caterers in. But she wasn't invited in there or into his OTT drawing room. Instead he led her down to the basement and closed the door behind him.

'Very well – to what do I owe the pleasure?'

He spoke in his fake upmarket lingo. Only when he lost his rag did he start to sound like the East End, Caribbean ghetto kid he'd once been.

Without waiting for an answer, he accused, 'It's money I suppose.' He took out his leather wallet and opened it up. 'How much do you want? Take it and clear off.'

Pearl was properly offended. Alright, half offended; the gift of free money was always a welcome thing.

'Don't want your dosh, I need help.' She knew a lecture was on the horizon and that she'd have to suck it up if she was going to make any headway with him.

His face twisted as if in pain. 'Help? You want help from me? That's a laugh.' He was in full ghetto boy mode, the bad blood between them out in the open. 'When did you ever give me any help? When I was a young man without any money, down on his luck and in trouble with the law, what help did you give me? Oh yeah, that's right, you dumped your kids for some numb nuts and farmed them out to social services. If I hadn't come along and taken them terrified youngsters into my home where would they be now, eh? Where would they be?'

He kissed his teeth and flashed his eyes lethally at her. 'No wonder they won't have nish to do with you. You're lucky some of your grandkids wanna know ya.'

By now he was pacing up and down like a boxer waiting to swing. 'Wrecking your kids lives, wrecking my life, yeah Pearl, you're a regular helping hand.'

She felt ashamed of what she'd done to her kids, but that didn't mean Lord Muckety Muck here had to keep pushing her face in it. She was grateful to him, from the bottom of her old heart, for taking her babies in and giving them a proper home, but she would also never forget that it was him who'd put the kybosh on her seeing them when she'd finally come to her senses. The one time she'd managed to get close to her kids, her eldest son had gobbed in her face and shoved her out of the way. A mother never forgot that type of pain. It knifed right through to your very soul.

Pearl pushed past regrets and hurt aside as she took him by the arm.

'I'm in trouble and you're the only one who can help.' She stalled for a moment. She didn't want to give too much away. 'Me and a friend had some property robbed.'

He fixed his strained gaze on her. 'Robbed? What do you want me to do about it?' He shook her hand off. 'I'm a businessman, not a fucking copper.' He went on with his sneering. 'You want help? I'd start dialling 999 if I was you.'

Pearl bowed her head. She knew he was really going to blow his stack when she told him what sort of help she wanted but she had no choice. She lifted her head and looked deep into his stormy eyes. 'The thing is, it was quite a valuable piece of property and I know…you know…'

He stared at her, his mouth half falling open. 'What do I know?'

Pearl's heart sank. 'Well, you know.'

'No, I don't know, I'm not a mind reader – that's your department, ain't it?' He drew breath and suddenly seemed to be trying. 'Alright, what was stolen?'

Pearl admitted. 'It was gold.'

His finely manicured brows creased together. 'Gold? That's easy, just find out who the local jewellers are who buy hooky tom off skaghead housebreakers and then pay them a visit. If you look in various shop windows you'll probably see your bits in there going cheap. Pop in and tell the guy behind the counter that you want it back or you'll call the law. Simples.'

Pearl's voice fell to a whisper. 'It wasn't gold jewellery that we had pinched…it was gold bars.'

Her brother gazed at her as if he'd never seen her before. 'Bars? Where the hell would you have got bars from? Bullion's a big boy's game. It's not a racket for a pound shop con artist like you.'

When she didn't reply, he absently rubbed a finger against his temple as if he had a raging headache. 'I don't know – and don't want to know – what shit you've got yourself mixed up in this time.'

His finger dropped. 'Tell you what I'll do; if a door to door salesman comes round trying to flog me some off the books gold bars, I'll give you a call, otherwise I don't want to know.' He opened the basement door and gestured impatiently towards the steps with his hand. 'Now, if you wouldn't mind, I'm busy.'

Pearl looked at the steps and then at her brother. She took the plunge.

'My mate and I need to find out who stole our gold, but we're not connected. Back in your bad boy days you used to knock around with loads of Faces, didn't you? Guys like Stanley what's his face and that Ingram bloke who owned that knocking shop in Mile End. And they were the tip of the iceberg from what I heard. Just wondering if you might still see some people socially from those days and you could put the word out.'

Her brother stared at her in grim silence before closing the door again. On one side of the basement was a wall covered with box files standing on shelves. He looked them up and down and then turned to Pearl. She could see another lecture was in the offing. Any other day of the week she'd tell him to stuff it, but she didn't have the luxury of behaving like she had the upper hand now.

'Do you know what these are sis?' He gestured at the boxes and files. 'They're twenty years worth of quotes, estimates, invoices, letters, tax returns and the like. For twenty years, I've been getting up at six in the morning and driving all over the country doing building work and then coming home when most are in the land of nod. Some days I was so knackered, I nearly fell asleep at the wheel. For twenty years I've been buying houses, doing them up, selling them on or renting them out. For twenty years I've been doing that and you wanna know why?'

Pearl knew to keep it shut. His voice rose. 'Because I realised after getting into bad company as a youth, you don't get anything out of life without grafting. And I've grafted enough for ten men. You can't trust or rely on anyone in life if you want to get on. You certainly can't rely on your own family or flashy, cheating, two bit crooks like Miller or Ingram—'

Now she butted in with confusion, 'Did you say Miller —?'

His bellow of rage had her snapping her mouth firmly shut again and stepping back in haste. 'And then you come round my fucking yard! And accuse me of being fucking connected to the underworld! Of hanging round with common crooks and thieves! Asking me to put the word out! You – who's just finished a stretch herself and who's never done a proper day's collar in her life!'

Pearl lurched backwards when it looked like her brother was about to clump her one. Instead he shoved his palm in her back to propel her up the stairs and down the hallway.

At the front door he pulled her close and hissed, 'Unless somebody in the family has pegged out I don't want to see your lying, children-dumping-self round my gates no more.' He opened the door and prepared to throw her out but thought better of it. He pushed the door to and held her close again. 'Who's your friend? The other crook involved in this bullion scam?'

'I can't say. And stop calling my mate a crook.'

'Was it just you and her who knew where it was being kept?'

'Never said it was a her,' Pearl slapped in quickly.

'Well, I've got some advice for you as a going away present. If no one else knew, that means either you stole it or she did. Personally, I'm guessing it was you.'

Abruptly, he turned his head as a motor pulled up outside the house. He peered behind the door onto the square. He loosened his grip on Pearl and smoothed down her crumpled coat as if he were the most caring brother in the world. Pearl twisted her lips. Yeah, right!

'That's my first guests,' her brother announced. 'He's an architect and she's the niece of a bloke who sits in the House of Lords – that's who I'm connected to these days. Now piss off.'

He threw the door open and gently edged Pearl out onto the steps. A man in a suit and a woman, who seemed done up to the nines as if for an awards ceremony, were getting out of a silver Merc.

Spotting him, the woman cheerfully waved. 'Darling!'

He became an English gent again. 'Josie! You look absolutely ravishing! Jack, good to see you!'

Pearl almost puked at her brother's bowing and scrapping and 'absolutely' and 'ravishing' bollocks. What an all time sell out he was. However, now there were witnesses, Pearl wasn't scared of him anymore.

She whispered, mischief dancing in her eyes, 'I bet Jack and Milady Josie Darling think you're connected. I bet you they say, 'that darky's a crook,' when your back's turned.'

He kept the all too bright smile plastered on his face as he shot back, 'I couldn't give a monkey's uncle what anyone thinks or says. I told you, I don't believe in anyone except myself.'

Pearl sucked her teeth softly as she turned her back on her fool-fool brother. As she walked down the steps, Josie gave her a curious look.

Her brother obviously noticed because he shouted, 'Thanks so much Pearl! The house looks so splendid when you've finished dusting and cleaning. See you again next week!'

His cleaner? Fecking cheek! An indignant Pearl almost turned and smacked him one in his lying mouth. She might be on her uppers but she was still his big sister. Was still the one who had held his small hand when they'd docked in Tilbury on the ship from Jamaica when she was thirteen-years-old.

No, it was time for her to put her baby brother 'under manners' as the Caribbean community would say when someone needed to be taught respect.

She took a startled Josie by the arm and in her rawest Jamaican accent whispered, 'You'll have to cut Mister some slack this evening. I'm afraid he's been arrested again for living off immoral earnings.'

'Living off immoral earnings?'

Pearl pulled her closer still. 'Yeah, you know – he's been caught pimping again.'

She tottered away from a horror-struck, jaw slackened Josie. Let her snob knob brother get out of that one.

Only when she hit the main road did she remember what her brother had told her:

'Either you stole it or she did.'

That stopped her in her tracks. Could he be right? Was Babs the one who had had the gold away?

Seventeen

'Mum, I'm off,' Courtney cheerfully shouted as she opened the front door.

'Say hello to Bella and her folks,' Jen called back. Her voice softened with happiness. 'That Bella's a really sweet girl.'

Bella was in the same class as Courtney. The reigning class pin-up who all the other girls cooed up to. Her family were loaded. Her mum had met Bella for the first time this week, after the assembly at school, and been completely bowled over.

'You can tell she don't come off The Devil,' her mum had whispered with stars in her eyes.

No wonder her mum was over the moon that they were hanging out. There was only one problem – they weren't mates. Truth was Courtney couldn't stand the girl. As far as she was concerned Bella was always chatting, 'me, me, me,' and going on and on about her parents flash pad in Monte Carlo – wherever the fuck that was – and their penthouse near Harrods. But Courtney had needed a cover to go out without her mum smelling something fishy. Saying she was going off to 'see' Bella had done the trick.

Once downstairs Courtney flicked her hood up and legged it across the estate. Less than ten minutes later she reached the Station Car Park.

The beat of music provided a fat arrow pointing to where Dodgy and her crew were. They were tucked up in a corner chilling to Gwen Stefani's 'The Sweet Escape'. Dodgy sat on the low-level wall with three other girls, all nodding their heads to the rhythm as Mandela, the dog, spun round.

Dodgy was puffing away on a huge spliff when she spotted Courtney.

She bounced off the wall, the spliff clenched between her teeth like Clint Eastwood in 'The Good, The Bad and The Ugly.'

'Glad you could join the party Courts.' Pulling the weed from her mouth Dodgy introduced her girl gang. 'That's Roach, Blinky and Strawberry.'

Courtney got it straight away why her dyed pink hair was how Strawberry got her nick. With the other two she didn't have a clue and just hoped Roach's didn't have anything to do with the skin crawling variety.

Dodgy offered her a tote. ''Ere, get your laughing gear round some Rasta blaster.'

Courtney shook her head with solid determination. 'Nah, you're alright.'

Her mum would have her, good and proper, if she returned home bonged out of her box, stinking to high heaven like one of Aunt Tiff's squats.

Dodgy's merry mood vanished in an instant, her eyes flashing red warning signals. She bared her teeth. 'You're not being a stiff are ya?'

It was one of the other girls – Blinky – who inadvertently

came to Courtney's rescue, waving a half-gone bottle of voddy in the air. 'Maybe she wants a slug of this?'

One look at the bottle had Courtney tied up in knots. Her mouth started to water. She licked her lips. She'd developed a taste for the hard stuff while her Nanna Babs was banged up. She'd managed to stay off the booze for almost a year now. But it hadn't been easy. A long, hard slog was what it had been. Sometimes she woke up with the taste of it soaking into her tongue. Stared longingly at the booze showcased in the window of The Devil's Offy like she was hypnotised. No wonder people called it the demon drink.

Courtney swallowed with true grit. She'd come this far and wasn't about to flush all her hard work down the bog.

So she did what Foxy, her former counsellor, had taught her to do when faced with gut-twisting temptation – she swiftly changed the subject.

'How come the station's staff don't run you off?'

The others roared with bellyaching laughter.

When Dodgy got her breath back she explained, 'they know better than to mess with us. Anyroads, we sell discount gear to the guy on the gate. He's happy.' She sucked deeply, and proudly, from her joint.

Out of the blue, a flash motor appeared. It stopped a couple of metres away and flashed its lights twice. Dodgy suddenly came to attention like she was on guard duty. She flicked the spliff and walked sharpish towards the car. Courtney's brows jacked up in surprise. She hadn't figured Dodgy for someone who moved to the beat of anyone else's drum.

Strawberry jumped off the wall and caught Mandela's lead. He whined and tugged attempting to follow Dodgy.

Dodgy hunched down on the driver's side. Courtney couldn't see who Dodgy was speaking to. Whoever it was the girl was paying attention to the max. Must be someone much higher up the food chain for the girl to be listening without any backchat. Suddenly she recalled the words Dodgy had use to see Tasha off with that day by the canal:

'Do you know who I'm covered by?'

Was this who Dodgy was chatting with now? The people she was covered by? Must be some scary people to have Bad Girl Dodgy at their beck and call.

Less than a minute later the motor reversed and drove away as a very cheery Dodgy re-joined the group.

'Who was that?' Courtney felt compelled to ask.

'We gonna tell her?' Strawberry added with a gleam in her eye.

Dodgy leaned her head to the side giving Courtney an appraising look. 'Nah. Well not yet anyways.' She pierced Courtney with an unsettling, cool stare. 'Court's gotta prove herself first.'

Eighteen

As jumpy as a tart in church, Babs took one last drag on her baccy as she lurked outside the impressive steel and glass office block. She'd almost lost her nerve. It wasn't going to be easy to sweet talk Kieran Scott into doing her bidding.

Their last meeting had been a real set-to. She'd told him, point blank, his antics put her in mind of her bastard, evil ex, Stan - and for her there was no greater insult. Babs had backed it up by slamming the door in his stunned face.

Hadn't clapped eyes on him since, but she didn't need gossip or the grapevine to keep track of him. These days he was In the papers, if you please, standing in front of flashy, new-build apartment blocks with headlines like, 'London's top property developer Kieran Scott…'

Kieran gone legit? Don't make me laugh. All this property malarkey was clearly a front for whatever rackets he had his sticky mitts in. Kieran on the right side of the street? Yeah, and Al Capone became a dustman.

His offices were near Canary Wharf, so she'd hopped on the Dockland's Light Railway and hung around near the front door until he appeared. Except that hadn't happened. Now she had no alternative but to enter a world that felt as foreign to her as walking into a garden party at the Palace.

She gathered her courage, chucked her butt and pressed the intercom button.

'I'm here to see Kieran…Errr, I mean Mr. Scott.'

'I'm afraid he's not in at present,' a woman replied.

Babs didn't have time for a brush off, so insisted, 'I'll wait for him, if it's alright by you.'

The reception area was filled with large, showy plants, a bit like the Day of the Triffids. Babs' face scrunched up as she checked out a big, square thing spewing water in the middle? What thc fuck was that about?

She took a seat, nicely placed under a tall tropical flower away from the prying eyes of the three receptionists. He must be doing well if he needed three bodies manning the front desk.

She didn't have to wait long. A dark motor, sporting blacked out windows, rolled up. Kieran stepped out looking every inch the successful businessman in a slim-fit charcoal suit and light lilac shirt. Maybe the rumours doing the rounds were true about him going legit because the Kieran she knew wouldn't have been caught dead in a lilac shirt. Babs didn't have a problem with it herself; it suited him.

As soon as he entered the building and walked passed her she was on her feet. 'Kieran!'

The gangster turned developer did a double take when he clocked her.

'Babs? What are you doing here?' He looked around at his people who were ready on high-alert for him to give the word to fling her tail out on the street.

Coldly, he ground out, 'What do you want?' His tone would've had many a man wetting his underpants. Babs was made of sterner stuff.

'I need a word.' No way was she going to be intimidated by him, the boy she'd saved from a life of neglect and abuse on The Devil. She stood her ground.

'I've got nothing to say to you. Now if you'll excuse me.'

He set off.

Babs chased after him shouting, 'I wouldn't have come if it weren't important.'

'I'm a busy man - call my PA.'

She caught up with him and grabbed him by the arm as two security guards bore down on her.

'Do you want me to make a scene in front of your people? And you know what kind of scene I can make. I'm sure you remember how I took your mum on when she belted you one.'

Kieran's nostrils flared at the memory. He might be able to say this 'n' that about her, but her sticking up for her kids – and he'd been like a son to her – he couldn't fault her on. He gestured to security to back off. Looked at his Armani watch.

'You've got ten minutes.'

He took her up to his suite on the top floor. It was almost a replica of the offices he'd had at his one-time club in Wapping, but slicker, smarter and crowded with works of art and even more exotic plants. The view went down the river towards the City. 'Alright Babs – what do you want?'

He took a seat in a large, leather swivel chair but didn't invite her to sit down, which filled her with sadness. How had it gone so wrong between her and her darling boy?

That seemed a good enough place to start. 'Well, first off, I'd like to apologise for the way we parted last time. That was uncalled for.' His brow hitched up in surprise. 'Don't get me wrong, you were bang out of order, but that wasn't the way to deal with the situation.'

Kieran eased back, staring intently at her. 'Blimey, you really must want something if you're coming over all sorry for comparing me to Stan.' She inwardly flinched at that. 'Anyway, don't worry about it, I've heard worse, a lot worse. Now what do you want?'

Babs moved to stand at the edge of the wall-to-ceiling window and stared down the river. She had to tread very carefully. She didn't want Kieran to twig that it was about the gold that he'd actually blagged in the first place, that she'd then stolen and now been nabbed by someone else.

Finally she faced him, remaining by the window. The distance between them made it easier for her to talk. 'Me and Pearl have had something stolen from us – you remember Pearl?'

'Vaguely.'

'It's quite a valuable bit of property actually. And seeing as you're in the business, we was wondering if you could help us recover it. I mean, obviously there'd be a drink in it for you if you could lend a hand.'

It was only when she'd set her stall out that Babs realised how pathetic it sounded. She was asking him to help her recover something without actually saying what it was and in the certain knowledge that if he found out, he'd go bananas. But she and Pearl were desperate, especially if Pearl's brother didn't come up trumps.

Kieran leaned his arms against the padded armrests. 'What is it that's been half-inched? A TV? A DVD player? An old motor? You're gonna have to fill me in on the particulars.'

Babs broke eye contact and tried to think of a way around the problem.

She was startled when he let out a small, mocking laugh. 'It's the gold, isn't it?'

'You what?' Bollocks! She hadn't seen that coming. No way could he have figured out what she and Pearl had done. She toughed it out.

'How can it be the gold? I was behind bars when it all went down.'

He stood up and took his time walking over to join her by the window. Kieran gazed thoughtfully at the commanding view. 'The Babs I know wouldn't be scared out of her wits to chat to me about anything. The only thing that would leave you shaking in your shoes is the thing that split us up in the first place – the gold.'

Babs was surprised Kieran seemed so relaxed about the news and on the strength of that she snapped back, 'Well, it weren't your gold either was it? You stole it too.'

'Yeah, that's true enough. How did you do it?'

'Never you mind. Will you lend a helping hand or not?'

He finally gave her his full attention. 'So, Babs from the block is dealing in stolen bullion is she? Who else is involved in this little caper asides from Pearl?'

Babs let out a resigned huff. 'Just us two. As far as I'm concerned that gold can rot in hell, but Pearl don't see it that way.' Her heart started racing. 'If my girls find out I'm done for. We've finally managed to become a proper family again and I can't have nuthin mucking that up.'

His face had the decency to sting with shaming heat, no doubt remembering his pivotal role in almost breaking up her family.

She carried on, almost pleading with him. 'Look luv, if you could find out who took it and get it back, perhaps we could come to some arrangement?'

Kieran shook his head slowly. 'No can do and I'll tell you straight out why. I've moved on. I don't give a tinkers cuss about the gold. I'm making far more money flogging flats in London to Russians and Arabs than I could ever expect to make out of the bent metal racket. While some people might think the prices I charge for properties are criminal, it's still all totally legit.'

He moved away and resumed his seat as if to emphasis his new status.

'Plus, I'm not in the 'business', no more. I'm as straight as the barrel of a gun now. My company deals in the stock market not in the basement of a shop in Petticoat Lane. I don't go to the old haunts and I don't meet the old crowd. I pay my taxes, fill in all the government forms, insure my motors. It's all one hundred per cent kosher. I don't care about the gold or what's happened to it. Got it?'

Babs looked in his eyes. He was obviously and completely sincere. She'd pinned all her hopes on him and now she'd been blown out. 'I see. In that case, can you recommend anyone else who might be able to help?'

Kieran's face tightened. 'You're not listening, are ya? I'm out, I'm done with all that.'

Stunned, Babs turned in a daze towards the door. She couldn't take it in. It really was curtains between her and Kieran. What was she going to do about the gold? She didn't have anyone else to turn to. The only other person who might've done the trick was Dee with her links to John's underworld contacts. But Dee was the last person she could turn to. If her daughter ever sussed she was the one that filched John's gold, regardless of John and Kieran being in cahoots blagging it in the first place...No, Dee was not an option.

As she reached for the handle Kieran asked, 'By the way – how's Dee doing?'

As well as going legit was he a mind reader now too? 'She's alright. Doing good after what happened to John.'

Babs was already thinking about what she was going to tell Pearl. With no help from Kieran their treasure was gone with no hope of getting it back. That was unless Pearl's brother came through for them.

There was a tiny hesitation before he asked, 'How's that kid of hers? Had a son didn't she?'

Babs wasn't in the mood to play happy families after the knock back he'd given her, so she absently answered, 'Yeah. A boy. A real beaut. Called Nathan, but we all call him Natty.'

'Natty. Nice name.' His voice was achingly soft. Probably wishing the kid a better childhood than the one he'd been dealt Babs concluded.

'Dee's opening a club by the way.'

Kieran seemed lost in thought. 'So I heard. A business associate has been invited to the launch on Saturday and wanted to know if I'd tag along as his guest. I hope she's paid off whoever she needs to give a backhander to. The club scene can get a bit lairy if you don't pass a few brown envelopes around.'

'Don't worry, my Dee knows about these things. She was married to John remember.'

'As if I'd ever forget.'

Babs frowned hard. What a strange thing for him to say. She knew there'd been toxic blood between him and John about the gold, but there was something in Kieran's voice that suggested it was something else. Whatever it was Kieran wouldn't confide in her; their close relationship seemed to be at an end.

Nevertheless, she still enquired, 'Are you going to take your mate up on his offer to go to the launch?'

Kieran seemed to collect himself. 'Probably not. I'm a busy man.'

He got up and escorted her back down to reception and then onto the street.

'The gold,' he whispered, 'are you sure you didn't blab to no one else about it? Or maybe Pearl did?'

'Not a soul. We were very strict about that.'

Kieran gave her a knowing stare. 'Did you arrange to have it stolen behind her back?'

Babs was outraged. 'I think you've had too many liquid lunches with your new friends at the stock exchange. 'Course I never!'

Kieran looked at her meaningfully. 'In that case, the answer to your problem is simple. If you didn't take it, then Pearl must've done.'

Nineteen

'What's up Vi?' Pearl patiently asked. 'You've been looking like a soggy weekend since we got here.'

Here was Izzy's Hairdressers off Stratford High Street. Vi and Di, accompanied by Pearl and Fred, came once a month to take advantage of the half-price special for OAPs. The twins did love a good ol' wash and set and Pearl couldn't blame them. Dying slowly in some scuzzy armchair, waiting for the undertaker to cart you off was how many saw the lives of older people. Pampering and sprucing yourself up was a young person's game. Well, two fingers to that! Older folks had as much right to a sprinkling of glamour just like anybody else. And anyone who said different she'd shown them about their business with a hard bash of one of her bottles of Wrey and Nephew about their bonce.

Isabelle, the owner, was doing a bang up job of styling and shaping Vi's Diana Dors look while her twin was under the dryer. Pearl would've been thrilled to have her hair done too. That was never going to happen. No one, absolutely no one, got to see what was under her headscarf.

An opened copy of Cosmo lay in Pearl's lap as she sat next to Fred who gazed at Vi with star struck eyes. Pearl almost handed him a hankie to wipe the drool from his chops.

When Vi pressed her lips together avoiding answering, Pearl quickly closed the mag and shuffled to the edge of her seat. 'Come on Vi, tell me what's got you so upset.'

Fred jabbed Pearl, not hard, but not gently either. 'Leave off. Let Vi enjoy getting herself tarted up.' Realising what he'd said he went bright red and sputtered, 'Not that you're a tart or nuthin—'

Vi let out a laugh that sounded like music. 'Even if I wanted to be a tart I don't think anyone's going to take me up on the offer.'

'Don't know bout that,' Pearl piped in. 'Knew this old bird who was on the game most of her life and taking all comers until she was well into her seventies. Apparently she had this thing she did with her belly button—'

That didn't go down well with Fred. 'Oi! Wash your filthy mouth out with soap and water. Vi don't need to be hearing about some arthritic Tom's fuzz hole.'

The ladies looked at each other and sputtered into peels of high-pitched laughter. God knew Pearl needed some laughter in her life. Her brother's words of advice were like a splinter in her thumb. Babs ripping her off? Pinching the gold and then playing all innocent? Nah. Babs would never do that. Would she?

Pearl bounced back to the present and caught Vi's fretful gaze in the mirror. Pearl gently persisted in getting to the bottom of what was going on. 'A problem shared is a problem solved.'

Vi tilted her head to look up at Izzy who got it straight away that her customers wanted to be alone.

Izzy shook her glorious black hair back as she announced, as soon as she'd taken Di from under the dryer, 'I'll be round the back making myself a brew.'

Once the four of them were alone Vi opened up her handbag with trembling fingers and pulled out a letter. 'This came in the post this morning.'

She handed it over to Fred whose lips moved silently as he read.

'They can't bloody well do that,' he exploded.

Pearl snatched it from him and as her eyes scanned the letter her insides churned with dread. 'It says the management of the care home will have to ask you to leave if you don't pay your fees which are due next Friday.'

Vi seemed to crumple in on herself. 'I'm already behind by two months as it is—'

Her twin forcefully cut in, 'I've already told you that my Glenda is good for it. She'll pay for us both.'

Vi straightened, her gaze flashing with defiance. 'I've told you I won't take a penny from your girl. Anyway, she doesn't like me. She's always resented how close we are.'

'She'll do what she's told,' Di snapped with the authority of a mother.

Her sister stubbornly kept her thoughts to herself on that matter. Then said, 'If I don't pay up they said they'll transfer me to Dead House.'

They all gasped. Dead House was the nickname for the Council run care home down the road. The stories coming out of that place were sickening. Old folk left to rot in their piss and shit for hours on end. A man with dementia who'd wandered off and somehow managed to get as far as Southend. And plenty more. It was no care home but a dumping ground for people who society should've been looking after with love and respect.

Fred's face boiled red as he blew his stack. 'I'm not having that. Over my dead body. I'll sort it out, just you wait and see.'

'It's all my fault,' Pearl admitted mournfully.

Vi's delicate hand waved in the air. 'I know what you're going to say. If you hadn't introduced us to that con artist I'd have enough money to pay my way. But, like what I said at the meeting, no one twisted my arm.' A breath shuddered in her thin chest as a stricken expression took hold of her face. 'I don't want to go there. I don't want to leave my friends behind.'

Di patted her sister's hand sharing her strength. 'We've been together for years now. You're not going anywhere without me.'

Their attention was diverted by the sound of something being shoved through the letterbox of the shop's front door. They didn't have time to figure out what it was because there was a flash followed by an explosion.

The twins screamed with terror as Fred and Pearl cursed. The sisters dived for cover, crouching on the floor with their arms protectively covering their heads.

A horrified Izzy ran out from the back. 'What the fu…?' She never finished. Another one came hurtling into the shop.

Flash! Bang!

That's when Pearl sussed what had been thrown – rockets. The twins desperately tried to curl into balls under a chair. They openly sobbed, clutching each other petrified to the core. Fred threw his body near the chair trying his best to protect them. Although she was bricking it, Pearl had long ago realised that crying did no good. She remained where she was.

The door burst open and five youths, hoods over their heads and their jackets zipped high up their faces, waltzed in. One held a vicious-looking, steel baseball bat, which was pointed with menaces at them.

'Penny for the guy! Remember! Remember the fifth of November! Oh fuck, it ain't November is it? Never mind, everyone loves a firework display, don't they? Now which one of you fuckers is Izzy?' the youth carried on.

Pearl dared to growl, 'Clear off or I'll have the coppers on ya.'

'I'll tell you what grandma, why don't you shut the fuck up before I really give the cops something to investigate? Now where's Izzy?

Izzy scrambled to her feet, her face ashen and pasty. 'Please, leave my customers alone. Take what you want from the till and go.'

The youth swaggered forward making Izzy take two steps back. 'Are you calling us thieves? That's slander that is. I should take your legs out for that. We're not crooks, we collect insurance and It appears that this month's payments have slipped your mind.'

Izzy's eyes widened as it dawned on her what this was really about. 'I was gonna pay it tomorrow.'

'Wazza ain't gonna cut it.' The thug laughed like a demented hyena. 'Cut it. Get it.'

The baseball bat bashed violently into a display of conditioner and shampoo. The products and shelving crashed to the floor.

'I've got it in the back,' Izzy hurriedly cried knowing she'd do anything to stop her beloved shop from being trashed. She'd worked herself to the bone to turn this place into her dream after she'd divorced her cheating husband, packed up her kids and started all over again.

As she rushed off the youth fixed a dangerous glare onto Pearl and the others cowering on the floor. 'Nice hair-do you got there missus, suits your face.'

Pearl knew when to leave it alone, but Fred didn't. 'You cowards. Why don't you go and pick on someone your own size?'

The bat was waved at him. 'Do you want some of this because I've got plenty. Come and have a go if you like?'

Fred could see the odds and nothing more was said.

The goons sniggered, apart from, Pearl noted, the one nearest the door. That one looked like they wanted to run for their life.

An out of breath Izzy reappeared and shoved a bulging envelope in the youth's hand.

'That's more like it.' The envelope was stuffed into the terror's back pocket.

But the thug wasn't finished. The bat was back pointing at Izzy. 'Take a seat.' The bat shifted to indicate a chair.

Pearl had enough of this. They had their money, anything else was unnecessary. Fury rose up with her words. 'She's given you the cash. That's enough.'

Fred wasn't having it either. 'Mugging people off, what they teaching you kids these days in school, eh?'

The youth didn't appear to take offence, just twirled the bat. 'Well, if it ain't ebony and ivory.' Calmly the thug turned back to Izzy. 'Now if you don't wanna watch your premises go up in smoke you'd better tell the Golden Girls to shut their gobs and mind their own.'

Izzy pleaded with Pearl and Fred. 'Please! I know you want to help me out, but the best way to do that is to stay out of it.'

She swallowed, then walked on legs trembling like jelly towards the chair and sat tensely in it. The youth searched the equipment in the shop. Then smiled with wickedness. Electric clippers were held triumphantly in the air like a trophy.

Fred started to move to intervene but Pearl snapped him back and whispered, 'Izzy said leave it. Don't you worry, they'll get what's coming to them one of these days.'

Suddenly the youth at the door walked slowly towards Izzy. The leader of the gang plugged in the clippers and passed it to the youth.

'Right, leave her a reminder for next month.'

The clippers buzzed on. The youth cut a path through Izzy's gorgeous hair like a mini lawnmower. The result was obscene. Her shiny, black hair hung on both sides with a bald strip running from back to front in the middle. Izzy struggled to hold back the tears.

The youth chucked the clippers on the floor as if they were on fire.

Baseball bat goon looked this way and that at Izzy's new hairstyle. 'If we come back next time it won't be a clipper that's used but something a lot more sharper and on other body parts.'

The bastard had the brass to mockingly bow to Pearl and the others. 'We won't charge for the fireworks display, that was free.'

Then they were gone.

'You alright girls?' Fred asked as he helped a shell-shocked Di and Vi to their feet.

Pearl was more concerned with Izzy who hadn't moved a muscle. She got to her feet and quickened her pace towards her. Izzy was in a trance, transfixed by the reflection of the horror story her hair had become.

Her almost dead eyes caught Pearl's in the mirror. 'They could've done anything to me, *anything*.' Her voice was dead too. 'But this.' She shook her head with feeling. Her hand caressed the right side of her hair. 'This is all I've got. This is why people come here coz my hair looks so great. Who's gonna want a hairdresser that looks like this?'

''Ere,' Fred said from across the room. 'Get a wig. There's some very nice ones around now and your barnet will soon grow back.'

The woman all cried with despair, 'Fred,' but it was too late.

Izzy burst into floods of tears mumbling, 'I'm so sorry,' again and again.

Just as Izzy had looked after Vi and Di once a month now it was all their turn to take care of her. They got her sat down on one of the comfy chairs with a cuppa touched up with a lick of Pearl's rum.

A Knowing Pearl asked, 'You having to pay protection money to someone?'

Fred squinted at her in surprise. 'How do you know anything about that?'

'Wish I could say the spirits told me, but truth is I've seen this one too many times with my own two eyes.'

An exhausted Izzy said, 'I've been paying hand over fist

for the last nine months.' She looked straight at Vi. 'It seems you ain't the only one with money troubles.'

Courtney was the only one not creasing up as they took the central line back to Mile End after the rumble at the hairdressers. Seeing those old people terrified out of their wits on the floor put her in mind of her Nanna Babs. Worst still it put her point blank back in her grandmother's sitting room when her granddad had Nanna on the floor choking the life out of her. Just thinking of that awful incident made her want to retch. Courtney had been involved in a few tussles in her time but what had gone on in that hairdressers was bang out of order.

She hadn't wanted to cut that woman's hair, but Dodgy had told her, in no uncertain terms, that was the only way she could become a member of her crew. So she'd done it and still felt shit about it.

Dodgy looked at her. 'You done good Courts. Thought you were gonna bottle it.' When she pulled out a fag and lit up, a mum with a kid sat on her lap looked disapprovingly at her.

Dodgy snarled, 'You gotta a problem with this missus?' She stabbed the ciggy in the woman's direction like a blade. The woman tutted and turned her face away.

Strawberry whispered, leaning into Dodger, '*They* won't like us calling attention to ourselves.'

A confused Courtney asked, '*They*? Who are *they*?'

'Never you mind,' Dodgy responded. Nevertheless, she snubbed out her fag heeding Strawberry's words.

Then she slowly smiled and Courtney had to admit she was a very attractive girl when she did that. 'All you need to know is that you've passed the test for getting into my Dodgy crew with flying colours. You're now officially a Dodgy Girl.'

The all cheered, Courtney's being half-hearted. She had a strange feeling she was going to regret falling in with this lot.

And, as if to pile on that strange feeling, Dodgy informed her, 'Gonna need you at the Station tomorrow night.'

Courtney was relieved. Saturday night was Aunty Dee's club launch and her mum was expecting her to stop in to look after Little Bea.

'No can do,' she bravely answered.

Dodgy stared at her dead in the eye with an expression that trumped loudly you didn't want to get on her bad side. 'Yes you will do. You're a fully paid up member of my Dodgy Girls now and you'll do as told.'

Twenty

What the fuck am I doing here?

Babs asked herself the question for the umpteenth time as she stood in front of room fourteen in the hotel in Finsbury Park. This was a mistake. An all-time loser mistake. The last time she'd been her was back in '78. And what a fucked up year that had turned out to be.

So, if this was such a mistake why have ya tarted yourself up like some blowsy piece selling her wares on Commercial Street, eh? Put on one of your best frocks and heels? What the flamin' hell are you doing here? Haven't you made enough cock-ups in your life?

But, like a magnet was forcing her hand, she raised it to knock. It wavered in the air. She couldn't do this. Just couldn't. The only road it led to was one with a street sign named Disaster. Decision made, Babs rushed to go back the way she'd come.

But she was too late.

The door opened. And there he stood – Tricky Dickie.

He'd hounded her with messages on her mobile to meet him. She'd ignored them but the Herbert wouldn't leave off. He was a persistent bollocks alright. If she didn't feel so low after Kieran's brush off and trying to figure out if Pearl had betrayed her she wouldn't have given him the time of day. Well, that's what Babs convinced herself.

But one look at him and she was away with the fairies. Her heart squeezed and leapt with pleasure. He was rigged out in a plain T-shirt and black jeans and a welcoming smile on his gorgeous, lived-in face.

Babs anxiously coughed and swallowed. 'Look Tricky Dickie…'

She squealed as he grabbed her hand pulling her inside.

He kicked the door shut with the back of his heel, took her face gently in the palm of his hands and kissed her.

Just like that! No 'Hello', 'How's it going?', 'Fancy a cuppa?' Simply plunged them into a place they hadn't been in almost three decades. Babs heated up with the power of a tropical storm. It felt soooo good. No, better than good. Took her zooming back to that time in '78 when they'd made love here. And it had been making love, not a bit of how's your father, getting your leg over or having a shag. It was the first time in forever Babs had felt that she deserved to be loved.

Babs reached up on tiptoes, tugged his head closer, threading her fingers into his hair and almost sucked the life from him.

Alright, so he's got a tongue and lips on him to die for, but you know you shouldn't be here. Babs willed her mind to shut it, but the warnings wouldn't let up. He might be retired, but once a copper always a copper.

Babs snatched her mouth away and stumbled back, gasping for air. 'Patrick,' for once she used his real name, 'there's no point to this luv—'

'So you admit I'm your love?' His voice was gentle, his face frank and open.

Babs clucked her tongue and rolled her eyes. 'You know what I mean. They say 'love' all the time where I come…' She harshly sucked the rest of the words back. The time for pussy footing around was over.

She took a bracing breath. 'Yeah, I fancy you something rotten. Some might say that's called love. I dunno. What I do know is that you can't have all the sweets in the sweetie shop.'

'I beg to differ.'

He swept her into his arms. Babs squealed louder this time. The fool was going to break his friggin' back. Then tears pricked her eyes. This was the type of romance she read about in Mills & Boon, the sort not meant for women living on The Devil's Estate.

She smiled away as he made a beeline for the bed. 'Patrick, you'll give yourself a bloody hernia, you stupid man.'

'As light as a feather.'

He laid her down and that's when her guard shot up again. Babs crossed her arms protectively over her boobs. Her cheeks glowed hot with embarrassment.

'My body ain't the same as it was all those years ago. Things have gone a bit south, know what I mean?'

He stared back at her as if she was a feast before a hungry man. 'I don't care if you've gone south,' he kissed her left ear, 'north', kissed her right ear, 'west', placed his lips on her forehead. 'Babs, wherever you're going I aim to be there too.'

Her face lit up into a cheeky grin. 'Well, I hope your truncheon is still heading north.'

Gently he helped her with her dress. Then her bra. Babs went scarlet again as she slapped her hand over her boobs. 'I really don't look the same. Things ain't what they used to be.'

He didn't answer, simply took her hands away from her chest. And there they were – her boobs for all the world to see. Babs wasn't even sure she was breathing as she watched his face. Please don't let him be disgusted! I'd die of shame on the spot!

Tricky Dickie couldn't take his eyes off them. 'Babs, they're fucking beautiful.' His hands softly palmed them. 'So smooth. So soft. So edible.'

His mouth was on her right nipple. He sucked. He licked. Babs thought she was going to burst a gasket. Ohhhh! What a feeling.

He pulled his head back. His eyes were on fire. 'If we don't get down to it I'm going to embarrass myself.'

Giggling they got his kit off in record time and spent the next hour getting reacquainted with each other very well indeed. Making love and cuddling each other tight like a couple of teens surprised they had private parts that actually worked.

Then he went and spoiled everything, at least in Babs' eyes.

'I want us to get married.'

She was out of his arms and off the bed quicker than a bride could say, 'I do.'

Babs started flinging her clobber on as she spoke. 'That ain't gonna happen. My girls would have a fit, probably turn their backs on me.'

And the gold. Fuck me! How could she have forgotten

about the gold and him being the law?

For the first time he looked like the serious copper she had met years back. 'My son and daughter have known about you for years, ever since I parted company with their mum in '98. And they're happy for me and actually want to meet you.'

Babs looked at him wildly as she did up the zipper of her dress. 'You know why we can't be officially together.'

He got angry. 'Oh, I get it, I'm good enough to taste but not swallow.'

'I'm still the girl from The Devil and you're still the fella in blue.'

'Former blue. You can't keep living life through your children.'

She swiped up her bag in a huff. 'My kids are all I've got.'

'You've got me.' His voice was hard but there was hurt there too.

Babs couldn't deal with it. She shot out of the room, couldn't remember the journey down the stairs and only stopped rushing when she hit Finsbury Park tube. The pain was so intense she had to hold on to the wall as commuters hurried by. Why had she opened her heart – again - to a man she couldn't have in her life?

Twenty-One

'Now, don't forget what I told ya about what time to put him to bed,' a flustered Dee instructed Natty's new nanny on Saturday evening.

Dee cradled him way too tightly to her breast. She stood in her state of the art kitchen in her larger than life house in Essex as she faced Miriam. It was the nanny's first day with Natty and suddenly Dee couldn't – wouldn't – let him go.

She was dressed to impress, heading off for her club's launch party. If she didn't shift it she was going to be late. But she couldn't let go of her darling baby. Stop being a right div part of her brain reasoned while the other half warned, 'what do you really know about this woman?'

'Mizz Dee?'

Miriam's voice brought her crashing back to the present. Dee had to admit she liked the sound of the nanny's voice – quiet, sweet and soft. Natty would like that.

The nanny continued as she reassuringly smiled at her. 'I know exactly how you're feeling. You would not be a normal mother if you didn't feel some level of anxiety about leaving him for the first time with what is, essentially, a stranger.'

Hearing it spoken aloud Dee felt even more of a Wally.

She needed to cut the apron strings and stop behaving like the world was coming to an end. She looked adoringly down at the son that she and John never expected they would have. He was kitted out in an all-in-one sky-blue baby suit with cute bears on the front and matching socks. Gucci o' course.

His eyes sparkled, giving her that million-watt smile that made her heart melt. Dee had a soft spot for kids. Hearing about abuse cases made her want to tear someone's head off. How could anyone look at a tiny baby and want to do them harm? It was a sick world, no doubt about it.

'Mizz Dee, if you don't leave now you'll be late for your big night.'

Dee looked up to find Miriam holding her arms out ready to take Natty. 'He'll be in the safest pair of hands you could possibly think of.'

Dee gave her little man a kiss as light as a feather on his baby-soft forehead to last him until she came home.

She whispered, 'Now you be a good boy for Miriam while mummy's off earning an honest crust.'

Dee straightened and took a shaky breath. Right, here goes! Finally she passed her much-loved son into another woman's arms. Miriam cooed to Natty as they followed Dee out into the spacious hallway, passing the large photo of Dee's long dead, much-cherished cat Banshee, who wore a pink bow in her fur. Dee reached for her coat and black leather Versace studded tote handbag. Once she had her coat on she gazed back fretfully at the nanny holding her son.

Miriam held Natty in the crook of her arm so that his mum could see him. 'Wave good-bye to mummy.' She held his hand up and moved it in a wave.

'Don't you worry Mizz Dee, me and Natty are going to become the best of friends. The very best.'

'Finally,' Miriam whispered in a sweet tone to Natty as his mother's convertible drove away. 'Didn't think the fucking bitch was ever gonna shut that filthy gob of hers and sod off.'

She rocked him as they took the stairs to the next floor. God, it was pure bliss to have a baby back in her arms. There was no feeling like it in the world.

'Now, what shall we do today? Play with some toys? Watch Teletubbies on the DVD? Oooo, I do like that Tinky Winky.'

Bagging this job hadn't been easy but the effort she'd put in had paid off. Miriam had doshed up the teen junkie to chuck the brick through the club's window and while Dee was called away she'd gone on the hunt for the list of applicants for the job. Thought she'd have a right job on her hands hunting it down. Who would've thought it would be all ready to go on the bitch's desk. There were four names, including hers with accompanying contact details. Two names were crossed out in thick red - she assumed that meant they were non-starters - which left only one other person in the race. Pamela Caruthers.

Once she left the club she'd given this Pamela a little tinkle.

'This is Mrs Black's assistant—'

'I didn't get the job, did I?' came the deflated interruption.

'I'm happy to say that Mrs Black would love to offer you the job.'

There was a gasp at the other end, followed by a quick and grateful, 'you don't know how thankful I am. This was my twentieth interview since being made redundant from working as a teaching assistant. Been working at that school for going on twenty years…'

Miriam rolled her eyes. If there was one thing she hated it was a bleeding heart sob story. 'Before we can dot the i's and cross the t's, Mrs Black needs you to know that the job offer is subject to one condition.'

'Anything.'

Miriam's smile was genuine this time; she was going to enjoy this.

'Every second Saturday you'll need to be available to join in her S&M parties—'

'I beg your pardon?' came the horrified response.

'The blokes do like a lot of begging, but nothing too kinky. A couple of the guys have been on the lookout for an older woman, you know fleshy boobs and wobbly belly.'

'Well I never!' Miriam could almost feel the woman rising to her feet in righteous indignation. 'I've never heard such filth in my life. And my tummy doesn't wobble, thank you very much.' Steel entered her voice. 'You tell Mrs Black she can stuff her job.'

The dial tone rang in her ear as the call was cut.

So easy. She looked down at the baby. Now she had the little prince all to herself.

They reached the landing. 'I know,' she said in a mock-surprised voice, 'we'll have us a great adventure and go find that cow's room and see what's inside.'

Dee had given her the grand tour of the tacky house from the lounge, which the stupid moo called the Hollywood, to the gym and swimming pool in the back. The only room that had remained off limits was Madam Dee's bedroom.

'No one, apart from me and the housekeeper, who pops in Wednesdays and Fridays, goes into my boudoir,' was Dee's firm instruction.

We'll see about that! As if a slag like Dee Black even knew what a boudoir was!

The room was huge, with a generously proportioned skylight above the king size bed, which was covered in a leopard print duvet and frilly cushions. She thought the pillowcases would be leopard print but they had a design she couldn't make out from where she stood, so she moved herself and Natty closer. They were imprinted with a photo of a laughing Dee with her arms around the shoulder of a much older man, who Miriam took to be the late, departed John Black.

Her lips rippled in disdain. 'Trashy, totally trashy, that's what it is my poppet. The deluded woman has got zero taste.' She rocked him closer to her chest.

Miriam pursed her lips in distaste as she took note of the partially opened door that led to a dressing room. 'We'll leave mummy's clobber for another day coz it's time for us to get to know each other a bit better.'

She kissed him on his cheek, which made him gurgle with pleasure. Miriam laid him on the bed. He kicked his cubby legs and arms in the air as she walked with attitude towards the leopard print – yes leopard print - dressing table.

She half turned to the baby and with scorn uttered, 'Can you believe this lady? No fucking class, that's what.'

She rifled through Dee's make-up until she found a bright-red Mac lipstick. Miriam took it and sat next to Natty on the bed. Poor thing looked wiped out.

She gazed down at him with a glazed expression in her

eyes almost as if she wasn't really there. 'Now I've got you back Andy I'm never gonna let you go.'

She tickled his tummy, but Natty didn't smile this time letting out a piercing wail as if he was trying to tell her his name wasn't Andy.

She ignored his desperate cry. 'I want you to say after me – mummy.'

He continued to wail, which made her nerves wear thin. 'Come on, say mummy.' More wails. Her face set into a stiff, stern mask. 'Not to worry my gorgeous boy, I've got a great way for you to remember who mummy is.'

Miriam undid his body suit and pushed it back exposing his soft baby belly. Abruptly his wailing stopped as he looked at her with the helpless innocence of a child.

'This will also help you to learn to read and write of course.'

She took the lipstick and scrawled one word in large, red capital letters across his tummy.

MUMMY.

Twenty-Two

'Mum, you look like a million large ones,' Little Bea gasped in star-struck wonder as she stared at Jen.

Courtney gave the thumbs up too. 'No one will be able to touch you tonight.'

That nearly brought Jen to tears as she stared back at her reflection and her girls who lounged back on her bed. Last year her eldest would've been spitting bile at her no doubt screaming her head off that she was doing a great impression of a scrubber. That had been a terrible time, one she took pains not to dwell on too often. With the help of the rest of the Miller clan they'd been able to claw what love and affection they had back. They were a family again.

Jen self-consciously straightened the hem of her knee-length, sleeveless, silver brocade dress and then looked down at her silver box heels. She looked the part of a woman who was the manager of a club and heading off to its grand opening, but inside there was a corner of Jen that still felt ugly.

'You're a minging, pitiful mess. Let's see if my hand can knock some beauty into ya.' That's what the girl's father would yell at her, along with a host of other degrading shite, before he'd beat her from one end of the room to the next.

Jen knew she wasn't ugly, but if someone battered you with it enough times that's how you started to view yourself. She tried to hide it beneath this harder looking Jen, but this feeling of not being worthy enough wouldn't go away. She never talked to her mum, sisters or mates about it. They'd only insist she was living in the past and needed to put Nuts, her former husband, behind her. That was all good and well, but what they didn't get was once you'd been a battered woman it took years to get your groove back.

Jen shook off the past and asked, with a mischievous lift of her lips, 'What earrings shall I wear?'

Her daughters eagerly scrambled off the bed to help her decide. Five minutes later Jen looked the biz as she grabbed her knock off Stella McCartney jacket.

As she put it on she stared at her daughters. 'Courtney—'

'I know,' her eldest cut in rolling her eyes with half-hearted annoyance, 'look after Little Bea. If anyone comes to the door, scream the place down.'

'Or get on the blower to me, got it?'

Jen opened her arms and gathered the two people she cherished most in the world as close as possible. For a moment she closed her eyes and felt their twin hearts beating against her as one.

'Mum, you're gonna be late.'

Courtney was right. Jen let them go and got into club manager mode. Her daughters waved her off, grinning for all they were worth. Then Jen headed to Mile End tube, head held high ultra confident that the club launch was going to be a night to remember.

As soon as her mum shut the door, leaving a cloud of Opium perfume in her wake, Courtney swung into action. The last time she'd sneaked out was during last year. She'd done a runner back then causing all kind of ructions including ending up in the same naughty kids' secure home that Dodgy had bossed.

Her sister, Little Bea's searching gaze flicked just above the book she was reading, following Courtney's every move as she quickly slung on a dark-blue Velour tracksuit and the same hooded jacket Dodgy had given her to wear during the smash up at the hairdressers.

Little Bea's gave her the once-over as she let out a resigned sigh. 'Oh! It's gonna be one of *those* nights.'

Courtney flipped her hood over her head. 'Ain't gonna be long, an hour tops.'

The old Courtney would've told her baby sister to shut her noise and mind her own, but she'd done a wagonload of growing up since then. She felt guilt-ridden leaving her sister all on her tod like this. Plus, her mum would have her guts for garters if she ever twigged. But that was a preferable fate to Dodgy coming looking for her, banging down her door shouting the odds about her no-show.

'I mean it,' she emphasised to her baby sister. 'Be back in a jiffy. But if anything goes on, you get on your blab-slab as quick as to me, got it? Don't try none of that shit you keep reading in those cop books if someone comes to the door.'

Her sister loved reading. More to the point she couldn't seem to get enough of true crime books. She was currently reading, 'A-Z of Forensics'. Having become a true crime statistic herself, Courtney found her sister's grisly obsession unsettling and downright weird. Their mum only allowed it because Little Bea was the top of her class in reading.

Ten minutes, or so, later Courtney heard Beyoncé and

Shakira's 'Beautiful Liar' before she saw her new mates. When she caught sight of them, in their customary all-over black, Courtney nearly did a double take – they were dancing. And it wasn't none of that prancing about some of the kids did but serious moves to the rhythm of the music. Fancy that, Dodgy being a beat freak, she would never have believed that. But then again there was loads of stuff she didn't know about Dodgy.

When the gang spotted her they abruptly stopped.

'Wotcha Courts,' Dodgy greeted. 'Thought you weren't coming.' She lifted an eyebrow, 'Thought I was gonna have to come fetch you for a minute. Believe you me that wouldn't have been a good look.'

Courtney worried her bottom lip. The other girl was on the warpath. Courtney scrambled around for something to say. 'Where's Mandela?'

Dodgy's face came over all soft; she did cherish that dog of hers. 'He's stopping indoors with my Nan.'

'I didn't know you had a Gran.'

Dodgy's soft expression deepened. 'We've all got Grans. It's just mine's alive and she looks out for me.' Courtney was about to ask after her parents when the other girl supplied the answer. 'My old man and girl fucked off years ago. Suppose they didn't want a kid tagging along for the ride.'

Those words revealed the little girl inside who hurt like so many other little girls, Courtney being among their number. Her own dad was long gone and she hoped to never clap eyes on the worthless prick again. The thud of his fists against her mum's skin were sounds that would remain with her for life.

Dodgy got back into Dodgy mode. 'Right ladies, time for us to hit that rave.'

Courtney was puzzled. 'Party? But we ain't togged out for a party.'

Dodgy winked. 'We are for the type of wing-ding we're going to.'

Courtney took the plunge and gave it to her friend straight. 'See, the thing is Dodge, I ain't gonna be able to go.'

In response, Courtney got a stone-cold stare that almost stopped her heartbeat.

'I'll just pretend my ears never heard that.'

Courtney shook her head with feeling. 'I can't. My mum's gone out and I've gotta take care of my little sis.' She did feel a bit of a Muppet saying she was obeying her mum to girls who didn't conform to anyone's rules. 'I mean, if you had to look after your gran you'd have to stop indoors.'

Dodgy leaned her head to the side considering Courtney's statement. 'You got that right.' Courtney smiled with relief which soon went down the lav when Dodgy added, 'But there's sod all wrong with her which means I'm going off to a blowout with my mates, which includes *you*.'

Courtney nervously swallowed, her eyes blinking like crazy. 'I can't leave my sister alone.'

Dodgy took a menacing step closer. 'Remember that home for girls we met in?' Courtney didn't want to do it but she nodded. 'Remember that day I got into a ruck with that lizard-looking fuck-tart in the common room?' Another nod, more shaky this time. 'And I got her by the hair. Now she thought that I was going to bash her brains in, but that wasn't what I did, was it?'

Courtney's mouth went completely dry as she filled in the rest of the story. 'You took out a pair of scissors and cut off her hair. On her eyebrows.'

'Funny what you can do with a pair of scissors in your hand.'

Courtney got the message and didn't bring up the idea of not going again. But she figured out that when they got to the rave, she'd stay for fifteen minutes and then sneak off.

But when they reached the party less than an hour later, her plan went out the window.

Courtney stood with the Dodgy Crew, hoods up, on the other side of the road and stared in shock at the long line of excited people queuing up outside a building. Blue, pink and green laser beams slid and swayed over it.

'You'll need this.' Dodgy held out a pair of Jackie O style sunglasses.

Courtney's hand trembled as she took it. 'I can't go in there.'

'Why's that then? Got homework to do?'

Strawberry, Blinky and Roach sneered along.

Courtney's horrified gaze was transfixed by the name on the building.

'But it's the Three Sisters Club.'

Dodgy dished out a dirty look and got sarky. 'They teach you how to read in posh schools? I really missed out, didn't I?'

Her young face turned back to the club. 'Alright ladies, it's showtime!'

Twenty-Three

'Thanks, big time, for turning out for the Three Sisters tonight,' Dee said with the broadest smile she could muster as she shook the hand of a Posh & Becks wannabe couple. Take That's 'Shine' boomed from the dance floor in the background.

She and Jen had been giving it the personal touch, meeting and greeting people at the entrance of the club since its doors had opened. If the long, snaking line outside was any indication, it looked like the club had smashed it for pulling in the punters. Dee was cynical enough to know that this might be the case because drinks were priced at a quid for the first hour. But, hey, who gave a monkey's! As long as the punters made this a night to remember and spread the word.

She felt like a kid in a sweetie shop. Everywhere she looked was colour, glamour, glitz and wall-to-wall party people.

'OMG Dee,' Jen squealed almost jumping with joy, 'I can't believe it. This is the dog's bollocks.' Her voice wavered as she choked up. 'I want to thank you for putting your trust in me and making me manager. No one's ever done anything like that before for me.'

Dee answered affectionately, 'Stop blabbing, you silly moo. We're blood family so we're in it together.'

'Shame 'bout this blood family member stuck in the cloakroom,' Tiff bitched behind them.

After Tiff's shenanigans the other day behind the bar Dee had made some slight adjustments and put her in charge of the cloakroom instead. Tiff had moaned to high heaven, but Dee had slapped her down so she got it through her loaf she wasn't putting up with Tiff's bad girl ways. If she did a bang up job tonight then Dee might see her way to installing her back as MC at the bar.

'Take no notice of Moaner Lisa,' Dee declared to Jen loud enough for Tiff to get the message.

She forgot all about her baby sister when a flash, white, stretch Limo rolled up. A wave of excitement rippled through the queuing clubbers as they stood on tiptoes to get a glimpse of the celeb putting in an appearance. A uniformed chauffeur got out and did the honours with the passenger door.

A slightly embarrassed, giggly Babs took his proffered hand as she tried to get out the back with as much grace as possible. And didn't her mum look a treat in a stunning, black, sparkling evening dress that Dee had insisted they go shopping at Selfridges for.

Dee's pleasure died when she clocked another person get out as well – the original bad penny Flo Miller.

Flo started posing this way 'n' that in her skimpy white dress with cut outs that put more flesh on display than Smithfield's Meat Market. Dee was not pleased, not one bit. This was meant to be her mum's big moment and that girl had taken every ray of limelight. You only had to look at the men with their tongues hanging out and the ladies slit-eyed with seething envy to know who had their attention.

Babs hugged both her girls, dizzy with delight at the crowds in and outside the club. Looked like it was going to be a right, royal knees-up tonight! She was over the moon for Dee. She deserved this after all that had happened with John.

'Got the shock of my life when the limo turned up to pick me up,' Babs gushed to her eldest.

'Only the best for my ol' mum.'

'You should've seen the faces on The Devil when it turned up.' She winked. 'Told 'em I was off to have fish 'n' chips with Prince Philip.'

Flo reached for Dee's hands, 'what a fabulous night, sweetie. I hope the glossies are coming to cover it for their diary sections.'

Dee shoved her hands behind her back twisting her lips as she looked Flo up and down. 'Looks like you came ready for your paparazzi shots.'

Babs quickly took Flo off to the cloakroom to avoid any more words being traded but soon realised her mistake when she saw Tiff manning the counter.

Flo and Tiff eyes hissed as they sized each other up.

'Will you please play nicely,' Babs snapped.

'Whatever,' Tiff replied, her lip curling.

'Of course Babs.' Flo's response was full of treacle.

Babs deposited her coat and turned wanting to separate these two as soon as. She needed this to be the one night she could put the trouble with the gold aside and have a good time. But Flo had other ideas.

She delicately searched in her Alexander McQueen

clutch bag. She gave Tiff that special feral smile she reserved for her and said, 'Here you go for your troubles.' She placed fifty pence on the silver tip tray.

Tiff's whole face flamed a solid red. She barred her teeth as she leaned forward, almost falling over the counter in her haste to get at her unwanted half-sister.

'You wanna be thankful this chunk of wood's in the way. Now why don't you fly off on your downmarket broomstick.'

'I'd rather be on a broom than a human coat hanger.' Flo blew Tiff a stick-that-in-your-pipe kiss.

Babs snatched her arm and marched her away. 'Where's a girl get a drink in this joint?'

Tiffany eye-fucked a busty piece who stood all sleek and sexy outside the dance floor door. The woman was her type of girl right down to her electric blue toenails. The hottie fluttered her black, feathered false lashes and Tiff fluttered her own right back. Oh yeah, this sextastic honey was really into her. Dee had warned her to stay put in the cloakroom come hell or high water...but if she didn't make a move some other lucky sod was gonna snap up her potential shag.

She got ready to move, but paused when the whispers of people nearby reached her:

'What the hell's she wearing?'

'Think she's mistaken this club for Glastonbury?'

Tiff twisted her head. A small black woman was heading, with purpose, right for the cloakroom. There was so much colour in her clothes that Tiff had to rapidly blink to get her vision straight again. The woman was rigged out in overalls...or was it a Kaftan? And bangles up her arms and outsized earrings dangling from her lobes. Some aging hippie chick, Tiff decided, looking like she was on her way to San Francisco but instead of a flower in her hair she sported a Jamaican flag headscarf. The rigid set of her face stated clearly she wasn't in the mood for a turn around the dance floor.

'I wanna speak to Babs Miller.'

Tiff folded her arms. 'I believe Mrs Miller is a guest – why don't you go in? I'm sure you'll find her.'

The woman put her small fist on the counter. 'This isn't hide and seek darlin'. You've got a public address system, haven't you? Call her up on that. Tell her Pearl's waiting for her in the cloakroom – well, get a move on! I haven't got all night!'

Hippie chick Pearl looked like she was about to jump out of her headscarf. Tiff wasn't good at taking orders, especially from some oldster who should be tucked up in bed sipping her Horlicks.

'I'm gonna need to see your invitation.'

Pearl kissed her teeth. 'I ain't got time for this.'

She leaned over the counter, pushed Tiff backwards and grabbed the public address Mic. 'Babsie Miller to the cloakroom. Babsie Miller to the cloakroom. Pearl's here and she'd like a word.'

Her words echoed through the club.

Once she got her footing back together, Tiff scowled and through gritted teeth hotly warned, ''Ere, you can't do that.'

'I just did,' Pearl smartly threw back.

It crossed Tiff's mind to call security but it was only seconds later that her mum came marching through the reception. She zeroed in on Pearl who she eyeballed like a gunslinger who'd just emerged from a saloon.

'Wotcha Pearl. I was hoping you were gonna put in an appearance. Thing is, I want a word too.'

Pearl nodded in agreement. 'Then we're both on the same page.'

Babs stepped closer. 'My girl Dee's got some rooms upstairs off the balcony. Let's pop up there and have a chat - in private.'

'Suits me.'

Tiff looked at the two women. She knew Pearl by name. Weren't these two supposed to be good mates? Now they looked like two boxers at the weigh in for a grudge fight.

'You alright mum?'

Her mum's answer was clipped. ''Course I'm alright. Why wouldn't I be?'

In silence, Pearl and Babs headed off for the stairs that lead to the balcony. Tiff watched them knowing there was trouble in the air.

No one noticed Flo following at a discreet distance.

The music stopped, giving Dee her cue. She stepped onto the stage, near the DJ, her dress shimmering as she moved with the grace of a queen. Every eye was on her. This was the life! The real life! John would be made up for her. Moisture misted her eyes. John, babes, wish you were by my side.

The DJ handed her the Mic. Dee pushed back the memories and addressed the gathering. 'Is everyone having a good time?'

A roar of approval and wolf whistles went up from the crowd.

When they settled back down she said, 'I want to thank every last one of you, from the bottom of my crooked East End heart,' she winked, they laughed, 'for coming out to support the Three Sisters on its first night out on the town. And now it's time for the icing on our club launch cake.'

Dee deliberately held back as a wave of electric anticipation swept the ravers. She hadn't let on about this to anyone, not even Jen and Tiff.

'I give you.' Dramatically she raised her arm to point to the steel corridor above, everyone following her movement. Upstairs stood a figure cloaked in the dark.

'The man who's taking the music bizz by storm. Our special guest. Our very own home grown East End lad, Kujuk.'

A spotlight lit up the newest rap sensation. The clubbers went wild, into a frenzy of disbelief and delight. Lapping up the love, Kujuk dived straight into his act, eating up the Mic with his most popular track. He acted with the style of what his name meant in Turkish – big.

The place erupted, everyone singing along and rocking away; even the walls seemed to move. The rapper was a busy man but he'd owed Dee and John big time for connecting him to the right people, which had bagged him the gig that had shot him into the big league. That's what the East End was like; you never forgot the people who gave you a helping hand on your way.

Ecstatic, Dee danced her way off the stage and around the back. As she moved towards the dance floor a hand grabbed her forearm, making her jump. With a swift move she turned to find someone she didn't want to see.

'What the backside are you doing here?'

'We need to talk,' Kieran Scott answered. 'About our son.'

With indignation she wrenched her arm out of his hold. 'There's no *our* anything.' She slapped her fists onto her hips. 'This is invitation only so you need to keep moving towards the exit before I get security to sling you out.'

He was rigged out all in black – slim fit Levi's with matching jacket, polo shirt that bagged out from his waist and trainers. Trainers? Dee did a double take. They were forbidden within the four walls of her club. Why hadn't the security staff turned his arse away? She'd be having very stiff words with them after this.

He moved slightly closer to her. Dee held her ground. 'I want to see Natty.'

She jabbed her finger at him. 'His name don't pass your lips, get me? He's got sod all to do with you—'

'Now that's where you're wrong—'

Mad as hell she poked her finger into his chest. 'Back. The. Fuck. Off. You agreed to leave us alone. As far as the world's concerned Nathan is John's boy.'

They'd had a one-time booty one-night stand which he thought gave him an in into her life. Think again! Besides, even if she'd wanted to – which she didn't - the way she'd betrayed John still ate her up with shame.

A muscle in his cheek ticked with tension. 'I'm not saying I'll tell the boy or anyone else any different, right?' Strong emotion clouded his face. 'But I need to see him. I never had a dad—'

'Join the club, none of us did—'

He waved her words away. 'I know what you're gonna say. He's got a dad and his name's John. You ever considered how that makes me feel? Knowing my flesh and blood's out there and I can't even get near enough to look at his face.'

Dee was only half listening to him, her attention diverted by the sight of four hooded characters sporting large shades. What the hell! Kieran in trainers and now this? Her security was doing a piss-poor job.

She gave Kieran her attention again and made short shrift of their convo. 'Get out of my club. Get out of my life. If I see you within a mile radius of John Black's son, you'll rue the day your cock took it into it's stupid bellend head to sniff at my vee-jay-jay.'

Dee stomped off, intending to make a beeline for the hooded youths.

Problem was they had disappeared.

Twenty-Four

Flo pressed her ear against the door to the room Babs and her friend had just gone into. She didn't really think this would have anything to do with the gold, but the Commander had sent her on a mission and that's what she was going to do. Of course he hadn't believed a word of what Dee and Jen had told him. His gold gone up in smoke in Kieran Scott's club? Yeah, and Shergar the racehorse had started the fire! The Commander was the craftiest person she knew. Flo loved him to bits. And would do anything for him. Babs and her brood knew where the gold was stashed. Of course they did.

Flo earwigged carefully to the conversation…

Babs and Pearl faced off like a pair of alley cats ready to do some serious damage.

Babs got straight down to it. 'Did you have a word with you know who?'

Pearl snapped back, 'He can't help. I told you that was a long shot.' Her eyes narrowed, her mouth turned ugly. 'Although he did have one helpful suggestion that I couldn't really face up to at the time. Perhaps I'll have to now though - I'm not sure I've got any other choice.'

Babs' face burned red at the threat in the smaller woman's tone. 'If you've got something to say gob it out.'

Pearl waved her small hand in the air. 'It's not just him saying it, but also the spirits are telling me—'

Babs butted in with a nasty scoffing sound. 'Spirits my East End arse. The only spirits you commune with are the ones drifting drunkenly out of a bottle of rum.'

Pearl moved closer. So did Babs. They stood nose-to-nose. Toe-to-toe. Their hot, angry breaths bounced off each other's face.

'Listen Pearl, I don't know exactly what's gone on here,' Babs snarled behind gritted teeth. 'Maybe you got caught up in the moment. Or maybe someone's leaned on ya, I dunno. I don't care.' She wriggled her head provocatively. 'Let's just say if you put things right, I'll say no more about it. Let bygones be bygones, know what I mean?' That was supposed to be the end of it but her temper got the better of her. 'Which I think is pretty generous of me in the circumstances.'

Pearl lost it big time, her head rearing back in outrage. 'Me? 'You're saying it was me? You've got the nerve of the Devil and all the evil spirits in hell—'

'Oh, pack it in with your spirits malarkey, I'm not a mug down the fairground.'

Pearl folded her arms, tilted her chin back and looked down her nose. 'I should have guessed you were behind it all along. What an idiot I've been.' She slapped her forehead, her bangles jangling. 'Trusting you of all people! Are the rest of the Millers in on the deal as well? I bet they are – a right little coven of teefs, the lot of ya.'

Her Jamaican accent was righteous with molten rage as she pronounced 'thief' as 'teefs'.

Pearl's mouth wouldn't stop. 'No wonder your gangster boyfriend couldn't help, he's already helped you out with this, hasn't he? You get me? What kind of fool do you take me for? And you know what really hurts? You and the rest of the gang having a laugh at my expense – that's what really stings. You bitch! You utter, fucking bitch.'

Babs' jaw dropped south. She'd never heard Pearl turn the air blue before. Then she reminded herself that this woman hadn't been banged up with her, less than a year ago, in the prison cell next door for being an angel.

Babs got right into her face. 'Now you listen to me. I've tried being being upfront but you ain't having it. You're gonna put things right, whatever it takes. And if you don't you'll be bloody sorry. I'll chase you down to the gates of hell if I have to…'

Crack!

Babs' head rocked back with the force of Pearl's considerable slap to her face. She could've dealt with the blow – it wasn't the first and no doubt wouldn't be the last time someone took a swing at her – what tipped her over the edge was the smug, self-satisfied expression of glee on her former mate's face.

'Right, you've gone and done it now!'

Babs flew at Pearl, grabbing her headscarf and dragging her to the floor, arms flailing as if they were two girls hating on each other in the playground. Babs went down with her. Pearl might be in her sixties but she gave as good as she got. The pair of them wrestled on the floor, grappling and spitting venom instead of landing blows.

'You piece of crap!'

'You two-faced slag!'

'Fuck you!'

'No, fuck you!'

A roaring fizz and whistle sound shuddered with an almighty thud against the outside of the closed door, followed by an explosion that sounded like a hand grenade going off.

The two women froze in shock staring straight into each other's eyes, more like lovers than enemies. Babs hurriedly shook herself free from Pearl, rushed over to the door and threw it open. People were screaming and shouting. Hooded figures attacked anyone that didn't scarper quickly enough.

Complete, fucking bedlam.

Dee's eyes bugged out of her head. She couldn't believe what she was seeing. Chaos spread through her beloved club like smoke from a blazing building. It was hard telling who and how many scrotes there were but they seemed to be everywhere. They were dressed in bad boy street style, their faces hidden by hoods, zipped up jackets and large sunglasses. Some were wrecking the bar, some were launching random attacks on the guests and some were overturning chairs and tables. For a few moments, Dee was stunned. Where the hell had these kids come from? Why hadn't the bouncers kept them out?

That bastard Kieran whispered in her ear, totally unfazed, 'don't know who you paid off to keep this party safe Dee – but it was the wrong people. Plus, your security seem to be a no-show.'

She hated that he was right, but he was. 'Yeah, very comical.' She seethed, 'I ain't having this in my club. I'm running them out.'

Kieran showed what an old hand he was. 'Discover who's in charge and giving the orders. Whack them and the rest will scarper.'

Dee turned to him in shock. 'Aren't you pitching in to help then? I thought you was a guest?''

Kieran was shamefaced. 'I can't Dee. I've gone straight. I'm in the papers these days as a respectable businessman. I can't have the law running me in for assault or disorderly conduct, it wouldn't look good with my investors.'

'You wanker.'

As Dee hurried across the floor, she called out to various guests who were trying to flee, 'Come on, they're only kids, tool up and take them on!'

Some of the faint hearts ran, some hesitated and some came to join her. Tiff and Flo appeared like avenging twins and got stuck in with their fists and feet.

But when a shocked Babs and Pearl rushed breathlessly down the stairs Dee warned them, 'Not your fight ladies. Go and hide somewhere.'

But they decided it was their fight and armed themselves with bottles and looked for kids to teach a lesson.

In the bar area, Dee found a youth smashing the optics with a chair. Coming up from behind, she took off a shoe and began raining blows on his head with the heel. 'Who's in charge of your little caper? Tell me before I drag your turkey nuts all over town.'

The kid fell to his knees and yelping in pain. 'Fuck off, I dunno, I dunno…'

Dee clocked that the youth didn't have no nuts; he was a she. 'Who's in charge?'

The kid rolled on her back, floundering and crying in

pain as Dee kept up with the punishment. 'Dunno…Dodgy! Help me! Help me!'

At the sound of the name 'Dodgy', a figure at the bar – Dee would beat her life it was another girl - had a rocket in a bottle with a lighter in her hand and turned to look.

Right, I'm having ya.

Dee put her shoe back on and, with a final vicious kick at her victim's belly, screamed, 'Get outta my club!'

Then she took off towards Dodgy. But as she drew close, Dodgy pointed the bottle with the rocket at her with the lighter near the fuse.

'Back off babe before I barbecue you and your weave. Go on, back off!'

Loving her moment in the limelight Dodgy got cocky. 'Why don't you get yourself a drink and let us finish our little part-time evening job? And next time…'

Dodgy was hit across the head from behind by a bar stool wielded by none other than Mister Straight Himself, Kieran Scott. Dodgy flew several feet across the floor and ended up motionless, in a heap. Kieran picked up a soda siphon and sprayed the rocket. Then he waltzed over to Dodgy, yanked her hood back and sprayed her face. 'Wakey! Wakey sleepy head! You weren't hit that hard.'

Dee stood over them. 'Recognise her boat?'

Kieran shrugged. 'Don't matter. It's who's paying her that counts.' He straightened up never taking his eye off Dodgy. 'Who's pulling your strings? I want their name now.'

The sound of another bang distracted him and Dee. Seeing her chance Dodgy bolted out of the club. There were fights and chases going on all over the club but when Dodgy's crew saw their boss was done, they legged it. Only

Babs and her friend Pearl were still fighting, dishing out justice to a pink-haired girl in the cloakroom. Dee broke it up and the girl ran for it.

But then a strange thing happened. Although the two women had been acting as a tag team, when it was over, Pearl turned on Babs and sneered, 'This fight makes no difference. It's still on.'

Babs spat back. 'Bring. It. On.'

Dee had no time to work out what that was about. She headed to the door where she found her useless security team milling around.

She pointed a finger at them. 'After you finish your shift collect your cards. You ain't welcome here no more.'

The gaffer of the team started to argue the odds but Dee turned her back as she made her way outside where many of the shocked clubbers hung around in groups, whispering and pointing.

'Anyone called the Bill?' Dee's loud voice got their attention.

The crowd fell silent. No one answered. Dee smiled. 'Good. Drinks are on the house for the next hour.'

There was a stampede to get to the bar.

Dee felt washed out but knew she needed to keep it together. Time enough tomorrow to figure out what came next. But now she had a name:

Dodgy.

Her sisters, mum and Flo anxiously waited for her in reception.

'What was all that about?' Jen asked.

'Dunno. What I do know is we still need to put on a party. Tiff go back to the cloakroom. Jen and Flo mingle and smooth over any ruffled feathers.' She added for Flo's benefit, 'And put a cardigan on dear, you're distracting the staff.' That broke the tension a bit. 'Mum get me a triple gin cocktail from the bar.'

When she hit the dance floor she saw Rapper Kujuk spinning a track and singing along. Good lad. She mouthed 'thank you' to him and touched her fingertips to her heart.

Dee cried out, 'Get your groove feet on people. This party's going on, in the words of Lionel Ritchie, All Night Long!'

Twenty-Five

Dodgy knew she was fucked and she wasn't talking about the beating she'd just taken. Her gaffers were going to go ape. Clutching her forehead she slunk down a side road from the club like a wounded animal. When she was sure she wasn't being followed, she stopped and inspected her fingers under a street lamp. They were covered in blood from where she'd held the cut on her head. It was a hell of a hit she'd taken.

Her Dodgy Girls had bottled it, the lot of 'em. Including Courts. Her eyes narrowed. Come to think of it she didn't remember seeing Courts on the dance floor. Well, Dodgy was on her own now with a simple choice. Was she going to report back to the bosses that she'd fucked up and take a beating? Or run off and take a bigger bashing next time she saw them?

Her leg felt like some beast had got its gnashers in it. Gingerly she eased down her trackie bottoms and ran her fingers over her thigh. It was swelling up already. She limped through another couple of streets until she reached a road of terraced houses that stood forlornly amid all the new builds.

At the dark end of it, near what passed for a playground,

a black Bob Marley was parked up with two men sitting up front. One seemed to be asleep; the other was playing with his phone. Dodgy hesitated. If she reported back now with her gashed head and mashed up leg perhaps the boys would cut her some slack. Come on, she had the bruises and blood to prove she'd put up a good fight. As she walked the last few yards though, she knew what a really dumb idea that was. These guys didn't do slack.

The motor's automatic window wound down as she kept her balance on her good leg.

Pinky put his mobile in his pocket. 'The party's over I take it?'

When it came to it, Dodgy didn't have the heart to say that the oppo had chased her out and with added lumps. In the end, she couldn't say anything at all.

Pinky sighed, shook his head and muttered, 'Send a girl to do a man's job.' He dug his passenger in the ribs to wake him up. 'Styley – our girlfriend here has messed up.'

Styley yawned, stretched his arms and then peered out of the window. 'Is that right?'

Dodgy had learned young there was no point in lying to players like these two. 'Yeah.'

Styley made a nasty sound at the back of his throat. 'Should've guessed Dee Black would have you over. She's John Black's widow, she'll be good for a ruck.'

Pinky nodded. 'Yeah and she's going to be somebody else's widow if she carries on like this. We'll have to pay this cunt Dee a visit ourselves.' Pinky turned back to Dodgy and held his hand out. 'We want a refund.'

She tried to be the hard girl she was and keep the worry off her face. 'I ain't got it. I spent it already.'

'Well, in that case you better get your hands on some pills and start selling them fast. We don't pay for services that aren't rendered – you know that.'

'I'll get it, I promise.'

Pinky reached into the glove compartment and took out a silver pistol which he passed to his brother 'One for you…' he took out another gun '…and one for me.'

For a moment Dodgy thought she was dead meat. She tried to hang tough but she was on the verge of tears. Furiously she sucked them back. She was the leader of the Dodgy Girls. Dodgy Girls don't cry.

Pinky turned to her in surprise. 'Are you still here? Why don't you go for a walk girlfriend? We'll catch up with you another time.'

Dodgy hobbled away as they exited the car. She'd got away with it this time. But she knew every time you got away with it brought the time you didn't one job closer.

'We going in there Dirty Harry style then?' Styley formed his hands into a gun and went, 'Pow! Pow!'

Pinky and Styley were a few hundred yards from Dee's club and walking fast.

Pinky was in a hurry to get it over with. 'It's simple bro. On the dance floor we wave one of our pieces around and pump a few shots into the ceiling. So the Widow Black gets the message she needs insurance. Then, when the crowd starts legging it, we run with them. When the law turn up, everyone's done a bunk and anyone who's left never saw a dickie bird. No one wants to grass up people with guns, you know that.'

Styley stopped. 'I dunno about this Pink – you know

what the big guy's like when people shoot on his manor without his say-so. Biggin ain't gonna like it.'

Pinky was tempted to tap his brother very hard in the middle of his forehead to knock some sense into him. 'He's not gonna know, now is he? Anyways, we ain't shooting anyone, it's just a demo. A light touch spray and pray.'

His brother pinched his lips together still not convinced. 'Should've got Dodgy to do it.'

'We got Dodgy to do it and the damn gal pissed it up.' When Styley said nothing, his brother added with attitude, 'what's the matter with ya? Gone gun shy?'

Styley got shirty and growled, 'You keep running your bullshitting gob like that bruv and there really will be a shooting, right behind your two front teeth, get me?'

Pinky put his arm around his pissed brother's neck. 'So, what do you want to do then? If word spreads we were faced off by Dee Black, our rep's gonna be in the crapper. Now shift yourself, don't wanna be late for our pick-me-up at Charmaine's later.'

Styley perked up at that. He did enjoy rolling between some bird's legs at Charmaine's knocking shop.

They turned the corner and walked up the steps to the club where the bouncers were on high alert after Dodgy's earlier antics. Styley loosened his hood so they could see his face. Both men were gripped with terror. The brothers were well known around town and it wasn't because of their acts of charity.

'Alright lads?' Styley started brazenly. 'Room for two more at the inn?'

Indecision played across the face of one of the bouncers who was obviously calling the shots on the door.

He stood his ground. 'Normally there would be but it's invitation only now. Unless you're on the guest list?'

'Oh yeah, we're on the guest list alright…' Pinky unzipped his hoodie to reveal his 9 Milly in a shoulder holster. 'Know what I mean?'

Sweat dripped down the bouncer's cheek. 'Look Pinky, we don't want no trouble. If you want some advice, I'd be careful if I was you, your hostess for the evening will take anyone on, shooters or no shooters.'

Pinky's lip curled. 'You're wrong – we don't want any advice.'

The bouncers stepped aside and the two brothers waltzed into the club.

Outside the doors to the main floor, Styley pulled his phone out. 'I'm gonna give the big guy a ring, just to make sure we're squared.'

His brother's light, piercing blue eyes blazed with fury in his brown face. 'No, you ain't, you hear.'

Styley's temper rose too. 'You're too bold bruv, you're gonna get us shot one of these days.'

With a huff of frustration and shake of his head he put his mobile away.

The dance floor was wall-to-wall jammed packed, hot and heaving, everyone getting on down to KRS-One's 'Sound of da Police'. Felt like the Notting Hill Carnival. Styley had to give Dee Black this: my girl knew how to throw a rave. The boys weaved their way into the middle of the heaving dance floor.

Suddenly Pinky got into the groove and started dancing. Styley grinned and joined his brother bussin' some moves and whooping-whooping at the right time along with the party people during the chorus. Pinky nudged his brother and gestured upwards. Dee Black presided on the balcony, resting her arms on a rail, keeping an eagle eye on proceedings.

The brothers shared a crazy grin. Then Styley put one arm around his shoulder, jogged on to the music for a bit and then used his free hand to pull out the semi, raised it high and pointed it at the ceiling. Pulled the trigger twice.

Bang! Bang!

Paused. Let off two more rounds.

Bang! Bang!

Shrill screams nearly drowned out the last two shots as the revellers divided and scrambled for cover. The music stopped. The lights came up as the two gunmen ran for it, joining clubbers rammed up against the main doors trying to escape. When Pinky turned and looked upwards, he saw Dee Black was gone.

Trapped behind the panicking mass of people fleeing the front entrance, the brothers turned and belted towards the back exit only to find it too blocked by punters desperately trying to fight their way out of the club. They tried to blend in at the rear and that was when they heard the shout of a woman's voice behind them.

'Drop the gun or I'll blast you to kingdom come!'

Pinky turned to find Dee Black crouching, cop-style, with both hands clasped confidently round a revolver. Shit. He reached into his pocket and pulled out his shooter, but, in a panic, it slipped between his trembling fingers onto the floor. Styley shouted, 'Leave it. She won't shoot into a crowd of people!'

But Pinky wasn't going to be taken out like a pussy in

front of a wagonload of people; his rep would never survive. Someone ran in front of him creating his chance. He swiped his pistol off the floor, turned and fired wildly and blindly in Dee's direction. The sound of more shooting behind them made the people in front part in all directions like the Red Sea and the brothers made their escape towards a fire door.

Inside the club a horrified Babs staggered from behind the bar on legs shaking so badly she had to hold onto the bar for support. The place looked like a whirlwind had gone through it with terrified people running all over the shop. She felt dazed. Couldn't believe it. Someone had come into her daughter's club and sprayed it full of lead. She'd read about this type of carry-on in the papers. Never in a million years did she think she'd be in the midst of it.

A piercing scream ripped through the air, higher and wilder than any that had come before. Her gaze darted automatically to where the scream had come from. And that's when Babs' life started to tilt out of control.

It was Courtney.

Babs frowned hard. It couldn't be Courtney. Her granddaughter was tucked up safe and sound at home. She blinked. It was Courtney alright with her hands covering her mouth, sobbing uncontrollably as she stared at someone on the ground.

A premonition of overwhelming dread chilled Babs to the bone. Who was Courtney looking at on the floor? Babs' heart began racing, her chest rising high and hard. No…she shook her head. It couldn't be. Not…

Babs belted forward.

An arm snaked round her waist holding her fast.

She struggled and kicked. 'Let me go! Let me go!'

'No. I can't.' It was Kieran, his bleak words coming through gritted teeth. 'I don't want you to see this.'

Babs started sobbing. 'Please! Please!'

His answer was to tighten his hold.

And that's when someone confirmed the nightmare running through her head.

'One of the Miller girls has been shot.'

Another person added, 'With all that blood it looks like she's a goner.'

Part Two: 2007

'They decided to poison my daughter against me.'

Twenty-Six

'What the heck do you two want?' Charmaine, the brothel's madam, bit out at Pinky and Styley.

Christ almighty! The last thing she needed were these two cretins in her house of pleasure tonight of all nights. She'd only just doshed out a bundle to fix the room they'd smashed to bits the last time they graced the place with their very unwelcome presence.

She folded her arms in the reception area using her considerable bulk to bar them entry. 'Pay day ain't until next week by my reckoning.'

She'd been in the cathouse business long enough to know that protection money came with the territory. It was usually a quiet, hand over the readies transaction and all parties were happy, but when her last operation was busted and she'd moved across the river Charmaine had soon learned that protection in these parts wasn't quite the same. Instead of a brown envelope these two goons here wanted to dip their wicks in the girls. On principle she didn't have a problem with that but every time they came there was trouble.

Pinky or Perky, she could never tell who was who, swaggered up to her and pinched her disgruntled mouth into a very ugly, lopsided shape. 'None of your lip, you old trout. You know how it goes. Get 'em lined up so we can choose a couple of sweethearts to ease our weary souls.'

The other one hooted with laughter at that. She twisted her face out of the cruel grip and snapped her eyes at them. What had she done to deserve this? Their antics were enough to make her vow that the next business she opened up was going to be a care home for nuns.

But bollocks to them, they had an arrangement.

'Look fellas you know how it goes – you turn up the first Wednesday of every month in the afternoon and you choose the two you want.' She slammed her fists on her ample hips and got shirty. 'Now you might not have realised this but it's pitch black out there and it's Saturday night.'

The other one strolled over to his brother and did something that made her gasp – he pulled out a shooter.

'Listen up, fat bird,' he spat the words in her face, 'we can either re-decorate this knocking shop with bullet holes or you can get two cock inspectors to us pronto.' His finger touched the trigger. 'This barrel's still hot, know what I mean?'

Charmaine got busy and within five minutes Pinky and Styley were in her best room on the first floor with two of her newest acquisitions. Sonia from East Ham, who was doing a bit of extra on the side to supplement her job as an accountant and Rachel who had debts running a mile long. Charmaine didn't have no truck with trafficked girls. London had women a-plenty willing to make a living on their backs.

After she was gone it didn't take the brothers too long to get their kit off and start pumping away. Their adrenaline was already as high as kites after blasting up the club so it didn't take them long to blow their load.

Pinky spread some Special K around Sonia's belly button and inhaled. Wow, he felt like the King of London Town tonight. There was no high like spraying lead to make a man know he had a pair between his legs.

'You think that Dee Black has got the message?' Styley asked as he played with his lady's titties.

Pinky sniffed loudly as the drug hit his bloodstream. He raised his head slightly and eyed his brother, a cocky grin splitting his face. 'Let's put it this way – the next time The Salesman shows his boat, she'll have our cash waiting in ten seconds flat. That's if the law don't close her down in the meantime.'

They started laughing so hard that they never heard the thud of heavy footsteps on the stairs. The only warning they got that something was up was when the door crashed against the wall. The women screamed. Four, huge toughs marched towards the bed.

'What the fuck...?'

'You can't just...'

Pinky and Styley's outraged voices hit the room. Styley dived for his gun, but one of the men backhanded him sending him crashing to the floor, blood spraying from the side of his mouth. The same man pointed at the women in turn and then towards the door. They got the message and fled.

Unlike his brother Pinky decided to use his brain.

'What's going on here fellas? If there's a prob we can sort it out like gentlemen, eh? Why don't we—'

He never finished. Metallic tape was slapped over his mouth.

Now he started to fight, using every dirty trick he'd learned on the street, but it was no use. His hands were tied behind his back and his legs together like a hog going to slaughter. His brother was receiving the same rough treatment.

As naked as the day they were born, Pinky and Styley were viciously dragged along the ground by their feet out of the room and along the hard wooden floor of the corridor. No one peeped out of the other rooms. If you didn't see you couldn't tell. Both brothers cried out in muffled pain as their heads hit every stair as they were unceremoniously dragged downstairs.

Charmaine watched the proceedings from a crack in the meet 'n' greet room near the reception area with a smug smile. Finally, those two wank jobs were getting a taste of their own bitter medicine. About time too!

Pinky and Styley were lifted and chucked into the back of a van. Boots held them down as black hoods were placed over their heads. Pinky made a vow:

If this was fucking Dee Black's work he was going to make that bitch realise what real pain was. Very slowly.

Pinky and Styley were terrified now as they hung upside down, stark bollock naked, in the freezing early morning air. They still had no idea where they were or who had the balls to nab them. They'd been driven across East London, then bundled into a lift and taken to a roof. Then something had been tied around their ankles and they'd been hoisted like meat for sale in a butchers'.

The clip-clip of heavy, confident footsteps beat across the concrete rooftop. An awful quiet descended and suddenly their hoods were removed and the tape ripped off their mouths. Pinky let out a small cry of pain as the tap yanked out some of his midnight shadow.

From his upside down vantage point Styley saw the murky Thames rippling below and recognised that he was in Wapping. His first ever girlfriend had hailed from here back in the days when it was shifting from a poor man's East End into El Dorado. Once abandoned warehouses were brimming with light and tons of money. He didn't get it himself; the place was still a shithole as far as he was concerned.

One of the heavies placed a chair in front of them. A smartly suited man walked over and carefully sat down. When the brothers clocked who it was they knew they were in big, fucking trouble right up to their frozen toes.

'I don't remember giving you permission to carry out a shooting on my manor,' Biggin informed them.

He didn't shout, he didn't scream or yell. No, that wasn't Biggin's way. His menace came from the quiet, deadly way he'd always approached life. Why raise your blood pressure when you didn't need to?

Pinky opened his mouth before his brother could. If Sty blabbed they were dead meat.

'What shooting?' He let out innocently.

The older man drummed his fingers against his thigh. 'Oh dear, they're playing dumb. Although to be fair, they are dumb I suppose.'

Pinky spluttered, 'We're not dumb enough to pull a stunt like that. No one is.' He laughed nervously, his teeth chattering with cold. 'We'd never take you for a jester. Fact of the matter is we ain't got a clue what shooting you're going on about.'

'That's right,' Styley chipped in. 'We'd never do something like that without your say-so first, would we bruv?'

Pinky shook his head. 'No fucking way.'

Biggin let out a heavy sigh, his breath frosting in the air. 'So you two know nothing about a club getting shot up tonight?'

They violently shook their heads.

Biggin left his chair, turned and moved towards the edge to stare down at the river. 'Let me ask you both a question. What punishment would you doll out to some cunt who was taking the proper Arthur Bliss? Like say someone came into your gym and mashed the place up?'

Styley, as per usual, let his mouth do the talking instead of his brain. 'They'd be dead.'

If Pinky wasn't tied up he'd have booted his no-brain bruv right off the roof. How many times had he told him to have a good think before opening that trap of his, eh? Ever since they were youths growing up fast and hard in Bethnal Green his brother's gigantic gob had put them in bother.

He spoke quickly, hoping to shove his brother's words into the wind. 'Nah, we wouldn't do that, would we Sty? We'd get the facts and then have a quiet word first and—'

Biggin swung round and it was too dark for Pinky to see from this distance but he knew the older man's face was like thunder.

'I never taught you to have a word. You get in there and beat the shit outta them to establish order.'

Pinky could feel the bones already breaking in his body. 'I'm telling you straight Biggin we never roughed up that club near the River Lea.'

'Who said it was near the River Lea?'

Pinky could feel the piss leaking from his cock. Biggin was going to make mince meat of them, so he blasted out the truth. 'We only did it coz the rich bitch who owns the joint wouldn't pay the starter on her insurance policy. And if she don't cough up that means your books aren't straight.'

He cringed as Biggin strolled over. He was more embarrassed that he stunk of piss than the beating he was about to receive. 'Please uncle, we were only doing what was right.'

Biggin was in fact their Great Uncle. He had taken them under his wing and into his business when they had started to bunk off secondary school and refused to go back. If it weren't for him they'd probably be doing a long stretch banged up somewhere.

'I should batter you both for stepping out of line.' Biggin was growling now all pretence at being calm long gone. 'Now I hear that the Rozzers are sniffing around all coz you two nutters don't have a brain cell between you.'

He raised his hand and belted one brother across the face and then the other.

Frothing at the mouth he snarled, 'And you wanna know why the Feds turned up? You fucking capped some woman who's now in the ozzie and the way I hear it she's critical.'

Both brothers sucked in their breath at that. Rage pouring out of him Biggin boxed the other side of their stupid heads, leaving them swinging in the wind. He was beside himself with fury as he marched around.

'Now I'm gonna have to pay hush-hush money to some plain-clothed plod I know to make sure our names are kept out of the picture.'

Styley spoke up. 'I'm sorry—'

His Great Uncle bellowed, 'I'm sorry ain't cutting it.' He took a deep breath as he visibly attempted to calm down. 'The only reason I'm not doing a proper job on you is because of your mother. My niece don't deserve another funeral after your stepdad passed last year.'

The brothers both breathed easy. But Biggin wasn't finished with them.

He jabbed a finger. 'This ain't finished. Not by a long shot. Tomorrow I'm coming to the gym for an accounting of what went on. And if I don't like it even my niece won't be enough to save you.'

He pointed at one of his men who took out a knife and cut them down. They landed with a hard thud on the solid roof. They might be hurting but it was better than what would've happened to them if Biggin had taken a scaffolding pipe filled with concrete to them.

He turned from them and marched away his men following.

'We ain't got no clothes,' Pinky squealed.

Biggin didn't even turn as he scoffed, 'After the strokes you've pulled it seems to me that your nuts need a little airing.'

Twenty-Seven

A wild-eyed Babs grabbed the passing doctor and held on to him for dear life.

'Is my daughter going to be alright? Please,' she begged, 'I can't lose her. It ain't right a daughter should go afore her mother.'

The woman gazed at her bewildered. 'Your daughter? Is she one of my patients…err Mrs…'

'Sorry about that doctor.' That was Kieran's voice she registered. Her red rimmed eyes glanced at him. Why was he letting the doctor walk away? Was he outta his fucking tree?

As if reading her anguished thoughts he said, 'That's the wrong doctor Babs—'

'Are you sure?' she snapped back her face haunted. 'Coz—'

'Mum,' Dee interrupted, 'Let's get you sat down before you collapse.'

Like a zombie, she allowed her eldest to steer her towards a plastic chair. She stared into space.

Then Tiff's face appeared along with Flo's. 'Shall we get you a cuppa from the machine downstairs?'

Which one spoke she didn't know; Babs couldn't hear a thing. She was lost in the horror of what had happened. Still couldn't believe it. Her Jennifer had been lying there in a pool of ever increasing blood. Claret coming out of her everywhere, that's how it had appeared to Babs. She'd screamed with such chilling ferocity that those nearest had shuffled back. Then she was on her knees, slipping in blood as she cuddled Jen close.

Someone had shouted, 'Don't touch her, you could make things worse,' and had tried to pull her away.

Not touch her Jen? Were they having a laugh? Babs had fought them tooth and nail; punching, thumping, clawing, but she'd been dragged, sliding on her bottom, away. Oh my God, if her beautiful, precious Jen was going to pass into the next world she wanted her arms to be the last she felt embracing her with love.

The air ambulance ride had been hectic and horrendous. Babs had held her daughter's hand all the way while wiping tears back with her other. The staff at the hospital had swung into action as soon as they touched down.

'Let them do their work,' Dee had whispered to her when she wouldn't let go of Jen's frozen, still hand.

Babs came back to the present as she recalled something else. Abruptly, her head came up. 'Where's Courtney?' she asked listlessly.

Tiff had her arm round her niece whose face was stark - no blood in it - looking like her world had come to an end. She left the comfort of her aunt's embrace and walked on unsteady legs towards Babs. 'Nanna Babs?'

Babs shot to her feet and growled, 'What were you doing at the club my girl?'

Courtney took a startled step back. 'I was—'

'Up to your antics, as per usual—'

'Lay off her mum,' Tiff barked.

But Babs took not a blind bit of notice. She'd lost all her bearings after the gunfire. 'All you had to do was listen to your mum and stay at home and look out for your baby sister.'

She whacked Courtney around the head.

'Why don't you ever listen to your mum?' She landed another blow before Dee rushed at her and grabbed her arm in mid-flight.

'Let me go! Let me go!' Babs' voice sounded horrible to her own ears.

'Mum stop it,' Dee said, her voice hardening.

Suddenly Babs' body went limp, all the life drained away as an unbearable grief took hold.

She sobbed, 'My baby's gonna die. She's gonna die.'

Dee took her chin gently in her hand and made her mum look at her. Glowering, she vowed, 'No she ain't. Not on my watch. This ain't no one's fault, you hear? Not Courtney's, not yours, not mine. The only person to blame is the bastard who pulled the trigger.'

Babs' body shuddered as if the bullets were going through her. She wished that's what had happened. If it meant her Jen would be alright she'd take every last one of those bullets in a heartbeat.

'Mrs Miller?' a voice called.

Babs desperately wiped back the tears and moved out of Dee's arms as she saw the doctor approaching her. 'Is she going to be alright?'

The rest of the family gathered round as the doctor

spoke. 'You're daughter is in a very grave condition. She has sustained two bullet wounds.' Two? This was bad. Very bad. 'One entered her arm, which we should be able to treat without many problems—'

'But?' Flo punched in.

'The other bullet is very near her spine and hit a major artery.'

Dee swore and banged her fist against the wall. It must've hurt but her ravaged face registered no pain.

And that's when Babs realised she was going to have to be the backbone of this family again. If she fell apart, they fell apart. Simple.

In a calm voice she asked the doctor, 'What does this mean?'

'We've managed to remove the bullet. We don't know how much damage it will have caused and Jennifer remains in a coma.' The doctor inhaled deeply, a sure sign of more bad news to come. 'If she does recover your daughter may never be able to walk again.'

There was a collective gasp, but not from Babs. If her girl couldn't use her legs again that was better than Babs having to put her six feet under.

She took the doctor's hand in hers. 'You do what you can for my baby. She's a fighter and I know she's going to pull through.'

Dee was outside the hospital foyer, underneath a 'No smoking' sign puffing a ciggy like a woman possessed. She'd had to get out of there. All of a sudden it had been too stifling, too hot. Felt like she was suffocating. Her sister was in a coma and she knew it was all her fault. Plus, the last time the family had gathered in a hospital, apart from to celebrate Natty's birth, was when John had passed over. One minute the quacks said he was on the mend, the next he was dead. Her husband hadn't deserved to die neither did Jen.

'Can I join you?'

Dee tightened her lips against her smoke. The one person she didn't want to blah, blah, blah with was Kieran Scott. Typical of him to intrude on her memories of John. She'd carry the guilt of betraying John with this wanker until her last breath.

'Suit yourself,' she finally told him.

Kieran lit up one of his fancy fags. No doubt thought that's what he should be chewing away on as a legit businessman. Legit, my backside! She didn't believe a word of it.

'You have any idea who the shooters might be?'

Dee took a final puff and ground the butt under her heel. She had her suspicions, but wasn't about to share them with him.

'Could've been anyone. I remember what club land was like from John's days owning the Alley Club. Could've been a dispute between some guys or a couple of juiced up blokes who just got over excited and decided to loose off a few shots and, caught up in the moment, fired in the wrong direction.'

He stared at her in rank disbelief. 'You're forgetting Dee that I cut my teeth in the same club world as John, as well as owning one before it burned down. Those shooters were linked to the kids who tried to smash up your place beforehand.'

She folded her arms across her middle against the cold. 'Were they?'

'Those kids were a warning,' he persisted, 'and coz you saw them off the real deal turned up to make sure you understood what way the wind was blowing.'

Dee's face changed as she leaned into him. 'Butt out of my business.'

He flicked his half-gone smoke. 'It is my business when it concerns the mother of my son.'

She almost decked him. 'The nerve of ya to mention that at a time like this. And, for the record, my Nathan has got nish to do with you.'

He dug his fingers into her arm and breathed hotly into her face, 'I want to see my boy. More now than ever. Whoever you're mixed up with is a dangerous player and I don't want Natty anywhere near it.'

She yanked her arm back. 'Who the fuck do you think you are?'

'Natty's father, that's who,' he savagely growled at back.

Someone coughed nearby making them spring apart.

Dee turned to find a watchful Babs looking from one to the other. 'Is there a problem?'

'Nah,' Kieran spat as he shook his head. 'I'll be seeing you Babs. If anything changes you get on the blower to me.'

Then he was gone. Babs paused as she glanced with narrowed eyes at her eldest. 'What was that about?'

'Nothing,' Dee insisted.

Bollocks! Mum had better not have heard a word of it. The idea that Babs would find out whose blood heated Natty's veins filled her with crippling dread. She would never live down the disgrace and guilt that filled her if Babs clocked who her grandson's blood father was.

So she said the first thing that came into her head.

'Actually, I was trying to persuade him to help me find the shooter but now he's Mister Legit he don't wanna know. Says he's got his ears closed to that world now.'

'Yeah, he said the same thing to me when…' Babs snapped her lips shut.

Dee tilted her head and closely inspected her mum's face. 'Why would you need Kieran to be asking questions around for you? You in some kinda bother?'

Babs vigorously shook her head. 'Nah, nothing like that. Someone wanted me to bend his ear with a favour but he told me the same as he told you.' Her mum was chatting away too quickly for Dee not to be suspicious. Then again Babs was under the worst kind of stress a mother could be under.

'I came down to tell you the Old Bill have arrived. They want a statement.'

'Fuck 'em.'

Babs nodded. 'I know. But you're going to have say something - anything really. You're the owner of the club.'

Dee rubbed her temples. 'You're right. But I ain't telling them dick. Anyways, the shooters were hooded so you can't make them out on the security cams. I'm gonna fix this for myself.'

That was the East End way. You didn't need the boys in blue to fight your battles.

Babs suddenly stated, 'If you know what's what, you need to tell me why my daughter was shot.'

This was hard for Dee but her mum deserved the truth.

'This is between me and you, right? I can't be certain, but a few days before launch night some cute arse turns up trying to strong arm me into giving him protection money on behalf of the thugs he works for. 'Course I saw him off. So they sent those kids to break up the party and when that didn't work, they sent two guys in to shoot the place up.' Dee choked a little. 'Gonna tell the cops I didn't see nuthin. There won't be any other witnesses either; they'll all be too scared but it doesn't matter. We don't need the law anyway, I'll get this sorted, find who did it and then…'

Babs took a breath. 'So, you don't think it was anything to do with Pearl then?'

Dee's head reared back in astonishment. 'Pearl? She doesn't run rackets, does she?'

'No, no, of course not.' Babs waved her hand. 'Dunno why I said that. Sorry luv. I'm all over the shop.'

Babs got back into full mum mode, trying to be cheerful with her family in the midst of tragedy. She linked her arm with Dee's as they made the trek up to talk to the cops.

The two police officers left in a real strop. None of the family were playing ball. Babs felt light-headed and so weary all she wanted was to put her head down. A distraught Little Bea was tucked into her side. The poor mite had cried and cried until her throat was hoarse, but she hadn't uttered a word. The girls would stay at the hospital with Dee tonight and then Babs was taking them to hers tomorrow.

'Mrs Miller.'

Babs took Little Bea's hand and got to her feet. Her heart seized in her chest at the grave expression on the doctor's face. Please no! No! Not my Jennifer! '

Is she—?'

'Comfortable.' Thank God! Thank God! 'She remains in a coma but I think you can see her now.'

As head of the family Babs led the way into the white, sterile hospital room. Babs made no attempt to stop the tears coating her skin like acid rain when she saw her beloved Jen unconscious in the bed, looking as frail as a China doll. She was hooked up to drips and feeds, with machines beeping and flashing.

After a few moments she wiped her eyes and looked at her family. Tiff was weeping and even hard girl Flo was choking up. Only two people were dry-eyed. Both Dee and Courtney looked on with faces like flint. Babs knew that look because she'd felt it herself.

Faces that demanded revenge and were going to get it.

Twenty-Eight

Babs took a fortifying breath as she stood in front of the gorgeous house in North Chingford. Just after midnight her family had bundled her off home in a cab telling her that she'd be no good to Jen if she collapsed. She hadn't wanted to go, but knew they were right. So she'd told them to stop fussing, got into the cab, but instructed the cabbie to drive her here instead. By rights this was the last place she should be, but it also felt like the most natural place on earth. She just hoped the door wasn't slammed in her face.

The cold, early morning air chilled her to the bone when she pressed the bell. And waited. A minute later the hallway light popped on and the door opened.

'Babs?' Tricky Dickie's eyes widening with twin surprise and concern.

Her heart beat like a football chant making her feel wonky and all out of shape. She was about to apologise for the late call, but instead asked, 'you gonna leave me stood out here like a bottle of milk?'

When he ushered her inside she saw that he was holding a snooker cue in one hand.

'Oh, sorry about this.' He waved the cue. 'Just my

precaution against unwanted visitors.'

As she looked around the hallway Patrick couldn't take his eyes off her. He didn't like what he saw. Her eyes were glassy, puffy and red and her fingers were clenching and unclenching at her side. He didn't need her to tell him that something terrible had happened. No doubt concerning her family. That family of hers were going to be the death of her.

'Babs, what's the matter?' He said it gently, not wanting to rush her if she didn't want to talk about it.

She arched a brow. 'Thought you would know. You always know when I'm in a bit of bother.'

'You told me to stay away and I'll always respect what you want regardless of how it makes me feel. So I told my mates up at division to no longer call me if your name cropped up.'

Babs teared up. 'Oh Patrick.'

Then she was in his arms sobbing her brave heart out. He locked his arms around her like she was the most precious person on this earth as her story poured out of her. He shook his head feeling her terrible pain. What a thing for a parent to have to go through. He'd seen it enough times when he was still on the Force, parents crippled and dumbstruck when they were told the next time they'd see their kid was on a cold slab in the mortuary.

He lightly pulled away from her and used a finger to wipe the tears from her face. He gazed at her intently. 'Do you want me to find out who the shooters were?'

Babs' heart skipped a beat. Once Tricky Dickie started digging the gold was bound to come up and what would he think of his darling Babs then? He was the one person who had always believed in her. Lord above, he'd be crushed if he found out about the gold. And what if he got hurt? How would she ever live with that?

She glanced up at him and held those beautiful, grey eyes of his. 'I don't want you anywhere near this.' She grabbed one of his hands and squeezed it tight. 'Promise me you'll leave this alone. Promise me!'

Indecision flicked across his face. Her Tricky Dickie wasn't a man to walk away when bad things were going on.

But he finally agreed. 'I promise. But Babs, I swear to God, if anyone's trying to hurt you—'

'They're not. This is all down to something at Dee's club.'

He smiled weakly at her. 'Do you want a cuppa? Or something strong?'

For the first time in hours Babs was able to smile. 'I want something strong, alright. You.' She shoved her hand under his jim-jam top to feel the warmth of his skin.

Suddenly he picked her up as if she were his bride. She would've squealed at that normally or laughed with joy, but the mood was too sombre with Jen being in hospital. Instead she placed her arms around him and tucked her head into the side of his neck.

They made love with slow, tender sweetness in his king-sized bed. After, as she snuggled in his safe arms, it struck her that she wanted to stay here forever. She wanted to stay with the best man she'd had the honour of knowing. What had happened to Jen had bought the shadow of death closer. You only got the one life. You had to grab the good things because sometimes there were no second chances. And what would her girls say? Plenty no doubt. But wasn't it time for them to see her as a woman with a woman's needs? She was a person too who wanted – no, deserved - things in life.

If they could see her heart when she day dreamed about Patrick, they'd see happiness sparkling like diamonds. The sunniest day of her life. Her Tricky Dickie wasn't just a former cop, he's a man for crying out loud. The best man ever. Plus, she adored having her evil way with his body.

'I love you.'

Three simple words that left her mouth like the most natural thing in the world.

'What?' He rolled them over until he was on top. His face shone with disbelief.

Babs threaded her fingers through his hair. 'Will you marry me Patrick Tricky Dickie Johnson?'

He whooped and punched the air. With a sheepish grin he gazed at her. 'I'd tie the knot with you right now—'

She shushed his joy with a finger over his lips. 'This has to stay between me and you at the mo. I need Jen to get better first – and she will get better - and then share the good news with everyone.' Her finger left his mouth. 'But until then I wanna keep this between us.'

'Your secret toy boy?'

She tweaked his nose. 'Sugar Daddy, more like.'

'I love you Babs.'

'Love you too.'

As they kissed Babs hoped and prayed he'd never find out about her involvement with the gold.

Twenty-Nine

'What you moping about?' Fred asked Pearl as he plonked down next to her at the brekkie table in the dayroom the following morning.

Pearl didn't answer. Too consumed with the gut-wrenching rage she was still feeling from the night before. It was true. Babsie had betrayed her. For once in her life Pearl really wished she could commune with the spirits because she'd cast such a wicked spell Babs would never be able to use that lying tongue of hers again. How could Babsie have kicked their friendship and trust to the kerb like that?

Greed, that's what. Craven and red-eyed, that's what they called it in the Caribbean; always keeping your eyes on what others had because you wanted it. If there was anyone who knew about greed it was Pearl Hennessy. She'd perfected the art most of her adult life, cosying up to gullible folk and ripping them off. And now someone had done it to her for the second time; first that con artist Saint Aubin and now Babs. She was loosing her touch.

While doing bird on a shoplifting charge no one had wanted to know her, only Babs would give her the time of day. Even when Pearl had gone against her – she was still ashamed of what she'd done – Babsie had stuck by her. Pearl wasn't sure she would've done the same. She'd valued Babs' friendship so much because the truth was all her other mates had either long departed this world or turned their backs on her. Her shoulders slumped with the weight of growing old and bent without a true friend to lean on.

'Pearl?' She raised her face, remembering Fred was there. 'You alright old girl?'

Some of her stuffing came back as she bit out, 'who you calling old girl?' She opened her flask and poured a good measure of Wray and Nephew over her Weetabix.

'So, what's got you looking like your world's come to a full stop?' He bit into his toast slathered with rhubarb jam. 'You found out who nabbed your gold?'

The betrayal and hurt spewed out of her. 'My so-called best mate has mugged me off.'

Fred gazed at her intently as he put his half eaten toast back in the plate and rubbed the crumbs from his hands. His eyes flicked to the door as if to make double sure no one was earwigging. 'You talking about that woman who comes to visit you?'

Pearl's hands curled into fists. 'Yeah, that's her. Babs Miller. We've been in this together for months now.' Her mouth twisted with utter disgust. 'And all the time she's been waiting to knife me in the back.'

Fred's brows ruffled together with such sympathy she could've kissed his sweet, balding head.

'You can't let her get away with that.' He words were fierce. 'That's rank out of order, that is. Back in my day—'

'Yeah I know,' Pearl rolled her eyes knowingly, 'you'd have gone round there with a crowbar and shown her what for.'

His watery eyes narrowed. 'Nah, that's where you're wrong. You wanna make sure you get a pro on the case. I'd have slipped 'em a bit of drink money and got 'em to go round there and doll out some street justice, know what I mean?' he tapped a finger against the side of his nose.

'And then what?' She threw her hands despairingly in the air. 'I still wouldn't have my share of the gold.'

A crafty expression covered his whole face. "Let me tell you a story—'

Fucking hell! Fred and his bloody stories! 'Come off it—'

He moved so he was practically hanging off his chair. 'No, hold up, this might be of interest.' Pearl rubbed her lips together with annoyance but she let him tell his tale. 'Right, see back in '79, two geezers pull a fast one on a post office and get off with twenty grand. A lot of wonga back then.' The light in his eyes glowed with the excitement of going back to the ol' days. 'Ten a piece, fair and square, should've kept both of 'em happy, right? Problem was one of 'em scarpered with the whole effing lot.'

Pearl's heart was beating like a run away train. 'What happened?'

Fred lifted his eyebrows. 'The geezer with the empty pockets sent a certain Uncle Frank to get his dosh back—'

'Uncle Frank?' Pearl cut in with surprise.

Fred looked shocked. 'You know Uncle Frank?'

Now it was Pearl's turn to tap her nose. 'Let's just say I haven't been on my knees praying for absolution in a convent most of my life.'

'Well, you know where this story is heading. The man got his share of the blag and the other fella was never seen again.' His voice dropped. 'My point is this. Get someone on the case who Babs Miller and her kin don't know. Someone you can trust to retrieve what rightfully belongs to you.'

Pearl's brain got ticking away. Fred might have a point. Someone on the case...She almost slapped her forehead as the solution came to her. Of course: why hadn't she thought of this before?

She got to her feet, slowly to ease the ache in her knees, as the pieces of her revenge against Babs started to fall nicely - thank you very much - into place.

She told Fred, 'I know exactly who will sort this out and get my teefed gold back.' She rubbed her hands together with anticipation. 'Babs Miller won't know what's hit her.'

Fred frowned as he looked around the dayroom. 'You seen Vi and Di this morning?'

Fred the Red might be an old, windbag much of the time but you couldn't fault his devotion to Vi.

Pearl scowled as well. It wasn't like the twins not to be at breakfast. 'You get on with your toast. I'll pop in on them before I get ready to go out.'

When she reached their room she quietly knocked. No response. She did it again and the same thing happened. A big rule of the care home was never to enter anyone's room if they didn't ask you to come in. Privacy was a big thing here unlike the home Pearl had moved from in Ilford.

She broke the rule as she opened the door calling the sisters name. The curtains were still drawn making it hard for Pearl to see, so she stepped further in. The sisters were lying side by side on Vi's bed. That was funny; Di had her own bed in here.

'Ladies, you'll miss brekkie if you don't put in an appearance soon.'

Neither one moved.

A chill ran down Pearl's spine as she quickened her pace and headed to the window. She snapped the curtains open and flipped round to face the bed and almost tumbled over at what she saw.

The sisters lay side by side, their bodies as still as statues, their twin faces an unnatural white. They held hands. On the duvet cover were their numerous pill bottles completely empty.

'No! No! No!' Pearl chanted over and over again as she moved like a sleepwalker towards them. She didn't need to touch them to know they were dead.

As Pearl rushed towards the door to get help she noticed a piece of folded paper on Vi's side table.

It drew her back, and as she reached for it a voice asked, 'Are they under the weather?'

She twisted to find a worried Fred standing in the doorway.

Oh God, Fred! Pearl moved urgently towards him blocking his view. 'Fred, you can't be in here right now.'

He stared at her like she was bonkers. 'What you gassing on about?'

Pearl shook her head sadly. 'I'm sorry Fred.' Best for it to come from her than someone else.

'What are you sorry…?'

He drew in such a sharp breath she thought he was going to have a coronary. Then he was running round her towards the bed. There was no sound from him as he felt for the sisters' pulse. His silent grief dropped him to his knees. Gently he took Vi in his arms and started rocking her.

'They left a note,' Pearl told him and bit the inside of her lips.

'What does it say?' His voice was far away as if he was mumbling to himself in a dream.

'I don't think this is the time—'

'Read it!' he yelled as he twisted to her. He turned back to Vi. 'Sorry sweetheart, I know you don't like me shouting.'

Pearl opened the note and in a shaking, sick voice read:

'To all our precious and much loved family and friends. We shared the same womb, came into this world together, courted together, even when Di tied the knot Vi was close by. Now they want to rip us apart. After what that St Aubin bastard did Vi don't have any money left to pay the fees on this place. Yesterday she got a letter telling her there's a place for her at that disgraceful Council care home down the road. Pulling us apart would be like losing our hearts. Anyway, as we came in this world together we thought we'd leave it the same way. Don't cry for us. Remember us as the way we lived, two women who had the time of their lives.

PS Fred this is from Vi to you.'

Pearl raised her head, tears streaming down her cheeks, and looked with compassion at Fred. 'She's drawn a red love heart with your name inside.

Fred caressed Vi's Diana Dors hair and said again and again, 'I was too late, too late, too late.'

He made an awful, high-pitched, piercing sound that didn't sound human.

A sound of grief Pearl would never forget.

Thirty

Babs' legs felt like lead as she entered Jen's hospital ward, Flo and Tiff close behind her. She was emotionally so wrung out that she didn't even know how she was standing up. After she'd left Tricky Dickie's and got home the grief had overwhelmed her again. She'd cried and cried until her chest hurt so bad Babs thought she was going to end up in the ozzie too. A part of her wanted to turn around and flee because Babs wasn't sure she could face seeing her darling Jen again with all those tubes coming out of her.

Even if this was going to rip her apart she knew she was going to have to square her shoulders, stiffen her spine and face it. Babs was the mum in this family and if she fell to pieces so did everyone else. Sometimes the burden of being the head of this family was a weight she found hard to bare.

Her mobile pinged with a text message:

Missing you. Wanting you.

TD

She closed her eyes. Oh, how she wanted him to put his solid, loving arms around her and whisper that everything was going to be alright. That when she got to Jen's room her daughter would be sitting up in bed with a ready smile on her face.

'Who's that then?' Tiff asked.

Babs quickly shoved her phone away. 'Just someone from The Devil wanting to know how Jen is.'

The last thing she needed was more head and heartache by telling Tiff the truth.

Her breath hitched painfully in her throat when she reached Jen's room. Courtney and Little Bea sat quietly by their mum's beside. Poor loves looked drained.

Babs didn't want to think it but it felt like a morgue. Like Jen was laid out ready for her coffin.

'You alright girls?' Tiff greeted her nieces knowing full well they weren't.

'I've got some prawn and cocktail crisps for you each.' Flo waved the packets trying to look cheery.

Courtney wearily came over and took one, but Little Bea said not a word as she continued to gaze at her mum. Her tiny hand crept across the bed cover and clasped her mum's palm. Babs walked quietly over to her daughter and kissed her gently on the forehead. If only kisses had the power to wake her up. Ah, to be Sleeping Beauty.

She smoothed Jen's hair as she whispered, 'You're gonna be alright my beautiful girl. You're just having a little rest and when you're ready you're gonna open those gorgeous eyes of yours. And the whole family's gonna be here to give you a big Miller hug.'

Flo moved to stand at the foot of the bed. 'I still don't understand why someone would do this. Why attack the club?'

The veins in Tiff's neck stood with the force of her

promise. 'If I ever get my hands on them, I'll…'

Babs finally let the emotion she'd been hiding from come to the surface – guilt. What if Dee had got it all wrong about the protection racket and this had something to do with the gold? Someone had been gunning for her and got her beloved daughter instead? But who? Unless…

Babs swung to face Flo. 'Your granddad—'

Flo was horrified. 'The Commander would never do anything like this—'

Tiff jumped in angrily, 'Is that what you're doing here?' she accused rushing to get into her half-sister's face. 'Reporting back on our weak spots so your Captain Bligh Granddad can take his revenge coz he thinks we've got his fucking gold?'

Babs snapped out, 'Tiffany. The girls.'

But her youngest didn't take a blind bit of notice, hurting so badly that her sister was near death's door. 'It was you, weren't it?' She pushed Flo.

Flo's face twisted as she pushed back. 'Get outta my face. I'm not—'

'I know why.' Courtney said it so softly that the others didn't hear and the row continued until it looked like her aunts were going to go down kicking and fisting besides her mum's sick bed.

'I know why,' she practically shouted.

The door thrust open and a nurse popped her head into the room. Her sour look said that she'd seen family punch-ups a time or two and she wasn't putting up with it on her ward.

'Is there a problem?'

''Course not,' Babs said quickly, 'Matron…Sister…Nurse.

We're just a touch upset as I'm sure you can understand.'

She stared hard at each one of them and then firmly closed the door.

Babs turned to Courtney. 'Do you know why this happened babe?'

She said it softly because the poor thing looked she was ready to sob her guts out again.

'One of my mates on The Devil rang me—'

'Who?' Tiff butted in.

Babs turned on her. 'Shut. It.' Then switched back to her granddaughter.

'My mate said they heard that Aunty Dee wouldn't pay some men money—'

'What money?' Tiff got in there again.

Flo sent her a withering stare. 'Protection money of course.' Her gaze lightened as she settled it on her niece. 'Is that what you mean?'

Courtney nodded. 'And these men decided to teach her a lesson by shooting up the club.' Her face crumbled as her eyes jack knifed onto her still mum. 'And now mum's gonna die.'

Babs embraced her tightly. 'Who did your mate say these geezers were?'

Courtney pushed slightly away from her Nan. 'Said they're called Pinky and Styley.'

'You what?' said Flo, going into Stan Miller voice. 'Pinky and Winky? Someone's pulling your leg.'

Courtney pulled out of Babs' arms. 'Nah, it's true. Cross my heart.'

Babs abruptly searched the room, her eyebrows snapping together. 'Where's your Aunty Dee?'

'She had to leave.'

'Leave?' Babs' voice rose with righteous indignation. 'You mean she left the two of you here on your tod without no one to look after ya?' She was beyond fury. 'I told her not to leave you alone. What's she playing at?'

Courtney looked at her fizzing Nan through her lowered lashes. 'She said she was going to find this Pinky and Styley.'

The adults started going at it again forgetting all about Courtney.

She crept to the side and palmed a scalpel one of the doctor's had left behind.

Natty's nanny, Miriam, admired her slim figure as she stood in front of the full-length mirror in Dee's dressing room. Satisfied with what she saw she turned her attention to baby, who was upright in his carry-chair on top of the dressing table. Yet another dressing table! Mirrors all over the gaff! What a vain tramp! Hadn't even bothered to come back the night before. Called her up though with some fake up story about her sister being shot. As if! Putting it about in some diseased toe rag's bed that's where she was. Didn't deserve the title of 'mother.' But, of course, this wasn't that witch's baby. This was *her* baby. Her Andy.

'What shall I wear today Andy sweetheart?'

She stepped towards Dee's extensive collection of designer dresses.

'All knock off o'course. *That woman* pretending to be your old girl couldn't afford the real deal.' She half-turned back to the baby. And winked. 'Me and you know the truth.'

Miriam wrinkled her nose. He was starting to stink the place out. She hadn't changed him once this morning. Wet through, he was, from last night. She carelessly shrugged. No matter. There would be enough time to clean baby up before the slag-hag came through the front door. That's if Mizzery Dee decided to come back at all today.

Miriam turned back to the dresses and roughly snatched out a Michael Kors' above the knee, green ribbed number. She moved back to the mirror and held it up against herself. Her sullen mouth twisted as she posed this way 'n' that. Growling deep in the back of her throat she slung it with distaste to the floor.

She looked over at Natty. 'Cheap trash.'

Her beautiful little fellow started bawling. Miriam froze at the loud noise. Her heart rate hiked up and pounded away. She became fearful. If Andy didn't shut it *he* would hear them.

'Now I've told you Andy until I'm blue in the face what will happen if you make noise and *he* finds us.' Miriam's voice shook with fear.

She didn't want to do this but had no choice. She went to her bag and pulled the Sellotape out. The baby's tears abruptly stopped. His stare was full of terror. She'd had to tape his mouth on a number of occasions so he got the message loud and clear. It was either that or a pillow over his face for a few seconds. Miriam hadn't had to resort to that yet, but she would if it meant *he* would never find them again. He wasn't ever taking Andy away from her ever again. Never!

She got back on with finding a dress in that bitch's collection. A flowery print number that, as far as Miriam was concerned, wasn't even good enough to wipe Andy's arse, went the same way as the last one. A retro, fifties lilac, polka dot cocktail dress. She chucked that too. Trash! Trash! Trash! A pile of clothing, which must total a collectively price tag towards the ten grand mark, lay strewn on the gleaming wooden floor.

She checked Natty…Her eyes misted over. Natty? Who was Natty? He didn't look like Andy.

Terrified, she started panicking, her heart beating like crazy. Where was her baby gone? Desperately she shook her head until the mist lifted and Andy came back into view. The panic vanished. Her darling baby stared at her strangely; well that's what it appeared to her. Almost like he was telling her off for having the brass to touch his phoney mum's gear.

She tutted. 'It's not my fault *that* woman is as cheap as a Lidl's summer deal.' Her eyes lit up as she perked up and waved her hands in excitement. 'I'm gonna teach you all about how to dress to impress. You mark my words, those baby girls will be pulling each other's hair out to have first dibs at you.'

She cackled with pure delight. Gave her attention back to the dresses.

Her breath suddenly caught in wonder in her throat. 'Think I've found the one Andy.'

Gently she eased out a dress that was covered with a light, protective paper. She gasped as the dress was slowly revealed. Now, you couldn't call this bargain basement tat. Simply gorgeous. A shimmering, scandalous, scarlet, neck-to-toe creation. Thrilled to the core Miriam checked the label. Saint Bloody Laurent. Classic.

Miriam whipped it on in less than a minute. Despite it being made for a woman with a fuller figure, including in the bust department, she preened and strutted her stuff in front of the mirror. Oh yeah, she looked the bizz alright. Miriam suddenly imagined herself stepping out onto the red carpet at a celeb event. And Natty…

No, her mind screamed. No! No! No! This baby was Andy. He would be there right with her, securely, and lovingly, tucked up in her safe arms.

'Doesn't mummy look a picture?' she declared jubilantly as she twirled round and round until she stopped with bursts of frenzied laughter as dizzy as her head.

The merriment dropped off her face as quickly as it had come. 'Better get this off coz we still have to teach you to call me mummy.'

Once the dress was back on the hanger she maliciously yanked and tore the stitches from it part way down one side.

Thirty-One

Pinky pointed the shooter at Styley and curled his finger round the trigger.

His brother's eyes bulged. 'What the fuckurees Pink? What the heck are ya playing at?' His irate voice echoed around the gym like a shot had already been fired.

Styley opened his mouth again, but snapped it shut when he noticed the coldness glazing his brother's eyes.

Pinky had been proper moody, like a caged animal, since Biggin's open-air bollocking of the night before. They'd legged it, with their family jewels cupped in their hands, like two flashers fleeing the law. Even though they'd tried their hardest to keep to the shadowed, cobbled back alleys of Wapping they had still run into a Duchess type walking her pooch. She'd screamed like she was in the front row watching The Exorcist, her bow-wow lunging and yipping playing the badass of the doggie world. Styley had played it cool with an, 'Evening missus,' tipped his head like he was doffing a cap and then they had calmly walked on.

No way were they going to get back to their patch without being seen again or someone alerting the Feds. Besides, their rep would take a massive hit if word did the rounds they were out 'n' about with their nuts and bolt swinging in the breeze. Their rep was how they maintained order; any slip-ups and people started taking liberties, big time.

So they broke into a ground floor flat on the hunt for clothes. Turned out to belong to some old dear from the clobber on offer. Kitted themselves out like RuPaul without the fashion or flair. With a dash of pink, of course. Going out without any pink was not an option. Worse than being stark, bollock naked.

Then they pinched a tenner from her caddy.

They'd hit the streets rigged out in granny wear, one sporting a cherry blossom bobble hat the other a Barbie shade scarf. London, being London, not one person had given them a second look. The city had seen it all. Two guys kitted out like Hinge and Bracket wasn't even worth the time of day.

And now Pinky had taken leave of his senses.

'This is what we should do to Biggin when he puts in his appearance.' Pinky's words ground out so hard it sounded like his teeth were going to crumble in his mouth. The gun hitched higher making a bullseye of the space between Styley's eyes. 'We should shoot his fucking head off.'

'You what?' Styley gaped at him. His brother was losing the plot.

Pinky lowered the shooter to his side as his chest rose and fell. 'We need to take Biggin out.'

Styley rushed forward and grabbed his brother by the arm. 'You can't be saying shit like that.' He threw a hand in the air with disbelief. 'You're talking about the Biggin, our mum's uncle for fuck's sake. The big fella hisself.'

Pinky yanked away and rounded on him. 'We might have the same blood running in our veins, that don't give him the poxy right to string us up by our bollocks and piss in our eyes.' He spat on the gym floor. 'I'm fucking shit tired of his, 'Yes sir, me sir, three fucking bags full sir.' I ain't getting on my knees no more to suck his over inflated dick.'

With a roar he belted across the room and launched himself at the punch bag. He steamed into it with quick-fire jabs, snorting air like a horse while his feet danced from side to side. Styley held the other side of the punch bag while his brother pummelled it like crazy hoping Pinky would get out of puff soon enough.

Pinky did the thinking for the two of them, but what his bruv was raving on about was utter lunacy. Wasn't it? Biggin had helped grow them up, shown them the criminal ropes, set them up in the gym, treated them more like cherished sons than great nephews. Of course, it was his duty to cuff them up if they stepped out of line. Wasn't it? Styley scrunched his face in confusion.

As if reading his thoughts his brother lay off the punch bag and with sweat dripping down his face looked Styley directly in the eye.

'We're not two nippers with our arses hanging out of our trackie bottoms no more. We're geezers.' He inhaled deeply as the coldness left his eyes replaced by a fever of excitement. 'We don't need some has-been Face holding us with one hand and belting us with the other.'

Styley still looked puzzled. 'What you saying?'

A nasty smile erupted on Pinky's face as he moved and cupped his hand around Styley's neck. He bent his brother's head until their foreheads touched.

'I'm saying when he gets here we take him out with this.'

He tapped the shooter against Styley's temple.

Biggin arrived at the gym in his Japanese SUV. Big windows, big wheels just like the man himself. He checked his Rolex. Right on time. Timewasters should be shot, point blank, on the spot. His great-nephews were turning into the same breed taking the ultra piss out of his bloody time. Or was something else going on here? Were the pair of idiot-boys trying to tell him something? That spray and pray job at the club could be the lads signalling they had drawn a new marker in their relationship with him. A big, fat red marker. Knowing those dunderheads, they'd want to leave the Biggin nest and strike out on their own. And maybe he would allow it. Maybe…

Biggin smoothed out any creases in his indigo-wool Paul Smith suit and headed for the door. He used the key his great-nephews didn't have a clue he had. Always keep one or two aces up your sleeve going into a situation where you weren't sure what you'd find.

He opened up. Except for Pinky and Styley the gym was empty. A spliff did the rounds at their usual perch at the table.

'What the hell are you wearing?'

His mouth stretched with distaste as he clocked Pinky's pink bobble hat and Styley's even pinker scarf. What a pair of fashion criminals. Didn't this generation get it that if you wanted to be taken seriously you couldn't go around looking like two flamingos that had done a runner from London Zoo.

They sniggered.

Pinky, the one with the supposed brain cell, explained, 'Let's just say an opportunity came our way and we couldn't resist.'

Biggin stared daggers at them as they tipped their heads back and roared with laughter. He had to do a double take to make sure he had entered a boxing gym and not the funny farm.

Pinky kicked out a seat for him but he didn't take it.

'Look fellas, I feel bad about what went on last night.' He held back the smile as he took in their stupefied expressions. Yeah, they hadn't been expecting that.

'It nearly broke my heart to put you both in that position. My own flesh and blood.' He shook his head sadly and dramatically. 'Left a foul taste on my tongue. But you do understand my position, don't you?'

Before they could answer he stepped around the table until he stood behind them. Stupid wankers! How many times had he knocked it into their skulls never to let someone blindside you from behind? He waited until they realised their mistake. Or until Pinky did, the other one just didn't have enough up top to do the sums.

Pinky's breathing changed to shallow and rapid. His great-nephew started to rise, but Biggin got there first. He placed his large palms on both of their shoulders. Pressed down slightly so they understood to keep their selves where they were parked.

He squeezed. 'There's something that slipped my ol' mind last night.' He let it out ever so softly.

Silence, then, 'What's that Uncle Biggin?' Styley of course. He suspected Pinky knew what was coming.

And he was right.

'We're sorry Uncle Biggin,' Pinky shot out quickly.

He took his hands away and stepped back. As they turned to gaze at him Biggin searched them thoroughly to spot any signs of resentment. None in sight.

He smiled as he rubbed his hands. 'Right lads, you still got any of that Cockspur rum in the kitchen?'

Once he'd disappeared out back Pinky raised his fist to thump the table in furious rage. His brother caught it mid-air. 'He'll fucking well hear you.'

As soon as Styley let go of his clenched hand, Pinky dropped his voice dangerously low. 'We've gotta do it now or he's gonna rub our noses in the shit for the rest of our days.'

'But he said sorry, we said sorry. All done and dusted.'

Pinky could barely contain himself. 'The reason he didn't push his old goat backside in a chair was so he could lord it over us.' He pulled his shooter out. 'Now all we've gotta decide is how to do it.' His brother looked unsure so he decided for them. 'We get him sat down. I say I've got to take a leak. Then I get behind him and blast his brains across the wall.'

His bruv began to sweat, his gaze darting nervously about. 'I don't wanna do this no more.'

'Too fucking bad coz…He's coming back.'

They hurriedly settled back in their chairs as Biggin slowly reached the doorway. Funny thing was he didn't have a glass of rum in his hand. And then they saw why.

A stunning, black woman held a sawn-off against his back.

She shoved him forward as she growled, 'Which one of you soon to be dead bastards is Pinky and which one Styley?'

Thirty-Two

Bang!

Pieces of the gym's ceiling smashed down from the bullet Dee blasted into it so these cunts understood right off she meant business. She hadn't felt this volcanic, almost unhinged, in a long time. Two of these fuckers had tried to murder her sister. But what made it worse was Dee was riddled with guilt twice over. That was her club Jen had taken a bullet in and maybe, just maybe, she should've dolled out that protection money and none of this would've happened.

She kept her gun trained on the big, older bloke. He appeared to be the head honcho of this pack of wannabe murderers. If they decided to take a chance at least she'd take him out of this world for good.

'Toss any hard wear on the ground.' No one moved. She yelled, 'Do it now.'

The one wearing the pink bobble hat – what the fuck was that about? – chucked an automatic.

'Anything else?' She wrenched the shooter so it pointed squarely at the leader's face. She wanted to call it an ug mug but he was handsome and looked the part. 'Not even you big man?' Dee sneered.

He had the brass to smile at her and say, 'Am I correct in thinking this has something to do with a certain club in Stratford?'

Her sneer twisted into a deadly snarl. 'You ain't a brief and this ain't the Old Bailey so cut it with the cute words. I've asked a question – which of you pathetic fools are Pinky and Styley?'

She took a step forward and spread her legs slightly to balance the shotgun evenly.

Big man said, 'My name's Biggin—'

She cracked over him, 'Which means these two crap heads must be Pinky and effing Perky.'

'You're John Black's missus.' Biggin didn't ask, he told her, which got her attention.

That stupid smile of his must've been welded to his lips with Superglue because it didn't waver an inch.

'And what of it?'

'I was a good mate of his while he was still learning the whats and wherefores with Uncle Frank.'

Dee frowned. There weren't that many folk around anymore who remembered her John's early days back in The Green with Uncle Frank.

She cautiously said, 'Is that so?'

'He'd be proud of you.' Her gaze darted in confusion. 'He'd expect you to come around to sort things out.' That smile stretched. 'But you know what I admired about John? He never went in all guns blazing. He always took the time to understand every nook and cranny of a situation. Made sure he had the facts first.'

He was spot on; that was her John alright. Out of the corner of her eye she noticed the one with the crazy scarf start to move. 'Don't try it buster or it will be three of you leaving this crap hole in body bags.'

Biggin turned to him and snapped, in a broad Jamaican accent, 'Keep your skin quiet.' He flicked his gaze back to her. 'I'm going to pretend you're John. The facts are these. These two are my great-nephews—'

'Well, you didn't try very hard to keep them on a short lead.'

Pink Bobble hat didn't take that well. 'You wanna watch your big mouth gal before I bitch slap you into silence. I've taken on guys with shooters – no problem.'

Biggin huffed loudly. 'I said shut up.' An uneasy silence filled the gym. 'He's Pinky. As I understand it my nephews got a touch heavy-handed trying to collect the insurance money—'

'Protection racket more like.'

He waved his hand with a flourish in the air. 'Whatever you choose to call it. I will admit that they collect the money on my behalf.' Dee almost squeezed the trigger there and then until he quickly carried on. 'But I never sanctioned any shooting. Believe you me they've been punished.'

Dee let out a sick laugh. 'Punished? You been on the ol' crack pipe or something coz If they'd been dealt with they'd be in the obituaries column.'

He waved his hand at his great-nephews. 'If you think I haven't done enough, go ahead. Shoot them.'

Incredulous, Pinky and Styley blasted him back at the same time.

'Are you off your head?'

'You bastard.'

Before Dee could think on what to do Biggin continued. 'I heard what happened to your sister, Jennifer, and it makes me sick to my stomach. It shouldn't have happened and it wouldn't have happened if I'd been consulted.'

'My sister's name is too clean to be in your filthy gob.' Dee could feel the tears gathering at the back of her eyes and her tummy muscles knotting tight.

'All I'm saying is that there's no need for any more blood to be shed. John would have understood that.'

She ignored him and addressed the ones she'd come gunning for. 'My sister's got two kids. Two little girls who are terrified that their mum's never gonna wake up again. Do you have any idea what that must feel like?'

'Yeah, I do.' It was Pinky. His face looked like it was fixed in stone and his eyes were slightly glazed. 'Our dad chucked himself under a train at Mile End Station. Probably have been killed out right if he'd used the Central Line but he went for the slower Metropolitan Line instead. We saw him in the London. No legs. One arm gone. A fucked up mess.'

A hard, lump of emotion caught in Dee's throat. That couldn't have been easy for two little boys...but still...

'We've all got our stories to tell I'm sure and the one I'm interested in is someone, or two, have to pay the price for Jen lying in a coma in that hospital bed.'

Biggin tried to get his hooks back in her again. 'And how are those two girls – your nieces – going to carry on living normal lives if they not only lose their mum but their aunty as well?' He raised his hands slightly. 'Coz that's the possibility here. I don't want it to come to that. We need to find a way forward here. Something that works out for everyone; that would be a John type solution. '

Dee rapidly blinked trying to flush away the images of Courtney and Little Bea that Biggin had plastered in her mind.

She didn't want this man to be right, but he was. Her two princesses needed her. That's why she'd felt so awful leaving them on their own at the hospital like that, but when Courtney had dropped her news Dee had seen red, her blood running hot and justice for Jen became her number one priority. All of a sudden she felt knackered. Emotionally and physically done in.

She must've been stuck in her thoughts for a while because the next thing she knew Biggin was standing in front of her. Before she could move he wrapped his large palm round the front of the sawn-off.

His chest leaned forward. 'I'm gonna take this, put it in the corner and then we'll all sit down and over a glass, decide what to do.'

Dee's grip tightened but there was something about this man that…that…she couldn't put her finger on what it was. Maybe he reminded her of John and Uncle Frank, that old style Face who sometimes had another way of sorting shit out. Her fingers loosened and he took the gun.

Styley dived for his piece, but Biggin turned the shotgun on him with fury. 'You are dissing me big time now. This lady is the widow of one of the best blokes I ever knew and you want to fill her full of holes? Now find some respect and stop playing the bitch.'

His great-nephew stopped shy of the gun. Then backed off.

Biggin threw the shotgun to him and as he caught it said, 'Put it away somewhere safe.' He turned to Dee, 'Let me take you to the kitchen so you can powder your nose. Then we'll decide what to do.'

Pearl's bangles rattled as she pressed the bell on the door of the two people who she hoped were going to pull out all the stops and get her gold back. That's right *her* gold. Babs' betrayal meant she'd forfeited all rights to it.

The loss of her gorgeous friends Vi and Di was a crack in her heart. Money could drive you to death. Taking note of that somber warning, Pearl still wanted her gold back.

A guy, who she instantly threw her arms around hugging him tight, opened the door. She eased back to stare adoringly up at him. 'How's my beautiful Lennox?'

He shuffled his feet with embarrassment, but leaned down and kissed her on the forehead.

She stepped inside calling, 'Where's my other gorgeous grandson. Glenroy?' She sang his name.

He appeared from the other side of the boxing ring. He sent her an affectionate smile as he said, 'Grams, how many times we got to tell you everyone calls us Pinky and Styley.'

She kissed her teeth and mumbled, loud enough for them to hear though, 'Smurfy and Smoothy? What kinda names are that? Lennox and Glenroy are solid Jamaican names you should be proud to carry.'

Pearl popped herself in a chair at the table. Her gaze ran lovingly over her grandbabies. They meant the world to her and more. Her kids didn't want to know her but at least her daughter's two boys hadn't blanked her. It had been them who had unknowingly moved the gold from Babs' house, although she'd told Babs an untruth and said her sons had done it. Pearl hadn't lied out of malice; she'd wanted Babs to believe that her kids had embraced her once again. What mum wants to keep admitting her children don't want to know her?

'Wanna drink grams?' Lennox offered. No, Pinky. She made herself say it in her head. If that's what the boy wanted to be called so be it.

She shook her head and waved her hands. 'Come sit down, I need you to do something for me.'

Once they were at the table the story of the gold poured out. By the end their jaws were slack.

'The gold from that blag last year?' Pinky said in wonder, his voice low as if he thought someone would hear, but Pearl couldn't see anyone else about.

'More importantly,' Styley rasped looking very angry, 'this Babs Miller thinks she can double cross you and rob you blind.'

Pearl caught his sleeve as he got up as if to track down Babs right there and then. Once she had their attention again she slowly confided, 'I want you both to get it back for me.'

Styley grinned. 'As if you have to ask. We'll have it back within the next twenty-four hours.' He paused. ''O course we'll want a big drink out of it.'

Pearl's head shoved back in indignation. 'You want to take a cut of Granny Pearl's retirement money?'

Pinky leaned in and took her hands. 'We did help you move it from that house up Mile End way and, from what I remember of the blag, there's plenty to go round. Plus, a geezer has to put bread on the table.'

Pearl thought for a bit before she nodded. 'Don't tell my brother, your great Uncle though. He's living a life purer than Snow White now and told me to sling my hook.'

Her grandsons looked baffled at each other. 'He said what? But grams…'

'Who's that with you lads?' a voice boomed behind them.

Pearl swung round and kissed her teeth long and hard as she eyeballed her brother in disbelief. 'Well, well, well, if it isn't mister I don't get my hands dirty no more.' She twisted back to her grandsons. 'That's what you were gonna tell me, wasn't it? That he runs all your rackets. You are such a bastard.' She leapt to her feet.

Biggin snapped his eyes at her. 'Know why I told you that? Coz every time you come into my life something terrible kicks off. Like that time I nearly ended up banged up in a flea-ridden Turkish jail because you decided to make one of the embassy staff's daughters your mark with your Madam Pearl mumbo-jumbo. We were on fucking on holiday for Pete's sake.'

He stepped fully into the room and Pearl stumbled back when she saw he wasn't alone.

'What the hell's going on here?' There weren't many times that Pearl was stumped in her life but this was one of them.

'Pearl is that you?' Dee Black asked as her eyebrows lifted.

'What you doing here darlin'?'

'You two obviously know each other.' Biggin's gaze sharpened on both of them.

Dee supplied the answer. 'Pearl's a mate of my mum's. A close mate.'

Pearl looked pointedly at her grandsons. 'Her mum's *Babs Miller.*'

But it wasn't them who reacted but her brother. His usually smooth, brown skin looked pasty and a touch grey. 'Who did you say her mum is?'

Dee answered. 'Babs Miller.'

One of his hands clenched tight like he wanted to do someone some serious damage. 'Why didn't you say?' he growled at Dee.

'What? That my mum's called Babs Miller? I'm not sure that's any of your beeswax.'

'I'm afraid that it is.' He sat down heavily like his plug had been pulled out. 'Dee, you need to take a seat. There's something you need to know.'

Thirty-Three

'I ain't sharing a room with *that*,' Tiff ground out, shooting daggers at Flo. Her outraged voice was so close to Babs' ear it left a nasty ringing sound in her head.

Ignore her whinging! Babs clenched her teeth as she gave her grandkids her full attention. Aww, they looked like a pair of lost lambs in her sitting room. Little Bea hadn't uttered a word since seeing the dreadful state of her mum. That wasn't normal...was it? She wanted to wrap them in the deepest hug ever and never let go.

Tiff and Flo had gathered the girls from their mum's hospital bed and then went over to Jen's to pick up some of their belongings.

A social worker had appeared at the ozzie giving it all that about being able to put the girls in foster care if the family weren't able to look after them. Courtney had clung onto Babs for dear life, while Little Bea had stood there in wide-eyed silence. Her grandbabies in foster care? Absobloodylutelynot! Where she came from they looked after their own. They'd be stopping with her until Jen got better. And Jen would get better. Babs wouldn't allow herself to think otherwise.

'Mum, I'm talking to you.' Tiff's groaning and moaning sliced through her thoughts.

Flo took charge. 'Babs, I'll get the girls settled in your room.'

And that's why Tiff was kicking up a stink. The girls would be bunking in Babs' room, which meant she would take the settee and now Tiff would have to share her old room with Flo. In a crisis situation all had to play their part. If Tiff didn't get that - tough bloody titties.

Babs went into the kitchen. Tiff stomped right behind her gob going into fifth gear.

'I ain't kipping with that slag. That's my old room, that is, so by rights you should tell her it's time to sling her toerag toff hook and head back to Poshville.'

Babs kept her peace and took out a duster and bottle of cleaner.

She sprayed the counter and rigorously wiped it down as motor mouth kept on. 'Dad's wrong side of the blanket was only meant to be dossing here for a couple of days, tops.' Babs sprayed and wiped down the draining board. 'I mean, come on, she's got enough bling to put herself up in some swanky hotel, don't she? So why does…?'

Squirt. Clean. Tiffany talking.

Squirt. Clean. Tiffany talking.

Tiff kept giving it some but her voice faded from Babs' ear. Her fingers gripped the duster tighter and tighter. Her hand moved in manic, frenzied circles. Pain radiated through her hand, but she took no notice. All Babs knew was that if she made her home all spic and span everything would be alright. All her troubles would go away. She'd be in control of her small world again. Of course that was plain bollocks and she knew it.

The therapist in prison had called it a type of obsessive behaviour, Babs' way of dealing with the world when something went badly wrong. Apparently if she made her home nice and neat, shipshape and Bristol fashion, she deluded herself into thinking her troubles would go away. There weren't many people she thanked during the time she was doing bird, but that therapist was near the top of the list. Babs had been super proud of herself when she'd conquered it...now look at her, back to being some demented, domestic goddess.

Babs willed her hand to stop moving, but it wouldn't. Please stop! Please stop! Please fucking stop! Why wouldn't that bloody spot of dirt go away? She sprayed it three times. Scrubbed with all her might. Still wouldn't go away and it felt like her hand was going to drop off. Her heart was about ready to tear out of her chest. The hot sweat on her face was flowing like a waterfall.

'Mum?'

'Babs?'

Trembling she raised her head to find Tiff and Flo worriedly staring at her. In a daze she wondered what they were doing in the bathroom of all places.

Babs pointed desperately to the sink. 'That dirt,' she jabbed her finger, 'I can't make it go away.'

Tiff peered over her shoulder and then looked back at her. 'Mum, there ain't nuthin there.' She looked meaningfully at Flo. 'Why don't we get you sat down?'

Before Babs knew what was happening, the duster and bottle of cleaner were gone and she was sitting on her comfy, worn settee.

Flo whispered to Tiff, 'What's wrong with her?'

'Her way of saying things have got a bit on top of her.'

'This will sort her out.'

Flo lit up a spliff and passed it to Babs who greedily puffed away, hating the taste – weed wasn't her thing – but it did the trick and calmed her down. Tiff took it away and both girls sat besides her.

'I don't understand,' Babs started in a small voice bursting with heartache, 'why would anyone shoot my Jen?'

Flo answered. 'Why does anyone shoot anyone? It's an evil world we're living in.'

She gazed at Stan's daughter, her face riddled in confusion. 'But Jen wouldn't hurt a fly. She's so gentle and caring.' She shook her head. 'When my Jennifer was little I could leave her alone for ages and she wouldn't make a fuss. Such a good girl.'

Tiff put an arm around her shoulder and Flo did the same. Babs sank back into their much-needed comfort; her troubles felt lighter.

'Why is it always the good ones who end up paying the price?' she finally asked.

Before the girls could answer there was a strong, firm knock at the front door. Tiff started to get up, but Babs said, 'No, I'll get it.' She was starting to feel her old self again. She looked pointedly at Tiff and Flo. 'You need to sort out the camper bed in your room.'

If Tiff started shooting off again she was going to let her have it with both barrels.

Her daughter's mouth drooped unpleasantly at the corners, but she kept her sense of injustice to herself. Good!

Babs opened the door to find Ryan, the estate's resident drunk standing awkwardly on her doorstep. At least he wasn't swaying.

'You alright Babs?' His bloodshot, jaundiced eyes blinked at her.

She sighed, feeling so weary she could drop. 'Truth is Ryan, it's one of the worst days of my life. But my Jen's hanging on in there. She's a strong woman and it will take more than some arsehole to put her down.'

His cracked lips smacked together. 'They wanna bring back hanging, they do.' Suddenly he looked down at his scuffed shoes and then up again. 'It ain't much.'

His hand went into his pocket. He took her hand and placed something in it. Babs found a creased fiver resting in her palm.

She gazed, bewildered, at him with tears pricking the back of her eyes. 'I can't take this.'

He leaned in. If her eyes hadn't been watering before they were now with the booze fumes coming off him. 'It's half of my drink's money, but you know what Babs, I'd rather see it go towards helping your grand children.'

Babs almost cried her heart out then. All most folk saw when they looked at him was a fella so bladdered most days he could hardly stand. But underneath all that was a man who was strong in his own way and who felt the pain of others. That's why she didn't offer him the money back because he still had his pride.

'Thank you,' she croaked, choked up with emotion.

He almost bowed to her and then his thin legs took him away. As he reached the corner another figure appeared – Rani from number fourteen on the landing downstairs. She gave Babs a plateful of chicken and lamb samosas. Five minutes later Jan and Tom from the Knackered Swan boozer gave her a boxful of fizzy drinks and two bottles of brandy.

And that's how it went on for the rest of the day, people on the estate trying to show their support for one of its most respected and long time residents. Even her one-time arch enemy, Mel Ingram, sent over her girl, Stacy, with four packs of ciggies. The residents of The Devil didn't have much but they were willing to share what they had with her. People could say this 'n' that about The Essex Lane Estate – and they did – but when the chips were down for one of their own they showed the world what a tight, caring community they could be.

Thirty-Four

As Flo took the road down to Mile End tube she realised that a car was keeping pace with her. Its horn blew and she turned to see a vintage Aston Martin mounting the pavement. It looked like the sort of car her grandfather liked to collect. She did a double take when she clocked that it really was her grandfather, the old sea dog himself – the Commander.

He was rigged out in a navy blue blazer, a purple cravat and shades that made him look like an aging Italian film director whose shoot was going very badly.

He leaned over and opened the passenger door and said in a quiet, sly voice, 'Hello, my dear. Why don't you get in and then we can go for a little drive?'

He'd obviously been parked up near The Devil waiting for her to appear.

Flo was uneasy as she climbed in. 'I'm not sure you're in the right gear for a road trip around the East End. I'm afraid you'll either be laughed at or robbed.'

He drove off the pavement. 'Don't you worry about that my dear, I'm well used to navigating the mean streets of East London from the old days. It's rather like sailing round Cape

Horn. You just have to keep your wits about you and an eye on the wind.'

'I'm sure.'

The Commander drove off towards Whitechapel in silence as if waiting for an answer to a question he hadn't asked. Finally, he snapped. 'Well?'

Flo was nervous. 'Well what?'

'Have you found out what's happened to my gold? What have the Millers done with it?'

'Oh that. You should have rung - you didn't need to come down here to ask me that.'

The Commander's driving was becoming careless and he nearly took out an old lady crossing the road. 'I have been ringing my dear but you haven't been answering.'

'Well, I've been busy. Babs Miller's been taking me round the markets. I found some nice gear down in Petticoat Lane actually.' Flo couldn't figure out why she was lying. It wasn't like she cared about the Millers, now was it?

The Commander slammed the brakes on and the car ground to a halt. He turned and grabbed her by the arm. 'I haven't sent you down to this rat hole to go shopping. You're here to find my gold.' His eyes narrowed. 'I've heard all about what happened at her daughter's club and that one of her girls is in the hospital. Now then – what's happened to my gold?'

Flo avoided his eyes. She wasn't scared of many people but she knew her grandfather had a temper on him. Not that he'd ever vented it on her. He'd always been a pussycat with her, but there was a first time for everything.

'Well, nothing yet, I'm working on it. But I think their story might be true. It's disappeared.'

There she went lying again! What was the matter with her? She loved the Commander to death, so why was she not telling him the truth?

'Disappeared?' her granddad scoffed. 'The Miller family are professional criminals. That crook Kieran Scott stole my gold and then that crook John Black stole it off him. And now it's disappeared? Just like that? Don't be so ridiculous. One of those crooks knows where it is and your job is to find out which one and where they've hidden it.'

'I'm trying.'

After a silence the Commander's voice softened. 'Do you know my dear there are two types of people in this world. There are sailors and the landlubbers. The sailors go places. The landlubbers don't.' He gestured at the grim estate the car was parked beside. 'The sailors find buried treasure on desert islands while the landlubbers end up on ghastly places like those blocks of flats. Now you have to decide whether you want to be a sailor or a landlubber. Am I making myself clear?'

Flo slowly opened the passenger door and got out.

She turned back to her grandfather. 'Perfectly clear.'

But everything between her and the Millers was as clear as mud.

Natty, who was as naked as the day he was born, was screaming his head off as he lay dumped on the cold, kitchen floor. Oblivious to his distress Miriam sat at a high-backed stool, wearing Dee's fluffy, pink slippers, which she'd 'borrowed' with relish. She slugged back a whiskey and orange. The booze was straight from that shag bag's hard liquor collection in the snooker room cum bar. Mad bird had warned her not to touch her whiskey and then top it up with water. Fair enough. Miriam had topped it up with her pee instead. A good shake of the bottle, no one was any the wiser.

She angrily shook the glass at her crying charge. 'See, that's what happens to naughty boy's who don't learn to say mummy! I've given you ample time to tell me that I'm your mum, but you won't have it. Wilful, that's what you are.' She scoffed nastily at the back of her throat. 'I suppose you learned that from *her*? Learned! As if that whore knows anything about educashun. She couldn't teach a junkie how to stick the needle in.'

Miriam knocked the remainder of the drink back, banged the glass onto the counter, shot to her feet and waltzed over to stand over Natty. She felt no pity as she scornfully gazed down at him through squinty eyes. His face was blotched an alarming red and wet from the continued stream of tears. Playacting, that's what he was doing, trying to get one over her. Well, she was onto him.

'I won't put up with this nonsense, Andy. You need to learn who the real mummy in this house is.' Her tone took on a mad, ranting quality as she shook a finger at him. 'Don't you get it? If you refuse to say mummy they won't believe you're mine. Then *he's* gonna come back and take you away and there's nothing I'll be able to do about it.' She bellowed, 'He ain't ever gonna take you away from me again. You hear?'

His cries turned into tiny whimpers, the fear of God in him. Suddenly she inhaled and relaxed her shoulders. Her hand dropped to her side.

Her voice grew quiet, even gentle. 'Do you think

mummy likes doing this to you? I don't, my lovely. All I want to do is to keep you safe. Me and you together. Forever.'

She absently patted a hand against her wig. 'I'm going to leave you for ten minutes, not a minute less, not a minute more, to give you time to consider your antics.' Miriam blew him a kiss. 'Don't forget, mummy loves you.'

As she started to leave Miriam was startled by the sound of Mizzery Dee's flash motor in the driveway. Bloody hell. The bitch wasn't meant to be back yet. Good grief, if that slapper found the baby on on the floor…

She dumped the glass in the bin, along with her panic and scooped up a still howling Natty into her arms. The car door slammed as she bombed it up the stairs. As the front door opened she quickly dressed him in a pair of Roger Rabbit jim-jams.

She pointed sternly at him. 'Now, shut your noise.'

But he wouldn't. Instead his wailing got louder. She pressed her hand over his mouth and yelped in pain as he sank the few teeth he had into her thumb.

Astonished and bristling with anger she raised her palm. 'You little bleeder—'

'Miriam?' Dee's call froze her hand.

In her sweetest voice she answered back, 'Coming Mizz Dee.' She turned to Natty, 'Now look what you've done.'

Miriam left him crying as she smoothed her hands over her dress and went downstairs. She remained at the top of the final flight as a wiped out Dee Black stared up at her.

'Was that my Natty crying?'

Miriam put on her best fake smile and best voice. 'Ah, poor love has another tooth coming through I think.'

'Bring him to me?'

'What?' Miriam tried her hardest to keep the fear from her face.

'You lost your ears or something?' Dee snapped back. Then she took a steading breath. 'I'm sorry. I'm not having a go. I just want my son.'

Something had obviously upset the bitch. Good! She deserved all the misery life had to throw at her. By the time she handed Natty over he was whimpering, but, thank God, not blowing his stack anymore.

As Dee walked towards the lounge clutching her son Miriam sucked her thumb where Natty had bitten her. It was time to move up her plans for her and her darling Andy to become a family again.

Dee held her son tight as she sat in the dark in John's chair. Natty must've felt the coiled tension inside her because his tiny fingers twisted in her jacket for dear life. She kissed his forehead. She was still having trouble getting her head round what Biggin had told her. It couldn't be true. No way. Babs would've…wouldn't she? Her mother wouldn't have kept this from her? They had come such a long way as daughter and mother. They had a solid relationship now where there was no place for barefaced lies only straight talking. But what she'd been told at the gym…

Dee whispered to her treasured child, 'There's only one way to find out. I'm gonna have to, point blank, ask your Nanna Babs.'

Thirty-Five

'So glad you've put in an appearance coz since you're squatting in *my* room I've rustled together a few adjustments,' Tiff informed Flo with sly glee.

Flo stood in the doorway of what she referred to as 'our room' and was very careful to hide the WTF anger she felt as she ran an eye over Tiff's 'adjustments.' Running along the middle of the room was a wardrobe lying on its side, a chest of drawers and a bookcase. Either side was makeshift panelling consisting of laminate flooring left over from when Babs had redecorated the sitting room.

'Building your own cut price Berlin Wall are you Tiff?' Flo spoke calmly. The last thing she wanted was this bitch to suss that she was royally pissing her right off. 'Turning our one-bedroom des res into a two-bed flop house?'

Tiff was attempting to use duct tape to keep her laminate panels straight but it was looking a bit drunk.

She snapped, 'Got it right in one. If you're gonna carry on poncing off my mum – MY MUM – you can do it in your own space.'

Flo was not best pleased to see all her gear dumped on the other side along with the camp bed shoved at an angle.

But at least she had the window.

Flo pretended she was still taking this seriously. 'Actually, then it's not a two-bed apartment, it's more of a one-bedroom, one camper bedroom, apartment.'

Tiff went into full flight. 'If you think you're getting my bed, you can fuck right off.'

'Fair play, I'll give over the bed.' Flo inspected the work. 'But there is a problem here – how am I supposed to get to my room without going through yours?'

'Gonna divide the door in two and hang curtains from there to the wall.'

Flo knew her tone was winding Tiff up. 'Of course! Silly me! Well, I must say this looks like a very professional job. You should have been a developer – shedloads of wonga in that.'

Tiff stared at her with distrust. 'You're alright with this?'

That caught the Mohican-haired witch out. Took more than moving a few bits of furniture around to push her hissy fit button. She decided to play the caring sister.

'Is everything getting to you Tiffany? I mean have you got issues you want to talk to me about? I know we've had out differences in the past but I'm here to help if you need me. I'm your half-sister after all, so come on, don't be shy, let me help.'

Here we go!

She waited for Hurricane Tiff to land. It never came.

Instead her sister narrowed her eyes. 'Think you can wind me up, eh? Make me blow like a bottle of bolly?' Tiff contemptuously brushed two fingers against her shoulder giving Flo the brush off. 'You stop on your side of the room and I'll stop on mine.'

Flo was getting narked now, seriously considering kicking down the room divide when she noticed Babs putting on her coat in the hallway.

Flo moved into the hallway. 'Are you off to the hospital?'

Babs nodded. Flo never thought she'd live to see the day she felt sorry for Babs Miller. At one time she'd hated her with a passion. Now she felt so bad for her about what had happened to Jen.

'Take care of the girls while I'm gone,' Babs instructed as her hand reached for the latch. Suddenly her hand fell as she patted her coat. 'Bollocks. I've forgotten my mobile.' She looked up at Flo with tired eyes. 'Will you get it for me? I left it on the kitchen table.'

Flo found it where Babs said it would be. As she picked it up it pinged with a text message.

She read it. Her mouth fell open. 'What the fuck?'

'Florence,' Babs called, her voice laden with impatience.

'Coming.' She made her voice sound bright and breezy.

As soon as she handed the phone over Babs was gone. Flo didn't hesitate. She made her way into her newly refurbished room. Tiff was still fighting with the laminate flooring.

'Tiff?' She invaded her sister's half of the room.

'Oi! I've told you—'

Flo urgently grabbed her arm. 'Shut it! There's something you need to know.'

'Excuse me, do you know of any all-night shops round here?' Courtney asked in her best plummy-school voice.

The woman, pulling a laden shopping trolley, was happy to oblige. She pointed down the street. 'Turn the corner and there's a 7/11.'

Courtney had given her Aunts Tiff and Flo some BS story about going to see her mate on The Devil when in reality she was out hunting down that bitch Dodgy. The info on where Dodgy was laying low came by way of that lippy, knob head Ellis who fancied hisself something chronic. She'd never been to his gaff before on the estate but knew it was a favourite hangout for Dodgy and her crew. The guy's mum worked three jobs to keep hearth and home together, which meant she was rarely around and that turned it into the ideal tearaway teen haunt. Ellis had played the Big I Am until she pushed the scalpel, upfront and personal, in his boat and put him straight. He soon let on about Dodgy being holed up at her mad Aunt Tracy's in Romford, in a flat above one of those all-night stores.

Courtney thanked the woman and headed through Romford market, which was in full swing. Someone was yelling, 'Pound-A-Bowl,' to entice passers-by to his fruit 'n' veg stall. There was a huge bookstall selling romances run by a gorgeous woman with flowing blonde curls to die for. Trendy clothes stalls and even one selling glasses.

When she reached the shop, Courtney hurried down an alleyway to stairs leading to the flat above. But drew a blank when an elderly guy with a very strange ginger beard answered. He suggested another place though, over the road.

Courtney found the store, hurried down a passageway that ran next to it and up a flight of iron stairs to the door at the top. She gripped the handle of the scalpel in her pocket and noticed it had sliced a hole in the fabric. Courtney hated violence. Even when she'd saved her beloved Nanna from her monster granddad Stan all that blood had made her feel dirty and panicked deep, down inside. It was the right thing to do – that's what everyone repeatedly told her – but taking someone's life hadn't felt right to her for the longest time. But sorting Dodgy did.

She whispered in a low, menacing growl, 'I'll get you for this you slag. You're gonna pay for my mum. All the way.'

She hammered on the knackered brass knocker and then clocked a doorbell half hanging off the door. It was the face of a frog with scary, bulging eyes with the button inside its wide, open gob. She pressed it and nearly jumped out of her skin when the whirring noise of an air raid siren cried out. Courtney waited but no one came to the door, so she pressed again.

A female voice inside yelled, 'Hold your blimmin' galloping horses.'

She heard the slap-slap of backless slippers approach the front door. It was opened by a woman wearing a bathrobe, with a towel twisted round her head and a fag hanging out of her mouth.

Ciggy bouncing between her lips as she spoke. 'Look luv, if you're flogging tea towels, sponges, scouring pads or some new miracle to clean my stove I don't wanna know. Plus, you'll be trying to screw me over, charging a fiver for each, and let's face it the market's round the corner where I can get the lot for a tenner. I mean do I look like I'm this year's Easter Bunny, Eh?'

The words came at 90 mph. Courtney's ears started ringing. Dodgy's Aunt Tracy went on and on and on. In the end, to save her sanity if nothing else, Courtney butted in. 'You've got the wrong end of the stick. I'm here to see Dodgy.'

Dodgy's aunt tugged the fag from her mouth and gave

Courtney the once-over, her eyes squinting slightly. 'Oh yeah? Wha'cha want with her then?'

Courtney let out a long, sigh of relief; at least Dodgy was here. 'She asked me to pop over.'

'Really?' The woman scowled. 'Thing is, she's hurt her leg, poor thing. She didn't say boo to me 'bout anyone coming to call though.'

Courtney toughed it out. 'She gave me a bell and told me to pop over coz she hurt her leg. She wanted a bit of company.'

Satisfied, Aunt Tracy waved her impatiently in. Courtney was expecting the flat to be an ultra disaster zone but it was neat, clean, full of proudly framed family photos and, in the sitting room, a large cabinet with rows and rows of gleaming glasses.

And lying on a floral-patterned sofa, under a fluffy, green blanket, curled on her side facing the wall was Dodgy. Courtney's temper rose to boiling point. How dare she! How fucking dare she! Her mum's fighting for her very life, tubes coming outta her this way 'n' that and this…this…rank, out of order gang girl cunt was taking a kip.

'Shannon,' her Aunt shoved out with the bark of a Sergeant Major, 'you've got a visitor.'

Dodgy's whole body stiffened. Her sharp, indrawn gasp was loud in the room. She twisted round so quickly she nearly fell off the sofa. 'Look, Pinky and Styley…' Her head came up. Her words stopped dead as soon as she clocked Courtney.

'Dunno who Pinky and Blinky are,' her aunt let out all light and airy. The tension in the room had obviously gone straight over her head. 'But your mate here says you gave her a bell to swing on by. I've gotta get my hair sorted for tonight at the Tropicana so I'll leave you two beauty queens to get reacquainted.'

Neither girl spoke when she left the room. Courtney took note of her bloodshot, swollen eyes. She'd never associated Dodgy with crying. Bloody good! She'd be blubbing a wagonload more by the time Courtney had finished with her.

'Courts I…'

Courtney whipped out the scalpel and advanced on the other girl. 'My mum's at death's door coz of you.'

Dodgy reared forward, the scalpel inches away from her face. Courtney was shocked out of her socks by the girl's unexpected action.

'Come on then! Stab me up! That's what you're here for, ain't it?' She pulled her T-Shirt up. Pointed crazily at her heart. 'Go on. Stick me right there, that'll do the job.'

Courtney's hand wavered in alarm. She'd been expecting Dodgy to give her a load of ol' flim-flam, trying to wriggle her way out of trouble.

Dodgy screamed, 'Not got the bottle then? I suppose not, you're a good girl, ain't ya. Here – let me help.'

She made a grab for Courtney's hand, but Courtney stepped back shocked by Dodgy's death wish behaviour.

The other girl slumped back, tears rolling down her cheek. 'It weren't my fault, weren't my fault. How was I supposed to know? Eh? Tell me – how was I supposed to know your mum would be there?'

'You wanna see my mum? She ain't opened her eyes once.' The scalpel trembled in her hand. 'The doctors don't know if she will ever again.'

A heart-wrenching sob tore out of the other girl. She shook her head to the beat of the words that followed. 'I'd never have gone in there if I'd known they had plans to shoot the place up with your mum in it.'

'It weren't just my mum. My aunts were there too and my grandmother—'

'Your nan?' Dodgy wailed, no doubt thinking of her own beloved grandmother.

Courtney's grip tightened on the blade. 'I ain't gonna ask you who the fuckers are, you done it coz I heard you mention their names to Strawberry.' The blood drained from Dodgy's face. 'Pinky and Styley. They were the ones in that flash set of wheels you were chatting to that time in the car park.' It wasn't a question but a statement: Courtney didn't need Dodgy to spell out the truth.

Dodgy sniffed as she swiped the back of her hand against her dripping nose. 'I tell you what Courts, I've done nuff badness in my time but willingly setting up one of my mate's mum's – never.'

'My mum never hurt a fly in her life,' Courtney said softly. Dodgy looked shamed-faced. 'Now she's got all these tubes going in her. I think they're hurting her.'

'Nah.' Dodgy shook her head. 'She can't feel nish. My old girl was the same. It happened to her.'

That was news to Courtney. 'Yeah?'

Courtney still thought Dodgy had been bang out of order, but she wasn't the one who'd pulled the trigger. Plus she looked like she was paying in spades. Courtney put the scalpel away and cautiously took a seat next to her friend. And Dodgy was still her friend.

'Silly moo was so busy drinking the can of brew she

wandered into the road and a bus had her. That's the way my Nan told me coz, as you know, my old man and lady did a runner without me when I was a young un.' She caught Courtney's gaze. 'That's why I told the lads from the off that I don't do mums. That Izzy at the hairdressers was a special case. Don't get me wrong, I didn't much like mine, but that don't mean I weren't broken-hearted when she weren't there no more.'

A troubled silence covered them. Then Dodgy whispered, 'You do believe me?'

Courtney nodded. 'I suppose…yeah, I know it weren't your fault.

Dodgy pushed out her little finger and curled it slightly. 'Friends?'

Courtney curled her pinky around the offered finger. What else could she say? 'Friends.'

Thirty-Six

'Babs?'

Dee's hesitant voice plucked Babs out of her daze. She was sitting by Jen's hospital bed holding her unconscious daughter's hand.

'Any change?' Dee's voice was barely above a whisper as she came to stand by Jen's bed.

Babs shook her head, but truth be told, she was a bit worried about how Dee was shaping up. Her girl didn't appear her usual self. Dee never left her house unless she looked like a class act; primped and preened to the max with designer clobber that made many a-woman green with envy. Her jeans… Babs peered harder; there was a stain on them. Her girl didn't go around with stains like she was a homeless.

Babs couldn't stop from asking, 'You alright luv?'

Her Dee didn't answer straight away. Instead she ran her palm over her forehead like she had a fever. Babs was concerned properly now. 'Nothing's happened to little Natty—'

'No,' Dee interrupted sharply. 'Why don't we get a cuppa in the caff downstairs?'

That's when Babs saw Dee's eyes for the first time and

she almost gasped. They were bloodshot and puffy. Her girl had been crying? It was about Jen she supposed. But, then again, she wasn't so sure.

Less than five minutes later they were in the small caff on the ground floor not far from the entrance. Dee had one of them fancy coffees and Babs a bog standard builders' brew.

'Now tell me what's up?' Babs started. 'I know that you're not yourself just coz of Jen – we all are – but there's something else going on with you. You've said it ain't our Natty, so what is it?' She patted her daughter's hand reassuringly. 'You can tell me.'

It had taken them so many years to become the mother and daughter that they were meant to be. The heartbreak of Babs not bringing up her mixed race daughter was behind them. They were tighter than a jar of peanut butter at a squirrel convention. They trusted each other.

Dee gave her a strange, guarded look. 'I met one of John's mates from back in the day. You know how it is, we got chatting and stuff.' She crossed her legs as she eased back in the wooden chair and gazed at her mum from under her very curly faux eyelashes. 'Then he asks me point blank if I've got a clue about the gold. You know, what happened to it.'

Babs' heart nearly stopped. Stay calm, she willed herself, there's nothing going on. 'Bloody cheeky beggar. I hope you told him to stick his nosey hooter where the sun don't shine.'

Dee let out a low laugh. 'Yeah, something like that.' Her green-brown eyes fixed on Babs. 'You ever wondered what happened to it?'

Babs almost choked on a mouthful of tea. But no one knew apart from her and Pearl. And the fuckwit who had thieved it, of course.

'The gold?' she managed to say with the innocence of the angels. 'After all the cack it brought into our lives?' Babs thumped the table slightly with annoyance, not caring you might look over. 'I don't care where it pissed off to as long as it stays there.'

She shook her shoulders desperately seeking something to change the subject. 'Now tell me all about how my grandson's getting on with his new nanny.'

Dee didn't answer; instead she kept her gaze peeled on Babs. 'Do you think someone has got it?'

'Got what?' Babs was getting really uneasy. And frightened.

Dee pushed her cup slightly to the side to give her space to lean forward. 'I mean, what would you do if you had all that gold?'

Babs smacked her lips together with displeasure. 'Know what I'd do with it if it were sat here right now? I'd friggin' shove each bar down your throat coz I can't make head nor tail of why you're asking me these bollocks questions.' Not until she reached the end did Babs realise she was almost out of puff. 'What are you, the fucking police? I don't know where the gold is – OK? Satisfied? Unless someone's told you different.'

Dee grabbed her hand. Squeezed. 'Sorry Babs. It's just, you know, it vanishing like that. It's strange, isn't it?' She pierced Babs with a laser stare. 'So you don't know anything about it?'

Babs snatched her hand back and threw both hands in the air. 'What is this? Where's this come from? I've said till I'm blue in the face I don't wanna know. Have you forgotten that that gold was probably why your hubby keeled over and his toes turned up, poor fella?'

Her daughter's face drained of blood until her brown skin had the appearance of parched earth. 'I know,' Dee uttered softly. She closed her eyes and then stood up. 'I've got to go home now. I'll come back tomorrow Babs.'

'Go home? But you only just got here,' Babs protested as she scrambled to her feet. 'Come back upstairs with me, I could do with your strength by my side.'

Dee said nothing as she picked up her bag and walked off without saying goodbye. Babs felt her throat go dry and even swilling cold tea couldn't stop it. Only then did she clock she hadn't asked Dee whether she'd found those two characters who Courtney had said carried out the shooting.

Then an awful thought pushed her unsteadily back into her seat.

Did Dee know that she'd had the gold?

It was too terrible to contemplate. What if Pearl had got to her and blabbed the truth? Turning her own daughter against her? But Babs wouldn't allow herself to believe it. Even Pearl couldn't be such a total bitch. Could she?

Babs was on her mobile phone quicker than you can say 'bullion robbery.'

'Pearl? It's me—'

'Got my yellow for me yet?'

Babs chewed into the phone, 'Never mind that. You been grassing me up to my kid?'

'You what? I don't even know your daughters. Well, not really.'

Babs let out a calm breath. 'I got your text earlier and agreed where we should meet. I wanna get this sorted too. It's all getting out of hand.'

Silence greeted her request. Then, 'I think that's a good idea. The time and place good your end?'

'And we come on our own, no back up or silly games?'

'Works for me.'

Only after Babs finished the call did it occur to her that Dee had been calling her Babs, not mum. They'd got over that hurdle when John had passed over. So why was her Dee not calling her mum anymore?

Thirty-Seven

Ghosts. That's what confronted Babs as she stood outside the Bad Moon boozer in Shadwell. The ghost of Neville, Dee's dad, back in '72 as she manically searched for him here to tell him that fatherhood had come a-calling. The ghost of Stan Miller as he made dodgy deals with Faces and bent coppers, at a table in the back, away from prying eyes. The ghosts of proud, hardworking dockers whose livelihoods went down the crapper when the docks closed. The ol' place hadn't changed much from the outside. Still looked like a joint in a Victorian costume drama.

Babs peered through the grubby windows. No punters seemed to be in there. Mind you, it was never heaving even back in the day. More a meeting place for under the table business rather than on the table pints. But more importantly no Pearl.

Babs had timed it to arrive a good fifteen minutes before the agreed time for two reasons. First off, she wanted to check if Pearl had come armed and with back up. And second, Babs needed space to get her head straight, all her ducks in a line.

She walked in and up to the bar. 'You're quiet today.'

The barman was an old boy with very seasoned eyes who braced his hands far apart on the bar and his body forward as if he was a guard dog.

'What can I get ya?' A man of few words. Good! If anything untoward went down he'd keep his mouth zipped.

'I'll have half of something, Not fussed what.'

While he poured, Babs looked around the bar. There were a group of posh youngsters at a table trying to talk and act street, but no one else. There were two bars in the Bad Moon, the former Ladies Bar, which still had the word 'Ladies' written on a stained glass window and the really rough public bar.

The former Ladies Bar was empty. The perfect place to sit and hammer out a solution with Pearl. Light and Pale drink in hand, she took a seat in the snug, a part of the 'Ladies' which was neatly tucked away for those wanting to keep themselves to themselves, but more importantly, gave a view of the comings and goings at the door.

Babs knocked back a good portion of her drink and wiped her tongue across her lips. She was a tad nervous and not ashamed to admit it. Worse case scenario was that Pearl was a no-show. If that happened Babs was going to stomp down to that care home and have it out with her former mate. Whatever went on she was going to get it through Pearl's nut that she didn't have the gold.

Babs checked her watch and swore. Pearl was ten minutes late. If another ten minutes came and went that could only mean one thing – Pearl Hennessy wasn't putting in an appearance.

Restless, Babs drained her glass and got up and peered through the window like an urchin casing some tasty buns to pinch. That's when she spotted her. Pearl ambling along in a coat that appeared a couple of sizes too big and her customary headscarf. No Jamaican flag print this time though, it was black. Not a good sign.

Once Pearl entered they stood there staring at each other with the awkwardness of strangers meeting for the first time.

Pearl broke the silence. 'Hello Babsie.' Her eyes squinted. 'Checking the street to see if I'd brought my posse along for the ride?'

'And have ya?'

Pearl shook her head. 'I want to get this sorted as much as you do. We need to wash this bad blood away. Have—?'

'No, I haven't bought anyone to hold my hand. Now we've got the niceties out of the way shall we get down to business?'

Babs ordered the same drink again and Pearl a rum and black.

They sat for a few minutes in a choking silence before Babs lamented, shaking her head, 'How did things ever get this far? How did we ever let this get out of hand?'

Pearl's face softened. 'Dunno Babsie. We should have sat down from the off, even if you had the stuff…'

Babs' bristled, 'I ain't got it – let's knock that on the head from the get-go.'

Her former friend toughened up too, her small hand tightening so hard around her glass her knuckles were clear to see through her skin.

'I haven't got it either. Look Babsie-girl, I haven't come here to play she said-she said. I want this sorted out before someone gets hurt. You say you haven't got it. Fine. I say I haven't got it. Fine. So who else could have taken it? You must've said something to someone – that Kieran Scott for starters. Maybe he found out and wanted to get his hands back on the gold, the crafty little beggar.'

The flippin' cheek! As if Kieran would have it away. Babs ground her teeth together; she didn't like anyone taking the rise out of her boy whatever had happened in the meantime. She reminded herself they were here to make peace so she loosened the grip of her jaw.

'I never said nish to no one, got it? I was Stanley Miller's other half and let me tell you, I learned all about how to keep secrets. I know too many of them, know what I mean?' She took a breath needing her next words to sound neutral not angry. 'You must've let it slip to someone. Maybe not on purpose, but somehow it just escaped. These things happen.'

When Pearl opened her palms and held them high Babs thought, here we fucking go. She wasn't in the mood for one of Pearl's commune with the spirits moments.

Babs relaxed when Pearl shrugged. 'Those kinda things don't happen to me, let me tell you. You're forgetting I was the one hiding the stuff, I had most to lose if people came barging in looking for it.'

Babs leaned forward, her voice low with sympathy. 'No disrespect, but we're all getting on so maybe you were having a senior moment, so you forgot about it.'

Pearl kissed her teeth softly. 'Forgot about it, my back foot. A fox never forgets her hole. As if I could forget that there's gold under my backside every day.'

Babs wasn't giving up. 'Perhaps someone spotted it in your room—'

Pearl slapped her forehead. ''Of course. I forgot!' At last they were getting somewhere. Babs let out a long, noisy sigh of relief. 'I had Superman and his X-Ray eyes over for tea. Or is that Spiderman? I can't remember.'

Babs nearly screamed in frustration, her gaze dancing around the pub. 'Come on Pearl. There's gotta…' She trailed off her gaze fixed in the distance. Her mouth tightened. 'Could you excuse me a second Pearl, I gotta powder my nose.'

Babs got up and marched into the main bar. When she was out of Pearl's eye line, she hoisted herself up on the bar and let herself down the other side.

''Ere, what the hell are you doing?' the barman rasped, his gaze jumping.

Babs threw daggers his way. He knew exactly what she was doing. She crouched down and made her way along, pushing past the barman as she did so. He rapidly took himself to the other end of the bar and turned his back.

'What the fuck are you doing here?' Babs wanted to shout but she kept her growl to a minimum so as not to alert Pearl.

A very guilty looking Tiff and Flo were hiding by a crate of brew. Tiff avoided her gaze and it was left to Flo to whisper, 'We followed you—'

'Effing sakes mum,' Tiff punched over, 'Flo saw the text from Pearl on your mobile saying you were meeting her here - The Bad Moon of all places - about the gold.' Tiff's eyes bugged wide on the word, 'gold.'

Flo didn't seem so fazed. 'We were scared for you. That gold is bad news.'

It had been going well with Pearl or at least they were talking. 'I can't talk now. But I need both of you not to stick your oars…'

Her voice froze as she noticed their gazes fixed on something over her head.

Babs pivoted around. Shit! Bollocks! Pearl looked down on them, arms tensely folded.

She shook her head in disgust, her dark eyes blazing. 'I trusted you Babsie. What a fool I was.'

Pearl stepped back. Her hand reached under her headscarf and, of all things, she pulled out a small mobile phone. It didn't take her long to get it on. 'You were right after all. She's come mob-handed. My mistake.'

Babs and her girls shot to their feet as the front door banged open.

Pinky and Styley burst in. The brothers didn't zero in on them but on the upmarket lads at the table who were mesmerised by the unfolding drama like they'd bagged the best seats in the house.

'Out,' Pinky yelled at them.

One made the mistake of answering. 'Now, steady on—'

The brothers were on them in a flash and grabbed them by the collar and threw them out onto the pavement. Styley advised the barman to go for a walk. He didn't argue, slipping into the back.

Pinky bolted the door and joined his grandmother. The brothers stood on either side of her looking very pleased with themselves. Not to be out done, Flo and Tiff did the same to Babs.

'Came on your own, did ya?' Babs spat, her face filled with thunder to rival the changing weather outside. 'You're the biggest, all-time liar there is.'

Pearl proudly announced, 'While you're on your tod? Is that right? These are my grand boys, Pinky and Styley.'

'The bastards who shot my Jen?' Babs screamed. She rushed forward gripped with a raging madness, but Tiff pulled her back.

'What?' Pearl was stunned.

'She's chatting out of her bum hole grams,' Styley said. 'You can't believe a word she says as you've just discovered. We don't know no Jen.'

Pinky pulled a revolver from his pocket while Styley drew a heavy cosh from his trousers and tapped it in his palm.

'These two birds her backup? Not exactly the Sopranos, is it?' Pinky sneered.

Flo pulled out her own surprise - a silver pistol. 'I can match you shot for shot. I clean out plastic gangsters like you and then go for a burger and coke. You wanna shoot it out? Give it a try.'

It wasn't the right moment for Babs to think about her journey with Flo but she felt a surge of pride in the girl. She reminded Babs of Stan back in his younger, cooler days.

Pinky's features turned nasty as he looked Flo up and down. 'Tough girl, eh? Put your toy away, you're playing with big boys here.'

Flo laughed. 'Oh yeah, I'm tough alright. And I don't wear girly pink either.'

The strange thing was it was like Flo and Pinky were in their own little world, trying to match shooter for shooter, dirty look for dirty look. Neither was willing to back down. A wave of electric tension passed between them. They bared their teeth at each other. Muscles bunched with alertness, ready to spring.

A quick tap-tap-tap at the locked door grabbed everyone's attention.

Pearl nodded to Styley. 'Answer it.'

He was incredulous. 'You're joking, it could be the law.'

'It's not the Plod. I said answer it.' She used her 'grandmother knows best' voice.

As Styley walked over to the window his brother smiled at Flo and put his gun away so Flo lowered hers to her side. Styley looked outside. Then he pulled back the bolt and the door swung open.

In walked Dee Black. No! No! No! Dee couldn't be here. She couldn't find out about Babs and the gold. Not like this.

'Dee baby…' she started.

Her daughter cut her off as she questioned, 'What's happened?'

Babs was gobsmacked because the question wasn't directed at her but to that double crossing cow Pearl. Her tummy started churning. Something was deeply wrong here. Very wrong indeed. She looked desperately to Tiff and Flo for an explanation. One arched her brow, the other shrugged. They didn't have a clue either.

Pearl said with sarky pointedness, 'your mum brought her youngest girl and Calamity Jane here with the short. So, as you can see, we've got a situation.'

Dee was unfazed. 'Yeah, but you brought your fan club too.'

'Yes, I did, but I left them outside as a reserve in case I needed them, which it turns out I did.'

Dazed, Babs' eyes swung from one to the other in disbelief. 'Dee, what's going on?'

Then her heart nearly cracked wide open when her eldest daughter sauntered to stand by Pearl like she was her right hand. This had to be a dream, right? More like the worst nightmare ever.

Babs gasped, 'Dee luv, get away from that woman now.' In response Dee lengthened her spine and stood her ground. 'You're on the wrong side. You should be standing here with your family. What the hell are you doing?'

When the answer came, it didn't come from Dee.

The handle of the pub's office, behind the bar, turned. A tall, handsome, older black man stepped into the bar. Babs put her hand on Tiff's shoulder to steady herself.

No way.

It couldn't be.

'Neville?' Stunned she gulped as her legs turned to jelly.

As her world began crashing down around her Babs shouted, no question this time, 'Neville Campbell!'

Thirty-Eight

'That's right, you remember my dad, Neville, don't ya mum?'

Dee's voice cracked like a whip, her face contorted in a way Babs had never seen before.

It matched the ugliness growing in Babs at the nerve of this man. Turning up like an unwanted guest at the Christmas table. How dare he! And Dee standing alongside him like he was the Angel Gabriel after all she'd told her about this bastard.

Babs turned on Dee. 'Oh yeah, I remember him alright.' She was losing the battle to keep her voice under control. 'The man who had more of a crush on his hair than me? He left us Dee. Didn't wanna know. I'd never stop you wanting to get to know him, if that's what you choose, but what I don't get is why he's here. Now.'

Babs noticed that Pinky and Styley had stood to attention like a couple of soldiers when Neville had appeared. And if he was something to do with them then he was connected to Pearl.

She threw her accusation at Pearl. 'This chancer something to do with you Pearl, ain't he?'

'Younger brother.' Neville supplied the answer. 'And the

lads are my great-nephews, Pearl's grandsons.' He stepped fully into the room, his gaze never leaving Babs. 'It's been a long time.'

Babs laughed bitterly. 'Oh, you mean since you told me to fuck right off on Mile End Road, back in '72, when you got an eyeful of my big belly. You were a nasty piece of work then and I suspect that's still the name of the game.' Her furious gaze swung to her eldest daughter. 'Betcha he never told you that he was with some other woman and her baby when I bumped into him that day? Your old fella is a man who loves to spreading his seed far and wide.'

Dee raised her chin. 'Dad's told me all bout his ex-lady and kid.'

Dad...

Babs turned the flashing daggers in her eyes back onto her former boyfriend. 'Playing happy families were ya.' She clapped her hands with mock applause. Then abruptly stopped as a thought struck her. 'Oh, I get it. It's all becoming crystal clear. Pearl gets the grandkids as the muscle side of the operation and they're backed up by head honcho Neville here who's obviously moved a lot further up the criminal food chain since he legged it outta my life. *Our* life. And to keep it all in the family, they decided to poison my daughter against me. What's the matter with you Dee? You been hooking up and listening to this crowd of chancers? What's the matter with you?'

Babs angrily marched over to Neville. 'You wanna know about your old dad? I'll tell you about him. I'll tell you about how back in the day, a jury wouldn't hang a dog on his evidence, no matter how many Bibles he swore on. He's filling your head full of prime shit and you're believing every venomous word of it. I thought I brought you up better than that.'

Dee slowly moved to Babs. 'But you never brought me up, did you?'

If someone had twisted a knife in Babs' heart it couldn't have hurt more than Dee reminding her about their tragic history.

Dee carried on. 'Yeah, you're right. He did tell me a lot of stuff, things you never felt like talking about even when I asked. Of course, I didn't know whether they were true or not. But the one thing I could check turned out to be true.' Dee's voice shook with emotion. 'I asked you, point blank, if you knew what happened to John's gold and you insisted that you didn't. I gave you every chance to fess up and you fobbed me off. But it wasn't true, was it? You did know what happened to it. You and Aunty Pearl had it all along and you never said a word'

Babs shuddered at hearing her girl call Pearl 'Aunty'.

Dee continued, 'Even when I asked you flat out, you denied it. So when my dad tells me that you were ashamed of your little black baby, ashamed of its black father and you turned your back on the both of us, you know what? I'm inclined to believe him, not you.'

Babs wilted like a flower in winter. 'I hid the gold to stop it destroying my family—'

'Well, you did a good job of that, didn't you Babs,' Dee barked with such fury it was a wonder none of the glasses shattered in the bar. 'My John died because of that gold and all the time you were keeping it for yourself—'

'No way Dee, I'd never—'

Dee stepped back as her mother desperately reached out

to her. 'If you'd told me where it was maybe my wonderful husband would still be alive today.'

Babs stabbed her finger in the air, her anger building again. 'John was long gone by the time Pearl discovered he'd been stashing it in one of my houses.'

'Houses you got from Stanley Miller. You probably diddled him out of those as well.' Tiff gasped in outrage but didn't butt in as Dee's tirade gathered steam. 'You made sure I never knew my dad, pushed Stan out of your life so he never got to know his girls. What kind of mum are you? The Black Widow kind, that's what.'

Babs marched the remaining distance between them and slapped Dee hard and harshly across the face. The sound was a whip crack in a sea of blistering silence. Her fingers fluttered to her trembling mouth, the blood draining from her face realising what she'd done. 'Dee, babe, I never meant—'

Her words dribbled away as her daughter turned her face away. 'I'm grateful for everything you've done for me, but you're done, you're shot. I don't wanna hear anymore of your stories.' Her voice turned hard as steel. 'What I do want is John's gold back.'

Babs thrust her hand into her hair in utter frustration.

'How many times have I gotta say I don't have it? They're playing you Dee. Pearl's got it tucked away. All that hunched shoulder shit she does is a game. Wants people to feel sorry for her and then she goes in for the kill. Don't believe a word that comes out of her evil gob.'

Babs turned on Neville. 'You proud of yourself, are ya? Have a bit of fun reversing the truth. Because that's the only thing you were ever good at, wasn't it? Telling lies and scalping girls.

Neville's face said nothing but his eyes twinkled. 'You'd be surprised Babs. I've learned to be good at a lot of things since the days when you left me and dumped my daughter—'

'You...' Babs lunged at him, fists at the ready, but she was dragged back by Flo.

Stan's daughter urgently whispered in her ear, 'He's not worth it.' Her fierce gaze did a circle of Pearl's family. 'None of 'em are. Especially you,' she spat at Dee.

Dee lashed back at Flo, 'and you're here in training as the next Mother Teresa I suppose? Give me a break! Only one reason you gate crashed Babs' place and that's to report back to your granddad on any info on the whereabouts of the gold. You know I've hit the bullseye so fess the fuck up.'

Flo suddenly looked peaky, but didn't rise to the bait. She merely arched a mocking eyebrow.

'I knew the Commander very well back in our Soho days,' Pearl uttered softly as if telling a bedtime story. Her lip curled with bitterness. 'A flash, posh Harry full of lies and bullshit bollocks. Do tell Jimmy that Pearlie sends her love.' With disdain she blew Flo a kiss.

Neville gently took Dee's arm. 'Come on daughter, Babs' lies are stinking the place out. She just can't stop herself.'

He gestured at his great-nephews and then escorted his daughter out.

Desperate, like a teenager who'd just been dumped for her best friend, Babs ran outside after them screaming, 'Get your lying mitts off my daughter. Let's talk Dee. I can prove it was him who ran out on us, anyone will tell you. Let me tell you about the gold...'

Neville abruptly stopped and used his big hand to push her backwards. Babs stumbled to the side and fell in the road. She didn't get up, bowed her head and sobbed.

Tiff gathered her mum to her feet as Flo swore a blue streak and flew after Neville and Dee.

Pinky stopped in his tracks and twisted to face her. 'Back off little gal.'

Flo held her arms wide. 'Make me.'

He scoffed, scornfully taking the measure of her with those startling blue eyes in his brown face. 'Why don't you fuck off back to your yard and play with your dolls?'

'I see you anywhere near Babs again you'll end up as stiff as a doll, you shit-faced cunt.'

He cut his teeth at her, dissed her with his eyes and made his way to the car. Someone's mobile started ringing as Babs pushed out of Tiff's arms and ran desperately towards the departing car. With fury she thumped it.

The back window wound down and Styley warned, 'My cousin Dee wants her old man's gold back. Make sure she gets it.'

The car's engine revved, wheels turned and it sped off. Half mad with grief Babs tried to chase it down the street begging for Dee to hear her out.

'Mum!' Tiffany shouted.

Babs didn't hear her. All she could hear were the wheels of the SUV taking her daughter further and further away from her. Her hands clenched hopelessly at her side. She was losing her girl all over again. Probably never see her precious Natty either.

Suddenly Tiff was by her side. She took her shaking mum by the arm and whispered, face ashen.

'That was the hospital.'

As they drove triumphantly away Pinky's mobile went off.

'What do you want?' he growled, none too pleased at who was on the other end of the line.

'I've got something that might be of interest,' the Salesman stammered.

Pinky twisted his lips as the motor turned a corner. The Salesman knew how their relationship played out – they got on the blower to him not the other way round.

'You looking to get those delicate hands of yours mashed up?' Pinky threatened. Any mention of damaging this man's hands had him hightailing it for the hills.

'No.' Strangely the other man didn't sound like he was shitting a brick. 'But this is about my hands.'

Pinky's interest was peaked. He frowned deeply. 'What you chatting on about?'

Pinky could feel The Salesman smile. 'I might be able to get my hands on something for you…'

Thirty-Nine

One daughter had just waltzed out of her life and now the hospital was telling her another might do the same. How could life be so cruel? Babs wanted to howl her anger and rage to the heavens. Jen couldn't die, she couldn't. Babs wasn't ready for this. She only realised her legs were slipping from under her when Tiff caught and guided her gently to a chair.

The solemn-faced doctor stood next to her as Tiff and Flo sat by her side.

He said, 'She developed a blood clot and is in surgery as we speak. Our best surgeon is working on her.'

'How long will the surgery last?' Flo asked.

It was just as well Flo could speak for her because Babs couldn't utter a single word. The ensuing conversation floated around her. She didn't even know when the doctor left or when Tiff asked if she wanted a cuppa or a puff on something. Nothing mattered except Jen. What the heck was she going to tell Courtney and Little Bea if their mum never came home?

How long they sat there before Tiff shook her arm she'd never know. But she raised her head to find the doctor standing there again. Bloody hell it must've been hours.

'Mrs Miller we've removed the blood clot. Jen still remains in a coma. We are closely monitoring—'

'Will my girl wake up?' she croaked.

'We don't know Mrs Miller. We just don't know.'

What was that?

Flo woke up, on high alert. It was still pitch black. She strained an ear towards the bedroom door. Yeah, there it went again. Some kinda noise either in the hallway or another room. It's a wonder she could hear anything with Tiff snoring for all she was worth on her reclaimed bed. She slipped out of the camper bed and picked up Tiff's poker. If Pinky and Styley were in the flat there was going to be murder on The Devil tonight.

Travelling softly, the way her dad had taught her to creep up on someone, she opened the door and walked into the corridor. Stopped and listened. A snuffling sound, very faint, which was coming from what she called a lounge and Stan had told her folks in the East End called a sitting room.

It had become Babs' temporary bedroom. Flo felt the heaviness of the poker in her hand, her face grim. If some cunt was in there causing Babs grief she'd brain the bastard. She inched towards the lounge and listened. Sounded like the breathing of one person. Babs.

And she was crying.

Flo leaned the poker in the corner and opened the door. Babs was sitting in the dark. She was hunched over on her makeshift bed on the settee, head in her hands, her shoulders shaking with sobs. The sight of Babs in such a state left Flo feeling upset. Funny that; this was someone she'd once vowed to destroy.

'Mummy Babs?' she asked hesitantly, then realised what she'd called Babs. She didn't have a clue where that had come from.

Startled, Babs half twisted as Flo entered and closed the door quietly behind her.

Babs blew her nose with a tissue and said too brightly, 'this hay flippin' fever's killing me. You go back to bed girl.'

Flo nearly answered it was the wrong time of year for hay fever, but it looked like Babs would spring another leak if she put her on the back foot. Best keep it to herself.

Flo crept closer until she stood in front of the older woman. When she caught sight of Babs' face she sucked in her breath. Her father's former wife was the picture of a broken woman with marble-white skin and a lifeless, lost look in her cried out eyes.

Flo hunkered down on her knees beside Babs, her gaze searching her distraught face. 'Not that long ago I'd rather have chocked than say this, but you're a strong woman Mummy Babs, one of the strongest I know. Jen's gonna pull through, you mark my words.'

Babs looked like a wounded animal unable to lick its wounds. 'My baby's gone again.'

Flo frowned hard. 'What baby?' Blimey, this family had more skeletons than the royal family.

'My Dee.' Oh, that very big baby. Babs wiped her nose. 'I was already carrying her when I met your dad and he did me a turn by marrying me, which didn't turn out to be the best move of my life.' She shook her head. 'I won't tell you all of the ins and outs, but I didn't bring Dee up. I lost her.' Her voice caught in her throat. 'We re-connected again when she got big. Now I've lost her again.'

Babs started heaving and weeping loudly. "I'm a bad mum, aren't I? I must be to lose my darling Dee twice in one lifetime.'

Flo sprang up, shoved in next to Babs and took her in her arms. She rocked her as the other woman cried and cried.

'You're the best mum I've ever seen.' And Flo meant that. 'Dee will be back, believe you me. All she wants to do is to get to know her father. I know what that feels like, I've been there. But you know what?' Gently she pulled back so she could see Babs' face. 'When she realises what an colossal twat this Neville is she'll come running to the person she knows loves her the most – her mum.'

Babs pulled a packet of tabs out of her dressing gown pocket and stared hard at them. 'I called these my Annies, my anxiety pills. I fought hard and long in prison to get off 'em and haven't taken one in over two years.' Her face twisted in pain. 'But with Dee gone and Jen battling for her life I feel like I've walked over the edge of a cliff and maybe my Annies will help me cling on.'

Flo took on the mum's role. 'No way are you swallowing any of that lot after you moved heaven and earth to see yourself straight.' She stretched out her palm with a 'give me' gaze and, after a moments hesitation, Babs placed them in her hand.

Flo took Babs' hand and guided her to her feet. 'Time for you to get some shut-eye.'

Flo sorted the settee out until it resembled a bed and got Babs tucked up.

'See you in the morning,' Flo said softly.

As she made her way to the door Bab's voice stopped her. 'I like you calling me Mummy Babs.'

Flo froze. Then, without turning round, whispered, 'I do too.'

Only when she was back in bed did Flo realise there were tears in her eyes. She'd never had a close relationship with her own mum. If only she felt as close to her blood mother as she did to Babs. She picked up her mobile and scrolled through her texts until she got to the last one sent by the Commander:

Have those pirates got my pieces of eight?

The 'pirates' were the Millers. The 'pieces of eight' the gold.

Flo knew she faced a life-changing dilemma. Jen getting shot had changed everything. Jen was her flesh and blood. Her sister. She wanted to smash the bastards who had shot her. Plus, what Flo hadn't factored in was coming under Babs Miller's maternal spell. Babs dolled out kisses and hugs like they were going out of fashion, something Flo had never had in her life. Her granddad was an old rogue not a substitute parent. Her real mum a waste of space. It was never said but when her mum looked at her she had that glint in her eye that stated loud and clear Flo was the spit of her father, the man who had conned her into marriage. Who would've thought that coming to live on some poxy estate in Mile End she'd have found the family she'd always craved.

But she desperately loved the Commander too. What was she going to do?

Flo dry swallowed two of Babs' Annies.

Then texted her Gramps back:

Think I've found your pieces of eight.

Forty

'Are you sure this is what you want to do?' Babs asked her granddaughter the following morning.

Courtney nodded as she sat at the breakfast table next to her sister. Although Babs had been grateful for Flo's pick-me-up talk and giving her a shoulder to cry on she still hadn't got much kip last night. Dee would come to her senses; she had to. Her girl would soon find out her dad was a no-good user in the same mould as Stanley Miller.

Of course, Stan and Neville knew each other; two peas in a criminal pod. A couple of cheap crooks. Successful ones admittedly, but crooks none the less. She must've been giving off some kinda 'dumb girl' scent when she was younger; how else could she have attracted so many creeps? So fucking what if Neville was Pearl's brother and they were playing the Big I Am, spouting off about wanting the gold. They were going to be mightily disappointed; she didn't have it. And as for those two wearing pink…well, she'd seen better enforcers on Danger Mouse.

Babs put her troubles behind her – for now – and gazed at the slap up brekkie she'd put on for her grandkids. Their plates were arranged in smiley faces – poached eggs eyes, sausage eyebrows, tomato nose and bacon mouth. Only problem was Courtney and Little Bea weren't smiling. Plus, they were picking at their plates.

Babs plonked down in a chair and sighed. It was silly trying to pretend everything was normal and she knew it and that's why she quietly asked Courtney, 'You sure it's the right time to go back to school?'

Courtney lowered her washout eyes as her slim fingers tightened round her fork. 'I can't keep going to the ozzie.' Her voice was barely above a whisper.

All the troubles of the world showed up on Babs' face again. Where was a magic wand when you needed it? A bit of abracadabra to make her grandbabies smile again? Aww, wouldn't that be a blessing.

'Don't you wanna see your mum?'

Courtney raised her head slowly. She rubbed her lips fretfully together. 'But what if I'm there and she dies?'

Babs' heart thundered in her chest. 'No. That's not gonna happen. The only place your mum's going is back home where she belongs with you and Little Bea.'

Her gaze shifted to take in her other granddaughter and what she saw made Babs chew her bottom lip with worry. Little Bea's real name was Sasha, but when she was small she'd been her Nanna Babs' shadow, so one and all had started calling her Little Bea. Little Bea said nothing as she stared into space. In fact her namesake hadn't said a word since her mum had been shot. And, come to think of it, Babs hadn't seen her cry either: not one teardrop. That was strange, wasn't it? Especially considering the close relationship Jen had with her. Babs shrugged. We all have our ways of dealing with things even when we're little, so best leave Little Bea to hers.

Babs' lips flattened into a concerned line as she stared at the upside book next to Little Bea's plate. She turned her head slightly sideways to catch the title:

'Killers In The Night'

Fuck me! A shiver of alarm ran down her spine. A ten-year-old reading muck like that? Especially with her mum being laid up in the ozzie with a gunshot. It wasn't normal. She'd had it out with Jen once about the grisly tales she let her girl read and all Jen protested back was that they helped with her reading; in fact Little Bea was predicted to get a level 5 in her SATs reading test. That might be so, but Babs still didn't approve. Her grandbaby should be reading about little ponies and princesses with golden hair. Mind you, she'd read those types books and instead of handsome prince she'd ended up with a right pair of Jekyll and Hyde frogs.

'What about you hun?' Babs broached carefully with the true crime fanatic. 'You wanna go to school?'

Little Bea violently shook her head, but not a word left her little mouth. Babs didn't like this one bit. There was something wrong. Maybe she should get on the blower to that therapist lady that had ironed out Courtney last year. And Babs was good for it with the dosh from the sale of the her houses.

'I better go Nanna Babs,' Courtney said getting to her feet, 'or I'll be late.'

'But you ain't finished your brekkie.' The girl had hardly touched a bite.

Courtney lifted one side of her shoulder in a shrug. 'I only usually have cereal.'

'Cereal ain't food,' Babs muttered. 'You need something solid and hot in you to keep you going until lunchtime.'

Courtney suddenly launched herself at her, flinging her arms round her almost knocking Babs backwards in her chair. Babs clung onto her, holding on tight.

'It's gonna be alright, you hear. Everything's gonna come good,' she crooned over and over.

A few minutes later Babs waved her happily off at the door but as soon as Courtney turned the corner of the balcony Babs' cheer dropped turning into a fierce scowl. That girl was putting on a brave front if ever she saw one. What if Courtney fell to pieces at school? Jen had been on top of the moon at Courtney getting a place at that posh all girls' outfit in town, but Babs wasn't so convinced it was the right move. If Courtney went into meltdown that fancy headmistress would probably tell her to buck up and feed her some stiff upper lip shit.

Babs was distracted by an almighty row coming from inside the flat. She rolled her eyes heavenward. Give me strength. Looked like she was going to have to knock some heads together. Again!

She found Tiff and Flo going at it in the doorway of the bathroom. In their night clothes no less. Flo in a tiny T-shirt with enough sparkle and glitter for a glam rock band and Tiff almost in the all-together. Spitting and snarling with the back alley manners of two cats fighting over a fish bone.

'I got here first.'

'No, you didn't.'

'You always leave water all over the gaff.'

'Least I don't leave it smelling like a sumo wrestler's jockstrap.'

''Ark who's talking, the woman with half the black forest hanging outta her armpits.'

Babs couldn't tell who was saying what, insults flying left, right and sideways. Her head reared back as something suddenly occurred to her; their faces were almost carbon copies of each other. Thanks to Stan's oats spreading, it was his face that stared right back at her. They had been born months apart which made them almost twins really. The girls would go ape if she pointed that out to them.

Instead she fumed, fists flying onto her hips. 'Will you please knock it on the head, the pair o' ya.'

They took not a lick of notice. Right, that was it. Time to remind these two blockheads who was paying the bills round here. Babs marched into the kitchen, filled a bucket, stomped back and, with a gratified smile, chucked the water at them.

With pleasure Babs watched them gasp and splutter as the water dripped down their scanty clothing.

'What the fuck did ya do that for?' Tiff groused, shivering as she madly wiped water from her dumbstruck face.

Flo had the grace to keep it schtum.

Babs stabbed her finger at each in turn. 'I will not have this carry on in my drum. Got it? Jen's fighting for her life in the ozzie, her girls are stopping here, probably scared out of their young wits, and all you two numpties can do is go at it like spoiled babies. Give us all a fucking break will ya.' Only at the end did Babs realise her voice had risen to raise the roof status.

She threw the bucket on the carpet drained to her very bones. She meandered, like a sleepwalker, to the sitting room and plonked down on the settee. If only Tricky Dickie were here so she could lay her weary head on his strong shoulder.

'Sorry mum.' Babs looked up to find the pair looking sheepish in the doorway.

Flo added, 'Yeah, apologies Mummy Babs.'

Tiff took off with firecracker intensity again. ''Ere, she ain't your mummy anything, got…' She clammed up when she clocked the furious threat lighting up Babs' face.

Tiff leaned against the doorframe and folded her arms. 'What you gonna do bout Dee?'

The million-dollar question.

'What can I do?' Babs raised her hands hopelessly in the air surprised she had the energy to move them. 'She's a grown woman. A mother herself. Knows her own mind.' Helpless, that's what she felt. The family she'd built with her own bare hands crumbling right in front of her.

Flo stuck in her two pence worth. 'That Neville being her dad *and* Pearl's brother, what a turn up for the books that was.'

Fury piled high inside Babs just hearing that fucker's name. 'Ain't it just. That bastard left me in the right lurch back in the day.' Those weren't easy memories for her to dwell on.

'Don't want to say this mum, but you really know how to pick 'em…Oi!' Tiff finished on as Flo elbowed her in the side.

'The important thing is,' Flo began, 'how to we get Dee and her thieving relatives to understand you don't have the gold.'

A sharp rat-a-tat at the front door got in the way of Babs' answer. Flo moved towards the door, but Babs' sharp voice stopped her. 'What the heck you doing?' Her gaze roved over the younger woman's clothing, or lack there of. 'If it's the postman you'll give him kittens. Anyroads, you're both ruining my carpet and I only bought it down the Roman four months back.'

'Serves you right for being handy with a bucket.' Tiff having a snide.

Ignore her. Babs did just that and headed for the door. When she opened it her mouth formed an O; no one was there. But there was a good-sized cake box with a ribbon wrapped around it, lying on the ground. Her lips split into a grin. Probably one of the good people on The Devil trying to support her during her time of need.

Babs picked it up, took it inside and kicked the door shut behind her. Then an idea came to her.

'Little Bea,' she sang out as she moved towards the kitchen.

Her granddaughter presented herself, mercifully minus 'Killers In The Night'. Babs knew Little Bea had a sweet tooth.

'Look what I've got.' She held the cake box temptingly up and winked. 'Park yourself down and we'll have a slice or two.'

Little Bea nodded, but no light lit up her gaze as she sat down. No matter, she'll be grinning away when she took her first bite.

Humming away Babs placed the box on the table, gathered two small plates and a bread knife.

'I'm hoping this is a chocolate cake, your fav.' She said.

Babs flipped back the lid of the box and screamed when she clocked the contents.

A hand grenade and a handwritten note attached in capital writing:

'MILLER YOU THIEVING SLAG
WANT OUR GOLD
NOW.'

Forty-One

'Bout bleedin' time too, thought Courtney as the change of lesson buzzer screeched over the Tannoy system putting a merciful end to the mind-blowingly boring violin lesson. Hells bells, what would the kids on The Devil say if they saw her toting a violin? Take the proper piss outta her for one with some smart arse claiming you could smoke the strings and get high.

She loathed this school but it was better than stopping indoors at her Nan's. All that chat about what happened to her mum was doing her head in, big time. It hurt so much to see her mum lying there fighting for her very life and knowing she'd played a big part in it. If only she had stopped mad bird Dodgy from gatecrashing the club none of this would've gone on. The only person she'd confessed her part in it to was Aunty Dee when she'd coughed up about those two gun-toting tossers Pinky and Styley. Aunty Dee had pulled enough strokes when she was a young un and so hadn't given Courtney the third degree and, more importantly, promised to keep what she had told her hush-hush. However, it didn't lessen the guilt she carried.

'Right ladies,' Mr Baxter called out interrupting her

thoughts, 'don't forget to continue to practice those glide-like movements on your bow.'

Mr Baxter was one of the few male teachers and he was every inch the creative type with his floppy, brown hair, sun-tanned skin and standout baby blues. Courtney didn't fancy him herself but plenty of the other girls had the hots for him. Some of them now giggled behind their hands. Courtney rolled her eyes; what a bunch of rank babies, carrying on as if they'd never seen anything in trousers before. Mind you, he was such a lovely bloke, with a gentle manner and a voice as soft and as sweet as when he played his violin.

As the girls put their instruments away, getting ready to rush off to their maths class, Mr Baxter turned his kind eyes to her.

'Courtney, if you don't mind staying behind for a minute.'

If looks could kill Courtney would be stone dead with the vicious, envious gazes the other girls slung her way. She ignored the lot of them. They could piss off to high heaven; most of them didn't like her and were blatant about showing it. An East End girl coming to their school was too much to swallow. Well, tough tats; she'd earned her place fair and square and was going to do her Nanna Babs and mum proud.

'What do you want to see me about sir?' Courtney nervously asked as soon as they were on their own.

Crikey! He'd better not be getting ready to go into, 'I'm sorry about your mum' patter. She'd had a bellyful of that with the headmistress and nearly blubbed her heart out. She was bone tired of crying, all she wanted was for her mum to open her eyes and come home.

He gave her an encouraging smile, tiny, gentle lines creasing the corners of his eyes. 'I noticed that your left arm and shoulder still need strengthening to hold your violin properly.'

Courtney heaved a small sigh of relief that he wasn't going there about her mum. 'I have been practising sir.'

A big, fat, porkie, of course. She was a crap violin player, no two ways about it, so why bother practice? The screech she made was enough to make deaf dogs on the estate run for cover.

He moved towards her. His voice was soft and easy. 'I've got an exercise that will really help you. Place your violin in the usual position.'

She did so awkwardly, shoving the instrument under her chin. Felt like she was wearing a neck brace. Her mum in the ozzie flashed in her mind. Tubes coming out of her, face sickly pale, the life draining out of her.

'Courtney?' Her teacher's voice snapped her back into the music room. 'Are you OK?'

Her breathing was doing strange stuff in her chest. 'Yes sir.'

Mr Baxter smiled at her, didn't utter a word. He must've sensed how she was feeling but was in tune enough with her to keep it to himself. What a guy!

His hands suddenly fluttered nervously in front of him. 'Is it alright for me to touch you, so I can show you the correct position?'

'Yeah, o' course sir.'

He coughed timidly as he stepped behind her. His body leaned into her as he placed his hand over hers that held the violin to her neck.

His other arm snaked violently round her waist.

He slammed her back into his body and growled, 'You want to tell your grandma Babs to mind her step.'

Courtney shook with absolute terror not able to believe what was happening. 'Mr Baxter, what are you doing?'

She tried desperately to wriggle away but he held her neck so tight she could feel his hot breath gliding down her neck.

'You tell her that Pearl wants her gold back, you hear?'

His hand over hers jammed the violin hard into her throat until she was gagging for air.

'I said do you hear me?' he snarled like a man possessed.

Mr Baxter had turned into a raving loon and Courtney was trembling uncontrollable with fright. How did he know about her Nanna Babs? And how did he know about her fallout with her mate Pearl? Courtney shook from head to foot terrified of what he might do so she nodded her head as quickly as she could.

'You better tell her,' he did a horrible pause, 'or else this is what will happen to you the next time I see you...'

Abruptly he let go of her taking the violin with him. He snapped the neck off it and chucked the broken instrument on the floor.

Courtney gasped for breath as she stumbled away. On shaking legs she grabbed her bag and belted out of the music room.

Mr Baxter, aka The Salesman, calmly lifted a satisfied eyebrow as he watched her go. He didn't earn much as a part-time music teacher so when Pinky and Styley had approached him with the proposition to clear his gambling debts to earn some ready cash he'd jumped at the chance. In return all they wanted was an ordinary looking Joe with an upmarket accent to help get new customers to sign up to their protection racket. As soon as he'd realised that one of his girls, Courtney, belonged to the Miller family the brothers were feuding with he'd got straight on to his mobile to Pinky. Now they'd added a new bow to his work for them. Now he was a proper villain. He was threatening people not flogging insurance. A new bow…He laughed at that. Clever!

It was happy hour for Courtney as she emptied the last drops of a bottle of a supermarket own brand of voddy that she'd half inched from a store during lunch break. She sat in the toilet cubicle still quaking from her dust up with Mr Baxter. Tears ran down her face as she curled over and sobbed until her chest hurt. All she could see was him snapping the neck of her violin and then threatening to do the same to her. Some kind of hard man he was putting the frighteners on a young girl like her. Just like her dad who had battered her mum black and blue whenever he felt like. Her granddad Stan had been the same, trying to choke the life outta of her Nan. She'd put a stop to her granddad but who was going to put a stop to Barmy Baxter?

Courtney put her hand over her mouth as she gagged. This paint stripper taken on an empty stomach was trying to make its way straight back up again. She was going to have to tell her Nanna Babs what he'd….but she didn't want to. She didn't want any more bother, but what choice did she have? It was either let on to her nan or her neck was going to end up like her violin.

Courtney stiffened as footsteps briskly click-clacked passed the loo's main door. She was too off her face to tell the time but she knew she'd been gone from her geography class way to long. She stood up, swayed like a sail in the wind and held on to the wall to get her bearings right. Courtney dumped the empty bottle in the toilet cistern and quickly chewed two soft mints as she set off to class.

Mrs Pringle, the geography teacher, was going on about tropical rainforests or something when Courtney entered. The room went silent as every eye landed on her. Courtney tried to look sober. It didn't come off though; she was too far gone. Fuck the lot of 'em. She gave one and all the evil eye.

Most of these poxy girls hadn't ever taken the time to be her friend. They all thought she was the wrong girl in the wrong place, just because their families were doughed up and hers wasn't. Being the scholarship girl was like having a red cross on the door during the plague.

'Miller,' Mrs Pringle snapped, 'you've been gone for nearly twenty minutes. Lessons in this school aren't optional you know.'

'I went for a tipple miss, in the karzie miss – it's the only way I can face your lessons, you know what I mean?'

Some of the girls tittered while others gasped.

Mrs Pringle went red in the face and with outrage bellowed, 'I beg your pardon?'

Courtney could see why drunks started fights; it was all too easy when you'd had a skinful.

'A swift half litre of the rough stuff miss down in the john or the saloon bar as I prefer to call it. Ere, you ain't got a sandwich on you babe? I think I need something to soak it up.'

A collective, horrified gasp went up so she turned to

them. 'And you lot can fuck off 'n' all with your homes in the country and your pony clubs. Bastards…'

The geography teacher was looking nervous now; she wasn't used to backchat in her classroom. Her tone softened. 'I see – well, perhaps we should go and see the school nurse? I can see you're intoxicated.'

'Intoxicated? Why is it no one in this school can speak English proper? I'm not intoxicated babe, I'm pissed, three sheets, Brahms and Liszt. Fucking intoxicated? Fuck me.' Courtney swayed slightly which jogged her memory and she remembered what the question was. 'School nurse? Nah, you're alright love, I'll stay for your lesson. I could do with a nap and nothing says the land of nod like you droning on at the whiteboard.' She looked at a girl in the front row. 'Oi, move your arris, I'm having that seat.'

The girl shifted herself. Courtney plonked unsteadily down and then slumped forward onto the desk where she closed her eyes. There was a lot of whispering going on around and above her.

It seemed to go on for a very long time before a man's voice said, 'Courtney? Shall we go for a walk and then perhaps we can go and see the headmistress?'

When Courtney looked up, she saw that a posse had been put together. There was Pringle, the school nurse, another teacher and the caretaker.

He was the one talking to her so she answered him. 'Nah, fuck that mate, I'm alright.'

More whispering and then hands fastened around her arms and she was pulled upright.

'Oi! Oi! What do you think you're doing? Get your filthy mitts off. That's assault, that is, I know my rights.'

The teacher, nurse and caretaker dragged her to the doorway where Pringle was holding the door. The teacher had recovered her bottle now she had some backup.

'I'll be waiting for an apology from you young lady. Then again, perhaps you won't get the opportunity to give me one as I expect the headmistress will decide you've delighted this school for long enough. Good luck at whatever chav comp you end up at.'

Courtney managed to drag her right hand free and to her mouth where she stuck two fingers down her throat. It was the time-honoured method used by bladdered teenagers down the ages. Courtney choked and gagged and then, although she'd had nothing much to eat, she managed to throw up the contents of her stomach. It wasn't much. But it was enough to coat Pringle's spit-polished shoes in yellow and green puke.

Forty-Two

'I'm afraid it's not possible to see Mr Scott,' the receptionist told Babs.

The young woman, who wasn't the same receptionist that Babs had met the other day, wasn't rude but there was something about the way she held her body that told Babs not to try it on.

Talk about trying, she'd been calling Kieran non-stop but he wasn't answering his phone so she'd gone for route one and headed straight down to his offices.

Babs tried again. 'Look luv, all you've got to do is bell him upstairs and mention my name, he knows me.'

The receptionist smiled this time, almost cracking her face. 'I'm sorry Mrs Miller, you can't just walk in off the streets and ask to see our CEO, it doesn't work like that. Now, I wish you a good day.'

'Does this look like a good day to ya?' Babs carefully placed the hand grenade on the desk.

Fair play to the girl, she didn't panic. As calm as you please she picked up her phone and pressed a number.

'Mr Scott, a lady has arrived in reception asking to speak you. She's also put an explosive device on my desk. It looks like it's disarmed. She says her name is Babs Miller.' After a few words at the other end of the line, she looked over at Babs. 'There's a security camera behind me Mrs Miller. Could you take a couple of steps back and wave at it.'

Babs did as she was told. Well nearly. Instead of waving she gave the thumbs up sign.

'You can go up Mrs Miller.' Babs set off for the security gates but the woman called her back and pointed at her desk. 'I think you've forgotten something.'

Babs could've slapped her forehead: the grenade, of course.

Kieran was waiting for her outside his suite on the top floor. Babs thought he'd be pissed at her for turning up like a bad penny, but his face was creased with worry.

'What do you think you're playing at? Waving a pineapple at my staff?' Seeing the confusion on her face he elaborated,' A fucking hand grenade. Why didn't you get on the blower to me?'

'I tried, you weren't answering,' Babs belted back. Then drew breath. 'Any chance you've got anything I can wet my lips with?'

A few minutes later they were on opposite sides of his desk, Babs nursing a small glass of sloe gin. She licked the liqueur from her bottom lip and started her story.

'This,' she placed the grenade on the desk, 'arrived at my gaff in a cake box.'

They both stared at it as though it was a third person in the room and they were waiting for it to give an accounting of itself.

Kieran reached for it and almost made Babs' ticker give out when he threw it from hand to hand like a ball. 'Fucking hell! Be careful Kieran, for fuck's sake!'

'Relax Babs, there ain't no detonator in it. You could play tennis with this and it wouldn't go off.' He held it up. 'See?'

It had an empty space down the middle. That's odd. She frowned. Babs could've bet her life there'd been something in that space when it had arrived. But then again she'd been in such a state trying to protect Little Bea no doubt her eyes had been playing tricks on her. Plus, it was Kieran who knew about these things which is why she'd come.

He sighed and put the grenade down. 'Pearl was it?'

'Gotta be.'

She placed the note on the table, his way up so he could read it. 'First of all she steals my gold and now she has the brass to accuse me of taking it. The nerve! Then she tries to blow me up.' Her voice shook with fear and unleashed anger. 'Little Bea was right there. My own granddaughter. What if one of the kids had got to it first?'

Kieran raised his gaze from the note to stare intently at her. 'Come on, you know better than that, it's just a warning. Just trying to scare the piss out of ya. You know how it works - bullets through the letterbox, a boom device in a cake box, an RPG fired through the window of an empty house, it's all pretty standard stuff.'

Babs took offence and got miffed. 'Nice to see you being so relaxed about it. Since you know the ins and the outs perhaps you can suggest what I do now?'

Kieran shrugged. 'Well, you could go to the Bill o' course, tell them.'

Babs was tempted to slap him one. 'Oh yeah, I can just picture the scene: 'Excuse me officer, me and a mate have been hiding the gold from that blag last year and now it's done a Houdini. Now my mate is trying to blow me to smithereens coz she thinks I double-crossed her. Can you find it in your heart to help me?' Have you gone soft in the head mate or something?'

Thoroughly narked off, Babs grabbed the grenade and note and put them in her bag. She got up so quickly the chair rocked back on its legs. 'Thanks for sweet FA,' she bit out and headed for the door.

His voice stopped her. 'You could deliver a counter warning—'

She twisted around, eyes blazing. 'Oh yeah, like knock on her door and when she opens it stick my thumb on my nose, waggle my fingers and go 'naar, naar, na naar naar?''

He eased to his feet and walked over to her. 'Why don't you arrange to meet your old mate Pearl on neutral ground and get this sorted before it all gets out of hand?'

Babs was outraged. 'I tried that and it didn't work out ...' Her voice wobbled thinking about Dee and that daddy-come-lately Neville.

'What happened?' he asked softly.

She filled him in on the reappearance of Dee's dad in her life and his connection to Pearl.

'Negotiate with Pearl? Never! She tried to blow me fucking up. Are you going to help me out here or not? With this counter warning?'

Kieran shook his head as he shoved his hands in his trouser pockets. 'Look, I've already told ya, I don't want sod all to do with it. I'm a model citizen me. I help old dears across the road, I could pretty much join the Sally Army.'

Babs folded her arms. 'Yeah, you're so respectable that your receptionist doesn't blink when I put a grenade on her desk.'

'Well, obviously my key employees are aware of my past, that goes without saying and clearly I need the right bird on my front desk.' He smiled slightly. 'Canny girl she is. You know how important loyalty is to me.'

Babs struck. 'That's touching. Now how about you show some loyalty to me?'

She took a step towards him and pinched his cheek with affection as if he was a naughty boy. 'I've wanted to do that since I shut the door in your face last year.' Her hand dropped to her side. 'You'll always be my lad, no matter what. Now you've gotta decide - will I always be your second mum, no matter what? Coz let me tell you Kieran I'm in a right, tight spot here,' her voice became husky, 'and I don't know what to do.'

They stared at each other, a reversal of the first time they'd met in the washhouse all those years ago, with Babs doing the rescuing back then.

Kieran looked shame-faced. 'Alright, I'll make some calls and see what I can do but it'll just be a counter warning mind. And you'll need some security—'

'Wha'cha mean? Like a bodyguard?'

He shook his head. 'More like someone to mind the fort back at your flat. Keep an eye on who's coming and going.'

Babs left satisfied. Not only was Kieran a man of his word, she also knew once he got involved, he wouldn't be able to back out. For the first time in ages her face broke into a smile.

Her boy had finally come back to her.

Forty-Three

'Do you know what the penalty for mutiny on the high seas is, my dear?' the Commander casually asked his granddaughter.

Flo knew telling her granddad that she was no longer willing to help him get the gold back wasn't going to be a walk in the park.

She sat in the drawing room of the Commander's villa in Notting Hill, surrounded by mementoes of his naval career including the model ships he made. And while it was a long time since he'd captained a ship, he treated everything in life as if he was still on the bridge giving orders. His eyes were flashing, his face so white with glacial anger it looked like the Titanic's iceberg.

Flo sighed. 'No, I don't.'

The Commander stood up and poured a large glass of rum from a decanter. 'You hang from the highest yardarm in the Royal Navy, that's the reward for mutiny!'

Flo ran her fingers through her long blonde hair and said quietly, 'I don't think they hang people for that anymore.'

The rum in his glass looked like a rough sea because his hand was shaking with fury. 'No, that's right, they don't!' He took a slug from his glass. 'No wonder the country's going to the dogs!'

He paced the room. 'I suppose you've been got at by *that family*, have you? Is that it? They've filled your head with a lot of silly nonsense and lower class sob stories to get you on their side?' The Commander always referred to the Millers as 'that family' rather than by their name, although he had some other, rather more fruity and naval words for them too.

'No, that's not it. It's just I'm starting to think Mummy Babs is right. That gold is cursed. It's caused murder and mayhem wherever it's gone. I don't want anything to do with it anymore'

The Commander was shocked. 'Mummy what?'

Shit! She hadn't meant that to slip out. 'I mean Babs Miller.'

She jumped when the Commander threw his glass into the fireplace where it shattered into pieces. Her granddad didn't lose his rag often but when he did it was time to take cover from the incoming storm.

'Mummy? You're referring to that cockney fishwife, that East End oik, that Al Capone in petticoats, as your mother now are you? You think that family is your own family now? My word, it's worse than I thought.'

But Flo didn't take cover. She clenched her fists. 'Yeah, that's right – mum! Coz she's been more of a mother to me than that your daughter, that spineless bitch with paintbrushes up her rear end who hates me.' She screeched with all the pent up emotion she'd been carrying since a child. 'Hates the very sight of me because I look like my father.'

Flo shook. If she was shouting the odds about home truths she was taking it all the way. 'And while we're on the subject of crime, perhaps you'd like to tell me how you came by that gold in the first place? Because you've never let on about that, have you Commander?'

He seemed to wither slightly and avoided her eyes. 'It was come by perfectly legally, I have all the paperwork.'

'Yeah, I'll bet you do. That's why you got John Black to hide it up in that villains vault. Talking of which, how did you come to be an ol' mucker of a Face like John Black in the first place?'

The Commander looked unsteady on his feet. Flo loathed what she was doing to the one person who had loved her with all he had her whole life. But now was the time for the truth to have its way.

'You meet a lot of different kinds of people in the navy,' he replied, 'and anyway...that's none of your concern my girl.'

Flo folded her arms in triumph. 'That gold was bent from the off—'

'The off?' His mouth rippled in distaste. 'How many times have I told you to stop using that awful, gutter slang?'

She ignored him. 'Admit it! You nicked it! So tell me then, what would Admiral Nelson up on his column have made of one his officers being a common thief? He'd have hung *you* from the yardarm! Because that's what you are bruv, a common thief with a posher accent!'

The Commander took a deep breath and walked over to fetch himself another glass of rum but his hand wasn't shaking anymore. He turned to face his granddaughter. 'That gold was for you, you know that. It was to be your inheritance. I wanted to leave something for my darling Florence.'

The anger drained out of her. 'I know gramps. But I

don't need it, nor do you. You've got money coming out of your ears. A house in the country and one in New York. We don't need the trouble this gold is bringing. Please let it go.'

He retook his seat next to the ship model he'd been making. 'You really want me to forget about it?'

Flo eagerly sat down at the table. 'More precious than gold is that I've found the family I've always wanted. I can't explain it. I've searched for such a long time to find the place I really belong. And I think I've found it.'

The Commander was silent. Then he picked up the glue and a piece of the model ship. He bent to do his work as he gently said, 'Well, you'd better tell me all about this new family of yours.'

She was about to plunge on when she remembered something. 'Oh yeah, this old biddy, calls herself Pearlie—'

The Commander stiffened. 'Pearl?' His voice sounded so strange Flo got worried about him. 'Pearl Hennessey?'

'Don't know her last name.' Flo peered at his paling face. 'Do you know her?'

He took a long swallow of his rum, the skin around his mouth strained. 'Never heard of her before in my life. Now come on, tell me all about the Millers.'

Flo didn't believe him but she knew when to leave off.

In a happy, eager voice she dived in. 'Let's start with nutter Tiffany who's always spitting her dummy out...'

When Babs got indoors the first thing that caught her eye was a jacket she'd never seen in her life on the coat rail. A Puffa jacket, black, bulked out with enough lagging to do the trick in a padded cell. Her body stiffened with fear. After the grenade she wasn't taking any chances. Babs searched quickly for a makeshift weapon to do some serious damage. Problem was she couldn't find anything. Silently she cursed a blue streak. She did a double take; on the floor was a sports bag with a carrier full of lager cans sitting on top. And from the sitting room came a voice she knew all too well:

'Just think Tiff, it ain't been that long since I was giving you a kicking in that scuzzy squat!'

What the heck was *she* doing here? In a panic, Babs chucked her handbag down and threw the door open to find her youngest sitting on the sofa while Knox sat opposite. They were drinking from a bottle of duty free brandy.

'What the hell are you doing here?'

The big woman drained her glass. 'Well, that's a nice way to welcome your new security detail, I must say me ol' mucker.'

'Security detail?'

Knox put her glass down, none too gently, on the table. 'My little brother gave me a tinkle and told me to get tooled up, get my arse over to Babs' and take care of business. And he'll sort out any expenses.'

Babs couldn't believe her ears as she dropped, stunned, into an armchair. As much as she appreciated what this woman had done for her while they were banged up she didn't want her anywhere near her life on the outside.

'Kieran never said he was sending you.'

Knox sent her a cold, hard stare that had made prisoners tremble and run for their hated cells. 'You'd prefer someone else? You got a problem with me parking my good self on your sofa?'

Babs took one look at her clenched fist and carefully answered, ''Course I ain't.' She had enough trouble on her hands without Knox doing a moody. 'If Kieran had told me it was you I'd have made sure the kettle was on.'

Knox's fingers unrolled and she grinned as she settled back. She turned to Tiffany. 'Bet your old mam here never told you I was her eyes and ears back doing bird, eh? Saved her neck a time or two I can tell ya.'

Tiff gave her mum a sly smile that made Babs want to box her ears. 'Nah, she never said a word. Told me she fought all her battles herself. Had the other girls quaking in their boots when they knew she was coming.'

If only they knew, Babs thought. None of her family or Knox knew what she'd had to do while on remand in the first prison she'd been locked up in before Kieran had sorted out protection for her. And it wasn't pretty.

Knox threw her head back and barked with laughter. 'As if! There was this one time—'

Babs smartly cut in, 'How was it you happened to give my Tiff here the kicking of a lifetime?'

Knox's merriment drained away. 'That was business with another boss. Confidential, you get my drift? Which is what it's gonna be between me, you and Kieran.' She stood up and cracked her knuckles. 'Now then, put your feet up and don't worry about a thing. As you'll remember from the slammer, no one manages argy-bargy better than your old mate Knox!'

Forty-Four

Courtney held on tight to the glass of water as she awaited her fate in the headmistress' PA's office. Her tummy rumbled and flipped over threatening to make her chunder again. She bit the inside of her mouth managing to hold it down.

Her defiance had long gone replaced by a feeling of doom. Mrs Elliot, the headmistress, had given her the bollocking of a lifetime and told her to wait outside her office while she called her family. There was only one way this was going to go – being expelled. Other girls at the school had parents who knew all the tricks when it came to defending their kids against the Elliots of this world. But her family only had one – deck the bastard. She knew when her Nanna Babs turned up there'd be a cry of, 'You calling my grandkid a liar? I'll show you what it's like, you stuck up witch,' and then Babs would pile in with her fists flying.

It didn't bare thinking about and was only going to end one way; expulsion for her while her grandmother was dragged out by half a dozen coppers.

Courtney's head sank when there was a knock at the door. Had to be Nanna Babs. Only when the door opened, it wasn't. It was her Aunts Tiffany and Florence. She did a double take at the way they were kitted out.

Flo wore a tweed, skirt suit, a headscarf tied under her chin, sensible shoes, gloves and string of pearls round her neck. She looked like she'd just come from inspecting her horses in the stables, proper Country Life. Tiffany, meanwhile, was following a pace behind in a black business suit with a briefcase. Her hedgehog hair was slicked down to hide the shaved sides. She winked at Courtney as she went by.

Mrs Elliot's PA stood up behind her desk her expression pinched obviously disconcerted with the way the newcomers had bowled into her office.

'May I help you?'

It was Flo doing the talking. 'Yes, I wonder if you can? My name's Florence Bordeaux – that's the Hampshire Bordeaux family incidentally – not the Suffolk ones. I'm afraid they're frightfully common. They've only got one house and it's only Victorian – can you imagine?'

Whenever Courtney had heard Flo's voice before she'd sounded like a right cor blimey merchant although her mum's side of the family was supposed to be worth a few bob. Now she was talking so posh, she made the queen sound like an oik.

Flo went on, 'and this is my solicitor, Tiffany Lake of the firm Lake, Lake and Lake in Mayfair. I presume you're familiar with them?' She pronounced Tiffany's name as Tiff-Annie.

The PA frowned, baffled.

Flo looked wildly surprised. 'You're not?? Well, Lake, Lake and Lake are very exclusive of course. Anyway, I'm

Courtney's aunt. It's all rather embarrassing, I'm afraid. Her mother was my younger brother's cleaner and you know what these upper crust boys are like, they can't keep their friend in their trousers and Courtney was his wrong side of the blanket. It's all frightful and ghastly but I suppose despite everything, all things considered, she's still family. Now – where's this Elliott woman? I want a word with her and I want it sharpish.'

Courtney's gaze darted between her two aunts, not a clue what was going on, but she kept it zipped.

The PA hopped to it and rushed to enter the headmistress' door. As she did so Courtney's Aunts came over to her.

'What's up babe?' Tiff asked, sitting down and placing a comforting arm round her.

Courtney gave them both a fretful stare. 'I've been necking booze again.'

Flo was talking street again. 'Don't worry 'bout it. All these nobs are piss heads. They're notorious for it.'

Tiff shook her head slightly. 'The problem here is our Court had a really bad problem with it a year back. She promised her mum she weren't gonna do it no more, know what I mean?'

Courtney hung her head feeling like the lowest of the low. She'd promised her mum to stay off the sauce.

The PA came back. 'Mrs Elliott will see you now.'

Tiff whispered to her niece, 'Don't worry bout a thing. Flo knows how to deal with these people. She'll sort it out.'

The two sisters marched into a room that was all wooden panels, rows of books and light coming from a huge skylight. Behind a gleaming, teak desk sat the headmistress.

Everything about her was pristine and perfectly in place – her greying bob, Liberty floral blouse with a huge, tidy bow in the front and neatly, manicured, short nails.

Flo took charge. 'You're Elliott are you?'

She took a seat opposite the headmistress without waiting for an answer and without being asked.

Flo dramatically tugged her gloves off. 'I trust you don't mind if my solicitor joins us? If I'm forced to resort to legal action, I want an accurate record of this conversation – make notes for me Tiffany darling.' Flo tilted her head back and looked down her nose while Tiff stood with a pen poised.

Mrs Elliott stuttered, 'Legal action? I'm sorry, I don't understand.'

Flo sounded as if she was talking to the butler. 'Yes, legal action. You needn't think you're defaming my family and getting away with it. And if it comes to it, I might ask my uncle, Judge Humphrey Bordeaux, to hear the case. We all know Humph likes a snort but he's never let the family down at the high court yet. Now then – what seems to be the problem here? Come on woman – spit it out.'

Mrs Elliott spat it out but she didn't seem very sure of herself. 'The situation is this Mrs Bordeaux—'

Flo bristled. 'Lady Bordeaux.'

'Yes, Lady Bordeaux. The situation is that I'm afraid your niece was found to be under the influence of alcohol, which is strictly against school rules of course. Normally she would be let off with a warning but I'm afraid this fits a pattern of behaviour with Courtney and that has left us with no choice but…'

Flo cut her short. 'You mean she was pissed? Let me ask you a question – why do you think parents send their children to a school like this?'

Mrs Elliott huffed, 'We provide an first class education, that's why, Lady Bordeaux.'

Flo shook her head slowly and tapped the desk with her fingernail. It was more and more difficult to tell which one was the real head teacher. 'No. They send their children to a school like this to make friends in high places and get pissed. Girls like that don't need an education; they just need to meet the right people. Look, I'm willing to be generous here; I don't want to waste time in the courts. If you're willing to reconsider, I may be able to overlook the matter.'

The other woman's body stiffened in indignation. 'I'm not sure I can, you see…'

Flo butted in again. 'Tiffany, can you tell me what my options are here please?'

Tiffany sighed. 'I think we can argue the school has breached Courtney's human rights. We could go all the way to Stratford…' she coughed, 'that's Strasbourg with that one. Of course, by then the school will be bankrupt anyway, so a judgement won't make any difference.'

Flo seemed pleased and rose to her feet. 'Fine. So - see you in court Mrs Elliott.'

The headmistress rose too panicking. 'Let's not be hasty. Perhaps if Courtney were to agree to alcohol counselling, we might be able to be flexible.'

Flo shook her head. 'Courtney's not agreeing to anything. No expulsion, no counselling, no nothing – are we agreed?'

Mrs Elliott made the best of her defeat. 'Very well, but this is her last chance and I mean it. But, obviously due to her current condition, she needs to go home for the remainder of the day. Good afternoon Lady Bordeaux.'

When they were outside, Courtney dashed up to Tiffany, grabbed her by the arm and whispered, 'What happened?'

Tiffany looked at Flo who was striding out of the office like a proper madam. 'Do you know something? I'm sorta warming up to my half-sister.'

Courtney begged, 'Did you get me off?'

Tiffany looked at her and wore a cocky grin. 'We sure did. Flo burned the bitch!'

As soon as they got into Flo's hired soft top, from the back seat Courtney burst out, 'I won't do it again. I swear. It's just…' Her lips glued together. The message was for her nan not anyone else.

Tiff twisted round, her gaze narrowing as she checked out her niece. 'What's going on Court? I know you're worried bout your ol' mum, but I can tell something else is going on here.'

Flo nudged her. 'Leave the girl alone. Can't you see she's been put through the wringer.'

'Nah.' Tiff shook her head. 'You better spill Court or we ain't leaving until it's out in the open.'

Courtney's gaze darted from one to the other. Then it gushed out of her. 'My violin teacher…' She gulped as her fingers locked tightly together. 'He said…he said…'

Her voice got higher and more breathless as she went on.

At the end Tiff lunged for the door, doing her nut. 'I'll fucking teach Tambourine Man to put the frighteners on little girls. By the time I've finished he won't be plucking strings for a while.'

Flo grabbed the back of her jacket and hauled her back into the passenger seat. 'That ain't gonna work—'

Tiff waved her fist. 'One of these speaks volume every time.'

'No,' Flo shook her head as her fox eyes squinted. 'You go in there and tight-arse Elliott calls the coppers. Then you'll be banged up and Courtney here will deffo get the ol' heave-ho.'

Seeing the sense of what she was saying Tiff slumped back. 'So what we gonna do? No way is Fiddler On The Roof getting away with this.'

Flo sucked her bottom lip as she thought. Then slowly smiled. She tucked into her bag and pulled out Babs' Annie pills. She passed one to Tiff. They gulped down their tabs at the same time.

Tiff said, 'we keep this between us Court. Your Nanna Babs would only start fretting.'

In a cunning tone Flo added, 'What that bastard needs is a lesson he'll never forget.'

Forty-Five

'Come on Fred,' Pearl said as she caught him before he could fall flat on his face as they entered the care home.

Poor sod was ten sheets to the wind. They'd just got back from Vi and Di's funeral. There hadn't been a dry eye at the funeral except Fred. He'd been as still as a statue and equally as quiet, that is until the drinks arrived. He'd knocked them back as if drinking was going to be outlawed tomorrow. Now he was as pissed as a balding skunk.

'Why she do it?' His rheumy, bloodshot eyes searched Pearl's face as if the answer would be written there. His gold tooth had lost its shine. 'Why didn't she wait for me?'

Vi wait for what? Pearl didn't have a clue what he was going on about. He didn't have a skullcap to wear at the Jewish funeral, so he'd covered his head with one of his many hats, a fedora, which lurched precariously to the side.

His face crumbled and he started to bawl, awful, heartbreaking sobs that made Pearl's heart ache too. Falling in love wasn't a pretty sight sometimes.

The receptionist kindly offered, 'Shall I take him to his room?'

'Nah, you're alright darlin',' she answered, 'I'll get him sorted.'

Fred was no light burden but she managed to shift him along the corridor. A door opened and Lin Chen's head appeared. As soon as she clocked Pearl she scampered back in and slammed the door. Pearl had tried a few times to dig away at her to get the truth of who'd nicked the gold from her room, but Lin always clammed up.

Pearl got Fred to his room, shifted a black photo album lying on the bed and managed to get him horizontal. Thank God he was snoring by the time his head hit his pillow.

'You old soak,' she whispered tenderly as her heart squeezed.

Pearl pulled off his hat, kissed his forehead and quietly left his room.

She headed straight for her own, desperate to take off her black mourning dress and slip into one of her usual colourful kaftans. She'd wanted to attend the funeral in her most colourful kaftan because they should be celebrating her friends' lives with colour and joy. But it was to be a very traditional send off which meant only somber colours allowed. She bowed her head as she reached her door; she would miss Vi and Di so much.

Pearl entered her room and went rigid with shock. Someone had been in her room and rearranged it. Her double bed was in the middle of the room, her bedside table under the window and her comfy armchair was right near her by the door. Her hand flew to her mouth as she found the precious photo of her children not on the wall where it had held pride of place but propped up against her portable telly.

Panic rising, she rushed over to the framed photo and got down on her knees and gently picked it up. That someone had been in here and touched her kids sickened her very soul. It was a family portrait taken at Griffiths and Sons photography studio in Roman Road. If you were black and lived in East London that's where you got her family snap done back in the early days.

They all wore their Sunday best with Pearl sitting on a chair with baby Carl in her arms, six-year-old Leticia, Pinky and Styley's mum, on one side and five-year-old Johnson, on the other. Presiding in the background, tall and strong was her husband Clifton. He was the only one with a small, smile on his face. He'd loved a joke. He'd been such a handsome man, someone she could always lean on. A year after this picture was taken he was wasting away in bed dying from lung cancer. Pearl liked to tell herself that it was his death that had made her go astray but the truth was she'd long been leaving her kids in the arms of others while she gallivanted about in Blues parties and Soho clubs. What a mess she'd made of her life.

Still clutching the beloved photo she straightened and looked around the room. She was still making a right, royal muck up of it. And this time some bastard was sending her a clear warning.

'I want it to stop. Right now, do you hear me,' Pearl ordered her grandsons as she sat with them at their table in the back of the gym. She waved her hands around to emphasise her demand.

The boxing gym was busy today and baking. Pearl nearly had to take off her scarf because the place was that hot. Apparently the heaters and radiators had been on full blast so that the men sweated to achieve a good workout. She was sweating buckets just looking at the guys go through their paces.

Pinky stared hard at her as he stroked the pink trim on his shirtsleeve. 'You just told us that some numb nuts has been in your gaff and rearranged your gear to put the frighteners on you, playing mind games and that.'

'Yeah, no one does that to our grams,' Styley punched in. 'I should go round to that wank hole estate in Mile End and bust open that Miller slag's head until her brains are all over the shop.'

Pearl thumped her fist on the table. 'No one is mashing up anyone's head, you hear?' Her hand went under her kaftan, to her garter, and she pulled out her flask of Wray and Nephew. She took a deep swig and then wiped her mouth. 'That gold is evil. I don't want nothing more to do with it.'

Styley gazed at her as if she was the one with the mashed head. 'Are you for fucking—?'

Pearl's swiftly whacked him across the head. 'Remember who you're speaking to boy. You're not chatting to one of your ragamuffin mates now.' She kissed her teeth very hard showing how upset she was. 'Cuss off at me? I'll put you under manners with my belt if I owned one.'

He quickly glanced round the gym to see if anyone had seen what had happened. Everyone was avoiding his gaze, which meant they had seen alright. Only a fool was going to repeat it to another soul.

His brother said, 'No, grams is right. We leave this alone now.' He touched her hand. 'Whatever you want we will do,' he caught his brother's eye, 'won't we Sty?'

A disgruntled Styley rubbed the side of his head. 'Yeah.

Whatever you want. But what about Biggin and Dee? She ain't gonna want to let it go that easy.'

Pearl took another lug of the rum and then put it away as she thought long and hard about his question. 'Well. I haven't figured that one out yet but you leave them to me.' She stood up. 'Now I've got to get back. My friend Fred—'

Styley's eyes lit up with mischief. 'Your friend, is he?'

Pinky joined in. 'Oooo, has gramsie got herself a boyfriend?'

She tried to swat them both but they jumped up and danced good-naturedly out of her reach.

'Boyfriend?' she muttered to herself so they couldn't hear. 'I haven't got my leg over since 1998.'

Styley hailed one of their guys over to drive Pearl home. She hugged them tight at the door. She wished she'd never started any of this. If anything happened to her grandbaby boys she'd never forgive herself. Now all she had to do was to get Neville to persuade Dee to pack in in. Problem was he hadn't listened to her in over thirty years.

'We really gonna leave it alone?' Styley asked as he and his brother watched their grandma Pearl being driven away.

'Walk away from a shed load of gold?' Pinky scoffed. He laughed and then became deadly serious. 'Hell will freeze over before that happens.'

'What's our next step going to be?'

Pinky rubbed his chin. And grinned. 'Didn't grams say that there's some hanky-panky foolishness going on between Babs Miller and a former copper?'

'You mad? We can't have a fucking Fed anywhere near this.'

Pinky put his arm round his brother's shoulders. 'Don't sweat it. All we're gonna do is create a little bit of trouble in paradise that might bring the gold to the surface.'

Forty-Six

'You've done well for yourself,' Dee slowly acknowledged, as her gaze leisurely took in all Neville's expensive chintz and whatnots in the gorgeous sitting room of his house.

Fuck me! She was a nervous wreck. This bloke was her dad, her flipping old man. Never in a million years, and some, had she ever believed she'd clap eyes on the fella who had helped give her life. Seeing him in the flesh, realising that she looked like him to boot overwhelmed her so much she wanted to weep with joy. The corners of her mouth turned down remembering all the bad, nasty things Babs had told her about him. Not one good thing had Babs told her. Not one. Dee resented the bloody hell out of her for that.

Neville nodded his head in approval as he smiled and waved at a deep-blue antique armchair. 'Take a seat my daughter.'

Daughter. An electric thrill charged through Dee.

As she plonked herself down, crossed her long legs and popped her Chloe Paddington bag on the polished wooden floor he poured them both a glass of bubbly. And not any old crap. Rose Lafitte. Now that was class! One of Dee's big worries had been if she did ever meet her old man he'd been some scuzzball, a proper down 'n' out on his uppers only wanting to know her so he could get his light-fingered mitts in her purse. Not only did Neville pass the tacky test he had plenty of wonga to burn.

'So,' Dee drew the word out, 'where's your lady and kid? You're married, right?'

His house hadn't shown much evidence of either, but you never could tell with a bloke. He might have them tucked up in another gaff.

'I've never tied the knot.'

Dee's brows shot up. Now that surprised her. Neville was a handsome geezer so in his day he must've been a real babe magnet.

Seeing her astounded expression he shrugged and chuckled. 'I'm not saying I was a saint, coz I weren't. I'm as red-blooded as the next geezer.' He sipped from his glass. 'Truth is Babs was right, when she was carrying you I had a little boy with someone else.'

'And you didn't marry his mother?' Dee couldn't hide the disapproval in her tone. If there was one thing she couldn't abide it was blokes who sprayed their seed left, right and friggin' centre without looking back to see if it had taken.

He put his glass gently down on the nearby table. 'You young kids nowadays it don't matter what colour you are, you all mix it up and mingle. Not back then. You stayed with your own. There was no way in hell I could've ever introduced Babs to my family. Now my son's mother, on the other hand, was black. My mum really liked that girl and thought I'd settle down. But, if I'm truthful darling Desiree,' She loved the way he said her full name, 'and I'd never tell you a lie – I couldn't stand her.'

Dee stared hard at him. 'So how did you end up doing the duvet dirty with her?'

He rubbed his jaw and Dee noticed how perfectly clipped and manicured his nails were. 'I met her at a Blues party.' He kissed his teeth lightly. 'One thing led to another and before I know it my son's on the way.'

'Do you still see him?'

His face became serious. 'I did until he was ten, then his mum moved to Toronto and well…' His lifted his palms. 'She married and let's just say he's got another father now.'

He got up and moved behind her chair. Placed his hand on her shoulder and said, 'that's why you're so important to me. I've already lost one child and now I've found you I can't lose you as well.' She heard him swallow. 'It would crack my heart in two.'

Feeling his grief Dee got up and wrapped her arms around him and hugged tight. He was trembling, poor guy.

'Now I've found you I'm not going anywhere.'

His large hand rubbed her back in a hypnotic motion. 'I'd never say a bad word about Babs, but that gold…' The movement of his hand deepened as his voice dropped hypnotically low. 'Babs is bang out of order. She lied to you, the same way how she lied to you about me.'

He pulled back and held her gaze. 'Look around you. I'm a man of means. I'm not saying I was minted back then but my darling Desiree I was on the right track.' His nostrils flared with barely suppressed anger. 'You know what really hurts? Knowing my own flesh and blood was out there living with people who weren't her family when all the time I could've given you a good life.'

Dee hated seeing him like this. Crippled with guilt and

almost destroyed. How could Babs have done this to him? Done this to her? God knows she hadn't wanted to believe him but when Babs had blatantly lied about the gold she'd started thinking what else could Babs be lying about, eh? If Babs had wanted her so much how come she'd let Aunty Cleo bring her up? Let some other woman grow up your kid? What kinda mother was that? And what if…? Dee couldn't think it. Much less say it; the one thing that had been eating away at her heart with the power of poison…

As if reading her mind Neville spoke it. 'Babs never wanted to bring up no brown baby.'

Her hands tightened around his because Dee felt like she was going to shatter like glass. All the old insecurities she'd felt growing up slapped her in the face. As a kid it had taken root in her head that her white mum hadn't wanted to be seen with her black kid. Her mum was ashamed of her, couldn't bare to look at her. Dee was the visible evidence that Babs had gone against the rules of her world and been with a black guy. It was one of the reasons why young Dee had been so angry in life, so wanted to show the world – by hook or crook - she was somebody. And then she'd finally met Babs and been told a different story. Been told that her mum had fought for her, wanted her, loved her. Now Neville was planting those old, rotten seeds again. And they were growing.

A furious banging at the door made them jerk apart.

He said, 'I don't like the sound of that.'

A furious voice outside yelled, 'Neville Campbell I know you're in there. You better give me my daughter back and don't come with your nonsense that she's not there coz her motor's parked here for all the world to see.'

'For crying out loud,' Dee growled through her teeth as she stomped towards the window, but Neville grabbed her and held her back.

'You let me deal with Babs.' He stiffened his spine. 'Us having this out is long over due.' His hand caressed Dee's cheek. 'Stay in here, don't go near the window. You leave this to me. That woman has hurt you long enough with her lies.'

Babs was hopping mad on Neville's doorstep. And scared. Terrified that she'd lost her firstborn forever. One of Neville's neighbours opened the door, popped her head out and looked at Babs disapprovingly. Stuck up cow.

Babs clamped her fists on her hips and with a curl of her lip shouted, 'You got something to say?'

The woman looked down her snooty nose and quietly shut the door. Babs reached up for the knocker again when the door thrust opened and that evil bastard loomed in the doorway.

He had the cheek to smile smugly in her face. 'Do yourself a favour Babs and fuck off back to that miserable, crime-ridden estate you call home.'

Her head reared back. 'Crime? You'd know all about that, wouldn't ya? Sending a grenade to my gaff to get your mitts on the gold.'

He looked at her as if she were a sack of shit. 'I think you mean Desiree's husband's gold. I suspect that was my great-nephews trying to help their newly discovered first cousin get it back. Fair play to them.'

'As if!' She sneered. 'You want that gold for yourself.' Babs spun around to face the square. 'Wander what all your lah-di-dah neighbour nobs would think of that? Maybe I should tell them?'

As she opened her mouth to broadcast the news, he wrapped his arms round her and lifted her up. Startled she kicked and screamed as he carried her round the corner of his house and slammed her into the wall.

As pain tore into her back he stabbed his finger into her face. 'Now you listen to me, you washed up old, pathetic woman. No one gives two fingers about what you've got to say? Know why? You're not even worth farting on.'

If he thought he could put the frighteners on her, he didn't know Babs Miller. She shoved into him. 'You give me my daughter back.'

'You hand over the gold and she's all yours.'

The man was bloody un-fucking-believable. This goon was still the same selfish prick he'd been all those years ago.

'I know what you're telling her about me and you know it's bollocks, every last lot of it. You're stringing her along coz you want the gold.'

He gave her a fake, sweet smile and leaned down to her ear. 'You better believe it doll. She's lapping it up like a kitten with a saucer of milk. I've got her like this.' His hand curled into a fist. 'In the palm of my hand and I could crush her any minute.'

It hit her like a punch to the face. This wasn't the young, charming Neville whose only care in the world had been his hair and having a good time. No, *this* Neville was hard and dangerous.

Fearing for Dee's life she tried to bolt past him to get to her daughter, but he banged her into the wall again.

'Funny thing is Babs babe,' he tiled his head and keenly

watched her, 'of all my ladies I ran with back then you were my number one. But you had to go and spoil it by getting in the pudding club—'

'Like you never had nuthin to do with that,' she countered outraged. This wanker had the nerve of the devil.

'I had plans, you see.' The greed blatantly stamped on his face. 'Plans to make it. Now how's a fella meant to do that with some kid round his neck like an albatross that needs its nappy changing? Eh?'

'You're disgusting,' she spat. 'The effing pits. You deserve to burn in hell for all eternity.'

'No doubt. But believe you me that daughter of yours is going to be there right along side of me.' His voice was filled with menace. 'Give me the gold and you can have mush-brained Dee back.'

Wearing a smile, part corruption, part triumphant pleasure, Neville left her and waltzed, as easy as you please, back to his house. The very idea that Babs Miller thought she was any match for him wasn't even worth the time of day. She was as thick as a villain's police record just as she'd been all those years ago.

Back then all he'd had to do was crook his little finger and she'd been panting after him ready to drop her drawers on his says-so. Babs hadn't been a slag – he'd give her that – because he'd been her first, but so what? Birds were all the same, claiming to love you to bits and then looking for their moment to get their heels permanently under your table.

He'd loved his big sister, Pearl, to death when he was young. And where had that love got him? Nearly in the shitter in a Turkish prison. Then she'd gone on her merry way and he'd had no option but to take care of her kids. He'd surprised himself how much he'd taken to those kids because, let's face it, the ones he'd helped create he didn't give two fucks about. And that included Desiree Black. The girl must be missing a couple of screws if she thought he really wanted to play happy daddy after all these years. Come on! As if! But Dee Black was an essential part of his plan, so he tore the collar of his Armani shirt and flattened his mouth into a grim line.

And, of course, just as he'd figured, Dee went ballistic when she clocked his ripped shirt. She slammed her glass of fizz on the table and shot to her feet.

'Did Babs do that?' She was already heading for the door.

He managed to drag her back, although it wasn't easy, the fury she was feeling was that strong.

'She's not worth it.' He caught her other arm and turned her to face him. 'I asked her to give you John's gold, but she weren't having it.'

'So she finally admitted she's got it?'

''Course she did. She wants to keep it all for herself, that's what she told me. Cross my heart darling Desiree.'

Dee snapped out of his arms. 'That bitch. All this time...'

The window smashed as a brick sailed through it making them duck down.

'Don't believe a word that comes out of his lying, toerag gob,' Babs bellowed, her voice hoarse with emotion. 'He's evil Dee, pure evil. If you think this is over, you cunt Neville, you're living in La La Land.'

Then Dee heard her mum's sobs as she moved away. Hearing Babs cry still hurt but she hardened her heart. Her mother had stolen John's gold and then lied about it. And she would never forgive her for that.

Forty-Seven

When Patrick Johnson saw the two guys blocking his path on his way to the newsagents he didn't even turn a hair. For years now he'd had a simple solution to any argy-bargy he might run into on the street - pull out his old warrant card, wave it around and warn, 'Police officer!' For those who weren't hardened crims that was usually enough to make them scarper. Those that were knew it meant he could have a carload of his uniformed mates on the scene within minutes laying the law down with their truncheons if necessary. Mixing it with the cops was not a good look.

The men wore hats that covered their faces and baggy dark clothes. One was directly in front of him the other standing to one side providing back up if needed.

The one leading the trouble held up his hand like a highwayman. 'Alright mate? You couldn't lend us a tenner, could ya? Only my mum's in hospital having a baby and I can't afford the cab fare to get up there.'

Patrick stopped a few inches from the bloke's hand and maintained his cool. 'So, your mum's having a baby, is she?'

'That's right.' His lip curled with cocky arrogance. 'I'm sorry, you saying she ain't?' He turned to his mate. 'That's a bit rude that is, him calling me a liar.'

The other bloke got leery too. 'That's well rude. And with you being so polite 'n' all and your poor ol' mum going into labour.'

This pair of likely lads looked like they were having the time of their lives.

Patrick decided to nip it in the bud; he wasn't in the mood for any aggro. 'My apologies for upsetting you and best wishes to your mother. Now if you wouldn't mind getting out of my way, I'll be about my business.' He kept his voice easy, calm with a respectful tone they didn't deserve.

He tried to move around them, but the thug in charge used his hand to block him again. 'Woah, one minute there cowboy – what about my tenner? I was trying to be nice. Was gonna ask you for your address so I could pop it back through your letter box later.' His voice changed to a growl. 'But now you're trying to piss all over my shoes I think I'll keep the readies you're giving me - you know, teach you some manners 'n' that.'

Being a regular polite guy was getting him nowhere so Patrick reached into his pocket for his warrant card. But it wasn't there. Shit! It must be in one of his other jackets. Going up against these thugs wasn't going to be easy; he wasn't as handy on his feet these days.

The front man drew out a long hunting knife from his waistband when he clocked Patrick's hand come up empty from his jacket.

He sneered, 'Oh dear! Thought you might be keeping some sorta switchblade in your pocket, only it turns out you weren't. That's careless that is.' He was grinning like the village idiot now. 'The streets ain't safe no more for unarmed people! You should carry something on ya.' He turned to his mate. 'I'm right bruv, aren't I?'

'You got that right. You never know who you might meet.'

Patrick considered legging it, but quickly thought better of it. That would only add fuel to fire and one of the biggest lessons he'd learned on the job was to keep the situation under control. Let the bad boys think they had the upper hand until you saw your moment to strike.

So he allowed the ponce to tap him in the chest with the tip of his blade as he used his free hand to expertly frisk Patrick until he located his wallet. He jerked it out and threw it to his partner in crime.

Patrick saw his chance and took it. He swung a punch at the knifeman's head. Even a few years earlier, there would have been more than enough power in his arm to deck the bastard. But not anymore. The bloke staggered backwards slightly but remained on his feet,

The other man blocked Patrick's exit route. He was caged. No doubt about it, retribution was going to be paying him a call.

The man he'd slugged inched closer and closer to him. He hissed, 'He's rude and getting ruder!'

He whacked Patrick across the chops with a powerful, right hook. Patrick tumbled backwards onto the pavement, banging his head as he went. He stayed down. His vision was fuzzy and blurred. Felt like he was seriously pissed after a stonkin' night out. Above, two misty figures bent over him. They were speaking, but he couldn't make head nor tail of what they were jabbering on about. He knew he should curl into a ball to protect himself from the blows that were about to fall but his arms and legs felt like lead. The only blow he felt was something landing on his chest. Something soft not heavy.

His mind went in and out, out and in. How long he lay there for he didn't know, but when his vision refocused the goons were gone. Instead a middle-aged woman peered down at him, her forehead creased with concern.

'You alright luv?'

Alright? Did he look alright? 'Yes, I'm fine,' he answered instead.

She offered her hand to help him sit up. 'Took a tumble, did you?'

He winced as red-hot pain shot through him. The side of his face hurt like a hammer had been taken to it. 'No, I got roughed up by a couple of muggers.'

She clucked her tongue. 'What's the world coming to?' She passed him a bottle of the water from her bag. 'I'll call the police.'

Patrick took a swig and felt his trouser pocket. They hadn't taken his phone so perhaps it was worth putting up a fight after all. 'No, don't worry, they'll be long gone. I'll call the police later.'

The woman picked something up. She seemed surprised and held it up for him to inspect. 'Is this yours luv?'

'Yeah, that's my wallet.' He sighed. 'They'll have had the money away and then thrown it.' He decided that must have been what was dumped on his chest.

He took his wallet and looked inside. Strangely all his cards were there. And the money. He'd had fifty quid and change with him when he'd set out. Quickly he took out the notes and counted.

Seventy quid.

That couldn't be right. He counted again. Definitely seventy smackers. What the fuck was going on here? Who'd ever heard of a mugging where the victim ended up with more money?

As the woman gazed on with open curiosity he took each note in turn and checked them out. It was on the third twenty that his pulse rate increased. On the back was a message scrawled in black, felt tip:

'Tell your mate Babs to back off.

Give us what we're owed.'

It was signed best wishes and the cheeky beggars had added three big kisses.

Patrick sat there flummoxed. The woman asked him urgently if he was alright again, but he didn't hear her. All he could think about was his beloved Babs was in a wagonload of trouble. Again.

Babs heard the ruckus and raised voices outside on the balcony just as she got the girls and Courtney's mate Dodgy sat at the kitchen table for their tea. She was still exhausted after the confrontation at Neville's and missing her eldest daughter like crazy. It was beyond heartbreaking that the only thing that kept her mind off Jen was the split with Dee.

''Ere,' she told the girls in a light voice trying to sooth over their concern, 'probably just some of the kids trying it on with Knox.'

Kieran's sister was doing a bang up job of playing guard dog and had become the latest curiosity for many of the kids on The Devil who would peep around the corner of the balcony in awe to get a sneak peak at the huge woman sat in a chair usually with a brew in one hand and a baseball bat in the other. They'd never seen the like.

'I won't tell you again mister to back the fuck off,' Knox loudly warned. Babs could imagine the froth foaming at the corner of her mouth.

'You better get out of my way before I pitch you over the balcony.' A man's voice. Babs' brows snaked together. His voice was muffled, which was odd because Knox's was so clear.

Babs smiled down at the girls. 'You tuck into your haddock and chips.'

Then she left them and rushed towards the door. Opened up and gasped sharply at the scene before her. Knox had her Tricky Dickie in a headlock, the muscles of her arm bulging round his neck.

She shouted as if at a dog. 'Knox! What do you think you're playing at?'

The other woman gritted her teeth as she increased the pressure round his neck making his face turn a horrible purple. 'This toerag tells me to push off so he can see ya. I tell him that ain't the way it works round here no more. So he decides to come it and I've got no choice but to show him who's daddy of the landing.'

'Let him go,' Babs cried.

She was properly mortified at the way Tricky Dickie was being done over. First time he'd been to her gaff in years and the poor bloke was being mauled by one of the wildest animals known to man.

'He's my…' Babs searched for the right word, 'gentleman friend.'

'You mean your shag?' Knox took away all the romantic

gentleness Babs had used. 'He should have said.'

Knox let him go and he started coughing and drawing in much-needed air.

When his colour had calmed down he turned blazing, avenging eyes on to Knox. 'If I was still wearing a uniform I'd take you down to the station on a charge of assault and battery.'

Babs heard a gasp, but it wasn't Knox; Courtney, Little Bea and Dodgy had their faces pressed against the kitchen window watching proceedings with wide-eyed nosiness. They scrambled away when they realised she'd caught them at it, but she wasn't fooled; they'd probably be hiding beneath the windowsill still trying to get an earful.

Knox, on the other hand, froze as if a pail of ice-cold sick had been chucked at her. She stared with disgust at Patrick like he smelled bad. Really, really bad.

'You a plod?' Her broad fingers tensed near her baseball bat leaning near against her chair. Her gaze swung to Babs. 'You letting some copper dip his wick in ya? You wanna watch that Babs, he could be infectious.' Knox gobbed on the balcony at her feet.

Babs' spine went ramrod straight. She'd had enough of people telling her who she could and couldn't see. 'He's a former policeman, Patrick Johnson, not that it's any of your beeswax.'

Knox scoffed. 'He's your Johnson is he?' Then she cackled with laughter. 'Johnson? Get it? His name?'

Babs ignored mad girl Knox as she ushered Patrick – she was still getting used to thinking of him with that name – into her home. She felt all fingers and thumbs and could barely make eye contact she was that embarrassed.

'Sorry about that.' She smiled nervously. 'Let's get ourselves into the living room and then I'll make us some Rosie Lee.'

His mouth twisted. 'I don't want any flippin' tea.'

Babs took a half step back at the ferocity of his words and the expression on his face. He looked fit to murder someone and by the looks of things that someone was her.

'Patrick, what's up?'

The muscles in his jaw twitched. 'Why have you got some she-cat heavy doing sentry duty outside your front door?'

Babs could barely breath. She should've sussed that him being a retired cop meant he'd twigged straight off what Knox was doing. She tried to brazen her way through, her gaze dancing around. 'There's been a couple of break ins in the block so my mate Knox is—'

He leaned down into her. 'Why are you lying to me?'

The last time he'd spoken to her so harshly was back in '78, in his motor, trying to convince her that Stan wasn't the man she thought he was. Babs wasn't scared of him, but it hurt so bad inside her to hear him talk to her in such a manner.

Another lie came to her lips, but she swallowed it down. How could she say she loved this man, promised to tie the knot with him and blag to his face at the same time?

Her shoulders slumped. 'I'm not at liberty to tell you.'

His hand ruffled furiously threw his hair. Then it reached down into his pocket and he handed her a twenty bill. 'Does it have anything to do with this?'

Her face turned pasty as she read the message. And read it again.

He began to pace. 'Know how I got that? It wasn't posted nice and neat through my letterbox, let me tell you that. I got jumped in the street and was left with that calling card.'

Her mouth formed an O as she reached out to him, but Patrick stepped back.

'Are you alright?' Now she understood how he'd got the bruise on his jaw.

His voice lowered as he pleaded, 'Babs tell me what trouble you're in. Let me help you.'

She was desperate to. But she couldn't. Her family were stuck with it but he wasn't. He could still walk away. If anything happened to him she would never forgive herself. 'I can't.'

He shook his head like the sadness of the world was squarely on his shoulders. 'I can't do this. Can't marry you.'

Her heart missed a beat as her harsh breath caught in her throat. 'Wha'cha mean?'

'You were right. We live in different worlds. I can't go through life looking over my shoulder wondering who might be waiting for me on the street because of this.' His hand waved round the hallway.

'But it will be over soon—'

'Until the next thing. And then the next.' She let him walk to the door though she desperately wanted to snatch him back. Hold on to him forever. Never let him go.

He gazed at her in a way that no one could doubt she was the most precious thing to him. 'I love you Babs Miller. Probably always will. I know it's a cliché, but love sometimes isn't enough.'

Then he closed the door in her face the same way she'd done to Kieran last year.

'Nanna, you alright?'

She heard Courtney's soft voice and half turned to find the girls staring at her, their bodies a hair's breath from running to her. She'd love nothing more than to feel their arms around her, comforting her, giving her their unconditional love when the bottom had dropped out of her world. Nah, that wasn't going to happen. No way was she going to fall apart in front of them. She had to remain the strong one in this family.

Babs wiped her nose with the back of her hand and put on a brave smile. 'I'm fine. Do me favour Courtney luv; in half hour bring a cuppa to my room. This stays between us and Knox, alright?'

Head held high Babs went to her room and closed the door firmly behind her. Then she flattened her back against it and slid to the floor. She thrust her fist into her mouth to muffle her cries of anguish. The love of her life was gone for good.

And there was nothing she could do about it.

Forty-Eight

Fred seized Pearl's arm, something fierce, his voice low for their ears alone.

'I don't like this. Whatever it is, don't open it. Bring it to me first and I'll take it out into the gardens and have a gander at it.'

They were in the dayroom where 'Escape To the Country,' was showcasing properties on The Costa on the telly. Fred's warning came off the back of the receptionist informing Pearl that a postman with a package for her was waiting at the front desk. He couldn't leave it because she needed to sign for it. The receptionist waited, none too patiently, in the doorway like she had to get away to do her nails.

Pearl was jumpy after having her room rearranged but even she thought Fred was going over the top. 'What you saying? It might be a bomb or something?'

'I'm just warning ya. No harm in me having a proper nose at it first.'

Pearl had a think about. Then patted his hand in gratitude and got to her feet. Even if there turned out to a problem she didn't need her hand held. Plus Fred needed to rest still looking worn down by Vi's death.

Fred clucked his tongue in irritation but she ignored him. She followed the receptionist out front where she found a postie in a uniform and baseball cap waiting for her. Outside was his GPO red van. On the desk was a shoebox-shaped package.

'I need you to sign for this,' the postman said.

Somewhere between the dayroom and reception, Pearl began to wonder if it really might be a bomb. She'd warned her grandsons to knock it off but that didn't mean that Babs wasn't going to still try it on.

'I dunno, what is it?' she said cautiously.

The postman huffed as if he'd missed his tea break. 'I'm a postman darlin', I just deliver stuff. If I'd looked inside I'd be committing a criminal offence. Tampering with Her Majesty's mail is against the law.'

Pearl gave him an arched look. She had a right smart aleck on her hands.

She edged closer. The parcel seemed legit but she still wasn't convinced. 'Who's it from?'

The postman obviously wasn't used to the public refusing packages. 'Look luv, do you want it or not? Only I'm running late and have got targets to meet. I can take it back to the sorting office while you make your mind up but then you'll have to come and fetch it yourself if you decide you want it. And bring ID.'

As Pearl examined the label she noticed something. 'This isn't for me – it's for Pearl Holland. I'm not Pearl Holland, I'm Pearl Hennessy. The address is wrong as well.'

The postman looked at the parcel and then at his notebook. He went scarlet with embarrassment. 'Oh right –

that's the wrong parcel. My mistake. Your one must still be in the van. Hold on a minute.'

He picked up the package and walked out, muttering to himself and then opened the shutter on his van and threw the package inside before climbing in.

The receptionist went back to work and Pearl stood with her arms folded waiting for the guy to come back with her delivery.

Postman Pat is taking his time, Pearl thought with impatience as the minutes ticked by. She waited some more and more still. In a huff Pearl walked over to the doors and peered out. How many parcels did he have in there for it to take this long? She opened the doors, rubbed her arms against the cool breeze as she walked outside. The shutter on the van was pulled low with only a few feet open so she couldn't see inside. There was no noise either.

'Hello?' she called hesitantly.

The postman's voice came, all jolly and jaunty. 'Wait there a minute luv…Ah, here it is. Found it.'

The shutter flew open startling Pearl. Four arms flew out and grabbed her under the armpits. Lifted her up and yanked her into the van. She opened her mouth to scream but a determined palm slammed over it keeping her sound of terror locked in her throat. The hand belonged to a woman, but with thick fingers like a navvy.

Pearl was forced to the floor, like a ragdoll. Then the woman sat on her. A fist banged on the inside of the van. It took off like a bat out of hell.

The woman pulled her hand from Pearl's mouth. She gasped and spluttered for air. Her lungs burned as she struggled to fill them, hyperventilating from shock and the weight of the ten tonne bitch. Then honest to God fury consumed her. Fury at herself that she could have been so dumb as to be lifted in this way by a couple of chancers.

'Ere – put this mail bag over her head and tie her hands up.'

Her body stiffened at the male voice. Did that mean there were three of them? Two in the back, one up front? Whoever this bloke was he wasn't the pretend postman. His accent was pure East London and sounded like he was used to being Top Dog.

'Stop with the wriggling, you dopey bint,' heavy moo ordered, 'or I'll make the knots so tight your hands will drop off.'

The woman sounded like the kind of bird who appears on reality TV shows explaining why the neighbours on the estate hate her kids.

The man sniggered, 'don't worry about her hands. She won't need them where she's going.'

'She will, she's gotta do some digging.'

The guy was laughing now. 'Oh yeah, I forgot. We should have brought some gardening gloves.'

The van rocked with their twin laughter.

Pearl tried to sound defiant but her nerves got the better of her and her words trembled. 'I suppose this is Babs' doing, is it?'

The man mocked her. 'Never you mind; you just think of some famous last words.'

Pearl couldn't actually believe that Babs was behind this. She couldn't believe her one-time mate would stoop this low.

'Is it about the gold? Babs knows I don't have it – she

has. Why's she doing this? I...I...' But she couldn't get the words out.

Pearl wanted to cry. Not because she was scared – she'd had enough near-death experiences in her life to face the darkness – but because she wouldn't see her grandsons again. Never hear her kids finally forgive her for abandoning them. As the awful thoughts tumbled inside her Pearl didn't even realise she was hiccupping with sobs.

'Oh shut it with blubbing.' That's the first time Pearl realised the woman's voice sounded vaguely familiar. 'I mean, we've all gotta go sometime. How old are you – sixty? Sixty-five? That's nearly your three score and ten anyway. A woman of your age taking a long walk off a short pier, let's face it, we're not talking 'taken from us too soon' here, are we?'

The man's next words made Pearl hold her breath. 'What's the best way of getting rid of a body?'

'Chainsaw. Mind you that would be really messy. Imagine all that gory blood and shattered bone. Yuk! What bout an acid bath? Ain't that how the Mob got rid of their unwanted?'

'A mail sack, some weights and a fishing boat, were the only tools you'd need,' he insisted with what sounded like first hand knowledge. With triumph he added, 'and look! I brought a mailbag with us! Who says I don't think ahead!'

As the journey went on and on Pearl was goaded by their taunts and she began to hit back. 'You won't get away with this. I know people, people who'll track your murdering arses down and make you pay.'

The man was unimpressed. 'Do ya? Where are they then? I'm afraid you've gotta face it old girl; you'll just be another missing person on police files. There's millions of 'em, nobodies who came and went and no one ever knew where. It's quite sad really. All those missing persons fading from their loved one's memories with just a few photos to remind them as they get old.'

The van seemed to have left the main road and was bumping over potholes and cattle grids. That gave way to the sound of branches breaking and the vehicle swaying as it drove over rough ground. They grinded slowly to a halt.

The guy explained, sarky to the hilt, 'here we are then – Epping Forest — the gangland cemetery! '

The only sound was the wind in the trees and a hooting owl. The shutters crashed open. Pearl was unceremoniously dragged out. The bag jerked off her head, the rope round her wrists cut.

She squinted in the full beam of the strong headlights in the gathering darkness. The two figures wore balaclavas and looked like ghouls from a horror film. One of the ghouls was carrying a shovel. The man.

'Alright Pearlie Queen, I'd like you to dig me a hole please, about six foot long and a few feet deep. I mean that's just a rough guide, there's no need to get it exactly right, I'm flexible.'

'Dig your own fucking hole, you cocky, evil monster.'

The bloke sighed and pulled a shooter from his jacket and held it to the side her head. 'If you don't dig me a hole I'm gonna plug my brand of holes in you and I know exactly where to place them to cause a lingering and very painful death. Now get fucking digging.'

Pearl knew she didn't have a choice, so she picked up the shovel and did as told. They watched her like hawks. Her knees and back ached and she'd only been going for ten minutes. Well, fuck the pair of them, no way was she stopping and pleading for her life. She'd grown up tilling the land in Jamaica and knew all about getting her hands dirty.

In the end it wasn't much of a hole that Pearl dug, but it seemed to satisfy the gunman. He pushed her into it and then hunched down beside her.

He held the pistol to her temple. 'Right, this is your last chance or this is goodbye. Now then – where's the gold?'

With the blinding light from the headlamps, his covered face and the gathering darkness all Pearl could see of him was a menacing, black shadow.

'I haven't got the gold. Babs knows that. If she's promised you a cut, you've been had.'

'Oh dear, that's disappointing…' The pressure of the gun increased against Pearl's head.

He waited for a long time before she finally felt the gun shake slightly. She gripped her hands together and prayed for her children's forgiveness.

He pulled the trigger. Click. Nothing happened. But he wasn't done with her. He pulled the trigger again. Another dull thud of the empty chamber.

The ghoul looked at his gun with mock surprise and then up at the woman who loomed over them. 'Would you fucking Adam and Eve it? I only went and forgot to bring any bullets.'

The woman sneered, 'Some gangland boss you are!'

And that's when Pearl recalled who the woman's voice belonged to. That twisted, bully-girl Knox. She'd been Top Bitch of the wing Babs and Pearl had been banged up in. Inside Pearl raged. She'd teach that slag to mess with her.

Pearl kept schtum about her new knowledge.

The bloke continued to rabbit on. 'Well, in every criminal scheme, there's always one fatal flaw. Mine was to forget to bring any shells.'

He rose to his feet and looked down at a secretly seething Pearl. 'Alright, this is your final warning. I haven't got time for this kind of Drury Lane theatre. If you don't return my client's yellow stuff, the next time you see me will be to the tune of gunfire. Real gunfire.'

The two figures walked back and climbed in the van and sped off.

Pearl clambered out of her grave screaming, 'I haven't got the gold, you fucking idiots!'

Forty-Nine

'Courtney Miller! The headmistress would like to see you in her office at once please!'

The deputy head had barged into her classroom, mid-lesson, and called out to Courtney like a prison warder. Mrs Freeman was a very attractive woman and knew it. Word was she'd been putting it about with any dad who was worth a million plus.

The history teacher looked at Courtney with sympathy. 'You're excused Miller.'

Courtney went limp. She knew there was going to be comeback after Flo had trashed the headmistress with her milady routine. No way was Mrs Elliott going to take that lying down.

Resigned, she closed her book and got up to go.

The teacher snapped, 'what are you two girls smirking at? Is that your mobile?'

One of the two girls hurriedly dropped her phone into her pocket. 'No miss.'

There was a lot of sniggering going on that morning as girls looked at their mobiles but no one had let Courtney in on the joke. Most likely a cat video that had clocked up a trillion hits or some girl hating on another on social media. She'd dared not check her phone because she was already in Elliott's bad books. She didn't need the grief.

Mind you, she was in no hurry to get there either, so she took the long way round, dawdling in corridors and checking her locker. When she finally arrived outside the headmistress' PA's office all she could hear were raised voices. Courtney's heart sank. Whatever was going on she prayed had zilch to do with her.

Mustering her courage she tapped gently on the door, hoping the knock would go unnoticed and she could slip away. Instead, it swung open and the PA clutched it so tight her knuckles were white. Her face was as pale as her hand. There was an almighty row going on inside Mrs Elliott's office. The headmistress' voice was dialled up to the max.

Her PA guarded the door like a Rottweiler. 'What do you want Miller?'

Since her aunts had flounced in here and lay the law down the PA had taken against her. No problem since the feeling was mutual; Courtney didn't give a monkey's toss about Missus Twin Set and Pearls too.

'Miss said she wanted to see me.'

'Does she?' The PA was jumpy and all nerves.

Courtney craned her head to see if the door to Elliot's adjoining office was open. It certainly sounded like it was. But it wasn't.

'She's too busy to see anyone. Now run along.'

The door slammed shut. Courtney hesitated for a few moments. She wasn't interested in history and she was coming over a bit nosey. It wasn't like Elliot to normally lose her rag like this. Even when Flo had worked her over the headmistress had kept it cool.

Intrigued, instead of going back to class Courtney went outside. With a burglar's step she crept along the side of the school until she was under the headmistress' window. Elliot was still going at it hammer and tongs.

'Do you think Mr Baxter, that parents are sending their daughters to this school at ten grand a term in order to have a pervert for music teacher?'

Courtney grinned with supreme satisfaction. Barmy Baxter was getting it in the neck, was he? Served him right. She'd kept well out of his reach since he'd tried to throttle the very life from her. But 'pervert?' What was that about? His voice was quieter. Courtney picked her ears up. She could just about make out what he was saying.

'This is obviously a set up Mrs Elliot.' Sounded like he was wetting his pants. 'You only have to look at that picture to see it's been photoshopped. It's obvious some of your pupils who've decided to have a malicious joke at my expense—'

'My girls?' Her voice was like thunder. 'My students come from some of this country's most respectable families.'

Courtney so wanted to peak through the window…She restrained herself.

'You can't seriously believe that I, of all people, would put myself in such a position. It's absurd. I'm a musician, an artist.'

Elliott's voice became even louder. 'Well, it looks genuine to me.' She cried with horror. 'And not only is it on the school's website but it's on the achievement and standards page. That's the one page prospective new parents find out about the standard of education in *my* school and make their decision about whether to send their child here.'

Courtney could feel Elliott vigorously shaking her head. 'I'm afraid I'm not in a position to give anyone the benefit of the doubt. The welfare of my students has to come first, not to mention the fact that I'm not willing to have my school turned into a laughing stock.'

'Let me have another look at that image please.'

A few moments of silence before Baxter pleaded, 'Look! Can't you see? The woman's hand doesn't fit on my thigh properly. It's obviously fake.'

The penny dropped for Courtney. She leaned against the wall and pulled out her phone where she found a dozen alerts from other girls through the morning. She went straight to the school's website.

On the achievement and standards page was a banner with huge black letters announcing, 'Naughty Nights At The Glam Gran's Parties (Uncut).'

It featured two naked wrinkly women, each one posing on the lap of a bloke who was sat on an easy chair. He leered at the camera with a drink and a cigar wearing just a pair of y-fronts. There wasn't much light at this Glam Gran's porno party but there was no doubt it looked very like Barmy Baxter.

Courtney slapped her palm over her mouth as she creased up laughing. Her tummy hurt so much she had to hold her chest.

In the office Mrs Elliott was back to her glacial, sniffy self. 'Since you are on a short-term contract I think it's best we terminate our arrangement now. Best for all parties. You need to leave the premises now. All your belongings will be forwarded to your address.'

He began to shout the odds. 'This is outrageous. You

haven't heard the last of this. You'll be hearing from my solicitor.'

The office door opened and then slammed. Courtney raced round to the front door to catch him in the corridor. No way was she missing this moment of total triumph. As he went by red-faced, she pulled some paper out of her pocket and collared him. 'Please sir, I'm wondering if you could sponsor me? I'm doing a five mile walk to help old-age grannies.'

Baxter looked at her with hatred. He pushed her out of the way. 'Fuck off Miller!'

'Here he comes.'

Tiffany and Flo were at the wheel of a hired car when the man who had dared terrorise their beloved niece emerged from the electronic school gates.

Flo drove up along side him as he marched down the street.

She leaned out of the driver's window. 'Oi Oi!'

A still fuming Baxter peered at them. 'Do I know you?'

'No, but you know our niece Courtney. Look mate, what you get up to in your private life is your business but don't you ever, *ever*, put your hands on her again – do you understand?'

Baxter clenched his fists. 'You faked those porno photos, did you?'

Flo's lips shaped into an innocent O. 'Dunno what you're gassing on about mate but we will say this: If you threaten our kid again, we won't play for laughs next time. It'll be more like this.'

She chucked a photo at his feet. She turned to Tiff and

laughed as they high-fived. Popped an Annie each. With backslapping laughter they drove off at speed.

Mr Baxter, aka, The Salesman, snatched up the picture. It showed a gravestone with his image on it and the words:

'Mr Baxter

RIP'

Fifty

It was bound to happen.

Pinky and Styley – the morons should be shot for the names alone - would twig soon enough he was the one backing Babs. And when they did...they'd come after him, blasting on all fronts. That's why Kieran was looking out of his huge, office window with a sharp eye checking the comings and goings below.

He stiffened, shifting into high alert, when he clocked a motorbike, driver plus pillion passenger, pull up outside. The guys peered into reception before slowly backing the bike up and checking out the building.

They wore helmets, trainers and black overalls with baggy tops. Gunman's clothes. Looked like they were on a reccy to him, casing exits and entrances, alarm system, security guards, the whole shebang. And after that they would lie in wait for him when he was coming or going.

And then...Bang! Bang! Bang! He was a dead man.

He watched them rev up the bike and zoom off up the street. Ordinary Joes probably wouldn't even notice the bike or think the guys were lost. But Kieran had been in the business way too long not to know better. Or maybe they really were lost, you never knew, especially on the Isle of Dogs.

'Mr Scott?'

Kieran had forgotten that he was doing an interview with a hack from one of the money mags to big up his business. His PR people liked him doing this but he didn't. The press thought he was a crook and he didn't like that. He turned back to see the journo sitting on one side of his teak desk that he'd brought back from a trip to Italy – no expense spared. He could see she thought he was a bit odd, jumping up and going to the window when he heard a noise on the street.

He smoothed his palms over his Hugo Boss jacket and walked with purpose back to his desk. 'Sorry Jane, I'm expecting someone.'

'My name is Martha,' she corrected him, her lips curdling like soured cream at the edges. Tetchy!

Alright looking woman, nothing to write home about, with long, bronzed hair and soft skin, but the hungry glint in her light-brown eyes spoke volumes about her ambitions. He'd worn that same look once upon a time.

'Martha, 'o course – now where were we?' He eased deeper in his chair to give her the impression he was relaxed.

'I was hoping to ask you a question that gets asked from time when your name crops up in the world of finance and development.'

Kieran clasped his hands together and said, 'shoot' before wishing he hadn't.

Martha avoided his eyes. 'Only – it might be considered a bit rude.'

Kieran shrugged. 'Ask me anything you like sweetheart – I haven't got any secrets.'

She toyed with her pen. Made eye contact. 'Well, as you're no doubt aware, there are rumours that you made your fortune by running with friends who come from the London underworld. No doubt that's just nasty gossip from some of your rivals and there's no truth in it – but...umm...I was wondering if you'd like to comment on those stories?'

London underworld? Cheeky fucking bint.

Kieran gave her a dirty look and then reached across his desk for his antique cigarette box. He lit up an expensive brand of charcoal filter, gold tipped fags and blew out a puff of smoke. Her face scrunched with distaste. A bleeding heart ciggy hater! Well, tough jiggly puffs, she was in his space now.

Kieran sighed as he leaned slightly forward. 'Do you know what really pisses me off about this country Jane? It's the way everyone assumes that a poor boy from the back streets can't make a few quid for hisself without sticking his fingers in someone else's till. These chinless, public school prats can't accept that a geezer from the East End can beat them at their own game, so they start up with the muck spreading at their poncey parties. All them Ruperts and Simons, they can't hack it, know what I mean? So I'll be frank with your readers sweetheart.'

He pulled hard on his smoke and practically blew it in her face. 'Yeah, I come from a tough neck of the woods. Did I meet a few villains while I was growing up? O' course I did. Did I get in a few barneys and the odd ruck when I was a nipper? Fair play, yes I did. But let me tell you this; I made my money by honest toil and hard graft, not by 'running with' anyone, as you put it.'

A button on the desk phone lit up. Kieran pressed it and snapped at the receptionist, 'Not now darlin, I'm doing an interview.'

She sounded out of puff and harassed. 'Mr Scott, we have intruders in the building. I have alerted security.'

He stubbed his fag out with a hard grind. 'Are they wearing crash helmets?'

The receptionist's tone sounded surprised. 'Yes, that's right. They rushed the barriers in reception and we think they're heading upstairs.'

'Alright, tell everyone to keep their heads down.'

Kieran jumped out of his chair and pulled open a drawer in his desk. He took out a Glock, loaded a magazine and pulled off the safety catch.

He turned to Martha who looked at his gun in bug-eyed horror. 'You better get under the desk.'

'I beg your pardon?' Her lips moved like that of a beached fish.

'Are your deaf? I said get under the fucking desk!'

As she scrambled to do his bidding Kieran picked up a golf club that was propped up against a wall and tucked it under his arm. He opened the office door a touch, mentally did a three-count, then peered outside. No one around. He ran out and hid in a stationary storeroom that was nearby. He held the shooter tight with one hand and the club with the other.

This one was going to be down to him. His company security people would run like rabbits when the gunplay started and he couldn't really blame them. They weren't paid to risk their lives. What a right idjit he'd been not to have hired a couple of tooled up heavies from the old days as bodyguards and put them on the payroll as caretakers or something. He knew his past was going to catch up with him sooner or later and now he had to deal with all this crap on his own. At the same time, he felt a spark of excitement. This was how he really rolled, not having working dinners with Rupert and Simon.

He listened intently until he heard a door open at the far end of the corridor and the soft footsteps heading for his office. A single set of steps. The other ponce was probably covering the stairs. That was good; he could deal with them one-on-one. As the guy went past his hidey-hole, Kieran gave it a second and then threw open the door.

He levelled his Glock at the man who now had his back to him. He had the fucker bang to rights.

'Drop the hard wear, get on the floor or I'll cut you in two!'

Even though his head was covered by a crash helmet, Kieran could tell this wannabe killer was taken totally by surprise.

The geezer half turned and fumbled in his pocket. That was enough for Kieran. He fired twice. The force of the bullets struck so hard he was blown up against the wall where his head banged before he bounced backwards onto the floor. But there was no blood.

'Help! Help!' Martha screamed from the office.

Kieran ignored her. He moved forward slowly and used his foot to flip up the guy's top. Kieran knew what he'd find, and he was right - a BPV. The wanker was out for the count. Kieran found his shooter in a pocket. Slipped it in his own pocket and thought about using his club to break the bloke's legs but then remembered that there was another one about. This joker could wait.

Running at high speed down the corridor, Kieran peered through a glass pane in the door to the stairwell. The other gunman was waiting at the top of the stairs, shooter ready for action, looking downwards. Kieran thought the bloke looked a bit on edge as he shifted his weight from one leg to another.

The guy made towards the door, changed his mind and went down a few steps on the stairs. These two weren't professionals, but he'd give them that, they had some front, rushing his office like fucking commandos. It crossed Kieran's mind that it might actually be the brothers themselves, Pinky and Styley. They were young and stupid enough to try a stunt like this. And they'd probably want to take personal revenge for him and his sister's kidnapping their grandmother.

Kieran kicked open the door and raised his pistol. 'Your brother's dead! Drop the gun or it'll be double bubble down the undertakers!'

Stunned for a moment, the guy seemed to be doing as he was told. He stretched out his arm but then twisted and loosed off a volley of shots. Kieran ducked as bullets hit the wall behind. A piercing burn sizzled down the side of his leg.

Enough with the playing games.

He fired only one shot back which hit the other man on his helmet. He tumbled down the stairs like a stuntman and then rolled, topsy-turvy, down a second flight. Kieran rushed over to the railing to see his target struggling to his feet and fleeing down the stairwell. He set off in hot pursuit but he took only a few steps before the wound in his leg kicked in and each step became an agony. By the time he staggered down to reception the only trace of the second hitman was the sound of a motorbike tearing down the street at high speed.

His receptionist's stark-brown face peeped over her desk. 'Did you call the law?'

His staff knew the golden rule – never, ever get on the blower to the cops.

'Of course not.' Her voice shook.

'Good.' Kieran turned to see frightened staff huddled around reception. 'Alright – back to work. Nothing to worry your pretty heads over. I'm not paying you to stand around looking scared, am I?'

Then Kieran remembered. He limped over to the lift as fast as he could and went back up to the top floor, Glock in hand. But by the time he reached the corridor outside his office, the other gunman had legged it. Kieran stumbled back to his office, ripped the sleeve off his shirt and used it to bind what he could see was only a flesh wound on his leg.

As he put his shooter back in the drawer, he looked under his desk. 'You still there?'

A terrified Martha was still hunched in her hiding place. 'You can come out now, they've gone.'

A badly shaken Martha was shivering as she put her notebook and recorder in her bag. She looked at him, her mouth opened as if to say something. Then, thinking better of it, she left his office as if the hounds of hell were after her.

As she went, Kieran called after her, 'don't forget, all that stuff about me and the Underworld - it's complete pony.'

Fifty-One

The following afternoon the totally miffed barman of the Bad Moon lay down the law to Babs, vigorously tapping the tip of his finger against the bar to ensure every word got through her loaf.

'I don't want no argy-bargy this time round, you got it?'

'I'm just meeting my mate,' she answered sweetly.

'Yeah? That's what you said the last time.'

Before they could exchange more crossed words the door swung open. A breathless Pearl stepped inside.

'Alright Babs. Mister Barman.' She sounded cheery which Babs cautiously took to be a good sign.

The still narked barman sorted them out a half lemonade shandy and a neat Bacardi and they took themselves off to the snug to keep prying eyes at bay.

As soon as Babs got word that Kieran had been hurt – though he protested it was nothing but a flesh wound – she made up her mind that this carry-on had to stop. So she'd got on the ol' dog to Pearl, swallowed her pride, and said it was time to negotiate. Pearl couldn't agree quick enough.

Now they drank in silence each wary of the other.

Pearl was the first to speak. 'I take it there's no surprises hiding behind the bar this time?'

'Or outside?'

They each shook their heads. Babs added, 'Cross your heart—'

'And hope to die.' Pearl hesitated. 'How's Jen?'

'Still hanging in there. We go down there every day and pray she wakes up.' She didn't add, 'Which is another reason I don't need all this'. But then she didn't need to.

Pearl worried her bottom lip. 'I was sorry to hear that your fella walked away from you. I never told my grandsons to drag him into this. Or that grenade…or Kieran…' she shook her head.

Babs couldn't even answer because Tricky Dickie dumping her was still so raw. Instead she leaned forward and lowered her voice even more. 'I was gonna bring the grenade and throw it in the river.' She frowned, 'but the strangest thing is I can't find it.' She shrugged. 'I think Flo or Tiff must've got rid of it.' She took a deep breath. 'I swear to you, on my grandkids lives, that I never took the gold.'

Pearl leaned in too. 'Babs I didn't take it either. I know I can be a touch free with the truth sometimes, but this time I've been straight up all the way.'

Babs considered her one-time friend, searching her face for the slightest indications she was trying to pull a fast one. Pearl's skin was strained and her eyes full of sadness.

Babs asked, 'So if we didn't take it - then who did?'

Pearl picked up her glass, took a deep lug and then sat back. 'The way I see it, the only way that someone could've pinched it is if one of us blabbed to someone.'

Babs spluttered, 'Well, don't look at me coz I never say boo to no one.'

Pearl's defences were back up. 'Well, nor did I.'

They were at stalemate again and the last thing Babs needed was another major league row. So she tried to calm things down.

'There's no point going at each other's throat, we need to think this through calmly.'

She paused, swallowed some shandy as her brain ticked away. Gently, she popped her half-pint glass on the table. 'The only explanation can be one of us dropped a clanger, not on purpose mind. Might be it slipped out and we didn't realise.'

Pearl frowned, her fine-boned fingers locking together. 'I don't usually make those kind of mishaps…but still…'

'I definitely didn't tell one of my girls.' Babs started thinking out loud. 'I kept it to myself that I was visiting you. And no way would it have come out in their company coz the whole reason I had anything to do with that soddin' gold was to keep them all safe.'

Pearl's eyes roving round as she joined in. 'When I saw my grandsons I was always guarded about what I spoke of—'

Babs got impatient, leaning forward again. 'We need to think long and hard about this. Go through every last person…' Abruptly she stopped seeing the expression of shock cover the other woman's face. 'What is it?'

Pearl shook her head as if trying to wake up from a trance. 'Nah…Couldn't be.'

'Who?'

Pearl's expression turned twisted and ugly. 'Yes, he mentioned the gold that time. But how did he know? I never told him that it was gold that had been teefed from my settee.'

Babs was liable to drag Pearl across the table if she didn't stop speaking in riddles. 'Who you rabbiting on about?'

It was as if Pearl couldn't hear her. 'Said he had underworld connections. Even claimed to be a burglar in his day, though we all thought he was chatting outta his behind. Warned me about that package.'

Babs thumped the table. 'Pearl!!"

Pearl looked up at her with rage darkening her eyes. 'I'll tell you who. Fred the bloody Red.'

'You sure he's out?' Babs asked quietly as she stood with Pearl outside Fred's room.

'Some of the others have taken him out to Bingo to keep his mind from thinking about Vi, God rest her kind-hearted soul.'

Babs still couldn't get her head around this. Some geriatric had nabbed the gold? She'd only clocked this Fred one time and the old boy looked like all he wanted to do was rest his bones in a deck chair on the beach with a pint of stout by his side.

'Are you sure about this Pearl?'

The other woman looked fit to explode. 'That crafty bugger has been holding one hand out in friendship while the other's behind his back ripping me off.'

Not reassured – Babs still thought this was a fool's errand – but she got on with the job. Plus, the sooner they could eliminate Fred from their enquiries, the sooner they could pop their thinking caps back on.

'His door's probably locked.'

Pearl gave the handle a go. Babs was right. She sneaked a look down the corridor and then stuck her hand under her headscarf and pulled out two hairpins. Babs arched her brows; Pearl was a regular box of criminal tricks.

Pearl expertly placed the pins in the lock. Click. 'Easy peasy,' she muttered and then opened the door.

His room wasn't choc-a-bloc full of stuff like Pearl's, it held only the bare essentials – a bed, armchair, built in wardrobe, chest of drawers with a small telly on top and a night stand with a lamp. The walls were bare of photos or any pictures. Fred the Red looked like he lived the life of a monk.

Babs took in the room with a dubious eye. 'Can't see where he'd stash the gold, unless it's under the bed o' course.'

Pearl squinted, a cunning expression settling on her face. 'Nah, Fred wouldn't have the goodies in here.' She turned to Babs. 'My guess is that he didn't do the job alone.'

Babs rolled her eyes getting thoroughly fed up of this caper. 'Oh, maybe he's in league with some shape-shifter?' She smacked her lips. 'Come on, Fred clearly hasn't got sod all to do with this.'

Pearl wouldn't have it and sidled up closer to her friend. 'Nah Babsie, just listen to me. He was always going on about how he was connected in the biz, even knew Uncle Frank.'

'Uncle Frank?' That got Babs' attention. 'You saying that Uncle Frank had a hand in this?'

'What I'm saying is there's gotta be evidence in here that shows Fred's in cahoots with another teef. We look through his drawers, under the bed, in the bathroom and I betcha we find the thread that will lead to our gold.'

And that's what they did for the next twenty minutes, riffled through Fred's worldly goods, hunting high and low.

'Babs?' Pearl called as she parked herself on the edge of

the bed holding what looked like a black bound book.

'What's that?' Babs plonked down besides her frowning at the book.

Pearl laid it in her lap. 'This,' she tapped the cover, 'is a photo album. I was in here the other day and I had to move it off the bed. Maybe it can shed a bit of light.'

The first couple of pages showed a very youthful – and handsome – Fred with his long departed wife and his sons when they were young uns. Then the photos changed to him in clubs and parties.

'Fuck me sideways,' Babs rasped, not believing her eyes. She touched a figure in a black and white snap. 'That's my Stanley. And look…' her finger moved wildly on, 'that's Uncle Frank.'

Suddenly Pearl sucked in a huge breath, her gaze riveted on another figure in the shot. 'No way—'

The door swung open. Without realising what she was saying, Pearl nodded. 'Hello Fred.'

'What the fuck are you doing in my room?'

Fifty-Two

Pearl was up and off the bed so quick there wasn't much evidence of the arthritis she claimed to have in her knee joints. She was in his face, her fingers flexing and moving like she couldn't decide whether to throttle him or crush him between her twitching fingers.

'You vile bastard Fred. You conniving, donkey-brained, dog in a manger bastard.'

His face grew red as he shut the door. He looked her directly in the eye. 'Don't know what you're going on about sweetheart—'

'The gold Fred,' Babs calmly jumped in as she stood. She kept her distance from them, not wanting to be any closer in case Pearl kicked right off.

'Gold,' Pearl underscored at the shocked expression on his face. What a fake up artist.

'Don't know nuthin bout no gold.'

Pearl clucked her tongue and shook her head as if he were a naughty boy whose mummy had caught him with his hand inside the drinks cabinet.

'Don't give me none of that innocent shit. You mentioned the gold the other day. I should have twigged,' she placed her finger beside her mouth as if she were deep in thought and in a baby voiced said, ''Ooo, how did Fred know bout the gold? Coz I never told him *what* I had hidden in my settee'. You knew all the friggin' time.'

Her finger fell away as sadness changed her face. 'I know we've had our ups and downs, but I thought you were my friend. My mate.'

Like a man defeated, his shoulders slumped as he moved to the bed and almost fell on it. His head was bowed. 'I only did it for Vi. I'd have never done it otherwise.'

Pearl's jaw dropped south in shock. 'Vi helped you—'

'No, no.' He raised his head. His eyes glittered with tears. 'Back in the day I was a burglar, but not your bog standard variety, I did jobs for hire. If someone didn't wanna get their hands dirty I was your man. Word got around and before I knows it I'm doing jobs for some of the biggest Faces in the smoke.' A long sigh escaped him. 'Give it all up when my Lizzie took bad and once she'd passed on to live with the angels I had my boys to see right.'

His eyes sharpened. 'But that instinct for finding stuff folk think they've tucked securely away never leaves ya. It's like you've got an extra sense, another trigger in your brain.' He looked at Pearl. 'And when you moved here and got those bars put up I knew you were hiding something.'

Pearl opened her mouth with indignation, but Babs caught her forearm to allow him to continue.

'I came in your room one night when you were sleeping. I still had a pair of sandman feet that moved as soundlessly as walking on air. The settee was a good hiding spot but the problem was something was making the bottom of it sag to the floor. Something heavy.'

'So you took the gold?' Pearl couldn't hold back any longer.

He shook his head. 'Nah, I only wanted to see what you were keeping back from prying eyes.' His face became strained showing his age. 'I didn't set out to rob ya. It's only when I heard Vi talking about her money worries a month back to her sister that I got the idea of taking the gold to sell it on to dosh her up.' His face crumpled. 'But I was too late. Too late. She should've waited and I would've seen her right.'

Understanding dawned on Pearl's face. 'So that's why you kept saying you were too late after Vi and Di died.'

His voice was wretched as he barely kept the tears at bay. 'If she had hung on for a couple of weeks more I would've had the money all ready for her to pay to stay here. But she didn't wait for me. I was only going to take a cut that was enough for her, didn't want none for meself—'

Babs cut in, hardening her heart to his distress. 'I know you think you were doing a kindness but it created a wagonload of badness. That was a lot of gold. So if you were only gonna take enough to help Vi who was gonna keep the rest of the money?'

Pearl punched in, 'and don't deny it coz we know some other fucker was involved in this. The job happened when we were in Liverpool Street, so you got someone else to do the nicking.'

'It's still here,' he said quietly.

'What? The gold?' Babs and Pearl shouted.

Fred took them to the boiler room in the basement. He crouched down in the middle of the room. 'Whoever built this place did a right Jerry job of it.'

He started uncovering and shifting some of the fireproof floor tiles. When they were piled up, they could see boxes that had once contained tomatoes from a supermarket. The cardboard was torn, ragged and stained. Fred pulled open the flaps from one box. Inside was several bars of gold. They were kept higgledy-piggledy and covered in dust and muck from where they'd been carried from one hiding place to another before finally coming to rest in this boiler room. There was no sheen on them and they looked like a job lot of materials left over from a building job.

Babs looked down and wrinkled her nose. It seemed right. These bars had long since lost their alluring glow for her. They were dirty alright.

Pearl lent over to pick one up but Babs pulled her back. 'Don't touch it. It's cursed.'

Pearl straightened abruptly. 'You're right. If I had one of my sage sticks I'd purify all the evil spirits.'

Babs huffed. 'Don't think even that will turn this gold into good.' She looked down at Fred. 'So who's your Batman to your Robin in all of this?'

The blood drained away from his face. 'If I tell you I'll be seeing my beloved Vi a lot sooner than I banked on.'

Pearl pulled the photo album out from where it was tucked under her arm. She urgently flicked the pages until she found the one she was after. Shoved it in Fred's face and pointed to a figure in a photo. 'That's him, ain't it?'

The look on his face told her everything she needed to know. She kissed her teeth with violent intent as she shared the photo with Babs.

Babs rocked back on her heels in shock. She was incapable of speech for a few seconds she was that stupefied.

When she did finally find her tongue she blustered, 'But I thought…I can't—'

'Since Fred's keeping his trap well and truly shut there's only one way to find out for sure,' Pearl asserted with authority. 'There's one other person who knows who stole the gold.'

Fred weaved to his feet, his turn to be gobsmacked. 'What you gassing on about? No one else knows nish.'

'See, that's where you're wrong.'

Pearl stomped out with Babs and Fred following close behind. She only stopped when she reached Lin Chen's room. She knocked. No answer. Did it again, same thing. Pearl knew she could've got her grandsons on the case to make Lin spill the beans, but as much as she loved her boys, they could be cack-handed and this woman was a delicate thing with a heart condition. Blimey, she'd have been dead after they'd got through with her.

'I know you're in there Lin. Stop playing dead or—'

The door eased open and the other woman's face appeared. 'I don't know anything.'

Pearl ignored her. 'I'm not asking you for a name. Is this the fella?'

She held up the photo album. Lin's eyes widened as her bony fingers tightened on the door. That's all the answer Pearl needed.

Then she caught Pearl off guard by unexpectedly spitting, 'He did business with my husband. It did not end well.' She shut the door quietly.

Babs and Pearl stared at each other as all the pieces of the puzzle fell into place.

Babs folded her arms and announced with lethal determination, 'It's about time we turned the tables.'

Fifty-Three

'Who's going to grow up to be a strapping lad like his granddad?'

Neville used a man's deep, rambling voice as he looked down at his grandson in his arms. Instead of his usual sweet smile Natty grizzled at him and flayed his legs. Must have wind, Neville decided.

'You're not full of yourself,' Dee responded to his comment, the twinkle in her eyes showing she was joking.

They sat in the large lounge of her house, which Neville had to admit was an impressive piece of property. But then he'd expect nothing else from John Black's missus. His girl had done good for herself.

He peered at the baby. 'He don't much look like John.'

Dee looked upset at the remark, her mouth twisting with displeasure. 'I never did ask how you met my John.'

So she wanted to change the subject, did she? He stared harder at his wriggling grandson and thought, what secrets are you hiding, eh little boy?

Neville answered her question. 'I met him at a club in Soho part-owned by Stanley Miller—'

Dee's brows shot up. 'You knew Babs' old man?'

'Everyone knew Stan Miller. He was one of those geezers who put himself about to make contacts. A very ambitious man was Stan. A man with big dreams.'

His gaze gleamed at the end as he thought back to times past when he'd been a young man running around town trying to make a rep for himself. It hadn't been easy for a lad from the Caribbean to stake his claim in London's underworld but he'd learned how to duck and dive in both its black and white worlds.

Dee's mobile went off. 'Yeah…What? Look I don't wanna know. I told ya…' Whoever was on the other end of the call was ruffling her feathers big time. She pulled the phone from her ear and laid it against her chest as she stood up. 'Sorry about this.' Then she left the room looking like she was about to tear the world apart.

Neville turned back to the baby. 'You need to toughen up my young man. It's a big, wicked world out there and pussy-boys end up mashed under the boot heels of others.'

He tickled Natty's tummy, which made the boy squirm and whimper. Neville touched his soft tummy again, this time more gently, and Natty winced. Neville frowned. Looked like the baby was in pain. He eased back his grandson's little top and sucked in his breath when he found a red bruise just above his belly button. Neville inspected it closer. No, it wasn't a bruise but a red rash. He didn't like the look of that. No wonder the boy was squealing and carrying on.

'It's time for his nap.' Neville looked up to find the nanny hovering over him.

He checked her out, slowly, from head to toe. There was nothing remarkable about her except he'd swear that mousy-brown hair of hers didn't look right.

'How did this happen?' He soothed the pad of his finger over the rash.

She smiled brightly at him. Neville noted only her lips spread the rest of her face remained frozen like ice. 'Babies are delicate things and susceptible to all manner of ailments.'

She leaned down to take Natty, whose fussing increased no end. Neville's big hand flashed out and she yelped as he grabbed her by her pretty blouse and yanked her close.

His hot breath and heated words smothered her face. 'If it comes to my attention that you've been causing mischief to my grandson I'm going to make it my business to saw your hands very slowly from the ends of your arms.'

Abruptly he let her go and she stumbled back. Drawing in quick breaths she stammered, 'I have never...ever...been treated in such a fashion ever in my life.'

'Then why don't you pack your gear and go?'

Her lips snapped shut. Thought as much, Neville sussed. He didn't know what Little Miss Nanny was up, but as soon as his daughter came back he was going to tell her to fire the bitch.

But he never got the chance.

When Dee came back, Natty and his nanny long gone, the angry strain on her face made him get to his feet.

'What's up? Who was that on the blower?'

His daughter hesitated, then shoved her shoulders back. 'Pinky and Styley. They know where the gold is.'

'How did Pinky and Styley find it?' Neville asked as Dee's motor pulled up outside the boxing gym.

Her dad had been bombarding her with questions most of the way and she answered the same way she did now.

'They didn't say.'

Neville rubbed his jaw. 'This better not be no fool's errand coz I will knock their empty heads together.'

Dee had no doubt he would. They got out of the car and walked towards the entrance.

Suddenly Neville held back. 'That's odd. The lads always have some muscle on the door.'

Dee shrugged. 'Probably don't want any unnecessary eyes getting a gander at the gold if they have it.'

As soon as they entered Neville froze when he clocked the scene before him. 'What the fucking fuck?'

Chairs were arranged in a circle with Babs, Tiff, Flo and Kieran sitting on one side and Pearl, Pinky and Styley on the other. In the middle of the circle was an empty chair.

The door banged forcefully behind them. Dee and Neville twisted around. They found a stone-faced Knox guarding the door with a sawn-off by her side.

Dee quietly told her newly discovered dad, 'You need to park yourself in the chair in the middle.'

He did a double take at her as if she'd lost the bloody plot. 'What the fuckurees are you going on with?' He turned back to the others. 'What's going on here?'

He felt the barrel of Knox's shooter in his back. 'Do as you're told mister. We don't want no claret spilled here today.'

'Are you in on whatever this is daughter?' he asked Dee.

'Let's just say I've given Babs the benefit of the doubt.'

It hit him. 'That wasn't Pinky and Styley on your mobile before. They don't know where the gold is at all.'

It was a highly-strung Pearl who shot out, 'Give him ten out ten for having a brain.' She slapped on her older sister voice. 'Get your skin in that chair.'

Neville weighed up his options and seeing none he did as he was told. Dee took a seat next to her mum.

'So, is someone going to tell me what this witches coven is all about? I've got a very important appointment with some business associates in an hour.' The charming, confident Neville was back in play.

Babs spoke. 'Funny you should mention your business associates coz we've got one of 'em right here.'

Pearl placed two fingers at her lips and whistled. The back door opened and out walked a very nervous Fred.

Neville threw his head back and laughed to high heaven. 'Does that look like someone I'd do business with? The guy doesn't even look like he knows what day of the week it is.'

Pearl patted the seat next to her for Fred. Once he was sat down the circle was complete.

He looked at Neville, his Adam's apple bobbing up and down. 'I didn't tell 'em, they sussed it out.' His shoulder slumped. 'To tell you the truth now that Vi's gone I don't care about the gold no more.'

Neville folded his arms and stubbornly tightened his lips.

Pearl said, 'Fred's explained it all. How you knew each other back in the day. How he used to do jobs for you. This time it was the other way round – he needed you to do a job for him—'

Neville snapped over her, 'Keep talking bare bollocks Pearl if it makes you feel good.'

Pinky and Styley were on their feet bristling with rage.

Pinky took out and waved a wicked looking blade as he warned his great uncle, 'you can chat to us any way you like coz you're the bossman. But keep running your gob at our grams like that and we won't need no shotgun to sort you fucking out. Got it?'

Kieran spread his hands to calm the situation down. 'Put the knife away. Sit down.' The brothers hesitated, but then did what he asked.

No one else saw but Pinky caught Flo's eye and she caught his. She arched her brow, her way of telling him she approved of his coming to his grandmother's defence.

Babs started speaking. 'All this time Neville you've been playing your family against mine. Making sure we were at each other's throats so we didn't twig you had the gold all the time.'

He sneered, 'Everyone is playing everyone darlin', you should be old enough to know that.'

There! It was out in the open.

He carried on, 'The people who succeed in this life are the ones who seize a business opportunity that comes their way.'

'And, was I just part of that opportunity?' Dee bit out. 'I told Babs she was talking outta it when she got on the blower to me and insisted you were involved.' She sneered, 'The long, lost daughter who you could twist and turn any which way coz she was desperate to know her blood father?'

Pearl said softly, 'A father should know his child, but Neville this is a bad way of doing it.'

The 'so what' expression on his face told her all Dee needed to know.

'OK, so I threw a few lies out there about Babs and what went down when you were born,' Neville admitted. 'When the stakes are high you do what you do to reel in the prize. I looked after my sister's kids when I had to.' He ran his eye rudely over

Pearl. 'Don't get me wrong, I don't regret a minute of it, but I'm a lone wolf. Always have been, always will be.'

Dee leapt from her chair and rushed him. She walloped him a powerful one in the face. 'That's for my mum.' She backhanded him across the mouth. 'And that's from me, you fucking, selfish low-life.'

All hell broke loose as Neville raised his hand to her. Everyone piled in trying to restore order. Even Knox.

And that's why no one noticed the door open. Noticed the newcomer walk calmly and silently across the room.

It was Babs who clocked the newcomer first.

'Little Bea? Babe what you doing here?'

The room fell silent as Little Bea carried on walking.

'What's this Babs?' Neville scoffed, wiping the trickle of blood from his mouth where his daughter had belted him. 'Getting your grandbabies to do your dirty work now?' He ended on a snigger.

'Bug. Off,' she blasted at him. There was something awful about Jen's daughter's face she didn't like. Still and stony, almost like she wasn't really there.

Dee must've felt the same because she lunged for her niece but Little Bea danced out of her reach.

'Sasha! Sasha!' Babs bellowed her granddaughter's real name.

But it was no use, the girl kept walking forward, her steps quickening until she reached Pinky and Styley. She stood between them.

'Come to join the family reunion?' Styley joked with confidence, chuckling.

His sarky patter stopped dead when Little Bea pulled something out of her pocket and held it up.

The hand grenade.

Fifty-Four

Little Bea looked like a schoolgirl who was about to do a 'show and tell' at school assembly. But this was one show the adults definitely didn't want to see.

The whole room let out an appalled, collective gasp as she placed a finger in the pin. Babs could feel herself falling backwards with the shock. And she would've fallen if Flo hadn't quickly rushed over to prop her up.

'What is this?' Neville growled.

Little Bea looked him square in the eye. And spoke for the first time since her mum's shooting.

'This, Mister Biggin, or as Nanna Babs calls you, That Fuck Face, is the grenade you and your nephews sent to her.' Her gaze switched to her grandmother. 'I disarmed it for you Nan. Took out the detonator.' She said the last word slowly and carefully trying to pronounce it properly. 'I know how to from one of my books. Then I found out where you'd hidden the grenade and put the detonator back in it. It was all easy peasy really.'

Babs couldn't even speak as the worse terror she'd ever known gripped her.

When Pinky started to move Little Bea calmly cautioned, 'Don't move.'

No one did.

The little girl carried on. It was scary how she spoke with adult confidence not like a young girl at all. 'Know what this is?' No one dared respond. 'In one of my books it says it's a military grade grenade. M67 or baseball grenade because of its shape. Mainly used by the American army—'

Dee cut in slowly, 'Babes, I want you to put it down. Then walk towards me.'

Little Bea didn't blink as she continued. 'It has has loads of this B type of explosive stuff. Did you know that it can be thrown 30 to 35 metres by a soldier?'

Babs was sobbing wildly. 'Please Sasha—'

'But I won't be throwing it. I'm going to stand here until these two cunts tell me why they shot my mum. Nanna Babs, I'm sorry you got scared like coz I weren't talking, but I needed to watch and listen to find out who were the per…per…' She licked her lips and tried again. 'Perpetrators. That's what my books call bad people. That's what a good detective does – watches and listens. Examines the evidence.'

Pinky made a move to grab her.

'No!' Everyone screamed out as they dunked for cover.

Little Bea jumped out of his reach. Pinky tumbled unceremoniously to the floor.

All of a sudden she burst into tears, her shoulders shaking and shuddering. 'I don't understand why you would do that to my mum?'

Her chest heaved as each rapid breath rasped out, her small face scrunched up. 'No one thought I could hear a thing, but I could. My dad…bashing up my mum. That's why I started reading those crime books, so I'd know what to do if anyone dared thump her one again.'

Her wet gaze flew wildly to Pinky and Styley as her small chest rose and fell with emotion. 'If she dies she'll never read me a story again. She'll never have another G&T, though I think the booze is bad for her. She'll never tell Missus Brown to fucking keep her kids in line.' Her voice twisted into open anguish. 'She'll never kiss me goodnight.'

Everyone slowly straightened up, but it was Flo who took a step forward. 'I know exactly how you're feeling.' She spoke in a voice for grown ups, not little girls.

Little Bea shook her head. 'No you don't. You're mum ain't in the ozzie.'

Flo took another step. 'But my dad died—'

'He deserved that,' Little Bea spat with venom. 'He tried to strangle Nanna Babs.'

Another step. 'Yeah, I know. That don't mean I don't miss him.' One more step. 'Don't miss the way he'd throw his head back and laugh like a drunken sailor.' One more. 'Don't miss the way he'd teach me to palm cards so I could cheat when I played.'

Little Bea's lips trembled. 'But they should pay for what they've done.'

Flo clucked her tongue. ''Course they should. A right pair of wankers and morons and prats all rolled into one.' Her voice took on a soft edge as she finally stood in front of her niece. 'If you pull that thing you'll be going right along with them. And what's that gonna do to your Nanna Babs, eh? What about your mum when she wakes up?'

Flo held her palm out as someone's phone went off.

Little Bea rolled her lips around thinking hard. Then she placed the grenade in her Aunt Flo's hand.

Flo carefully placed it on the floor and then wrapped Little Bea in a tight embrace.

Pinky yelled, 'That little gal needs some licks.'

'Oh yeah?' Flo shot back. 'I'd like to see you try, you pink bastard.'

Pearl piped up, 'She's got a point. That's what happens when you send dangerous things to people instead of cake.'

'Will you all shut up,' Babs yelled.

Only then did they realise she was on her mobile. She gave the call her full attention and nodded. Then she cut the call and clutched the mobile so hard her knuckles turned white.

'That was the ozzie.'

Babs was crying hard in the hospital room. There were tears in Dee, Flo and Tiff's eyes too. They stood around Jen's hospital bed.

'Can you stop with the boo-hooing,' Jen rasped in a small voice. Her throat hurt like heck. 'You'd thing I'd kicked the bloody bucket.'

Her daughters were all smiles and joy as they held her hand tightly either side of her bed.

Babs leaned forward and kissed her middle child on the forehead. She smoothed Jen's hair gently away from her cheek. 'I have missed you something chronic. I thought…' She couldn't say the rest of the words because they were too awful to contemplate.

'Mum, it's alright,' Jen soothed. 'The quack said my legs are in working order and I'll probably be home in a couple of weeks.' She looked around at her family. 'I've gotta take it easy though so I'll need all of you to give me and the girls a helping hand.'

'In a heartbeat,' Tiff announced.

'I'll drop and collect the girls from school,' Flo added.

'And my little princesses can stay at mine anytime,' Dee offered.

Jen gave each of them a grateful, but tired look. 'So what's been going on since I've been in here?' She gazed at her girls. 'You two been behaving yourself?'

No one spoke. In fact everyone tried to avoid her eyes.

Alarmed, Jen tried to sit up. 'What the bollocks has been going on here?'

Once they got outside Dee threw her car keys to Tiff. 'Me and mum will catch up with you two in a mo.'

Tiff and Flo headed off arguing loudly about who was going to drive Dee's motor, not that she'd said either of them was up for the job.

In the cooling air she turned to Babs. They stood stiffly avoiding eye contact for a time.

Dee broke the silence. 'Mum, I'm really sorry about —'

Babs didn't allow her to finish. 'You've got nish to be sorry about. That bloody Neville was always a master manipulator.'

Dee looked like her heart was about to shatter. 'But I believed what he told me all too quickly. I should've trusted you.'

Her mum vigorously shook her head. 'Every kid wants to get to know their dad, so it was understandable that you'd swallowed every last one of his lies.' Babs pulled in a deep breath. 'I don't blame you. I only wish he could've been the old man you deserved.'

Then they were in each other's arms, hugging each other tight, their troubles behind them.

'Promise me one thing,' Babs whispered in her daughter's ear.

'Anything.'

Tears prickled behind Babs' eyes. 'Whatever might happen in the future, you'll never call me Babs again. Will always call me mum.'

Fifty-Five

As soon as she got home Dee headed for John's whiskey collection in the snooker room cum bar. She poured a large Iron Dram, the name John had given to the really strong stuff and knocked it back in one. Dee shook her head as it burned a hot path down her throat and made her eyes water. Just what a girl needed after the shocking Miller-Campbell-Hennessy clash that had almost exploded in their faces. Till the day she died she'd never forget seeing that grenade in Little Bea's hand. And the words that Pearl had softly spoken:

'A father should know his child.'

Alright, so Neville didn't want to really know her, had only been using her to divert everyone away from the gold, but that didn't mean that Kieran was stringing her along. What if he did really want to know Natty? Was it right that she keep them apart? Dee knew deep inside the pain that it caused never knowing one of your blood parents and even when they turned out to be a full-time, selfish, me-me-me wanker like Neville at least she'd clapped eyes on him. Could point him out in a crowd instead of blindly walking past him in the street without knowing they shared the same blood.

She slammed her glass down. No! She couldn't do that to John. Couldn't have people laughing and nudge-nudge-wink-wink-winking at him for not having the juice to create a child and a missus who'd opened her legs to all-comers. Not that that's what she'd done, but those who got their rocks off on behind the fence chat loved to make up their own stories. And poor John not able to defend himself from the grave. He'd become a laughing stock and she wasn't having that, no bloody way.

Dee let out a long, noisy sigh as she wearily left the room. Tonight she just wanted to lie on the bed, her little man cuddled to her breast, close her eyes and leave any other troubles until tomorrow.

But when she looked in his cot he wasn't there. Dee rushed off to Miriam's room. Empty.

A bad feeling chilled its way down her spine as she stumbled onto the landing and bellowed, 'Miriam! Miriam!'

No voice came back.

Heart racing, gut clenching she belted down the stairs and checked every room. No sign of her precious boy or his nanny.

'Oh my God! Oh my God!' Dee paced in panic. Couldn't believe it.

WHERE WAS HER SON?

Then it hit her with the power of a ton of bricks falling on her. That cunt! Bastard! Devil's spawn! Only one person would have the brass to take her child – Kieran Scott. And to think she'd finally been seeing things from his point of view.

Dee picked up a chair and flung it across the room as her body thundered with almost super human rage.

She clenched her teeth as she found her mobile. As soon as the line connected she growled, 'Have you got Natty?'

'He's here.'

She cut the call and headed straight to the kitchen where she found a bread knife. A serrated edge was what she needed so he felt agonising pain when she sawed his dick and balls off. Kieran wouldn't be planting his baby cream in any other bird once she finished with him.

As soon as Kieran opened the door to his plush pad in Chelsea Dee let rip with a solid fist to his chest. He rocked back on his heels, wincing at the flesh wound from the bullet that had skimmed his leg, but he managed to stay upright. She bowled in, her body vibrating with fury and kicked the door shut.

'You better not have hurt my baby,' she cried.

'Will you knock it off?' He flinched as his fingers massaged his aching leg.

'Knock it off?' Her chest rose and fell as she gave him a look that should kill. 'You have the nerve, the nerve—'

'You need to listen to me-'

'I ain't listening to dick. Just give me Natty and we'll be on our way.' She shook her head in disgust. 'And I don't wanna ever see your ug mug again.'

Suddenly he lunged at her and pinned her arms and wouldn't let go. She fought but couldn't get free.

He leaned in and spat in her face, 'Calm the fuck down. There's something you need to see.'

Dee's head reared back. 'What do you mean? Has something happened to my boy?'

It was then that she noticed the expression on his face –

haunted and shattered. Something was badly wrong here. Badly wrong.

'Kieran, you're frightening me.'

He manhandled her into the main room and her heart nearly gave out at what she saw.

There was her baby in the arms of the woman she knew as Miriam. Except the brown bun was gone replaced by flowing blonde hair and the fresh, clean face was tarted up to the max. What nearly did her heart in was the wicked looking knife that Miriam held in her hand right next to her son. Oh my God! Oh my God!

'Miriam?' Dee croaked.

The other woman let out an ugly, unhinged smile that did not light up her dead eyes. 'Ah, I see the bitch from Essex has finally put in an appearance.'

Dee could hardly catch her breath as she stared helplessly at Kieran. 'What's this all about?'

The skin around his mouth was pinched white, his lips a grim, hard line. 'Her name's not Miriam, it's Lisa and she used to be my girlfriend.'

Dee stared back, gobsmacked, at the other woman. 'What? I don't understand—'

Lisa waved the knife manically in the air. ''Course you wouldn't, you thick as shit slag. What Kieran ain't told you is me and him are a family—'

'No we're not,' Kieran butted in strongly. He tapped a finger to the side of his head gesturing that his former girlfriend was off her trolley.

That sent Lisa into a rage and she pointed the knife at Natty's tiny head. 'Why do you keep lying Kieran? You made a mistake pushing me outta your life, but we're together again. Me, you and our son.'

Dee rounded on him. 'You told this nut job that Natty was your son? You fucking half-wit.' In desperation she twisted back to Lisa. 'He's lying outta his bum hole—'

'No he's not.' Lisa's voice was firm. 'He made me check out his kid as your mum was wheeling him around that arse end of an estate she lives on.'

'You did what?' Dee nearly punched Kieran again.

'I've told Lisa that all she needs to do is hand Natty over and we'll forget all about this. Eh?'

But his plea fell on deaf ears as she stroked the edge of the blade lightly against the baby's cheek. Jesus, help me, Dee silently begged. Thank God there was no blood on her son's face and he remained asleep.

'That's why I became his nanny.' Lisa spoke as if talking to herself. 'To make sure you were looking after him. But you weren't. You weren't looking after my poor, poor Andy.'

Kieran angrily opened his mouth again but Dee held up her hand.

Andy? Who the fuck was Andy? This woman was obviously not the full ticket, but there was a tone to her voice that reminded Dee of Babs' voice back in the days when Dee was still giving her a hard time about giving her up when she was a baby. It was pain. Not any kind of pain, the type only a mother would know.

'Can I sit down Lisa?' Dee's voice was soft and calm. 'So we can talk mum to mum?'

The other woman narrowed her eyes and then pointed to the soft sofa opposite.

'Kieran, why don't you get us both a cuppa?'

That got Lisa hissing again. 'Don't tell my fucking fiancé what to do.'

Dee held her hands up in peace as she sat down. 'I'd never do that. Just thought you might like something to wet your throat.'

Dee caught his eyes and used hers to gesture towards the terraced balcony with the cor blimey view of London, which was behind Lisa. He caught her silent meaning, nodded and left.

Dee gave the other woman her full attention. 'I remember when he was born.' A little smile quivered on her lips. 'He was so little, the most gorgeous thing I'd ever seen in my life. Did you feel the same when your Andy was born?'

'Yeah.' Dee had to contain her triumph at hitting it right on the nail.

Lisa stroked Natty's cheek, the same place the blade had touched. 'My Andy was nine pounds—'

'Blimey, that's a big un.'

They laughed Dee's completely fake.

She urgently looked towards the terrace praying that Kieran could get something done soon.

Kieran looked at the drop from his bedroom window. Flippin' hell, if he fell he was a goner for sure. But he didn't have a choice; he had to do this for his boy. When Lisa had turned up carrying Natty and a blade he'd almost bitch-slapped her into next week. Not that belting women was his thing but anyone, anyone, who dared threaten his flesh and blood might as well start digging their grave. It was her holding the knife that held him at bay. One of the reasons he'd dumped her was she was way too clingy for his liking, going on about wanting to be a family, but he hadn't realised she was living that close to the edge.

Kieran stopped thinking and started doing.

He lifted himself up and froze out the pain in his leg. In three moves he was hanging from the window frame outside in the cold window. Didn't look down. Now all he had to do was somehow stretch or swing enough to grip the balcony rail…

'He took my Andy away from me,' Lisa uttered sadly as she looked down at Natty.

'Who's *he*?' Dee asked quickly wishing with all her heart that Kieran would move proceedings along. Come on Kieran! Come on!

'My ex-husband.' Lisa's gaze blazed. 'We broke up but I'd never keep him from seeing Andy. Used to come see him every Saturday and take him out. Except that Saturday they never came back.'

'What?' Lisa had her full attention.

The other woman's eyes were bleak. 'He said he was going to bring him back at three as usual. When they never come back I went looking for them.' She croaked, 'Couldn't find them anywhere.'

Dee thought she was going to vomit at the ugly tale being told. How could anyone do that to a mother? Run off with her kid as if she hadn't given birth to him?

Despite knowing this woman must've done some terrible things to Natty, an overwhelming wave of pity swept over Dee.

'Did you find them?'

Lisa's face went stark white. 'My ex was Italian. He took my Andy and left the country.' An awful sound left her mouth. 'I couldn't find them. I went to Italy myself. This private detective said he'd help me but —'

'The bastard ripped you off and ran off with your dosh,' Dee finished for her.

Lisa nodded and frowned. 'I thought you were doing the same thing to Kieran, running off with his kid. It ain't right.'

She started raising the knife. Kieran caught her wrist as he stood behind her. The balcony door was open behind him, cold, frigid night air creeping into the room. He twisted the knife out of her hand and dashed it to the wooden floor. Natty woke up and started screaming. Lisa collapsed into the sofa, crying and rocking.

Dee only had eyes for her beloved boy. She scooped a distressed Natty to her breast shushing and kissing him over and over. What would she have done if she'd lost her son? He and Nicky were the closest people to her heart. She'd fight tooth and nail against anyone who threatened them. She glanced over at Kieran's former girlfriend.

With bleak eyes Kieran stared at her. 'What do you want me to do with her? Call the cops?'

Dee quickly shook her head. 'I don't want the Bill anywhere near me. Or Natty.' She turned to Lisa. 'What your ex did to you and your boy is pure evil. He ain't getting away with it.'

The other woman wiped the tears from her eyes with the back of her hand. 'What do you mean?'

'Me and Kieran are gonna make it our business to hunt your ex down and get your Andy back into your lovin' arms.' Dee knew full well this woman weren't all there but no fella had the right to take a mum's child away from her.

'What?' Kieran was gobsmacked.

But Dee plunged on ignoring him. 'No man has the right to do what your former old fella did to you.'

Lisa started wringing her hands together. 'You'd do that for me?' Her momentary hope was dashed by bleakness covering her face again. 'But I had a break down and ended up in the nut house for a couple of months. I know I'm not right. I don't want to hurt my Andy.'

'What about your big sister Joanie?' Kieran asked. 'You use to talk about her a lot.'

'Joanie?' Lisa's face brightened. 'She looked after me when I came outta the hospital. Do you think she'll help me look after Andy?'

'Let's find out shall we,' Dee answered. 'Give Kieran her number. You gotta understand that we'll do our best to find him, but we might not be able to. And you've gotta do everything you sister tells you to get better.'

Lisa's voice shook. 'I can't thank you enough. I'm sorry, I think I did some terrible things to Natty. I can't really remember —'

Dee punched in savagely, 'And don't tell me coz I think if I hear what you did I'll have no choice but to kill you.'

Half an hour later her mortified sister Joanie and her husband gently led Lisa out of Dee and Kieran's lives.

Once they were alone Kieran and Dee sat in an awkward silence, their blood son once again sleeping in his mother's arms.

Kieran hung his head. 'All I can say Dee is sorry. I never knew—'

'Would you like to hold him?'

His head snapped up. His gaze landed greedily on his son. He couldn't even speak. He eagerly nodded.

Dee watched Kieran's face light up like he was touching magic as he held his boy. She'd felt the same holding a squalling Natty for the first time.

'A father should know his child.'

She couldn't get Aunty Pearl's words out of her head because Dee finally realised she was right. Still there was knowing and *knowing*.

'We need to come to an arrangement,' she told him.

'I know that.' He kept his amazed gaze on Natty.

'He's still John's son.'

'Know that too.'

'What say you became his Uncle Kieran?'

Kieran tickled Natty's tummy with delight. 'Hey little man, I'm your Uncle Kieran...'

Fifty-Six

Three weeks later

Patrick woke up in the night and a sixth instinct told him he was not alone. He took an easy breath, just the way he'd learned to do as an undercover cop, and slowly reached out for the lamp switch on his nightstand.

Four women stood around his bed all dressed in black. Two had large holdall bags at their feet while one was heavily propped up against another. He didn't need telling who had come to pay him a midnight call – Babs' girls.

He sat up as he calmly asked, 'Can I get you ladies a cup of tea?'

Dee, the eldest, held up a finger. 'We're gonna do the talking and all you've got to do is open your ears.'

There was a breath of silence before Jen, who looked pale leaning against Tiff said, 'Our mum ain't a happy bunny these days.'

Tiffany informed him, 'Mum keeps crying her heart out.'

'And we hear that's down to you,' chipped in Flo.

'Apparently,' Tiff joined in, 'we hear you've given her the boot coz you found out 'bout her and the gold.'

'Look, I—' he started but Dee snapped over him.

'Told you to stay schtum until we've had our say.' He closed his mouth. 'What you need to understand is she only got involved to save us. Tried to hide the stuff to keep us lot out of bother.'

'That's what mum's do,' Flo said as if he were an idiot, 'they help their kiddies out.'

Jen smiled weakly. 'Babs Miler's the best woman you'll ever meet.'

'She's loyal and good and loves to have a laugh.' That was Flo.

Dee punched in, 'She's kind and caring and will never betray you.'

'And she deserves loads of sex,' Tiff grinned. 'Lots and lots of earth shattering sex.'

Dee clipped her around the nut. 'Enough of that, thank you very much.'

Tiff rubbed her head. 'Well she does.'

Dee straightened. 'Anyways, we're not going to keep you from your kip, so this is the last thing we're gonna say – our mum deserves a great guy in her life. Now we think that guy's you.' Her foot kicked the holdall bag. 'And we're leaving this and the other with you coz we know that's what Babs would want.'

They left him and he didn't move for a full two minutes wondering if he'd just had a dream. No, the bags were still there. He got out of bed and crouched down by one. Unzipped it and whistled.

Inside were bars and bars of gold.

Fifty-Seven

Two months later

'Do I look the part?' Babs nervously asked.

Her four daughters – she'd claimed Flo as her own – all gasped as they looked at her in her bedroom.

'Stunning.'

'Gorgeous.'

'Out of this world.'

'Brings tears to my eyes.'

She didn't know which of her girls said what because they all gushed in awe at the same time.

Babs looked back at her reflection in the mirror. 'You don't think it's a bit over done?'

Dee walked up to her and placed her palms gently on her shoulders from behind. 'A bride should pull out all the stops for her wedding.'

For the second time in her life Babs was tying the knot. This time she was doing it with a man who worshipped her from the hair on her head to the tips of her freshly manicured toes. Richard had handed in the gold – anonymously – which had been reported all in the papers and the telly. A couple of bars were still missing but the Bill were pleased that the majority had turned up. Strange thing was though no one had come forward to claim it. The stuff was cursed, plain and simple, and her girls had wanted it gone from their lives. Babs was mummy proud of what they'd done. Especially Tiff. It couldn't have been easy for her youngest to turn her back on a wagonload of wonga.

Babs let out a private smile of pure pleasure as she remembered that warm day when she was drowning her sorrows in a bottle of mother's ruin down the Knackered Swan. Tricky Dickie had turned up, got down on his knee and popped the question in front of the whole flamin' pub. When Babs had given the thumbs up the customers had raised the roof with an East End cheer.

Now finally the day had arrived for Babs to make him her old man.

She was dressed all in white, the picture of a traditional bride from the veil to the sweeping lace train behind. Babs felt a bit daft in this get-up but the girls had insisted on taking her to Madame Dominique's swanky shop Up West to get something made especially for her.

'We better shift it,' Jen said. And grinned. 'We can't have the bride being late for her own wedding.'

Babs was a touch disappointed that no one from her block was on their landing to gawk at her and wish her well. Nevertheless, she would miss this place. She and Richard had bought a lovely three-bed out Essex way. She'd managed to wangle it with the council for Tiff and Flo to become the new tenants of her flat. Babs would love to be a fly on the wall to see how that panned out.

Once they got downstairs they made their way across the

estate towards the main road and the registry office. Babs' face screwed up in confusion as they instead headed towards the old washhouse, which had long ago been abandoned and boarded up.

What the heck?

''Ere? What's going on ladies?'

They all giggled in response and propeller her gently forward. Once they reached the door of the washhouse Flo opened it and push it wide.

Babs' hands flew to her lips. 'On my life.'

Jammed inside seemed to be most of the estate. And Pearl and Fred, who now owned the care home paid for in cash. They'd also given all the pensioners who'd been swindled their money back.

When Babs had asked in an arched voice where the dough had come from, Fred was cheerfully vague. 'Well, to tell you the truth, I had a bit of a lucky run on the gee-gees. You know - an accumulator and that. Soon mounts up.'

Babs was unconvinced. 'Did you really? I didn't even know bookies took gold bars as stake money.'

Fred gave her a twinkly look with his eyes and said no more.

And Nicky back from his travels Down Under accompanied by what his mum distastefully termed, 'a fast piece.'

The place was decorated up a treat. Balloons, banners, beautifully arranged tables, nosh and booze aplenty.

Babs' heart hitched in her chest as she spotted her groom. Wow, he looked a total knockout in his dashing, startling white suit with a red carnation in a buttonhole. His best man, his son, stood up with him.

A hush fell as Babs walked down the aisle with her

daughters and grand girls behind her. Flippin' hell, her heart was galloping like it was in the Grand National.

When she reached her groom he gripped her hands like he didn't want to let go.

'Finally,' he whispered.

She whispered back, 'finally.'

The Minister called everyone to attention and started the service.

He started the vows. 'Do you Richard Tricky Dickie Johnson…'

The place erupted into uproarious laughter.

'You silly sod,' Babs told Richard.

'I did it for you. Anything for you.'

Babs couldn't believe she'd wasted so many years when she should've been spending it with this one of a kind fella.

When they were pronounced man and wife everyone whooped it up. That was the signal for the piss up to begin.

An ecstatic Babs and Richard did the rounds of congratulations. Everyone ahhed when a horse and carriage appeared to take the couple away for the start of their honeymoon in a cottage by the sea in Cornwall.

Before Babs got into the carriage she let her gaze span over The Devil's Estate. She was going to miss the place. For all its faults and secrets this had been her home, the place she'd reared two of her children.

Under her breath she whispered, 'Good-bye old friend.'

Then, as Richard gallantly lifted his bride into the carriage, a disturbance broke out.

Someone drunkenly groused, ''Ere? I know him. Ain't he a plod?'

'And what of it?' that was Tiff's growl.

'Yeah,' Flo bustled in beside her sister, 'what you got to say about it?'

Patrick made to go back but Babs grabbed him as the argument started to get out of hand.

'Leave it. It wouldn't be an East End wedding if there wasn't a punch up.'

As the carriage rolled away Babs pulled Tricky Dickie's head down and gave him a smacker to last a lifetime.

Thank you!

Thank you for reading *Blood Secrets.* I hope you enjoyed it. We had a total ball writing it!

I adore hearing from readers, so please do get in touch with me if you'd like to.

You can contact me via
My website: https://dredamitchell.com
Facebook Dreda Facebook
Twitter: Dreda Twitter

Reviews: I write for you!
I love to hear what you think about the books.
So please leave a review

More Books

The Flesh and Blood Series

Blood Sister
Blood Mother
Blood Daughter
One False Move (Quick Reads: The Reading Agency)

Gangland Girls Trilogy

Geezer Girls
Gangster Girl
Hit Girls

DI Rio Wray Series

Vendetta
Snatched (e-novella)
Death Trap

All About Dreda

Dreda wrote five books before partnering up Tony Mason to continue her writing career. Dreda scooped the CWA's John Creasey Dagger Award for best first time crime novel in 2004. Since then she has written eleven crime novels. She grew up on a housing estate in the East End and was a chambermaid and waitress before realising her dream of becoming a teacher. She is a passionate campaigner and speaker on social issues and the arts. Dreda has appeared on television, radio and written in a number of leading newspapers including The Guardian. Some of Dreda and Tony's books are currently in development as TV adaptations.

Printed in Great Britain
by Amazon

27899533R00236